BF
HB
$24.95
N
signed
Colorado

# THE DEATH OF SPRING

*Silvio J Caputo jr.*

# THE DEATH OF SPRING

by

## SILVIO J. CAPUTO, JR.

Ashley Books, Inc.
Port Washington, N. Y. 11050

DEATH OF SPRING.
© Copyright 1984 by Silvio J. Caputo, Jr.

Library of Congress Number: 81-14952
ISBN: 0-87949-201-5

ASHLEY BOOKS, INC./*Publishers*
Port Washington, New York 11050

*Printed in the United States of America*
*First Edition*

9  8  7  6  5  4

Library of Congress Cataloging in Publication Data:

Caputo, Jr. Silvio J, 1951-
   Death of Spring.

   1.  Title.
PS3553.A628D4          813'.54          81-14952
ISBN 0-87949-201-5                      AACR2

# THE DEATH OF SPRING

# CHAPTER

# 1

The stillness of the night was broken by the screech of the ambulance siren. In the emergency room, the nurses began preparing for the patient. Over the intercom came the call: "Dr. Biber! Dr. Biber! Please come to the emergency room." Then silence.

A cool breeze pushed past the swinging doors of the emergency room to the reception desk where a nurse glanced up as it touched her. A moment later a tall, dark Italian in his mid-fifties approached her. "Excuse me, miss, has Jim Caputo been admitted?"

"No, he hasn't arrived yet. He should be here any minute."

"Thank you."

He turned and walked slowly to one of the chairs across from the desk. He took his watch from the side pocket of his bib overalls, glanced at it and slid it back into his pocket. He placed his canvas hat on the chair beside him and crossed his legs, moving his large work shoe slowly back and forth. He passed over his mustache twice with his forefinger and thumb and waited, staring past the floor and into a thousand yesterdays.

At the sound of the ambulance in the driveway, doors swung open and two attendants brought in an old man in a wheel chair. He writhed in pain, clutching his hip. The man who had been waiting arose and followed them. When they reached the nurses' station they stopped momentarily. One asked the nurse, "Have you found Biber?"

"Yes, he said to take him directly to the x-ray room."

The old man grasped the armrest of the chair and reached for the backside of a young nurse standing at the station. The man in the overalls saw and exclaimed, "Pa!"

The old man glanced at him and once more turned in pain. The attendants took him down the hall. His son returned to the waiting room where he was joined by his brother and nephew. The brother was younger, his son standing next to him was taller, closer in height to his uncle. The younger son spoke first. "What happened?"

"He fell."

"Where?"

"Coming out of Scavina's."

"I wish to hell he'd stay out of those damn bars. I don't know what we're going to have to do to keep him out of there," the younger man said.

"We're not going to. He's done it for a long time," the elder replied.

"For twenty years."

"He drank before Mom died."

"But that was different. It was wine then. It's that damn whiskey that . . ." He was cut off by a cold stare that reached back thirty-five years. The argument was old. The two stood in silence.

Dr. Biber appeared from the darkness of the corridor.

The younger brother asked, "What's wrong?"

"He broke his hip."

"What are you going to do?"

"Put a pin in it."

The doctor turned to leave when the elder son spoke. "Is he going to be all right?"

The doctor turned to look at him. He took a slow breath and began, "That old man has made a damn liar out of me for ten years," he said. "Every time I feel he's going to die, he doesn't. And most of the time I don't know why. Medically he's died six times. He should be . . . he could have died eight years ago when he broke his ankle and gangrene set in. I wanted to remove part of his leg. You were there when he told me to go to hell. At least that's what you said he meant. I should have learned Italian when I moved here. You were probably being polite."

"No, no," the son protested.

"He could have died from bleeding ulcers any number of times, or cirrhosis of the liver, or black lung, or emphysema. If you want to know if he's going to be all right, why don't you ask him? He isn't going to die until he wants to."

"When you are going to operate?"

"Now. He's in a great deal of pain. Fill out the necessary papers while I get ready."

The doctor turned and was gone. The two brothers went to the desk and began filling in forms. One of the nurses brought them the old man's possessions: his wallet, watch, and some loose change. When they were finished the younger took his brother by the arm and motioned him toward the back of the room. He told his son to go to the car and began speaking quietly to his brother. "Who called you, Tony?"

"Joe Serafino."

"What happened?"

"He fell trying to catch a cab."

"Did he . . . have the gun with him?"

"I've never seen him go any place without it. He thinks he's still in the camp. The police took it. They're always around when something happens. He doesn't put bullets in it. They know it. But they gotta take it. One of these days we're not going to get it back. Did you bring him any money this week?"

"He wanted eighty dollars. I brought it to him yesterday. He wanted to buy some chickens and feed."

Tony opened the old man's wallet. He found a five and two ones. He showed his brother and shook his head in disgust.

"They rolled him again. Even when he's hurt and lying on the ground they roll him. He thinks because they offer to take him home so he don't have to call a cab, they're his friends, but they roll him. Every time they take him home, the next morning he's broke."

Tony noticed a policeman standing near them. He stared momentarily, causing his brother Silvio to look behind him.

"How's your dad?" the policeman asked.

"He broke his hip."

"I'm sorry to hear that. When we found him outside Scavina's, we thought he was hurt. We had Sam call an ambulance. It's a good thing we were around."

"Yes," answered the younger brother, "you're always close."

"Well, we try to help the old guy out. He goes back a long ways."

"Did he have his gun with him?"

"No, I can't say as I saw it. You know he's gonna have to learn he can't carry that thing around with him. We've had a lot of complaints because of it. I know Jim doesn't want to hurt anybody but when he's been drinking, you never know."

The two brothers gave no reply and after a moment the policeman turned to leave. Tony said, "Mike, we'll be in for the gun in the morning." The policeman proceeded out the door without reply.

The brothers finished with the papers and left the hospital. The scarred body of the old man was once again prepared for the knife.

In the town, those who had robbed the old man divided the money. This would have made him angry at one time, but living was enough for him now. By morning he would have forgotten what had happened with these men the night before, and they would again be his friends. The whiskey often did this to him and it made it easier. But the whiskey had little effect now. The old man lay on his back, trying to force mucus from his blackened lungs. When he tried to pull himself up to spit it out, the pain was too great and he swallowed it. The drug they had given him was beginning to take effect. He folded his hands in an almost holy way, murmured a few words in Italian to his dead wife, and his arms dropped to his side.

The darkness which he hated, but knew too well, began to close upon his mind. He thought perhaps that he might not reopen them and that would be easier. He became peaceful.

The drug freed the old man from the present that he wished to escape only to return to the past that was mixed with the people that he loved and the hell he survived. The long hours of continuous labor with a pick caused his body to twitch even when it was at rest, and now, twenty years later, his body still quivered when he slept. His eyes moved as he returned to the caverns that produced the coal that he thought fired the furnances of hell. But the physical torments that he had suffered could not match the integrity that he had lost in compromising himself for survival.

Distantly the grinding of metal and rock echoed within him. The crashing thunder of mules' hooves kicking his temples made him return to the places where he had labored in blood and sweat, where his back had been bent by the low ceilings and his hands and fingers disfigured by strain. The old man seemed lifeless, but inside he continued to move and voices from the past brought him strength:

"People die here too easily. Every day death walks them

into the ground."

"This cannot be right. Look at their faces . . . they have to watch while the ones they love are brought out in pieces."

"It will take many caskets to bury all of them."

'They must continue to live."

"The living must continue."

"When dying becomes too easy, life becomes cheap."

"And if we do not struggle we will all die."

But the past was gone when the voices stopped and the old man lay asleep away from the many years in the coal fields. The underground rooms where he had worked were silent now. Their cold, dark, damp walls felt no steel picks digging into them. Their stale, moist air filled no lungs with poisons nor did they burn from explosions. There was no one left to work them. All were gone or buried and the pinon trees gave no evidence that they ever existed. Only a few that could never come to the surface again remained there. But there were still voices in the old man and they stirred him again . . . .

"If you don't wanna work, get the hell out, boy. It's too bad these mules can't dig so we would send you Wops back to where you came from—"

The old man was taken from the preparation room and wheeled down the corridor to the operating room. The lights on the ceiling flashed past his face as the lights of the mine had done so often. The memories of the long trip deep into the earth returned, and the sound of the wheels turning and clicking over the uneven track filled his mind again.

The next morning the two sons made arrangements for their father to enter the nursing home. It was a clean place and he would receive good care. He'd been there twice before and would stay only until the break healed.

The people at the home had grown used to his singing at four o'clock in the morning and his evil wink that had little meaning now. They had even gotten used to his keeping salami and wine in the refrigerator. They enjoyed watching him wheel his chair up and down the halls, stopping to talk with others. They talked of the past, the old country, the good things, "when people were people," they would say. Always they shared the past and the nurses would hear them laugh about things they didn't understand.

Once in a while they talked of serious things, of how little they had and how hard the work had been in those days. The times they suffered drew them closer together. Words such as, "We had to use everything from the pig, lots-a-times that's all we had," meant little to the nurses but it left such an impression upon the old ones' faces that they knew the closeness shared by the old people was a good thing.

The old ones would go on for hours talking of the picnics and the ball games, the sharing during the Depression years. Occasionally they would say, "God rest his soul." The dead meant a great deal to them. They knew perhaps soon they would be called, but it was of no great concern to them for they were religious and realized life was only a well traveled journey with many hardships and would end in heaven. There they would see their loved ones and would be with them without the drudgery of life. They were sure of this and it made it easier.

Their children came occasionally. This was their greatest joy. They bragged continuously about how their sons and grandchildren were doing so well and how they had gone to college and were making lots of money. They never grew tired of showing off their pictures and saying again and again how beautiful the little ones were, always ending with "God bless them." Their families meant life to them, for they all found the meaning of love. The less they had the more they loved. The harder life was, the easier to love.

The home was a good place and the old man healed quickly, although most old people don't. When Mike DeSanti would come to see him, the old man would cut a small Vienna loaf of bread in half and give one to Mike with a piece of cheese or salami. Mike would give Jim a paper bag with fresh eggs and Jim would say, "These froma my chickens?"

"I haven't been over there for about a week. I don't got no way to go. Joe and Tony, they work. They don't bring me. I can't go."

Jim shook his head in disgust and said, "They wanna sell 'um. They want me to stay here. I ain't gotta no goats, no chickens . . . They take the check, all of 'um . . . 'um . . .I go home."

"Jim, who's gonna take care of you?"

"A-a-a! I take care. The fava dies ifa you don' water."

"But you cana walk. Whata you gonna water?"

The old man took a cane from beside the bed and very shakily stood up. He smiled with a half-laugh anu the event was broken by a shrill voice. "Mr. Caputo! You know you're not supposed to put pressure on that hip. You have strict orders from Dr. Biber. You'll never heal properly unless you let that hip mend. Now where did you get that cane?"

Her voice faded into yesterday, and the old man was soon home. He sat upon a large rock, watching the baby goats wean from their mothers. High in the air a small dot revealed a chicken hawk that would be shot if it ventured too close. The chickens picked at the ground and at each other. A few yards away, where the base of the hill leveled out, grew his garden. It was no longer necessary for life, but the old man always planted it. He watched as the fava beans, the lettuce, the leaves of the carrots, the squash, the cucumbers, and the spinach swayed smoothly in the summer breeze. And he remembered the soil that would not yield.

# CHAPTER

# 2

Vicenzo Caputo was nine when he first heard his father Santino talk of America. He was old enough to realize that the land in Italy could not support all of his family and it was no surprise to him when his brother left for America. He remembered his father saying, "Nature treats us like orphans. She sends only enough rain to give us hope, then she takes away the crops. The goats are as scrawny as the vegtables that survive. The land here is too rocky and I have heard that America is a large country and there are not enough people to work." Vicenzo remembered too the man who owned the land in Italy.

Not long after his brother Augusto left for America they heard from him. He did not say much but he sent money home to help his father. Santino used the money for his family's necessities and, with what was left, he bought several small toys for Vicenzo while he was in Rome. The word passed quickly that Santino was spending money that he had not before. The landlord soon heard and he went to Santino to see for himself.

"Papa," Vicenzo called out, "it's the landlord, he comes again." Vicenzo's father went to the door and waited.

"Go and play," he told his son. "Hurry." When the landlord approached the house he was greeted by Santino on the front porch.

"What can I do for you today, Mr. Colonzago? I sent the rent money last week."

"I got the money. But I think maybe you're making a little more money off my land than you're telling me," he answered.

"I make exactly what I tell you."

"How do you go to Rome and buy such nice things as your son plays with?" As he spoke he looked down at the boy whose eyes widened with fear.

"It's with money my son sends from America, not with money I earn from this land."

"So if the land is no good, why don't you leave? Why don't you go to America?" The man laughed as he said this. He was a big, fat man and the gross ripples of his flesh shook when he laughed. The small boy looked with disgust at the large figure with sweat rings around his armpits and perspiration dripping from his forehead. "So maybe I'll look around and see how wealthy your son has become," he said as he began walking up the steps to the front door.

The boy's father took a step toward him and put his arm across his path, grabbing hold of one of the posts which held the porch up.

"This is my house. What's in it is mine. Nobody questions me in my house!"

The landlord stopped. He pointed his finger at the father and said, "You better not cheat on what you earn on my land or you'll get the hell off. You understand? I got friends who deal with people who cheat me." In a few minutes he was gone down the road in his cart.

For many days after the landlord's visit, the boy watched his father glance out the windows with a newvous fear. He kept his shotgun close at hand, and at night he and Carmela's father would sit at the kitchen table and talk of men who came in the night and brought death. Others had died for less than they had done. Even the warm summer breeze seemed their enemy as it pushed gently against the house. Everyday noises became magnified, things that had gone unnoticed became cause for concern. Vicenzo noticed his father walking about outside, watching him play near the olive trees. One day Vicenzo followed him.

When the boy passed the corner of the house, he saw his father turn quickly and pull a gun from his belt and point it directly at him. The double expression of surprise and shock came over the father's face as he dropped to his knees and motioned for his son to come to him. He hugged him, saying again and again, "*Bedo mio, bedo mio.*" The boy could feel his father's heart pounding harder and harder against his chest, his rough beard scratching the side of his face, and the sweat rolling down his own face from his father's.

"What's wrong, Papa?"

"Nothing, *bedo*, nothing. You musn't surprise your father that way."

"Why do you watch me, Papa?"

"Because I love you. Sometimes you can't understand things. You just have to accept them."

"Is it the landlord? Is he going to do something to hurt you?"

"No, baby. Don't worry. Papa will take care of anything."

He hugged the boy again, got up, took him by the hand and they went into the house.

The day-to-day drudgery of the fields became harder to bear with the lingering pressure of the landlord about the house. The men constantly looked about the grounds, their eyes moving slowly from one end of the land to the other. They even began speaking of hired protection.

"If we go to the *Black Hand,* we'll owe them the rest of our lives," Michael said.

"What do we do then, wait for them to come some night like a thief? We cannot pay them what Colonzago can. Every day I see the children go about the house and wonder if they will come after them. They have killed women and children before. If we defy him, others will also, he cannot let this happen. He will come," Michael said.

"Then we must take care of him ourselves," Santino said slowly.

"You mean kill . . ." Michael's words died away. There was silence.

"He thinks we have cheated him. Life for him is money. If we cheat him of money, we cheat him of life. He knows no other thing."

Several more days passed. The two men became more at ease and began working the farm as they had done before. Maria noticed the change and stopped her husband in the field. "The landlord?" she asked.

Her husband gave no reply.

"The landlord!" she insisted.

He gave her a hard look and answered, "He will not bother us."

She grabbed his arm and stared hard into his face. "You have not killed?"

Santino wiped his forehead with his arm. He casually looked at her and said, "He died from too much wine."

He turned and continued working the land. She stood watching, wondering and fearing. He moved slowly away from her, his back muscles flexed tightly against the plow.

When she reached home she could do nothing but sit in the kitchen, fearing what her husband might have done. She feared the authorities, who took care of the wealthy; she feared the landlord's friends, who were scum of the night and brought death; and she feared God. Each was a real thing to her and a threat to her family. She sat many hours when she heard the front door slam shut. Her husband? The Black Hand? The police?

"Maria?" Michael entered the kitchen. "Santino, he told you?"

"He told me nothing. Michael, what have you done? Santino says the landlord is dead. He says he drank too much wine. Did he kill him, Michael?"

Michael sat across from her and began, "Maria, you must understand what a man must do," he said.

"But killing!" Maria said. "It's murder!"

"Maria, Santino did not kill anyone. Listen and remember. We have tried to live from this land for many years. We have seen some good things but mostly bad. It is only because we have been close that we have managed to live at all. Now you must understand and again draw close together with your family. Men such as this landlord live by making other people miserable. They are like mushrooms feeding off the land, but it is we who make the land produce. It is easy to sit in a big comfortable chair and collect the rent. This was not enough for him. He had to take his share of what we work hard to grow."

"But we have always lived honestly," she broke in, "and the children will learn from us. If we do wrong it will be upon us and them."

"Maria, we have not done wrong. Listen, men such as this have many enemies. If we do wrong by protecting our families, then God must have pity upon us. We have spoken to many of the other workers. They too have suffered. One, his son disappeared because he refused to pay more than he was able. Santino feared that this would happen to Vicenzo. Another of the men had his daughter taken. He has never seen her again. The landlord committed many, many injustices."

"And if we live by death, if we solve our problems by killings, then we will live in fear and always be with death," she answered.

"Then we will live with what we must. Some things are worth killing for. We will respect death but we will not fear it," he said sternly.

She became silent. She knew that these were her husband's feelings. He had expressed them many times. She looked at Michael again and asked, "How did it happen?"

"A too proud man makes an easy prey. Often he had bragged of his expertise as a wine taster. Often he had become too drunk to tell the difference between wine and vinegar. Before Tuesday's celebration of the feast of St. Joseph we met Santino, myself, and others. Each brought his best wine. We met at the village square and pretended to be drunk. The landlord heard of the gathering and came quickly."

"At the feast of St. Joseph?" Maria said crossing herself. Michael continued. "'What is going on here?' the landlord shouted." "'Come,' I said, 'come and help us celebrate this great feast. Come and judge who makes the best wine.'" Michael's voice began to rise and his eyes gleamed.

"'Mine is without a doubt the best, Everyone knows this,'" I boasted.

"'Then let me taste it and see,' our fat landlord replied. He drank, swallowing but half the wine. The rest poured down the sides of his mouth like the pig that he was. He drank to the others until he came to Santino.

"'And how is your wealthy American son?' he said. 'Perhaps I will come tomorrow and see of his wealth.' Santino tightened his fists and smiled in hatred and calmly said, 'Yes, come tomorrow and see.'

"'He drank for over an hour. Finally I shouted, 'This wine is ox's urine. Come, let us go to Aldoline's.'"

"Aldoline's!" Maria broke in. "But that is where the catacombs are."

"Yes, and an old Roman city. It is the place where many were buried alive by the volcano. I told Colonzago that I had placed a keg of wine in the side of the earth five years earlier so the wine would age without being disturbed. 'Tonight we shall see who makes the best wine,' I said.

"'Excellent,' our pigeon shouted. 'Bring the wine, let me taste this nectar for the gods you boast of.'

"'I cannot. The keg has been placed in the side of the earth. If we try and remove it, it will break and all the wine will be lost.'

"'Then here, fill this with wine and bring it to me.'

"'I think we should drink alone, with our own,' Santino said. 'The wine is our sweat and our blood. He has enough from us.'

"'No, Santino,' one of the others answered. 'This man is our landlord, our protector. Our best wine is his.'

"'Our best in return for insults! For driving us to fear! For hunger! Gall should be his drink.'

"The landlord was sobered by the words. He looked at Santino and said, 'And if it hadn't been for the land, *my land,* what do you think your family would live on?'

"'Your land bought with blood money,' Santino answered.

"The insult landed upon the landlord like a fighter's best punch," Michael said. "He moved toward Santino and Santino clenched his fists but he knew that the men would stop him. I broke between them, 'Come now, it is the feast of St. Joseph. Let us drink and forget our differences for tonight. The best wine waits for us. Come, signor Colonzago. Judge for yourself if the wine made is not the best you have tasted anywhere.'

"'Yes,' Colonzago said, 'let's go drink the wine. I will deal with this man tomorrow.'

"We left the village square and headed toward the outskirts of the town. Soon we came to where the ruins of the once great Roman civilization now stood. We came to an opening in the earth. Two of them moved a stone from the entrance and the landlord entered, unthinking.

"Santino and another man had waited on the outskirts of town to make sure that they would not be followed. Two men approached them and Santino recognized the uniforms.

"'Hey, what's going on?' one of them asked.

"'Good evening,' Santino said, 'and how are the protectors of the people tonight?'

"'Never mind how we are. What's going on out there?'

"'Just a little celebration in honor of St. Joseph,' came the reply." Michael's story was so vivid that Maria felt she was there, seeing the whole episode.

"It looks like a little too much celebration to me, and where is this little party going at such a late hour?" One of the uniformed men asked.

"Away from the town, of course. We don't want to break the peace, so we will go where it is more private."

"And you won't mind if we join you," said the other officer.

Santino felt the tension. They knew too well that the police protected those who could afford it.

"Join us, of course. Have some wine," Santino cried, handing one of the officers a bottle of wine. The officer took it and drank slowly, watching Santino as he did so. He took the bottle from his mouth and handed it to the other officer.

"And how was your day, officer? A bit on the warm side, wasn't it? And too dry. If it doesn't rain soon the crops will dry out and be useless. Drink up," Santino said, looking at the man with the bottle. "If the crops dry up we'll all be dead and then turn into dust and leave only memories, just as these ancient ruins, and someone in the future will stand here and say that death was kind to us, that it came and relieved us of a world too harsh to be understood. Relieved us from the torment of others. Wine can do this. Ah! But your're not drinking, friend. Drink and let the wine relieve you of the worries of the world."

The officer held the bottle up so he could see the contents clearly. He looked at Santino cautiously.

"Drink up! After a short time you will feel the spirit of the past," Santino insisted.

"Here, you drink," answered the officer, returning the bottle to Santino. "I have no taste for this cheap vinegar you pass as wine."

"What's the matter, friend? You will not drink with us?"

"No, you talk too much and I don't drink with peasants. Go about your business, go with the others and get out of the streets or I'll take you in and not let you out until your flesh rots from your bones. Get the hell out of here and take your poison with you. Don't let me catch you around here again."

The men stood staring at the two officers. One of them cleared his throat, spat upon the ground and said, "You never know what these goddamn peasants will give you to drink."

"They do too much dirty work for the landlords," said the man with Santino. "They kill with no conscience, let them think tonight we have given them poison. Let the thought burn in their heads and let them think of death as we have to."

In the catacombs the men began their descent with the landlord leading the group. "This wine," he said, "it is the best of all."

"Yes, yes," answered Michael. "It has aged just right. There is no wine like it in all of Italy and it would be a great honor for us to share it with you. We all know how important you are here in Calabria."

"Santino doesn't think so. He doesn't realize that if it were not for my land, he and his family would be dead of hunger. I could have him thrown out tomorrow, then he would see. He'll give what he owes or I will not wait for hunger to take his life. You can't let these commoners get out of hand or they will think they are important. You must be firm!"

A strange silence settled over the group. The landlord had spoken as though he were with the other landlords. All of his pomp spilled out over the men like honey over an invading ant. A realization of why he was there with the men poured over him but he would not think of it. He had power over them and had nothing to fear. The land was his, he carried the politicians in his back pocket with the police, and if all else failed there was the Black Hand that he paid to do his dirty work. He had nothing to fear. The silence made Michael realize that there might be trouble if Colonzago suspected anything. "The wine is like no other. But I have been hesitant to brag of it until I had an opinion from someone such as yourself," he said.

"It is best to do so lest one make a fool of himself," Colonzago said.

The men continued on. The passage was cold, dark and narrow. The fat man nearly filled the passageway. The torches of the men burned dimly. Each flickered with movement. Then the small party stopped. The landlord had come to the burial chamber of some noble families of long ago. Several skeletons lay upon stone slabs in small rooms off the main passage.

"Who are these people?" Colonzago demanded.

"They are nobody who will hurt you," Michael answered.

"They are noblemen of the past, those who held power over the rest. This place is a tribute to them. They did not realize that justice meant nothing until they were dead. We may be miserable here but there is something more than filling the belly. See them, they die just like we all will."

"Yes, but if they were noblemen then they lived well."

"Yes, and at the price of many. But enough about the dead. We are alive and it is the time to celebrate."

Colonzago looked at the passage filled with men. He could not see beyond the last corner. The men stood looking at him and then he realized that there was only one way now, forward. It was then that he began to be aware of his helplessness. All of those who protected him were on the surface and the men that feared him stood between him and them. He continued down the passage, trying to dismiss the thought that they might do him harm.

Water began to fill the tunnel and Colonzago began slipping. Twice he fell and Michael helped him up. "Perhaps it will be better if we return tomorrow," he said after the second fall.

"But we have to work the fields tomorrow," Michael said. "And we know you do not want us to miss a day's work." The floor became treacherous with mud and Colonzago was forced to balance himself against the wall. He soon came to the end of the passageway. There it widened into a circular area, large enough for the men to gather around.

"The keg! The keg! There is the keg! Let us drink," said the landlord, crossing the area, his feet splashing water as he crossed. "Bring me a flask and let us drink!"

Michael handed him a flask which he filled. Turning to the men, he held it up and said, "To all my hard working tenants! I drink to your health."

"Don't worry, Colonzago, we will stay healthy. Healthy enough to work your land while you are in Rome talking with the other landlords about how to handle your peasants."

The landlord stood staring at nothing. Hope leaving his mind, he looked at the keg and said, "It's not set in the wall! The keg, it's not set in the wall!"

When Santino and the other man arrived, Colonzago was chained to the wall, the water rising slowly past his knees. The others stood apart, allowing Santino to go past them.

"You're too late," Michael said to him, "the wine has already done its work." Santino looked at the man standing in the dim light, the water creeping slowly up his legs, his limp arms chained to the wall.

"So we meet," he said to the landlord. "It is late."

"Santino, you have always been a fair man. Please talk to these men. Make them understand that this is murder."

"When your body is afflicted with disease, you kill it."

"In God's name, Santino, in your conscience you cannot murder! My blood will be on your hands. In God's name, my blood will stain your hands and your family!"

"No, my friend, the river will wash our hands of you and your blood. You see, I have grown tired of fearing the wind."

The water within the cave began to rise quickly and a cold chill passed over them through the cracks in the walls where the water seeped in. The men stared at the fat man chained against the wall.

"Bastards!" The landlord screamed. "You think by killing me you'll be better than you are! Bastards! Peasants! I spit on all of you. They will find me and you will all pay. They will come in the night and kill you all!"

The men began the ascent through the narrow pathway. They could hear the landlord's curses.

"He will grow tired of cursing soon, when the water covers his head," Santino said to Michael as they walked.

"Yes, tonight he sleeps with the fish," Michael answered.

"The malocchio on all of you! The malocchio on your families!"

The men stopped when they heard the words.

"To hell with your Sicilian curse! Suffer as we have suffered, and die with the curse you have been to us all of your life. You can curse hell when you get there. This curse means nothing to me," Santino said. "Just the same, tonight I will light a candle to Saint Anthony."

"Light one for me, Santino, maybe then I will sleep nights."

Maria looked at Michael as he finished. Her hands had become still.

"God cannot be happy with what you have done," she said.

"God does not have to live here. We do. Colonzago was a man, and we had to deal with him as men. Would you rather your children live in danger of their lives?" he answered.

She could not answer. She too was tired of living in fear.

Michael left the table. From the next room, Vicenzo looked at his mother's face and could tell by her expression that the situation was very serious. Young as he was, he could not understand the full impact, but he knew that the fat man who scared him and caused his father to act so strangely would never return.

When night came, Santino returned home. Nothing was said of what Maria had learned from Michael until they were in bed. Maria lay on her back and spoke softly. "I talked with Michael today."

She became hesitant and tried to begin again, "We talked of the landlord."

There was a moment of silence, then Santino turned from his side and looked at his wife. She did not return the look and he settled on his back. Again the silence came and she knew she must continue.

"I know what happened."

"Then you know more than I do."

She hoped he would say more. When he did not, she again tried to fill the silence.

"There is much I do not understand, and because of this I fear many things. If the police find the body they will begin asking questions. He had many friends in the Black Hand, and they too will seek revenge."

"A man who has friends such as his also has enemies, and they will be happy when they hear of his disappearance. He has been a cruel man and has died as he lived," Santino said directly, "and I know nothing of him, only that at the end of the month I will pay the rent."

"Santino, if someone comes . . ."

"Listen," he cut her short, "I will take care of anything that must be taken care of. I will protect my family the only way I know. You have work to do. Do it and do not concern yourself with my responsibilities. If I have to deal with the police or the *Black Hand*, I will do so. If I must settle with God, then I will do that too. He would not have made me a man if he did not want me to protect what is mine. As for Colonzago, you do not know anything. *Capisci?*"

"*Capisco.*"

Santino felt the force of his own words. He took his wife's hand and squeezed it gently and then embraced her.

# CHAPTER

## 3

It had been many years since Vicenzo listened from another room and watched his mother's face as Michael spoke. The words were not so important and he could not remember them, but the lesson he knew well and had learned many times. Now he was content to be home, and he sat on a large boulder near the bottom of the hill watching his chickens pick at the ground and at each other. In the distance a small dot appeared above the rocky face of the hill. The old man saw it and knew the vulture would soon come to eat.

"You will eat anything," he said to the chickens as he watched them pick at small rocks on the ground. "And he must have no less appetite if he will eat such a bird, and right now I am too tired to protect you."

The old man looked up at the vulture and said, "Yet these chickens are mine, and I cannot let you take them. After living here you understand that I cannot let you take them."

The old man gripped his cane and thought, I can at least throw this when he comes too close.

The vulture was still far away when the old man's grandson rode up the steep driveway to the house.

"Hello, *nonno*" he called out.

"Hello," the old man replied mechanically.

"How are you feeling today?" the young boy asked as he got off his bicycle.

"*Bene,* You seen you' daddy?"

"He's supposed to be here. He was going downtown and then come up here. I don't know where he is."

The old man shrugged his shoulders and turned to look at the vulture, leading the boy's attention to the bird.

"It's a chicken hawk. Do you want me to kill it?"

"Go ina the house. By the sink there's a gun anna some shells. You bring 'um."

The boy went into the house and returned with a small caliber shot gun and three shells. "I'll get him, nonno," he said as he passed by the old man, climbing between the strands of fence and beginning the ascent up the hill. When he crossed between the goats, they ran to one corner of the pen, the leader's bell clanging as he ran, the others crying out for protection.

The old man watched the boy go quickly up the hill. He could see little movement as the branches of the pinon trees swayed with a warm December breeze. The sun turns everything brown, he thought. It has been too long since it has snowed. The winter months are like no others anywhere. The sun would have me plant the garden in December and pick it in February, but tomorrow it may snow.

A few clouds began passing over the hill and the old man thought that it would snow soon. But it is warm and nature could easily catch us off guard if we did not prepare for her, he thought. He pulled his green cap down on his forehead so that the sun would not burn his eyes. His hair was pure white. None of the black that it once was could be found on his head or face. Only a discolored yellow on his mustache broke the completeness of it.

The old man remembered when he had stood on top of the hill and tried to reach up into the clouds that came quickly, his arms stretched out, reaching for the fine mist. It rained and then he came down from the hill without having felt the clouds, and the feeling went unsatisfied and it remained with him each time the clouds came. But now the sun was bright and there were only a few high clouds and they could not hide the sun.

The boy was near the top of the hill. The old man looked hard but he could not see him moving among the brown rocks. I cannot see as I once could, he mused. It is good a thing that the boy came, or the vultures would kill all the chickens. While the boy was hunting the bird, his father arrived. The old man heard him drive up, but did not turn. The old man's son approached him as he looked toward the hill.

"That's Sil's bike, isn't it?" he asked as he neared. "Where is he?"
The old man gestured toward the hill with his head.
"What's he doing up there?"
Again the gesture.
"Why didn't he wait for it to come nearer the chickens?"
The old man shrugged his shoulders as if to say, ask him. He smiled and said, "He isa young. You bringa the whiskey?"
"Dr. Biber says you're not supposed to drink."
"When I don' feel good, I drink, and I feel better."
"It makes you sick to your stomach. It irritates your ulcer."
"I'ma no talkin' abouta my stomach. Bringa the whiskey and the cigarettes."
A shot from the hill broke the conversation. Both looked at the sky. Neither could find the bird.
"He's a gooda boy. Helpa me into the house. I wanna talka to you about something."
"Pa, I don't think you should move. You've got everything you need here."
"It'sa too much. I canna take care no more. The rabbits need to be cleaned or they die. I killa two this morning. They're ina the box . . . take 'um."
"Let me give you money for them."
"Nooo! Take 'um."
"You give me rabbits, you give Tony rabbits, you won't kill any for yourself. Let me give you the money for them."
"Take 'um," the old man insisted. But the son would leave the money on the kitchen sink as he always did. He knew that the old man received more money now than he did when he worked the mines. He remembered the first time he received his pension check from the company. He held it out to his son and said, "Look ata what they pay me for no work. The firsta time I worka the mine they pay me sixty-four cents a ton. Somma times I no see that much." This, he felt, was for work that he had done but never been paid for, so it was owed to him. The first of the month the Social Security check came too and this also, he believed, was for work that he had never been paid for. And there was a third check, the one from the black lung fund. He knew that the pain would never leave his chest and the doctor told him that his lungs were black and rotten because of

the coal dust from the mine. When the doctor told him there was no cure, he pictured in his mind a piece of wood that had been chewed by termites and was waiting to collapse.

"Helpa me into the house," the old man said.

The two went into the house and the son went to the refrigerator to get the rabbits. "How do you feel?" the son asked.

"Eaaa," the old man answered shaking his hand." Sommatimes OK, sommatimes notta so good."

"You've got everything you need here."

"It'sa too much. I canna no take care of it. You remember whenna you mamma take care ofa house. Looka now. I tried but it'sa too much." The son did not answer. He began washing the dishes in the sink and put them where they would dry.

The boy came into the house with the gun. "I killed the vulture," he said putting the gun back where he had gotten it. The old man took the boy's cheek with his forefinger and thumb, squeezed it and said, "Gooda boy."

The old man had done that often and it did not hurt so much now as it once did.

"Sita down and have a little wine."

He motioned to his son to bring it from the refrigerator.

"Pa, it makes him sick if he drinks it this early in the day."

The old man looked at the boy and could see the disappointment in his face. He winked at him.

"Here are the four dollars for the rabbits," Vicenzo's son said, handing him the money.

The old man pointed to the door and replied, "Take it and go getta the whiskey and cigarettes."

The old man's voice was firm and the son folded the money into his palm, then turned toward the door. Before he reached the door, the old man spoke again, firmly. "Anda bringa some sausage. Anda don't geta lost."

The man turned as he opened the door to see his son smiling and said, "So that's where you got that."

He closed the back door and went through the back porch. When he passed by the window of the porch he heard through the open screen, "Go to the ice box and geta the wine."

That night the snow came. The old man did not see it begin to fall but he felt it. He sat in the Volunteer Inn across from a short Italian man playing a game with the fingers. The two flashed numbers with the fingers on one hand. As they did this they called out numbers that would equal the total number of fingers. They played the game quickly, turning the hand when neither called out the correct number. It was hard for one who was not used to the game to understand, for the numbers and fingers seemed to be continuous.

The old man's hand dropped to the table. The number he called out was equal to the number of fingers he and his friend had held out, and he had won. The other man motioned to the bartender to bring the old man another drink.

When the waiter brought the drink, the old man said, "Calla my son to come and geta me."

In a short time the waiter returned and told the old man, "Your son wasn't home but your grandson said he would come as soon as his mother gets home."

The old man continued to play the game and before long he was drunk. The noise around him began to fade. The pool balls in the next room cracked together and plopped into the pockets. The words of those around him became half-sounds, and in his stomach came the pain of whiskey pushing nausea into his chest. And from the past came voices . . . .

"What does it mean, this WOP."

"It means you have no papers."

"I gotta papers. They sign 'um when I come."

"No, you don't understand. He says a dumb wop, he means you're no good except to dig the coal. The mules are worth money, you're not worth nothing—you're a wop!"

"That somma na bitch."

"Who's a somma na bitch, Vicenzo?" the man across the table asked, half-drunk.

"That somma na bitch, he says I'm a wop," the old man came back, raising his voice. "Somma na bitch!"

"Sure, Vicenzo, you're a wop, I'm a wop, whata the hell does it matter?"

"Becausa we works lika animals anda we acted lika animals. They made us lika animals."

The old man put his hand to his forehead. The pounding began in his temples and a moment later he threw his arms forward in disgust. The table flew to the floor, the bar became silent.

"Somma na bitches!"

"Take it easy, Vicenzo. You're not in the camps any more," his friend said, trying to relax him.

The grandson entered the front door and saw the others picking up the table. Quickly he came to the old man.

"What happened, *nonno?*"

The other man answered, "He was trying to get up and knocked the table down." The old man motioned for the boy to help him up and said, "Let's geta the hell outta here."

Outside the bar the air was cold and damp. A thin layer of snow covered the ground. The old man's cane left small round imprints in the snow as he leaned heavily downward. The boy walked beside him, watching as he took short half-steps to the old pick-up truck. The seat felt cold as the old man got into the truck. He felt the cold penetrate through his pants.

The ride home was a slow one. The sound of the heater blowing hot air caused the old man to fade into half-consciousnesss, his body rocking slightly with the movement of the truck.

"How do you feel, *nonno?*"

The boy's voice went unnoticed.

"*Nonno,* you feel all right?"

"Bono," the old man replied, "justa tired."

The truck climbed slowly up the incline to the back of the house. The boy got out of the truck and hurried to the old man.

"It'sa very peaceful," the old man said. "Looka, you canna see the sky. The snow comes froma nowhere. It'sa gonna snow till morning, then the sun will shine. We are very fortunate here, the sun shines everyday."

"Yes, *nonno,* let's go into the house where it's warm."

The two began walking slowly to the back door, the old man leaning on the cane, the boy holding his right arm. When the old man turned the corner of the house, his cane slipped on the wet cement and he fell to his knees in pain. The boy reached for him.

"*Nonno! Nonno!* You all right, *nonno?* I'm sorry! I slipped."

"Giva me the cane."

"*Nonno,* I'm sorry. Here, take my arm."

"Giva me the cane!"

"Here, *nonno,* here's the cane. Do you want me to carry you in?"

"Helpa me to the house."

The old man rose slowly with the support of the cane and the boy. He leaned for a moment against the house and his grip tightened around the cane. The snow melted against his skin and he held the cane up so that small beads of water fell from his hand. He swung his arm toward the house so that the cane struck the wall and shattered. The boy stood silent.

"Helpa me inside."

"Yes, *nonno*," the boy replied calmly.

Inside, the old man rested on his back in bed, the boy at his side.

"Do you want me to call for a doctor, *nonno?*"

"No, I'ma all right."

The old man winced in pain and breathed from his mouth.

"How olda are you?" he asked the boy.

"Seventeen, *nonno.* I was seventeen yesterday."

"It'sa been a longa time since you' grama see you. She used to bounce you ona her knee. She says you gonna be a great musician becausa you' ears. She wasa very beautiful. You remember you' grama?"

"I think I do, *nonno.* I remember her sitting in the front yard by the trumpet vine."

"You were very young."

The old man began resting easier.

"Can I get you anything, *nonno?*"

"Go in the kitchen and get the gun."

"What do you want the gun for?"

"Go get 'um."

The boy left and returned with the gun.

"You keepa this, fora you' birthday."

"I can't take your gun, nonno."

"I give 'um to you."

"What if more hawks come?"

"You kill 'um."

The old man took the boy's hand and squeezed it and smiled with his half-laugh.

"A longa time ago, I come this country for something. I was never ina the right places or knew the right people. My brothers come too. I no heard froma most a them. Maybe they fine. But you' daddy no have to go inna the mine. He went to school and gotta gooda job. He's gotta nice house. He no hava to work like me. Now it'sa you' turn. Ita took us to you, that'sa why we came. You do even more than me or you' daddy. You understand?"

"I think so, *nonno*."

"You look atta you' daddy's hands."

The old man opened his hands, showing them to the boy, his bent fingers and scared palms shaking slightly.

"You hands no lika this."

"No, *nonno*."

"Gooda boy. You be a musician, playa the music you playa fora you' grama."

"How did your hands get like that, *nonno*?" the boy asked slowly.

"You wanna know about you' granpa?"

"Yes, *nonno*."

"Maybe it'sa no so good."

"I want to know."

"We worka longa time, like this." He began moving his arms as though he had a pick in them. "Every day we worka. Sommatimes all day and parta the night. Pretty soon you' *nonno's* hands no straighten." The old man held out a hand that looked more like a claw. The boy became frightened inside.

"Sommatimes they say you' *nonno* isa hard man. Many times you' *nonno* has to be hard, or he woulda no be here. I will tell you sommathing about you' *nonno*."

The old man talked for half an hour, then fell into a peaceful rest. The boy sat for a short time looking at the old man. He put his fingers on the old man's hand and felt the skin where it had been scarred by blisters. He repeated some of the things he had heard, then went into the kitchen and sat with his head on his arms and cried.

# CHAPTER

# 4

Early the next morning the old man sat at the kitchen table, gumming a piece of bread and cheese. Small air bubbles formed on the false teeth which were in a glass on the sink. I am very tired, he thought. I remember when a night's rest gave me strength, and now I only am tired.

Outside another chicken hawk circled above the hill not far from his house. The church bell tolled a short distance away. The goats moved to one side of the hill, the rabbits moved quickly in their cages, the chickens turned their heads and stopped their picking. In the house there was no change.

There were two holy cards stuck to the side of the mirror in the bedroom. The old man did not think of them now, but the names of the people on the backs were as familiar to him as his own.

He was the last of seven brothers. The first died before he was old enough to understand the finality of death. The others came to America at different times after him, and the dream that brought him here burned in all of them. But there were no dreams left now, only waiting. He remembered his father sitting on the porch, his head resting on his forearm, his fist wrapped around a letter. His mother stood over him, crying.

"I don't understand. What did Fortunato say happened?" Maria asked.

"There was some kind of card game and an argument. Augusto is dead."

"And will they send him home?"

"He is already buried."

Vicenzo's brother had gone to America before he knew him well. He barely remembered times that the two had spend together, but they were times that left a deep mark upon his young mind. Augusto had found work in America and he often sent money to Italy. And this, Vicenzo thought, was America.

"I must go to America," Santino said to Maria. "I must find out what has happened to my son."

"You will go to America?"

"I must."

"And leave your family?"

"Michael will see that you have what you need."

"And you will go to kill?"

"I will do what must be done. Fortunato did not say how it happened." Santino's face was puffed and reddened about the eyes from holding back the tears that he felt in his heart. He pushed himself back on the rocker that he had rocked his first-born in and came slowly forward. Maria wiped her eyes and spoke again.

"I do not think you should leave your family."

"I must go to my son. He was the eldest." Santino's face began to show the agony he felt in his heart. "I must go to the one that has been lost."

"If he was with Fortunato, the Black Hand was there too. And if you go, they will kill you too."

"I will have justice for my son."

"You will have revenge."

"What is the difference? If I were not a man I would not care."

"Augusto was my son also."

"Then you should understand why I must go."

Vicenzo's presence was then noticed.

"And what about him?" Maria asked, pointing to Vicenzo. "Would you leave him fatherless?"

Vicenzo's eyes met his father's for a brief moment the two stood motionless.

"He is your son too."

"And if such a thing should happen to him I would go also."

Maria motioned for Vicenzo and began to cry. Vicenzo went to his mother, his eyes never leaving his father. His mother pulled him to her breast. Still he looked at his father.

"I must go," Santino said quietly, and the boy understood.

Santino left for America shortly after that. His journey passed slowly and he thought of his son and the justice that he sought, the justice that Maria called revenge. She feared for him to leave for America as if the name held some curse.

Their first-born son was gone, leaving a void that could not be filled by their other children. Maria and Santino did not love the others less, but they remembered the first time that they made love and the first time their love brought forth a child. And now that was gone. Augusto was the one who had suffered for Santino's youthful mistakes, those first mistakes of a young father. If he could defy death and bring back his son, Santino would give his own life.

Vicenzo watched and listened to his father those few days before he left and he could not feel the tears of his mother. Instead he felt the power of his father.

The America Santino found was a nation trying to mold itself into an industrialized power. He followed his son's path to the coal camps of Colorado. From down in the black bowels of the earth came the source of the monster's energy. Here in the shafts of the mines, those who dared to remove the black coal from the earth risked death.

The small coal towns had been modeled on the cities of Europe. The streets were cobblestone and narrow. The church steeple towered above the buildings and could be seen from any part of the town. The town sat in a valley surrounded by hills, on one side mostly stony, their bare tops jutting out of the earth smooth and hard. To the south the hills were covered with evergreens and brown spots. These continued until they rose up to form a peak of such height that it made the town seem almost in a hole.

Deceptive autumn winds blew dried leaves about the street as Santino moved slowly down the walk, looking for someone to direct him to Fortunato Reno, the man who had informed him of his son's death.

The street narrowed into a pile of buildings as Santino walked from the train station. The chugging sound of the train slowly pulling away from the station left Santino in silence for a few moments. The picture before him faded like an old photograph. For a moment he felt the past that his son had been a part of. Slowly he stepped toward the middle of the street, looking about at the flat front of the wooden stores, the names and letters he did not understand. On his back he carried a pack which was strapped over one shoulder. His greyish-brown suit was covered with dust from the ride. The *berretto* he wore was slightly tilted and his thick, black, wavy hair surrounded it on all sides. His forehead sloped slightly and his Roman nose protruded over his mustache which curled at both ends. His jawline was stern and distinct, and his eyes were deep and dark as he looked about.

There was music playing somewhere in the distance. It came from the cluster of buildings about a quarter of a mile from where he stood. He began walking toward it. He stooped down and ran his finger over one of the red bricks that made up the street. The letters TRINIDAD had been stamped across each brick. He began to walk in the direction of the music.

"Hey, get the hell off the street!"

He glared up to see a line of men in dark suits turning the corner on the upper part of the street.

"You there, get the hell off the street!"

Santino turned and saw a man standing in front of one of the stores.

He stared at the man as though deaf.

"What's the matter with you? Can't you hear?"

The man motioned for Santino to move to the side of the street. Santino walked over to the man.

"You don't understand what I'm saying, do you? Must be another import. Well, you picked a hell of a time to come here. Those men up there," he said, pointing to the groups approaching in a slow, solemn march, "they mean business. Why the hell am I telling you this? You don't understand English."

He looked at Santino who shrugged his shoulders and gave him the deaf look again. It is better to pretend to know nothing, he thought. Even though I do not understand, I will wait and watch.

"Here, sit here." The man from the store motioned for him to sit on the ledge of his front window. "You will be out of the way here. There's been enough killing already. Hell you don't know what I am saying. Don't move, don't go out there. Understand? Stay here." He patted the window ledge and disappeared through the front door of the store.

When he returned, he had a rifle with him. Santino saw him place it just inside the door where it could not be seen from the street. By then some of the men had begun to pass in front of the store.

There were two lines of them extending back to the intersection of the T-shaped street. Santino watched as they began to move slowly by, the stern European face expressionless, walking as though the horse-drawn cart, which had led them, had some sort of hypnotic power over them.

Santino felt cold air surround him. A funeral coach led the procession. It appeared a shadow in the bright sun. The horses focused ahead, their eyes shielded on both sides by blinders, pulling the casket upon wheels, the doors on both sides not allowing entrance to heaven or hell. There was the *squeek—squeek—squeek*—of the wheels and the *kook—kook—kook—kook—kook* of the hooves upon the street—and then silence upon silence as the men passed. There seemed no end to them as Santino looked up the street.

"This must have been a great man," Santino said, half-aloud in Italian, "or a great cause."

"You don't speak any English?" the man from the store asked.

Santino had forgotten about him and again shrugged his shoulders.

"You're better off not knowing what has gone on here. This funeral won't go unanswered." The man's words were interrupted by the sound of horses galloping down the street in a head-on collision with the men.

The funeral carriage stopped as did the men. The horsemen came within thirty yards of them broke rank and formed a line the width of the street. Their commander led his horse to the front of the line and paraded his horse across the brick street.

The man from the store pulled at Santino's sleve and motioned for him to go inside the store.

"Come inside."

Santino shurgged his shoulders.

"It's better not to see some things. Come inside where it will be safer."

The neatly formed lined of troops impressed Santino. Each of the men sat upon a well-trained horse, its head tilted slightly downward. Here is the power of the landlord, Santino thought. Working men could not afford such fine animals.

The uniforms of the men gave evidence of great organization. Each of the esquestrians wore a khaki uniform with brass buttons which flashed in the sunlight. They have very fine boots, Santino thought, and their eyes are protected by fine hats. I would like to ride in such an army.

The leader of the men approached the funeral cart.

"You are not supposed to be on the streets today. Can't you read the posters?"

A man in the front of the procession answered in Santino's language. Santino looked at him and realized that he had been so taken by the uniforms of the others that he had not noticed that many of the men were dressed like himself.

"Speak in English. I don't understand your gibberish!"

The man stood silent. The leader turned his horse sideways and gave the command.

"Present arms."

The men drew sabers and positioned them.

The man who had answered the commander began to move slowly toward the funeral cart when another of the men spoke.

"Surely the order didn't mean for us not to bury our dead."

"The order said no one is to be out in the street organizing violence."

"We do not intend violence, we only wish to lay our friend to rest."

"Your friend has caused me more grief than I care to talk about."

"And now he is dead and he can cause you no grief."

"You know damn well he's become a martyr. You look upon him as some sort of hero. I read the papers. I know how people will look back at what has happened. I will be the scoundrel. I will be the killer. Get off the streets! Get off now!"

"We are not women who you can so easily scatter, Commander. You will have to pay to exert your power now."

The men had drawn very near the funeral cart. The commander looked at their faces. A battle here during a funeral would go against him heavily in the eyes of the state.

"I won't give you any more martyrs," he said, turning his horse toward his men.

He returned to the troops. They changed rank, this time lining both sides of the street, their sabers still drawn. The funeral march started again, moving between the ranks of soldiers. When they had all passed, the soldiers closed together and followed.

Santino rose. He thought I would like to speak to this man who stands so bravely before the saber. He began to leave the front of the store when he felt a hand on his arm.

"Where do you think you're going?" It was the owner of the store. "There's going to be trouble again, more people are going to die. You better leave here, get back on the train and go back to wherever you came from."

Santino extended his hand to the man and said, "Tanti grazie." The sky overhead was beginning to cloud. Dust swirled about the horses' hooves as the wind pushed its way through the street. Santino followed at a distance until the men reached the country. There, next to a hill, the gravestones stood in no pattern beneath the peak. The words the priest said were lost in the wind and Santino watched as the shadows of the clouds moved over the peak and across the land.

When the priest was finished most of the men started to filter out of the lot. Two men filled in the hole and three men stood watching. One of them was the man with whom Santino wanted to speak.

When he drew near, Santino asked the man, "Parla Italiano?"

The man turned and answered, "Si." Again he watched as the men shoveled.

"This man, was he respected much?"

"As all men should be," came the reply. This time the man did not turn.

"I am very sorry. He must have been close to you."

"Sorry for what, friend? He died doing what he thought was right. Death should be so kind to us all."

"And death was kind to your friend?"

"Death is kind to all those who dare to live. He has become even greater in his death."

"There is a burial ceremony for all types of men," Santino said, "and if he is so great, would he not be even greater to continue to live?" His words went unanswered.

One of the men next to the man to whom Santino spoke motioned for Santino to walk with him.

"My friend is grieved by the death of a man who stood by us all when we all might have died," he said to Santino, "and sometimes it is better not to know so much about certain things."

"The men on the horses?"Santino asked.

"Yes, the men on the horses. Where do you come from?"

"Calabria."

"And for what reason?"

"I come to find my son."

"Your son lives here in Trinidad?"

"The last I heard from him, he lived in a place called Valdez."

"Yes, it is up the river from here. And what was his name?"

"Augusto Caputo."

The two men continued walking and when they came to the funeral coach they stopped.

"Augusto Caputo. I think I know of Caputos that live up the river. There was one who was involved in the Valdez shootout a short time ago. I do not know what his first name was. Did he specify where he lived?"

"No. He said he had to move frequently to find work."

The man opened the back of the coach. There were many hand-guns and rifles inside.

"Is your son a miner?"

"Yes."

"I will take you to someone who will help you. I know a man who has helped many newcomers. Perhaps he will know something."

"There are many guns here," Santino said. "Many could have been killed."

"This is true," replied the man. "As you have said, there are many reasons for a funeral."

The man mounted the coach on one side, Santino on the other.

The air was beginning to chill. Santino pulled the upper part of his coat together. Soon tiny flakes began to fill the air. The coach rode noisily along a dirt road.

Soon they came to a river. As they crossed it Santino looked up the canyon where the river flowed and saw in the distance the snow capped mountains. This is a strange place, Santino thought. I have felt as these men do. It is a strange feeling. I know how they feel inside, it is in their faces.

The men rode for a distance down a road that had houses on both sides, most of which were small and looked like they had been stamped from the same mold. To the south loomed the peak over which the clouds came. After a short time the driver stopped the horses in front of a large white house which stood in contrast to the rest. The front walk was guarded by two clay pots, the contents of which had long passed with the summer and now stood empty.

The driver told Santino to wait for a moment and went to the front door of the house. He knocked several times until another man appeared at the door. The two men talked, the man at the door looking at Santino.

During their conversation, Santino sat thinking that it must be near dusk. I cannot see the sunset, he thought. These men are familiar yet strangers. They are Italian, I can see, but I will trust no one so that I will not be taken advantage of. I will find what happened to my son and those who are responsible will pay. I have dealt with more powerful men than these.

As Santino sat thinking, he heard his last name called from the front porch.

"Caputo? *Vieni qua?*"

Santino left the cart and went to the front of the house. "Come in, Mr. Caputo," the owner of the house said.

"I am wet and dirty," Santino answered. "Perhaps it is best if I stay here by the door. I will not take much of your time."

"You are not used to the snow and it is going to be a bad night. Please come in where it is warm," the man answered.

Santino went into the house. The warm air felt good. The man who had brought him said goodby to them and was gone.

"You have come a long way," the man said, turning to Santino.

"I have good reason," Santino said.

"So I have just heard," the man said. "My name is Frank Naccarto." He extended his hand.

"And mine is Santino Caputo. I have come here looking for my son."

"Your son lives here in Trinidad?"

"In a place called Valdez. But he does not live there any more."

"Then he has moved."

"He has died. I received this in the mail some time ago," Santino said, handing Frank the letter that he had pulled from his shirt pocket. Frank read the letter and gave it back to Santino.

"I know the man who sent you this. We shall go find him tomorrow, but it will not be easy to get him to talk."

"You know the man?"

"Yes, anyone who has been in Valdez on payday knows Fortunato. And how was it that you heard of your son from him?"

"We have known his family for a long time. His father is a decent man."

"Then let's leave it at that. Tomorrow we shall find him. Excuse me," Frank said. "I think that my wife has not heard me."

Frank left the room and Santino warmed himself at the fireplace. Frank's house was like the landlord's in its beauty but unlike it in its warmth. The times that I was in the landlord's house it was because he wanted me to know that there was a difference between myself and him. But this man is different, he does not act like there is a difference between one man and another. I can see it in his eyes and feel it in his voice. His home is very beautiful. I have never seen blue glass cover a table before or make up the doors of the china closet. The floors shine, and the wood must be well cared for.

"Here," Frank said, returning to the room, "it is not much but I think that you will find that my wife is a very good cook."

"I do not wish to be any trouble. Maybe it is best if I come back tomorrow."

"And where will you go on a night such as this? I would feel insulted if you did not accept my hospitality."

"Thank you, my friend. It is true I do not know anyone here and I have not seen snow like this since I was in the northern part of Italy. It is probably why I stayed in the south."

"Yes, I remember the beauty of the hills and the sweet smell of the sea. The sun warms the earth there like nowhere else."

"You have been there?" Santino asked.

"I was born in Grimaldi and my wife in Cozenza. My mother was from the north and my father was from the south too. The man who brought you here said that you were from Calabria."

"I am from Aiello."

"Then I could have thrown a rock and hit the town."

"Why did you leave Italy?"

"The land could not feed us all and we heard many things about America."

"Things are still the same and you have done well here."

"There are many ways of making money in this country. It is a strange country but there are ways of making money. Your son came here for that?"

"He did. Italy is sick with landholders and the rest of us who work can barely survive. And so many son came here to get what he could not get there."

Santino continued eating. The fire crackled and Frank fed it more wood. As the flames grew higher a large shadow danced behind the men on the wall.

"I saw a funeral in town today. It was a curious thing. In the middle of paying their respects to the dead, the men were willing to die. Was this for a cause?"

"The man you saw being buried today lived for the same reason that many of us live for, a right to live like a man in decency."

"And he was killed for this?"

"Many have, Santino, and it is for something worth dying for."

"I have seen men die for such things as you have here."

"You mean in the old country. There are men here in America that would do the same. It is a mistake. Decency isn't this house or the things in it. Only," Frank hesitated for a moment, "Only the family is worth dying for."

"Did you know my son? I was told you know and help many from the old country."

"What was his name?"

"Augusto."

"Tomorrow I will ask and see what I can find out, but for tonight, you rest. I have asked my wife to prepare a place for you to sleep." A woman had come into the room and Frank went over to her. "Santino," he said, "I want you to meet my wife, Marietta."

"It is my pleasure," Santino said, looking at Marietta. Then he turned to Frank. "I cannot impose on you like this. You have done too much for me."

"We have a big house," Marietta broke in, "and there are only two of us. I have already prepared a bed."

"Your kindness is difficult to refuse," Santino said.

"Come, rest tonight and tomorrow we will see what we can find," Frank said, putting his hand on Santino's shoulder.

"And maybe in the morning we can talk," Marietta said. "It has been a long time since I have seen Italy."

"I thank you again," Santino said, "and we'll be sure to talk in the morning."

Santino was taken to a room at the back of the house. There he laid down on a small bed and closed his eyes. He could hear the sound of the snowflakes scratching against the window and the murmured voices from the other room. Before fear and apprehension could again bother him, he was asleep.

The next morning Santino awoke with the sunrise. He lay in bed listening. He heard a sizzling sound coming from the kitchen. He felt the coldness of the bottom of the bed with his foot as he moved it between the sheet and blanket. Warm air passed over his face from a vent above him. During the night I sweat, he thought to himself. I hope that I did not stain the sheets. I will wash them if I have to.

Santino looked about the room. He saw furniture as fine as that in the room he had been in the night before. In one corner of the room stood a statue of Saint Anthony. Above the mirror was a picture of Saint Theresa holding an armful of roses. A crucifix hung above the bed and rosary beads were draped around the bed post. The chest of drawers across from the bed was made of oak with inlaid designs carved into the wood. Even the floor, he thought, shines where the rug does not cover. No man shows such kindness and does not expect something in return, yet what do I have that this man can want?

Soon Santino dressed. He dressed in his warmest clothes, remembering the snow from the night before. At the breakfast table Frank's wife asked many questions about the old country.

"I have been here five years," she said smiling, "and already the water has turned my hair dark. It was such a beautiful blond in Italy."

"But it has made you no less attractive," Santino answered.

Marietta blushed, putting her hand to the side of her mouth and turning her face slightly.

"To such compliments she would listen to all day," Frank laughed.

"Yes, that is one thing they all have in common," Santino answered.

"Now, my friend, tell me what you came to find."

In a low voice, Santino began. "My son worked in a place called Valdez. A short time ago I got a letter from America that says he was killed. I come to find out what is true."

"Your son was a miner?"

"Yes, how do you know?"

"There is little else one can do in Valdez. It is a mining camp. Fortunato sent you the letter?"

"Yes, Fortunato Reno."

When Santino said the name, Frank looked at his wife. They both became uneasy.

"You know him?" Santino asked.

"I have had aquaintance with the man."

"Is there something about him?"

"When a man works as hard as he does on earning a reputation, he deserves it."

"Is he Black Hand?"

"No, no. A man like him would not live long in the Black Hand. He is too loose with his tongue. But he would sell his mother for the right price. Did he ask for anything?"

"No. In the letter he said something about a card game."

"Then we will start looking for Fortunato. Finish eating and we will go."

Frank rose from the table and looked out the back window of the porch.

"The peak is clear," he said. "Today it will warm up."

"How do you know this?" Santino asked.

"The peak forcasts the storms for us. When the peak clears, the day will be good. "Come, Santino. Let us go up the river. But first let me get you a heavy coat."

"I will be all right," Santino answered.

"Dressed like that in Calabria perhaps, but not in Colorado."

Frank went to the back of the house to get the cart. Snow had covered the ground during the night. Cold air rose from it and left a burning sensation in Santino's eyes. He was not used to the cold. When Frank came back, Santino got into the cart. They headed into the hills on a narrow, winding road. Pinon trees grew between the evergreens. The ground between them was solid white. Many of the branches of the trees hung low from the weight of the snow, and occasionally a branch would snap back to its original position, the snow scattering to the ground. The wind swept drifts to the bottom of the trees. At the top of the drifts ridges sloped gently to the base of the trees.

Santino turned as the cart rounded a hill, exposing a shallow river. The glare of the sun made him squint. He said, "It is very beautiful and quiet. Yesterday it was so dark and the wind blew hard. And today it is all so beautiful."

"Perhaps Mother Nature does not like to be watched when she's at work," Frank answered.

Soon houses began to come into view. There were only a few at first, then more and more began to dot the hills.

"The houses are like boxes," Santino said. "Men do not have large families here."

"These are company houses. The men are miners."

"The houses belong to the company the men work for?"

"Yes."

"This company, it owns much land."

"All of this that you see here. To the right and to the left."

"It is very powerful then?"

"Yes, very powerful."

Santino sat quietly for a moment. "This company," he finally said, "how does it treat its workers?"

"It is not an easy question to answer. Many things have happened here between the company and the workers. There has been a struggle in which many have been hurt."

"And killed?"

"How did you know this?" Frank asked.

"Yesterday in town there was a funeral. Was this for one of the miners?"

"Yes, a very well known miner."

"These men are treated so badly that they are willing to die?"

"Many have left the old country to escape their sufferings and misery. Instead they found it here. There are men everywhere in the world who are willing to take advantage of other men's work. For the sweat of all these men there is some man who wears a tie and nice shirts and spends his time in fancy restaurants."

"I have seen this happen before in my country. I understand. When I mentioned Fortunato's name this morning, you and your wife both became uneasy. Your wife is not here now. What do you know about him?"

"Fortunato has been known to betray the workers to the company. They can not prove it, but somehow when the workers have made plans to organize against the company, they always find out."

"The workers have been unable to do something about this?"

"They fear that if something were to happen to him, their families might suffer."

"A family can give a man strength that he would not otherwise have, but it can also put him at a disadvantage. It is a different fear that can burn within a man when he thinks that his family can be hurt by his actions. And when a man acts out of fear, the advantage is always to his enemy," Santino said.

The cart rounded a sharp corner and came to a group of buildings. Frank stopped the cart in front of one of them.

"Where are we?" Santino asked.

"This place is called Segundo. I will ask where we can find Fortunato," Frank answered.

Santino watched Frank disappear into one of the buildings. It was still early in the morning and it had not begun to warm up as Frank said it would. As he watched, men began to appear on the street. These are working men, Santino thought. Each of them wore a leather cap with a small light in the front. They stood on the corner of the street with a lunch bucket in one hand and the other stuffed inside the pocket of their jacket. Santino could see part of the overalls that they wore underneath and the large work shoes. A cart came and several of them got into it and headed toward the hills.

The sun was beginning to warm the air and Santino loosened his coat. His exposed skin was wet from the heat of his body and it quickly turned cold. Santino pulled the collar of the coat back together again.

Frank returned and got into the cart. "He is supposed to live a little farther up, in Hell's Half-acre. We should be able to find him living in the back of a bar there."

As the two men rode up the canyon, the hills began to narrow so that the road ran alongside the river.

"The sun shines, yet it is so cold." Santino said.

"Life can be nasty, living in these canyons."

"Are there many canyons?"

"Yes, very many."

"There are young boys working in these mines?"

"Some are very young."

"There was one back there that looked Augusto's age."

"How old was he?"

"Twenty-two."

"Some are much younger than that." Then there was silence for a time.

Hell's Half-acre was not far from Segundo. Frank turned the cart onto a road that went into the hills. Then they crossed a bridge over the river and soon Frank stopped the cart again in front of a building. The smell of stale beer came from the entrance and was strong twenty feet away. Frank got out of the cart.

"I will go in with you," Santino said, getting down from the cart.

When the two men entered the bar, they were watched from the back corner of the room by a small man.

"'Scusa me, I wonder if you could help me find someone?"

The man answered, "In English. Say it in English."

"I am looking for a man named Fortunato Reno. He is supposed to live in one of the back rooms."

"Who is looking for him?"

"A friend of his."

"And who does this friend work for?"

"For no one. He has come a long way to see him—from the old country."

The man at the table began to rise slowly.

"And this man from the old country, is he from Sicily?"

"He's no Black Hander. This man has come a long way. If you know where we can find him I would appreciate it much."

At that moment the man caught the corner of Santino's eye. He turned and looked directly at the man's face. There was a frozen moment.

"Santino," the man said aloud, forcing a smile.

"Fortunato," came the reply in a low voice.

"It has been a long time since I have seen you," Fortunato said. Santino could sense an uneasiness in his voice. "I would say many years."

"You have come because of your son?"

"Yes, to find out what happened."

"It is like I said in the letter, there was a fight in a card game. Augusto lost his temper and it led to a fight."

"I knew my son too well to believe that he would let a card game become so serious."

"But that is what happened. You must accept it," Fortunato said nervously.

"He was my son. My eldest son. I will not leave until I know why my son is dead," Santino said in a stern voice.

Fortunato broke for the back entrance, Santino following quickly. The two disappeared. There was the rumbling sound of a struggle.

Frank moved toward the door. Fortunato burst from the entrance as though Satan were tearing at his back. Frank could only grab his shirt and, as it tore from his grasp, he flung himself upon Fortunato, pinning him on the floor.

Santino came from the room, wiping blood from his mouth. "The bastard has the room booby-trapped," he said.

"He's a madman! He's trying to kill me! Stop him!" Fortunato pleaded.

"Why would he want to kill you?" Frank asked, letting him up but holding on to him.

"I don't know him. He's mad!"

"Maybe mad enough to know what kind of a man you are. Sit down, Fortunato, we want to talk with you."

The men sat down at one of the wooden tables that filled the room. Fortunato moved his chair a slight distance from Santino.

"I knew you'd blame me. I knew when you walked in," Fortunato whimpered.

"Nobody's blaming you for anything," Frank answered. "We just want to talk to you, ask you some questions. Santino has come a long way, show him some courtesy. Now, Santino, what did you want to ask him?"

"You said in the letter," Santino began, "Augusto was killed in a card game of some kind. Over what?"

Fortunato mumbled something.

"Look," Frank shouted, leaning over the table and grabbing Fortunato by the shirt, "you act like a child. This man has come a long way to find out what has happened to his son. You may have no notion what a son means to a father, but I intend to see that he gets some answers. Now stop this childishness and answer him!"

Frank's face was flushed. The veins began to bulge in his neck. Santino watched and knew that Frank understood what was happening to him in this strange country.

"You men better settle down or I'll call the law," the bartender called to them.

"It's all right. Everything's under control. We would like to see this man alone for a short time," Frank said, looking at the bartender who went slowly into the back room.

"The bartender thinks you are from the Black Hand," Frank said to Santino. "He will not bother us."

Fortunato looked at Santino, "Mafioso!" Before Santino could answer the remark, Frank stopped him with a gesture of his hand.

Santino detested the way that the Black Hand treated the people in Italy. They were feared as killers but he understood Frank's gesture of silence. If Fortunato thought that he had connections with the Black Hand, he might be afraid that if he did not talk he would be killed.

"Now, Fortunato, what is it that you know about this card game?" Frank asked.

"You may not like what I have to say," Fortunato began.

"He was my son, I have the right to know."

"I remember when he first came here. He used to sit at the bar with a blind man who played the concertina. While he played Augusto would sing and the others would put coins in the man's hat. The blind man offered to buy Augusto a drink one night, but Augusto told him that his concertina reminded him of his home and family and that was enough."

"You knew my son," Santino said quietly.

"I knew him."

"And this card game?" Frank asked.

"One night they were playing and talking about some dynamite they were going to get from the company."

"Dynamite? For what?" Santino asked.

"He does not know what has been going on between the workers and the company?" Fortunato asked Frank.

"He knows what it is like to be treated as a peasant. And he has seen how intense the struggle has become. Continue."

"The company keeps a supply of explosives for blasting inside the mine but it is usually well guarded. One of the men who was playing with Augusto said something about it while they were playing."

"The men were not talking loud, but there was a small boy, nine, maybe ten. He was watching them play and running back and forth from the table. Augusto became angry with him because he kept saying aloud what cards he had in his hand. Then he hit the boy."

"Augusto hit him? Because of a card game?"

"No. Augusto hit him because of a foul mouth. When Augusto tried to get him to stop what he was doing, the boy called him a son-of-a-bitch and gave him the *fulva*. Augusto slapped him across the face and said his father should beat some manners into him. I am thirsty, I need a drink."

"I will get you one, then you continue." Frank returned from the bar with a drink. Fortunato started again.

"The men went to porthole three the next night where many of the explosives were kept. There were guards waiting for them."

"There was a fight?" Frank asked.

"Yes, there was much shooting. Most of it into the night."

"The boy informed the company?" Santino asked.

"He told them what the men said. The company would pay for such information. There were three men killed that night. Word got around that it was the boy who alerted the company guards, otherwise they would not have known of the plan that the men had. They entered the mine through an air shaft and came from the bottom up. The guards usually are placed at the entrance of the mine. Some of the other miners took the boy to Utah to a copper mine. I do not know what happened then."

"And how much of this were you involved in?" Frank asked.

"I only know what many others know."

"And could you have stopped this from happening?"

"I don't know what you mean."

"Were you there the night of the game?"

"I was."

"Who was the boy?"

"He . . . he . . . was the son of one of the owners."

"Did the men know this?"

"Probably not."

"And you did not tell them?"

"I mind my own business. They would not believe me anyway."

"And what was your business with the boy?"

"I knew who he was. That's all. You're blaming me for what happened, aren't you? It's easy to blame someone whenever something like this happens. You all need someone to blame, so you blame me."

"You always seem to be in a position to know what's going on and you never help the right people."

"I live back there with the prostitutes. If I am in a position to know anything, it is not by choice. I haven't the luxury to afford integrity. When I get up in the morning, I stink of cheap perfume."

"Why don't you live honestly?" Frank said.

"And go in that stinking hole? If I sell what I know, I don't have to live each day with a pick in my hand in that hole. The miners work like animals and they never pay them for what they do. They cheat them like children. At least the prostitutes are paid for their work."

Fortunato fell silent.

"Are you satisfied with what he has said?" Frank asked Santino.

"It is the truth," Fortunato said.

Santino looked at Fortunato. "If there were any way that you could have stopped my son from dying . . . ," he said. "But he is dead now and he cannot be brought back. It would be unjust of me to blame you. Augusto was a smart boy. If he believed that this was what he must do, then so be it."

"Let us go, Santino, your son died honorably," Frank said, rising. "As for you, Fortunato, you cannot buy integrity. May God have pity on your soul."

"Let God save his pity for those poor animals who don't know better."

"Yes, my friend, may He have pity on you."

Little was said on the journey home. Santino did not think of the cold, or the glittering snow, or even of the mountains. His thoughts were his own. Frank said nothing.

Santino stayed in America for a time, after he found what had happened to Augusto. Many from Calabria had come to America and there were still six more sons that must live under the landlords or leave. Three of them already talked of the new land. Santino knew that he would have to decide whether they would come to America or not.

With Frank's help he got a job working in the mine for a short time. There was something within him that drove him to do the work that his son had done. This made hin realize that Augusto had sacrificed much to send money to Italy. He met people who had known his son and he came to know the bitterness that the men felt for the company guards. But there were also Frank and others who were good men and had done well in America.

Then came the time for him to leave. "I must return to Italy," he told Frank. "Thank you for all that you have done."

"I wish that I could have done more," Frank answered.

"Perhaps some day I can return the hospitality," Santino said.

"The people here will remember your son."

"It is in God's hands now. If there is no God there is no final justice."

The two men hugged each other and Santino was gone.

# CHAPTER

# 5

When Santino returned to Italy he found that out of fear, the new landlord no longer lived in the district. He ruled the land from Rome and left in his place to collect the rent a man whose ties with the underworld were well known. Nothing else had changed, and he did not expect it to. In his mind he could see the vastness of America. He still had six sons who could have the chance of Frank Naccarato, with opportunities that would never exist in Calabria.

Maria had nothing to say when Santino arrived home. Her eyes asked all the questions. "Augusto died for what he thought was right," he told her. "The men with whom he worked are honorable."

"Was their honor enough to keep them alive?" she asked.

Santino did not answer. There were no words that could justify to her the loss of her son.

"America is a strange land," he continued slowly. "The men there struggle openly against those who take from them their honor and dignity. There is no shame in dying when a man can stand up for these things. America is a large country. There are many more opportunities there that will never exist here."

By the time he finished talking, Maria had begun to cry. Deep inside she had hoped that the letter from Fortunato had been a mistake. Now she knew that it was not and she did not hear what Santino was trying to say. In his mind were six sons for whom he wanted the opportunity of owning land, instead of being ruled by it. In her mind were six sons, none of whom she wanted to die as Augusto had.

Two years after he returned, Santino began to talk with another of his sons about leaving Italy. The boy was becoming a man. He realized that to remain in Italy was to submit to the landowners. Santino spoke of America with hope, but always buffered it with caution. Soon his son spoke of leaving. Maria said little when Santino talked of leaving Italy, but when her sons did so she began again to feel the loss of Augusto. She spoke to Santino.

"Your sons talk of America," she said one night.

"I have talked with them about it," he answered.

"You would have them leave Italy."

"I do not wish to discuss these things before I go to sleep," Santino said.

"How many do you wish to bury in America?" she cried. "No, we can not even bury then, all we can do is get letters from people telling us they are dead."

"And what would you have them do here? Soon they will be men and there is not even enough here for us. They will want families of their own and a house to live in. There are men who went to America and now have things we will never have. The land there is rich. All it needs are strong hands to work it and it will produce plenty, without the fear we live with. A man can own his own land there, and there is nothing to stop him if he has the guts to do it."

"And he may not live long enough to see this paradise. Do you wish to receive another letter?"

"Everything has a price. They will have to be willing to pay, if necessary. But if they do, they will become more than if they stay here. The choice will have to be made by them."

"There can be no choice after you have told them of America."

"I have also told them of the risks."

"But not the way you have spoken of the riches. They are young. Risks mean little to them. What young man would not want to go after the stars that you have made them see?"

"You do not understand. There is nothing for them here. The land can produce no more, and it is not even ours. We make it produce for someone who does not care if we are dead or alive. It will always be so. The boys will be men soon and they have a chance to own good land, land that will make them strong, and not fill the bellies of someone else. This is worth working for."

"Is it worth dying for?"

"Yes, it is worth dying for."

Maria watched her remaining six sons become men and, as they did so, they left their homeland. The first to leave reminded her of Augusto the day that he left. And a part of her left with him. Then the next one left and it was hard for her as before. The third son was close in age to the second, and soon he left too. Maria realized that this was something that she could never become accustomed to. There were only three sons left at home now, Vicenzo and the twins, and Vicenzo already talked of America. Often Maria would look at him with a look that only a mother can give.

"You would not hurt your mother, Vicenzo?"

"No, I could not hurt you, Mama."

"Would you leave your mother if you knew that it would hurt her?"

"Do you mean will I go to America?"

"I have heard you talk with your father, and I am afriad that you will leave as your brothers have."

"Papa says that there is more land there than all of Europe. That he traveled for days without coming to the end of it, and that there were men who owned big houses surrounded by their own land. Wouldn't you like to have these things?"

"Yes, my son. I would like you to have these things. You are much like your father. Soon you will be so much like him that you will have to do what you believe is right. It would hurt me to think that you did not have your father's heart. Come here, my son." Maria held her son close.

The time came sooner than she expected. When Vicenzo was fourteen, he began making preparations to leave. She tried as best she could to hold what was in her heart, but she knew that this was what he had to do. Santino and his wife accompanied Vicenzo to the dock where the ships for America left.

"Take care of yourself. Trust only those people who I have told you of. Remember, there are many men in America who are no different from the landlords here. Never trust anyone who is associated with them. Stay away from the coal mines. There is much treachery there. When you first get to Colorado, find Frank Naccarato. He will do what he can for you. Never take advantage of such men. Treat him with respect and honor. I have written him, he will be expecting you."

The father's face changed from an expression of concern to one of love. "Don't do anything that will bring dishonor to you or to the family. And don't forget that your home is always here."

"I won't, Papa."

"I wish that I could do more for you. There is little or nothing to gain by living here. This has been true for too long. Find the right opportunity. When things are going well, send for Carmela. Her father has assured me that she will save herself for you. You should respect what she is doing."

"I will, Papa."

"Say goodbye to your mother. Then you must leave."

Maria's eyes went to her son's. "Do not forget all that we have tried to teach you," she said, clasping one hand within another. "Make sure you get enough to eat, and that you have clean clothes. If you are not happy in America, you come home."

She could no longer use words and surrounded her son with her arms. She wished that somehow she could squeeze him back into her body where he would be safe from all harm. But he was no longer a child, and it was in his heart that he must leave.

"I will write soon. Please don't worry, Mama. I'll be all right," Vicenzo answered.

Maria began to cry. Between the tears she murmured softly, "*Bedu mio, bedu mio*—my little boy, my little boy."

"Go now, Vicenzo, the boat will not wait for you. Come, Maria. Do not make it more difficult than it already is."

"Goodbye, Papa," the boy said, as he gathered up his baggage. He turned and hugged his father and whispered, "We will dance the tarantella together again some day." He squeezed his eyes and from them came tears of love.

"Write your mother soon and often. Now be a man."

Santino wrapped his left arm around Maria and with the other hand waved to his son who had turned to wave before disappearing up the long wooden ramp to the ship's deck.

"He has made the decision of a man," Santino said. "He is in God's hands now. May God watch over him."

On board ship Vicenzo saw many strange faces. These people must be from the north of Italy, he thought. I have seen these tall, thin frames on the people there, and sharp jaw lines and pointed noses. They would resemble the Romans if their noses were not so pointed and were instead wider. He heard them talk and although he had heard the language before, he could not understand them. They almost sounded familiar, he thought. Perhaps they are from Tirole.

"Excusa, do you understand Italian?" he asked.

"I do not understand what you are saying. You must be Italian but I do not speak the language," the man said, shrugging his shoulders. There were others on board who must have been from Italy, he thought. It would be good to have someone to talk to. If not, it will be a long voyage.

Soon the movement of the ship made him give up his search for someone to talk to. The constant rocking made him sway with the rhythm of the ship and he emptied his stomach until only a clear fluid came out. He sat against a wooden frame that led to the lower deck, his head between his knees. He tried to think of home but his head began floating. After a few hours he fell asleep.

The morning sun warmed the deck and the ocean sparkled as the ship moved smoothly upon it. Vicenzo awoke to the strong scent of salami. It made his stomach tighten and he looked around to see where it was coming from. He saw a man sitting not far from him, cutting thick slices of the meat and holding them between his thumb and the edge of the knife while eating them.

"You want a piece?" the man asked.

Vicenzo shook his head no.

"You do not look well," the man observed.

"It is because I do not feel well," Vicenzo answered.

"Perhaps something to eat will help. I have some goat cheese in my sack, if you would like some."

"I have brought food for myself. I think it would only make me sicker."

"I do not think you can be much sicker than you already are. Perhaps you would like someone to talk to."

"That would make the time pass more quickly. I have been on board this ship for only a short time and already it seems like eternity. My name is Vicenzo Caputo."

"It's nice to meet someone who speaks the same language. Mine is Vito DiErcli. I have been called Shorty most of my life."

"I can see why!"

"My legs are long enough to reach the ground. So what the hell, they won't get any longer by wishing they were! Where do you come from?"

"Calabria."

"There has been much suffering there the last few years. I hear the drought there is very bad."

"There has been more than anyone's share of suffering. The land upon which the people depend has given nothing. The less we get from the land the more the landowners want from us."

"The situation is indeed a bad one. I am from Lombardy. Things are not good there either."

"Is this why you are going to America?"

"No. Mine is more of a personal reason."

"What do you know of this America?" Vicenzo asked.

"That an ambitious person can become wealthy if he knows the right people."

"That doesn't sound much different from Italy."

"It is a big country," Vito said, shaking his head. "When you are stopped in one direction, you can always go another. Are you traveling alone?"

"I am. But I have brothers who are already in America and friends who expect me."

"You are very fortunate."

"Why do you say that?"

"Because there are many here who have no one," Vito said.

"Do you have any plans?" Vicenzo asked.

"I have some relatives in a place called Utah. I will go there first."

"This Utah, do they mine coal there?"

"This is what I have been told. Why do you ask?"

"I had a brother who dug coal in Colorado," Vicenzo said."

"He no longer lives there?"

"No, he does not."

"Is this the work you plan to do?"

"I will not go into the ground. It is a place for the dead. I will do whatever work I can find, but I will not go into the mine. Your relatives, they will help you find work in Utah?"

"They own land there. Some kind of farm."

"It is good work. A man should stay close to the soil. It is God's will that man should make things grow. He can sustain life in that way, not only his own but that of others. You are fortunate to have such relatives."

"This I will not know until I get there. Then I will know how fortunate I am."

"You sound as though you do not believe that Utah exists."

"Life has a way of playing tricks on a man. Sometimes it is as though there is some force that does not want him to succeed."

"This is true. Yet it is these times that a man can truly find what he is made of and what he was meant for."

"It sounds easy to say, but we will both have to wait to see what is in store for us. At any rate, what will be will be. Let us both make the best of whatever the situation."

The two men remained together on the ship. Soon they became friends and shared what little they had to eat. The ship was old and sounded at times as though it were going to break apart. Vicenzo was doubtful of ever making it to America when the wood creaked and the ship rocked back and forth. But Vito reassured him.

"I have been on worse ships than this and they are still floating," he would say.

On the fourth day of the voyage, Vicenzo began having doubts. "This sea is not consistent," he told Vito. "On the farm you can feel the firmness under the feet. But out here, there is no solidness."

"Have patience," Vito told him. "There is much land in America. And it is as solid as anywhere in Italy."

Vicenzo recalled his father sifting the soil through his hands and saying many times, "It is here that we get our life. If only this land were ours, I would make it produce even if it did not want to. Nature is feminine and, if treated properly, she will yield much more than could ever be believed. In America there is much land. Get what you can live on, enough to make you independent from others for your livelihood."

It was not easy for Vicenzo to think of land while the boat rocked back and forth. He believed that what he was doing was right and that if it were not for him to reach America he would not. But he must try to do what he believed was right, so that when fate intervened in his life, he would be ready. The ship took three weeks to reach America. There was only one bad storm, and during it Vicenzo knew that land was the most important thing in life.

The day the ship arrived in New York harbor, the two men were standing on the deck.

"Who is the statute?" Vicenzo asked.

"It is for liberty," Vito answered. "The Sicilians have a saying about liberty, those that can afford it, have it."

Small ferry boats began pulling alongside the ship and people loaded into them. A small crowd formed at the entrance ramp.

"Do you speak any English?" Vicenzo asked Vito.

"A little. I think we can get by with what I know."

The two men stood in line until it was their turn to get into a smaller boat.

"Ask someone where they are taking us," Vicenzo told Vito.

"Excusa, *Signore*. Where do you taka us?" Vito asked one of the men who was sitting on the edge of the boat in an American uniform.

"To Ellis Island for processing."

"He says to a place called Ellis Island."

"What for?"

"He says for processing."

"What's processing?"

"Let me ask him."

"Excusa. Whatsa this prosseng?"

"That's *processing*. That's where you will be checked for disease or any undesirable characteristics."

"He says that if you are sick, they are going to check and give you something."

"I'm not sick."

"They're going to check anyway."

"All they have to do is ask and I'll tell them."

"He says they want to check."

When the boat arrived at the island, the people again started filing out of it and into a large building.

"I feel like a cow being brought in for the night. First we get on the boat, then we get off, then we get on another boat, then we go in here, with all these people. So far I don't like this America," Vicenzo said.

"Relax, Vicenzo. You become impatient too easily. Soon you will be on your way to Colorado. Then, when you are making all that money, you will look back and laugh at this."

People were directed into small sectioned stalls where they were examined for ringworm, leprosy, trachoma, and venereal disease. Those found to have any of these were marked with colored chalk and isolated from the rest in a cagelike area. Vicenzo was put in one such cage.

He sat on a chair, wondering why he had been put in such a place, and he became indignant. Vito, seeing that Vicenzo did not understand, slipped into the cage with him.

"What do they do now?"

"If you got it they will send you back to Italy."

"What the hell do you talk about?"

"You know, the disease."

"What disease?"

"You been to a prostitute house not too long ago?"

"I'll cut your tongue out!"

"I'm only telling you what they said."

"This place is crazy. I got this itch from the boat. If my mama could have seen the boat they bring us to America in, she would have said they were pigs to expect us to make a trip like this. If I have caught something it is their fault."

Another man entered the room wearing a white smock over his clothes.

"Do either of you speak any English?"

"I speaka a little."

"Tell your friend if he has the venereal disease, he will have to return to his country."

"He knows this," Vito answered.

The man began examining Vicenzo. "This is strange. But then again, I have seen so many strange markings on you people, sometimes I wonder just how the hell you live. Ask your friend how long he has had these markings on him."

"He saysa he gotta them on the boata."

"That's all we need, a whole goddamn boatload of venereal disease."

"He wasa with no woman."

"How do you know?"

"I wasa with him."

"And how do you know he didn't have it when he got on the boat?"

"Because he wasa just married. His wife isa in Italy."

"I swear you people breed like rabbits."

Vito looked at the man and said slowly, "I donna think I'ma tell him whata you justa say. He may thinka you insulted his wife. He donna like that."

"If you think that I'm going to be threatened by you can go to hell."
The man left the stall.

"What's going on, Vito?" Vicenzo asked.

"I told him you were married."

"I'm not married!"

"I know. I just told him because he thinks that you have venereal disease and that you got it from some whore. I just said it because of the way he talked."

"What did he say?"

"It's not important."

Soon another doctor entered the stall and addressed Vito. "Are you the one who needs to be cleared?"

"No. It'sa my friend." Vito answered, pointing to Vicenzo. "This man wants to check you," Vito said.

"Again?"

"Be patient, we will be finished soon."

When the man finished looking at Vicenzo he spoke to Vito. "Your friend has been bitten by fleas. We're going to have to detain him to make sure that the fleas were not carrying any disease. Please explain this to him."

"The other man who wasa here says that it no wasa fleas. He saysa that it wasa whata man gets in a whorehouse. There isa great deal ofa difference betweena the two," Vito said to the man.

"The other man who was here has done this often."

"Why?"

"There are people in this country who you will find to be a lot less friendly than him. They think that people come here to ruin the country, or perhaps take it over."

"I thinka that they comma here to do the worka no one else willa do."

"It sounds as though you have been here before."

Vito did not answer.

By this time Vicenzo had become impatient with the many words that were spoken that he did not understand. He motioned to Vito to tell him what was going on.

"The man says you have been bitten by fleas and that they will keep you here to make sure that you do not have any disease from them."

"I'm not even in the country yet and I have been tasted by the animal that rats hoard."

Vicenzo was taken to a small room that contained a cot and a small wooden table and chair. There he remained for several days, waiting for the doctors to allow him to leave. The time passed slowly and Vicenzo was without companionship. Vito had gone into the city to find work.

On the fourth day Vito returned and Vicenzo was cleared by the health inspectors. He was taken to a room where he was questioned on his past and his intentions for the future.

There were two men in this room. One of them spoke to him in Italian, asking him his name and where he was from. Then he asked him why he had come to America and what he intended to do. Vicenzo became uncomfortable. From experience, he had a distrust of governments and he knew that the less they knew about him the less he would be bothered. He was asked questions of loyalty to the government and he answered that he had no intentions of overthrowing the government.

The question seemed odd to him. He knew nothing of this new government, but he thought it strange that it should be so concerned with people wanting to overthrow it. Perhaps it is doing something that makes the people want to overthrow it, he thought.

When the men were finished, Vicenzo thought that he had answered the questions correctly and that they were satisfied.

"I have not seen you in three days," Vicenzo said to Vito as they left the island.

"I have been finding us some work in the city," Vito answered.

"You mean in the city here?"

"Yes, in New York."

"You are not going to Utah?"

"It is best if we get work here and earn some money. That will make it much easier when we get to the West."

"I do not want to live in the city. There are too many people in too little space. I came here because there is much land and I want to go where the land is."

"You are too impatient. There is plenty of time to go to Colorado. Believe me, it will be much better if you show up with money in your pocket. If there is one thing everybody respects in America, it is money."

Vicenzo paused for a moment. They were nearly at the dock. "What kind of work did you find here?"

"They are building a transportation system here and they need many workers. The rent is so cheap that we should be able to save most of what we earn."

"All right, I'll go with you. But remember, I came here to go to Colorado and I will not stay here long."

Soon they were in the city of New York, wandering down its streets and searching for a life that had eluded their fathers and grandfathers. This was Vicenzo's first look at America and it was the second time he wondered if he had done the right thing. The city was dirty, yet Vicenzo had known those who were dirty, and he knew well the times his mother had made sure that he was clean.

"There is always enough water to wash yourself. If you are dirty it is because you choose to be," she had told him. And it was the one promise that he made to her before he left that he would keep clean.

The streets were crowded with people. Men stood on the corners selling vegetables and meat and fish. Others hurried in and out of the buildings. Vicenzo heard languages that he had never heard before.

"There are people here from many countries," he told Vito. "I have never heard this many tongues, not even in Rome, where all Europe comes together."

"Many share your dream, Vicenzo. It will be difficult making it come true."

"The strongest will make it come true, Vito, and only if they want it bad enough."

The two men left the business section of the city and Vito directed them to the place that he had found to live.

"I think that it is better if we leave for the West," Vicenzo said.

"There is no West for me," Vito said, "I cannot go."

"You are going to live here?" Vicenzo asked Vito.

"All the places around here are the same. There are none better."

"There is no other work here?" Vicenzo asked. "Why have you changed your mind about going West?"

"Because there is no West. I have no money to travel anywhere."

"What about your relatives."

"They are as phony as the story I have made up about them. And yours? They really exist?"

"My father would not lie."

"Then you are very fortunate. As for me, there is only work on the pick and shovel gangs who build railways," Vito said. "The other work is ragpicking or work on garbage scows. They will hire us for the hardest, dirtiest, and lowest-paid jobs."

"Then we should leave. There are better places, my father has told me."

"Then you did not lie to me. There are people in Colorado who will help you."

"I have not lied."

"It is not as though I meant you harm, Vicenzo." Vito began to try to justify why he had lied. "Everyone has a dream. All those people who came here with us on that boat did so for a reason. One day I heard someone speak of a place called Utah and their relatives who owned a mine there, so I adopted their mine as my dream. The English I picked up selling goods on the black market, smuggling olive oil to this country."

"I cannot judge what you have done. If you want to come with me to Colorado you are welcome. It is supposed to be a big place. I'm sure there will be enough room for one more."

"Come, Vicenzo, let us sleep for the night. I have already paid for a cot."

The two men walked a short distance to a rundown building which had two entrances to it. Four wooden stairs led to the entrances which were supported by sacks of garbage and discarded pieces of trunks. Above the doors was a balcony made of old crates, all of which depended upon the others to stay suspended. The wall which supported the doors and roof had been faced with some kind of plaster which had been chipping away for want of maintenance. Inside three other men had also rented the same place. They had stacked their belongings along the wall and underneath the wooden shelves that were covered with trunks and bags.

"You can have my corner for the night," Vito offered. "I will sleep over by the door."

"It is most kind of you, but I think I will find someplace else to sleep for the night."

"It would not be safe in a strange country. This is not the best, but it will do for one night."

"If I am bitten by one flea during the night, I am going to hold you responsible," Vicenzo said to Vito with a straight face. Then he winked and smiled.

Inside the room Vicenzo tried to find a place that would be as comfortable as possible. The others had already occupied most of the room.

Two men slept on a wooden brace nailed to one corner of the wall with a thin mattress placed on top. Two more had cots laid out directly beneath them with a large quilted blanket for warmth. Along the wall with the scaffold bed was a stove, next to which were two cots. Above the stove were placed various chests that the men had brought from their native countries. There was but one man sleeping in the room at that moment.

"You lived here long?" Vicenzo asked when the man awoke.

"For five cents a night, it's not bad."

"In Italy, my father's pigs live better than this."

"Don't make the mistake of thinking you're in Italy now. You are in America and here you have to play their game by their rules. This is all you can get for the money that is paid for the kinds of skills we have."

"Tomorrow I leave," Vicenzo said to Vito.

"Yes, tomorrow leave, but for one night, rest."

Vicenzo began making a place for himself in one of the corners when a rat ran along the shelf above him. He watched it. It was followed by two more.

"I think that I would rather sleep outside on the steps," he said.

"It is not safe outside. Remember, you are in a strange country. You are no longer on your father's land," Vito warned.

"I think it is better to sleep out there than with the rats. I have already been bitten by the fleas."

Vito knew that Vicenzo would not stay inside. "Stubborn Calabrez," he muttered as he watched Vicenzo set his blanket on the stairs outside. "He will have to learn the hard way."

Outside, Vicenzo lay upon the steps. The day had been a long one and he was glad to see the night come. He could hear the noise from the city but he was tired enough to know that it would not prevent him from sleeping. Two of the other men who shared the room arrived and moved past Vicenzo without taking notice of him. Others moved past the front of the building but Vicenzo did not notice them.

Soon all the stirring from the room stopped and Vicenzo thought that the men were all asleep. I have been here a short time and already I do not care for this place, he thought to himself. These men live more like animals than men. I do not understand too many things here, he thought. I must learn how to read so that I will at least know where I am. An ignorant man is too easily fooled and taken advantage of. His last thoughts were of his home and family. Then he dozed into sleep.

During the night Vicenzo was stirred by a slight movement near him. When he opened his eyes he could see a figure moving inside a bag as a rat moves inside a sack of grain, half the body in, half out. Vicenzo lunged at the figure. He felt the body jerk away from him and a hard object come down on his head. The blow stunned him and he felt himself roll down the steps.

A moment later the man passed by him and Vicenzo got up and tried to stablize himself. A sick feeling rushed into his stomach. A sharp pain stabbed his head. He moved in the direction that he saw the man run but could only go for a short distance before he realized that he could find nothing in a strange place in the dark.

I must find out what has been taken, he thought, and he returned to the steps where his bag lay, half-spilled, upon the steps. He began slowly to go through the articles of clothing when the words *the box* bellowed up from his mind like hot lava gushing forth from a volcano. His search became frantic. *The box. The box.* His hands could not move fast enough. *The box.* He turned the bag upside down. There was nothing else in it. Waves of depression ran through him. He sank down onto the steps. He should not have been so careless. The box was gone. The words of his father rang clearly in his ears: "Do not trust anyone with those things that are vital to your life!" It was his own fault that the box was gone. There was no one else to blame. He had betrayed himself through carelessness.

In the morning the men began to leave for their jobs. Vito came out to find Vicenzo huddled over the bag he had brought with him from Italy.

"Come, Vicenzo, today we catch the train for Colorado."

"Today I catch the train for hell."

"What's the matter? Yesterday you could not wait to leave and now you sound like you don't want to go."

"Last night I was paid a visit by a thief. He stole the box that I carried in my bag."

"So get another box."

"Another box maybe, but not with a ticket in it."

"The ticket to Colorado was in the box?"

"It was. And the money my father had given me. There was little at home. Yet he gave me money to come here and now I have betrayed him."

Vicenzo did not rise nor did he look at Vito when he spoke. He felt as hopeless as a person feels when he believes himself lost with no chance of being found.

"So someone paid you a visit during the night?"

"Yes."

"Well, you have learned your first lesson in this country. Make sure you do not have to learn it many times."

Then there was a silence.

"The ticket can be replaced. Workers are always needed."

"You can go to hell, too."

"There is no reason for you to feel this way. What has happened cannot be changed. It is best to put this in the past and think about the future."

"You do not understand. I have failed!"

"What do you mean, failed? This is not but one thing in your life, and you are young."

"I have failed my father! He put his faith in me and it has not taken me long to betray him."

"Your father may have told you many things but you will have to learn them for yourself. Then you will know them. You will know them so well that the next time you go to do something foolish, the knowledge will slap you in the face so hard that it will knock you silly."

"You could have told me that these people roam the streets at night."

"And these people don't exist in Calabria? Besides, you're a hard head and probably would have told me to go to hell."

"I had been given a chance and threw it away."

"Listen." Vito sat down beside Vicenzo and began slowly. "It does not take a genius to turn gold into money."

"What do you mean?"

"If your father sent you here with pockets full of money and you made a good life for yourself, it would have meant nothing. Many men can do as much. But starting out without anything, now you are dependent upon no one but yourself. Now you survive, no matter what. You have to take a bad situation and make it work any way you can. Then you will always be proud of what you have done."

"I think if I had the money right now I would tell this stinking rat's nest to go to hell and return to Italy where at least some men have dignity."

"If I had the money I would tell a lot of people to go to hell! However, right now I cannot afford that luxury. Sometimes the price of integrity is too much."

"It can never be too much."

"I hope you can always feel that way. But for right now, come with me. There are some jobs to be had and they will not wait."

"I will not have any of your stinking jobs."

"You told me on the boat that it was your decision to come to America."

"This is true."

"Then it is your responsibility to see to your own existence here. If you had been brought here against your will you could struggle against those who were responsible for your being here. As it is, you are only struggling against yourself. And that is a battle you cannot win, for in the end you will have to destroy a part of yourself."

Again Vicenzo fell silent and Vito did not know if his words had had any effect.

"You do as you wish," he finally said. "As for me, I have to eat."

Vito left Vicenzo. The early morning sun had started to warm the air and soon it began warming the life within Vicenzo. Around noon a small boy approached the steps with newspapers under one arm. He had small, dark, round eyes and dark, curly hair. His shirt was torn and the overalls dirty. His feet were bare.

When he got close he asked, as though apologizing, "mister, you want to buy a newspaper?"

The dialect Vicenzo did not recognize but he understood the language well enough.

"I do not want to buy anything in this country, and I do not wish to be bothered."

The boy turned to walk away when a voice broke in. "Why are you so cruel to the boy? He has done nothing to you."

Vicenzo turned to see a large, hard-looking woman standing on the wooden balcony above him. She stared down at him, forcing a reply that he did not want to give but could not avoid.

"I did not mean anything harsh to the boy," Vicenzo began.

The woman would not let him finish. "Then why do you treat him like that?"

Vicenzo hesitated for a moment, then began again. "Things have not gone well for me today. They have not gone well since I left my home."

"And you think that they are going well for him? He probably has not had a decent meal since he's been in this country. This hasn't been the promised land for him either."

Vicenzo turned back toward the boy to see him walking away. "Hey" he called. "Do you want to sell those papers or not?" He took from his pocket an Italian coin and extended it to the boy. "I was saving this one for good luck, but you can turn it in for American money."

The boy took the coin and turned to leave when Vicenzo stopped him. "What about my paper?" The boy gave it to him and was gone. Folding the paper under his arm, Vicenzo looked at the woman for some kind of approval.

"Last year many children like that died around here. Just don't make the mistake of pitying them when you see them. Try to understand, but don't pity them." Then she disappeared.

Vicenzo wished that she had remained, for there was something inside him that needed to be said and there was no one to listen. He put what was left of his things inside the room. Then he went to the business part of the city. He could smell the food and it made him even more bitter than before. He returned to the room and waited for Vito to return. When he did, he carried a loaf of bread and some salami. "I knew you would be hungry," he told Vicenzo, "so I brought these."

"I would like to leave this street," Vicenzo said while they ate, sitting on the steps.

"All the places are the same. One is like all the rest. Some day all their work will make somebody a decent place to live, but I'm afraid it won't be us who will see it," Vito answered.

"This does not make sense. These men are sacrificing their lives so that some day others will live well."

"Maybe, maybe not."

"It seems like such a waste for one man to live like this so that another man may live easier."

"You have learned something else about America."

"It seems that I have had to learn too many lessons in one day. Nothing is right."

"And tomorrow you will learn the lesson of hunger unless you come with me and not spend the day sitting around doing nothing. I am tired and need sleep. If you want to sleep inside there is always room. The cost is five cents a night. If you still insist upon sleeping outside, that is your own business."

Vito disappeared into the room. Vicenzo thought about what Vito had said to him and the feeling that the woman from above had left him with. If a child could do what he must to survive, then he would also. He went into the room and tried to rest for the next day.

The next morning, Vicenzo went with Vito to the place where he worked. He was given tools to work on a road that ran underground. When he asked Vito to explain it that night, Vito said that some day the road would be used to move many people very quickly. Vicenzo was reminded of the road his uncle called the Appian Way. He remembered the times he had gone to the north to visit his uncle and he had seen great columns of polished stone and marble from ancient Rome lying in ruins. He had asked his uncle who had built such beautiful buildings and had been told that once the Italians had built many such cities and that they now lay in ruins like the great men who built them.

That first night Vicenzo could not sleep well. He seemed to see the marble columns and hear his uncle's voice speaking to him. "Many years ago there were men who were the civilizers of the world. The road they built connected Rome with the rest of the civilized world." The word *civilized* had puzzled him and when he questioned his uncle the answer too puzzled him. "It is where men live and act like men." "But are we not all men, made in the image and likeness of God?" "Yes, you have been taught well by your mother, little one. Some day you will learn that you must *earn* the right to be called a man, and when you do, you will find that there are responsibilities that are as important as the rights themselves. Because without them, the rights are lost. If a person does not act like a man, do you think he should be given the courtesy of being called one?" "I guess not." "You are still very young. Someday you will understand."

In the days that followed, the monotony of hard physical labor made Vicenzo's mind wander more and more into the past. He wielded the shovel again and again until it became a reaction. Again and again he heard his uncle's voice. "There is in your ancestry a great general who fought with Caesar." The shovel with dirt was heavy at first, but it became easier as Vicenzo learned the skill *"Your father is a good man. He has never had the chance to learn of the arts. It is a luxury and a hard thing to have when the necessities are so hard to obtain."*

By the third day his back ached, but he was young and strong and after working for a while the stiffness went away *"Your mind is the most important thing that you have. Use it well and it will free you of the harshness of life. Cultivate it like a garden so that it will produce more than you ever expected."*

By the sixth day Vicenzo worked like a machine while his mind returned to the past. *"Like these ruins, Vicenzo, if we fail to learn why these great cities came to such waste, then they are of no value.*" "Will you teach me more of these things, Uncle?" "*I have never been blessed with such a child. I will teach you all that I can.*"

Vicenzo could speak to Vito about these things for Vito knew the ruins of the north of Italy well.

"You have been to the great cities of marble and stone so how can you be satisfied with this work after seeing how great our country is? This cannot be our destiny. Destiny is reserved for the important people like this Caesar that you talk of. The rest of us fill in the empty spaces of time. And when destiny is ready for us, we do its dirty work."

"Then we live for nothing."

"How can you say this? Think of your family. That is what you live for. For your family! You all live for each other. There is no better reason for living. If Destiny would only leave us alone we would all be much happier."

"I do not understand you fully. What do you mean, leave us alone?"

"Perhaps it is this city's destiny to be great for some purpose, and it finds it convenient to use us for its purpose."

"And in the meantime we do what we can to make things as pleasant as possible."

Vicenzo felt the impact of what Vito had told him. "Sometimes things seem so important," Vicenzo said. "But it is not so hard to figure that we are all trying to get through this life with as little agony as we can."

"Don't let it bother you, Vicenzo. Sometimes it is better to just live and not think so much. Now, let's get some rest, or tomorrow we will not earn enough to fill our bellies."

As the days passed Vicenzo kept in mind the amount of money that he had to earn to pay his way to Colorado. He thought less and less of his uncle and Italy and more of the hole that he worked in. The days became a week and he realized that it would not be so easy to leave New York to get to Colorado. After he had been paid he bought food and little else. There was almost nothing left.

"I think that I am heading in the wrong direction," he told Vito. "I have been working all week to go West and now it seems to have moved farther away from me."

"Don't become impatient, Vicenzo. It is surprising how much a man can accomplish if he has time on his side."

"You have worked as much as I and have earned as little. And it does not bother you?"

"I am still here. Next week will have to take care of itself. After you are here for a while you will see what I mean." It was not long before Vicenzo learned what Vito was talking about.

A week later while Vicenzo was sleeping, Vito woke him.

"Vito, what's the matter? Why do you wake me? I need rest if I am to work tomorrow!"

"Vicenzo, listen to me. I have run into a sort of a problem. These two men have come to deport me. I must go with them." Vicenzo became aware that there were two uniformed men in the room with them.

"Who are these men? What do they want?"

"You see, it's like this. The papers I used were no good. That means that they stamped my passport WOP."

"What does that mean?"

"It means I am without papers so they are sending me back to Italy."

"What can I do to help?"

"Nothing, but I want you to listen to me. Here, take this box. In it is what you will need to buy the ticket to Colorado. If you do not wish to go there, use the money to return to Italy and your father and mother. The choice is yours."

"I can't take this."

"You would insult me and refuse a gift?"

"No, but this is all you have."

"I have plenty more, don't worry. I will get to it when I get back to Italy. Now take the money and do what you must."

Vicenzo thought for a moment, then took from around his neck a medal on a chain.

"Here, you take this."

"It is St. Anthony. I cannot take this from you."

"My mother gave it to me for protection. And it is a gift to you. Would you insult me?"

"No, friend, I would not."

Vicenzo wrapped his arms around Vito who returned the embrace.

"You take care, Vito. And may God watch over you."

"Never give up hope. Sometimes it is all we have."

The room seemed empty when Vito was gone. The rest of the night Vicenzo lay awake, trying to think of the day he left home, the days in the north with his uncle, and of the man he had known for a short time. Soon it was dawn. The men began to awake to go to work.

Then Vicenzo thought of the box Vito had given him.

# CHAPTER

# 6

The train pulled out of the New York station. Vicenzo sat in one of the cars, a bag with what was left of his belongings under one arm and the ticket to Colorado in his hand. He thought of his friend and what deportation meant—the long voyage home on another vessel, the sea, the rats, the disease. But he is not the kind of man that gives up easily. He will make the trip more than one more time, he thought.

Vicenzo sat near a window and watched the buildings pass as the train picked up speed. The movement of the train was soothing and the rhythm of the wheels upon the tracks made him drowsy. The sun rays warmed the car and soon Vicenzo fell asleep.

He was startled in the night by a stranger who stood over him, was poking him in the shoulder. Vicenzo opened his eyes and saw the man's uniform. Immediately he began searching inside his jacket for his papers.

"Your ticket," the man said, "I need to see your ticket."

Vicenzo continued his frantic search until he found his papers. He handed them to the man who looked at them and said, "I don't need these, I need to see your ticket."

"These are my papers. I have been passed through the island," Vicenzo said in Italian.

"You don't speak any English?" the man said. Vicenzo shrugged his shoulders.

"I need your *ticket*," the man repeated. "*Ticket*," he said again, this time taking from his jacket a ticket that he kept with him for such occasions.

He showed it to Vicenzo. Vicenzo handed him the ticket that he had held in his other hand. The man punched it and was gone.

Vicenzo's heart had begun to beat faster. Now he resettled himself and again fell asleep, this time tying the rope from his bag around his arm.

The trip on the train seemed long but it was not like the ship. Vicenzo gazed out the window at the land as he passed and never tired of the view. My father was right, he thought, there is more land here than I ever imagined possible.

Two days after he left New York, Vicenzo arrived in Trinidad. He got off the train and went into the station where there were other arrivals.

"You will have to go to the courthouse to have your papers checked," the man in the station told them.

"Where is this courthouse?" another asked, in Italian.

"Take this street here," the man said in the same language, pointing to a street just outside the station. "Go all the way to the top where there is an intersection. When you come to it, go left for three blocks and turn right. You will come to it. It is a large building of granite stones. There is a Statue of Liberty in front, like the one you passed when you came into New York, except it is much smaller," the man said.

The people left the station and began walking toward the courthouse. Vicenzo followed. He looked at the buildings, almost recognizing those that his father had told him about. Other people on the street took little note of the foreigners for they had seen many come up the street. Vicenzo could not help looking into the windows of the stores that he passed. The hills around the town gave him a sense of familiarity. For the first time since he left home, he felt comfortable.

It did not take them long to reach the courthouse. The others went inside and Vicenzo stood in front of the building, looking up at the columns of stone. I have seen columns like this before, he thought. He went up to them and placed his hand upon them. But the others were old and there was no use for them. These are alive.

From the steps of the building Vicenzo could see many of the surrounding hills. I know what my father meant, he said to himself. A sudden calmness reached out from within him.

I should go inside, Vicenzo thought, and make sure that all my papers are in order.

Vicenzo went into one of the offices and spoke with the man who was working there. "Excuse me," he said, "I'm looking for the office to have my papers checked."

The man did not understand what he said but he knew what he wanted. He motioned for him to follow, walked down the hall, and pointed to a room.

"Tanti grazie," Vicenzo said and went inside. The others who had gotten off the train were already inside. An official was speaking on the phone.

"I'd like to talk to Frank Naccarato," Vicenzo said, coming toward the man.

"Have a chair," the man said in Italian to Vicenzo. Vicenzo sat down.

When the man was finished he returned to his desk where he was met by the other man.

"Frank, these people arrived from the old country. If you don't sign for them, they go back tonight."

"What is the problem?" Frank said.

"Their papers are no good. I don't know how they have come this far, but it's happened before. Sometimes I wonder about the immigration office. They'll let just about anything through."

Frank said, "These men are human beings. It is not asking too much to treat them with a little respect."

"Look, I did you a favor when I called you to tell you that they were here! I didn't have to do that."

"This is true, and I thank you. Where are the papers? I will sign them"

Frank began signing them as the people waited in confusion.

Vicenzo watched him. Frank was not a tall man but he was well built. His short black hair was combed away from his forehead and there was something in his voice that made him sound self-assured.

"You know, Frank, sometimes I think you are crazy. You take responsibility for all of these people who you don't even know. If they get in trouble the police are gonna take it out on your hide. Unless maybe you have something going with the mine officials to bring in cheap labor," the man behind the desk said.

Frank looked up from the paper. "If there is any way to stop these people from going into the mine, I will be the first to do so. I am trying to keep them from having to return to the nightmare that they have left, not to start a new one."

"You better check that one's papers. He did not come in with the rest," the man said, pointing to Vicenzo.

Frank went over to him and said in Italian. "I need to see your papers." Vicenzo took them out of his pocket and handed them to him. "These papers are all right," Frank said, looking at Vicenzo.

"My name is Vicenzo Caputo. My father told me to come to see you when I got to Trinidad," Vicenzo said.

"I have been expecting you," Frank said, extending his hand. "I thought that you would be here a couple of weeks ago."

"I had trouble getting here," Vicenzo said.

"Help me get these people situated and then you can tell me what happened," Frank said. Then he spoke to the people in Italian and they all followed him out the door.

Frank and Vicenzo helped the people put their baggage in the wagon that they had come to town in. From the courthouse Frank drove down the street to a boarding house where they were put up for the night with Frank's personal word that they would be taken care of the next day.

On the way home, Frank and Vicenzo talked.

"How is your father?" Frank asked.

"He is good."

"And your mother?" The question sent Vicenzo back to the dock in Italy. He could hear his mother crying and he could see her face in his heart.

"She is good," he answered.

"You miss her very much," Frank said. "You show it in your voice."

"She has sent five sons to America."

"It is not an easy thing to do. When I came here I was three. My mother and father came when there were only a few Italians in America. Now many are coming and it is getting harder and harder for them. You say that you had some trouble getting here?" Frank hit the horses with the reins and they moved a little faster.

"I was kept at Ellis Island because I was bitten by fleas on the ship coming over."

"They try to be careful not to let disease in. They fear the plague," Frank said.

"I worked for a while on the . . . , " Vicenzo thought for a moment, "the subbaway," he said in English, "in New York," he finished in Italian.

"I have heard of it," Frank said. "My wife has prepared a place for you to stay."

"I do not want to intrude."

"You will not be intruding. It is a big house and Marietta is a good cook. She is from Italy too. She enjoyed your father's company and she'll probably wear your ear off with questions about the old country."

The cart continued at a steady pace down the old Santa Fe trail and turned to cross the Purgatory River. It was the same road that Santino had traveled, but it was not as familiar to Vicenzo as the street had been.

"Many things have taken place since your father was here. Things have not gotten any better. Sometime soon I am going to have to close the East Side Theatre. It is a movie house that I own."

"What is a movie house?"

"I will show you," Frank said, laughing. "It is hard to explain but I will show you. Anyway, it is a business that I own. I have made arrangements to begin working in Cokedale, a small town five miles west of here."

"Isn't Cokedale a mine?"

"Yes. Why do you ask?"

"My father said that my brother was killed because of those who owned mines and that I should have nothing to do with them."

"This is very good advice. Your father is a wise man. However, Cokedale is not like the other mining camps. This one is owned by decent men. I have made arrangements to work outside the mine on the tipple, where I can help see that the men who must go inside are paid for what they dig."

"But these camps are dirty and there is a great danger of death."

"Your father has taught you too well. Now I will further your education and make sure you understand me, because your father was not here long enough to learn what you have to do to survive. These mine companies have everything under their control. They make the laws for what you can and can't do. It was the government that stopped you when you arrived in New York, but these companies are a long way from the government. The marshalls pretty well run things their own way," Frank finished.

"In Italy we learned that it is better to know your own business and the government should do the same. Every time it does something for you, it takes more in return. Pretty soon it knows everything you do."

"Do not expect much from the government here. They are busy with other things. Tomorrow you will go with me to Cokedale. They are in need of men to work in the coke ovens. You will be able to work in the sunshine and the boarding house is the best you will find in any camp anywhere, so do not worry. If there are any problems, you come to me. Don't listen to anyone who wants you to join any type of organization."

Vicenzo looked at Frank. "What do you mean by organization? You do not mean the Black Hand?"

"No, not the Black Hand, but something that can kill you as easily."

That night, as Vicenzo lay in bed, he thought of all he had seen and heard that day. The house is beautiful and Frank owns good land, but he talks of organization and death. Always there will be the risk of failure and here it could mean death as it had with Augusto. I will survive, he thought, I will survive for both of us.

Vicenzo did not sleep well. Several times he passed into unconsciousness but each time anxiety awakened him. Morning came and soon Vicenzo was on the road that his father had traveled in search of the cause of his brother's death.

The cart moved up the narrow path between the hills. When Frank and Vicenzo neared Cokedale, the road dipped down and then crested, over-looking the entire valley in which the mining operation existed. The coke ovens stood in four rows, curving with the contour of the hills. A stream of dark smoke poured from the top of each oven, dispersing into a thick grey cloud. A black dot marked the front openings from which the coked coal would be pulled from the oven. At a distance they looked like ancient ruins that had been smouldering for centuries. The smoke from the ovens filled the small valley and made the land appear to be on fire. There were pinon trees spaced by patches of brown, dry earth, and a gully separated the camp into two parts. On one side the ovens burned, on the other there were several large buildings. In front of one of the buildings was a herd of mules surrounded by a wooden fence.

Another building sat upon a hill opposite the one that Vicenzo and Frank had just come over. It had a long, narrow structure connecting it to yet another building which was at the bottom of the valley, and a small engine pulled cars heaped with coal across it from the cluster of buildings to the ovens. Overlooking the camp were piles of small black rock. A line of carts ran from one of the buildings to the piles. Each cart was filled with black material and when it got to the top of one of the hills, it dumped its contents and then started the descent to the building. At the farthest end of the valley were rows of small white houses.

As Vicenzo neared the camp, he thought of his brother. He remembered his smile, his curly hair, the feel of his hand around his little brother's shoulders as he boarded the ship in Italy. Vicenzo felt down deep within him a longing to see his brother. "My brother," he asked Frank, "he is buried here?"

"No, not in this camp."

"In what camp was he killed?"

"Another one farther up the river."

There was a brief pause and Vicenzo spoke again. "You will take me there?"

"Sometime I will take you, but I better tell you something for your own good. First, the people who own this camp are different from the ones who own the others. Do not treat them unjustly and they will be fair with you. The others are dangerous. They kill without conscience. There is no law there but their own. They have the power of money."

As the two drew near the camp, Vicenzo's eyes began to water from the smoke and he could see the red glow coming from the entrance of each of the ovens. The cart that dumped the slack made a squeaking sound as it jerked along the cable and from each building came a particular sound. A grinding cracking came from the uppermost along the side of the hill, a splashing from the next as though someone had turned on a giant faucet and it had run into a lake. There was the monotonous hum of machinery inside the long tube which started at the far end of one building and continued down to the next.

The men continued down into the center of the camp a short distance away from the mining operation and came to a large house situated away from the other houses. Unlike them, it had grass growing in its yard. Frank went into the house where he spoke to its owner.

"It has been a while since I have seen you," Frank said as he greeted a tall, fair-skinned man.

"Probably too long. The theater business has not been so good."

"Sometimes good, sometimes not so. I think I need a break from the business. The men with whom I was a partner could not see things as I do, so until I can set something up for myself, I would appreciate the work."

"That will be no problem. The men around here trust you. Perhaps they will trust the company if you are working the tipple. Things haven't been so good in the other camps. Many are beginning to talk of strike again. The conditions here are not so bad but the talk spreads like fever. Once it starts it spreads everywhere."

"It is a bad situation," Frank said.

"It is becoming worse than that. You know how wretched the conditions have become in many of the camps. Now agitators have come among the workers here and are causing trouble. They are out for their own benefit and care nothing for the men."

"Who are they?"

"They call themselves wobblies. They are supposed to represent some worldwide organization for workers. They are foreigners."

"Yes, but at one time I too was a foreigner."

"This is something different, Frank. I have seen many different things brought to this country by many different people, but this thing is something different. They talk of some worldwide movement to take over the machinery that produces the coal."

"I have heard these men speak," Frank answered. "The men do not seem to be taken in."

The other man hesitated.

"I think that there is something also that is troubling the company." Frank tried to use the word *company* so that it would not reflect directly upon the man he was talking to. "It is the union that the company fears, and with good cause. I have seen these coal companies kill to keep the men from the union."

"I know what you are talking about. You know that is not true here. This company has always been good to its people."

"I know this."

"Then you will work the tipple?"

"Yes, I will do what you ask. Now, come here a minute. I want to show you somebody."

The two men went over to the window where Frank pulled back the curtains.

"Do you see the boy sitting in my wagon?"

The man looked out the window to where Vicenzo sat waiting. "Yes," he answered.

"A few years back, when the talk of strike was all over the area and the company from Valdez brought in strike breakers, there were many who were killed in the struggle."

"I remember."

"His brother was one of the men killed."

"Why has he come?" the man asked, glancing away from Frank. A look of fear came over his face.

"Not for revenge. He has come because his father has sent him away from the land struggle in Italy. Soon Italy will be involved in another war."

"I have read of such things."

"Many have come here to escape the conditions over there. Many did not realize that things here are not much better. The government refuses to recognize what the companies are doing to the people and would rather stick its nose in Europe's business. If war breaks out here between the workers and the company, there will be many in Washington who will wish they had tended their own backyard and left the other countries to themselves." Frank stopped, realizing that it was not the time to discuss politics. "If it is possible," he continued, "I would like to have a job for him working somewhere around here, but not inside the mine."

"Miners are in great demand right now."

Frank answered him with a slow nod. "I know."

"I do not know what jobs are available right now, but I will check."

"This is all I can ask," Frank said, thinking, There is always a job if you know the right people.

"Come, let us talk to your friend and see what he can do."

"First let me ask one more favor. He does not feel comfortable here, knowing that his brother was killed in a coal camp. Perhaps you could show him around the camp or say something that would help him relax."

"That should be no problem," the man said, moving toward the door.

Frank introduced the two and soon the workings of the camp were being explained to Vicenzo in a slow, tedious manner, for the tall, fair-skinned man spoke little Italian and that of a different dialect. Finally Frank took over the explanation.

"The coal comes from the mine there on the sides of the hill. The men load it in pit cars, like you see there, then it is weighed at the tipple."

"For what reason?" Vicenzo asked.

"To determine how much the miner will be paid."

"How do they know who has dug the coal?" Vicenzo asked.

"They have what they call a check. It is a small round piece of metal with a number on it. When a miner finishes loading a car he hooks a check onto it so that when the car comes out of the mine the man on the tipple gives him credit for digging the coal."

"The man on the tipple knows all the numbers and what man uses them?" Vicenzo asked.

"He has a list, and if he is honest he uses it."

The man with Frank and Vicenzo became uncomfortable at Frank's remark. "That is the job that Frank will have," he told Vicenzo in as good Italian as he could.

When the men reached the bottom of the valley, they turned toward the main buildings.

"That building on top," Frank said, "is where the coal is crushed. It comes from the mine and is emptied into a hopper."

"What is a hopper?"

"It's a large metal bin," Frank explained. "At the bottom of it are steel rollers with teeth two inches long. The rollers crush the coal into pieces this big." Frank made a circle with his thumb and first finger the size of a nut. "Then they pulverize it into power."

"They go through a lot of work for this coal. Why do they not burn it as it comes out of the mine?" Vicenzo asked.

"The ovens could not burn it like it comes out of the mine. After they crush it they wash it to take out everything that is not good coking coal. In the washhouse they float off only the coal, everything is dumped over there." Frank turned to point to the huge slag piles that they had passed on their way into the camp.

"It looks like a great deal of what a miner digs is no good," Vicenzo said.

"This has been a problem between the miners and the company for a long time," Frank answered. "The company does not want to pay the men for loading anything other than coal, but it is difficult not to load some of the other rock that is mixed with it. It is difficult to always see what you are loading down there."

Vicenzo again felt the memory of his brother. "It is difficult working in the mine?" he asked.

"Yes, it is difficult."

"I would like to go there," Vicenzo said. "I would like to see where my brother worked."

"I will take you sometime, but do not be in a hurry. It is not a good place to go."

The men were very near the buildings. Vicenzo could see the men with their faces and hands blackened from the coal dust.

"He asks many questions," the company man said.

"Yes, he is very inquisitive."

"He will not cause trouble?"

"What do you mean?"

"I mean about what happened to his brother."

"He has come here to live, not to cause trouble. His father came a few years back to find out what happened to the brother. He was satisfied. I see no reason for Vicenzo to want to carry any sort of vendetta against anyone."

"Well, sometimes these Italians are like that, you know."

"No, I don't know. What do you mean?"

"Something happens in the family and right away they start blaming someone."

"I am Italian."

"Yes, but you were born in America. You're different."

"My father was just like him. When he came he knew no one. What he had, he worked for. If something happened to him, someone would answer to me."

"I swear, Frank, sometimes when I talk to you I don't think that there's any difference between you and the men we send into the mine."

"That's because there isn't. The house I live in, the clothes I wear, the food I eat, all mean little when you talk about me as a man compared with these other men."

"Do you honestly think that these men would have taken the time to educate themselves the way that you have?"

"The difference is not that they would or that they would not. The important thing is that they *should* have the choice. What they do with it after that is up to them. If they refuse to take advantage of it then they must accept their fate."

"Well, we have at least given them more than any other company!"

"These men have not been given anything they have not worked hard for. Anything that they have, they have earned, but do not take me wrong. Your company has been good to the workers. I realize that much more and the company would not be able to operate financially. It is too bad that the situation does not allow for higher wages or better working conditions. This is not your fault or any one person's. I have seen some of the other camps where the conditions are barely livable. Something is going to happen that neither you nor I will be able to do much about."

"I am not stupid. I know that most of the workers here do not listen to those who cause trouble. But a hungry man who does not have enough to feed his family and must work under bad conditions makes a good listener and follower. And soon the talking is going to stop. It is only a matter of time and place."

"Excuse me, Vicenzo," Frank said in Italian. "I did not mean to be rude by interrupting my explanation of the camp. Where was I?"

"You were saying that the water floats off the impurities."

"Yes, after the coal is washed it is loaded in those cars over there on the railroad tracks. They are then taken over the trestle to be emptied into the ovens."

"What about the buildings over there, the one with the mules and the one that has the smoke coming from the roof?"

"One is the mule barn. The mules are used in the mine. The other is the machine shop where the lamps that are on top of the miners' caps are charged. They also take care of the pigs."

"They make sausage there?"

"No, no. The pig is a small engine that pulls the coal cars out of the mine."

A loud hiss came from the ovens and the air around them was filled with steam. "What is happening over there?" Vicenzo asked.

"They are cooling the coke so that it can be pulled from the ovens and loaded onto the railroad cars."

The men continued past the buildings and stopped in front of a bar. "That's more than enough talk of the mine for one day, Frank," the company man said to his guests. "Let's stop for a little refreshment and maybe a quick game of cards."

"That does not sound too bad. I'm sure that Vicenzo would not mind."

Inside the bar were many men who knew Frank and soon the three were sitting around a table covered with green felt. Smoke filled the room from cigars the men smoked.

"Vicenzo!" Frank cried in a loud voice, "what do you want to drink?"

"I don't know. I'm not used to drinking anything but wine."

"Have a glass of beer with a shot of whiskey. Bartender," Frank called, "bring a bottle of whiskey and a round of beer." He said to Vicenzo, "If you are to live around the camp, whiskey will help keep your lungs clean. The men who go in the mine breath coal dust so much that sometimes the whiskey is the only thing that will keep them breathing."

While the three played cards, other men began to enter the bar. Soon there were many and the noise of the place exemplified the liveliness and robustness of the men who worked in the mine by day and washed away the black coal from their minds and lungs by night.

It was not long before the whiskey took effect on Vicenzo. He had been accustomed to wine in his father's house but the foreign alcohol acted differently upon him. His mother was forgotten. The camp was forgotten. There were only the cards, the noise, the liquor. On the way home, the night air did not bring back Vicenzo's reasoning power. He sang to the moon over Italy, to the pinon trees and hills, and for the coming of spring— the song he had learned from his father. The words came easily and he did not think of anything or anyone.

But there was the morning and work that would keep him alive.

The ride to the camp next day was not as pleasant as the night before. There was little conversation and that only about the job he was to do with the coke ovens. There was one thing that bothered Vicenzo and he had not asked the day before because of the presence of the stranger. But he felt comfortable in his friendship with Frank. And it was more than this, there was admiration as of a father.

"I do not understand why you are leaving the theater in town to work in a place that you do not care for. Sometimes it is more than not caring for this coal business. I think that you dislike it very much.

"You are very observant, Vicenzo," Frank answered.

"You are much like my father. It was not hard to read how you feel."

"When your father was here he went into the mine to try and understand what your brother had done in there. Learn from him and your brother, God rest his soul, and do not make the same mistake. A person does not have to let a snake bite him to know that it is a bad thing. So learn this thing the easy way."

"You have not answered my question. I do not mean disrespect. If it is none of my business, I shall not ask."

"The men here need help. Working on the tipple I can help much more than by entertaining them. When the coal comes out of the mine they will at least have someone they can trust weighing the coal for them. Does that answer your question?"

"Yes. I should apologize for asking so much when you have been so kind. The man that I met yesterday, is he responsible for the job that I will be doing today?"

"Let's say that it is in return for a favor."

"I think that you have done many favors to help the people who have come from Italy."

"We help each other. You will see how much easier it is to help each other. We cannot survive otherwise."

In camp Vicenzo was taken to the place where he was to work. Frank told him that he would pick him up when the working day was over. Vicenzo was put to work with a man who explained the job he was to do.

"The larry cars will bring the coal from the wash house to the top of the ovens." Vicenzo watched the cars roll by them. "Come with me. I will show you. See there. The cars have stopped. Watch how the coal is placed into the ovens."

It is very hot here for such an early hour, Vicenzo thought.

"See how the coal forms a cone in the oven. First you smooth the coal out so that it will burn evenly. Then someone else will come and build a door, like this man over here." Vicenzo watched a man covering the front of the ovens with bricks, leaving two holes.

"Why does he leave the two holes?" Vicenzo asked.

"Two reasons. First, so that there will be enough oxygen for the coal to burn and so that it will reach maximum temperature evenly." When the man was finished the coal caught fire.

"The fire burns but no one has lit it?" Vicenzo said.

"That is because it is hot enough in the oven to start by itself. That is why they are made out of bricks. When the coal is done, another will come and break the door and begin pulling the coal like this man over here."

"See, you break the door and begin pulling the coal into the railroad cars that come along this track in front of the ovens."

"I should not have any trouble. I understand what to do," Vicenzo answered.

"Frank has taken care of the paperwork for you, so you are ready to begin work. I will put you with an experienced worker so that you will learn the right way. Just be sure you do the work. There are many around here who need the job, so be sure you do not waste the company's time."

The man introduced Vicenzo to another man who was Italian. The two men began pulling the doors and loading the coke. By lunchtime, Vicenzo felt sick. "I do not think hell is this hot," he said to Mario, the man with whom he was working.

"It is not so bad in the winter when the snow comes. You will get used to it. What did you bring for lunch?"

"A cheese sandwich."

"Let me see the sandwich."

Vicenzo handed Mario the sandwich. He placed it on the lip of the oven for a few minutes and then handed it back to Vicenzo.

"It is toasted!" Vicenzo said in surprise.

"You might as well make the best of the situation. The heat is more bearable that way."

The rest of the afternoon Vicenzo and Mario pulled eight ovens. Vicenzo's shirt would not hold any more sweat so the liquid dripped to the ground. Tomorrow I will bring a hat, he thought. At least my eyes will be in the shade. The day was nearly over and the next crew was beginning to arrive.

Vicenzo watched as one of the men finished building the door for the oven that he had pulled earlier. The coal caught fire instantly, and as several ovens began to burn again, others were sprayed with water and a cloud of steam rose above them.

Vicenzo began pulling the door from the oven that he hoped would be the last for the day. When the door was removed he took the long scoop and began scraping the coke from the oven into the railroad car. When all of the coke was removed he could see that several of the bricks within the oven had melted and had turned a shiny brown, like glass that has bubbled. He stepped back from the ovens where he could see the dark grey cloud begin to rise. This coke does not have the most pleasant smell, he thought. A shower would take the smell off of my body. Frank picked him up and in a short time they were on their way home.

"Next time I do not think I will drink before I go to work."

"You will get used to it before you give it up," Frank answered.

On the way home the sky began to darken. When Vicenzo turned to look at the hills around them, he could see the red glow from the ovens behind the hills. He lay back against the seat and fell asleep.

Soon Vicenzo was in the routine of going to the camp in the early morning and returning in the evening. He lived in the basement of the Naccarato home but was quickly becoming independent. He enjoyed playing cards in the bars of Cokedale and was becoming used to the whiskey. Frank noticed that Vicenzo was more comfortable in the camp and soon they spoke of his moving there.

"You have been very kind to me," Vicenzo told Frank.

"My wife and I have both enjoyed having you live with us."

"I will never forget your kindness."

Frank and Vicenzo stood in front of Frank's house. Marietta stood by the front door, watching them. They talked for a few minutes, hugged each other, and Vicenzo got into Frank's wagon.

"You be sure to stop and see us when you come to town," Marietta called out to Vicenzo.

"I will," Vicenzo called back and started up the road.

"He will do all right for himself," Frank said. "He is as stubborn as one needs to be in the camps." He noticed that Marietta was looking directly at him with an expression of surprise on her face.

"Why do you look at me like that?" he asked her.

"I think that it is from one *capo tosto* to the other that you say this." He watched her disappear into the house.

In Cokedale, Vicenzo made arrangements to move into the boarding house. The house had been built ten years before of adobe bricks and wood and was located on the side of a hill near the company houses. He was met at the door by an elderly woman.

"I . . . talka with . . ." he said slowly.

"You are Italian," the woman said in Italian, "so speak in Italian."

"How did you know I was Italian?"

"You've got the map of Italy on your face," she answered. "What can I do for you?"

"Some of the men told me that you had rooms for rent."

"I do," she answered. "I would like to talk with you. Sit down." Vicenzo went into the room, thinking of the men who had recommended her. She is not the kindly woman that they said she was, he thought.

"Where do you come from?" she asked.

"From Calabria."

"What town?"

"Aiello." Vicenzo became uncomfortable under her stare.

"What is your name?"

"Vicenzo Caputo."

"Have you been here long?"

"Not too long," Vicenzo answered, starting to become defensive.

"I don't think that you have been anywhere too long. You are very young. Tell me about Calabria."

Vicenzo was surprised by the request. "What do you want to know?"

"It has been thirty years since I have seen the old country," she said. "When I left the olive trees covered the land and the breeze from the sea was like a breath of life." As she spoke, Vicenzo could see in her eyes the many times that she had throught of Italy and had pictured it as she spoke.

"There are still many olive trees and they greet the sun each morning with their leaves moving back and forth with the breeze from the sea. And when they're full of olives they cover the ground with them, and all of us, my mama, my papa, and my brothers, we gather them in the baskets."

"The olive trees will not grow here," she said. "Only the pinon trees, and they give seeds once every seven years."

"I think that I will miss them," Vicenzo said.

"I will show you the room now," the woman said, rising to her feet.

"You don't want me to tell you more about Italy?" Vicenzo asked.

"It will take a long time to tell me of thirty years. Right now there is no time, but tonight you come to me here and tell me more."

The woman went upstairs where there was a hall with many doors. She stopped in front of one. "This is a good room," she said. "Out the window you can see the mountains." She turned to leave. "If you need anything, come and see me."

"Tanti grazie." he said and she was gone.

Vicenzo talked with her that night, and for many nights after that. She never tired of asking questions about Italy. One night she told him that he should learn to speak English. "It is good to know the native tongue," she said. "It is much more difficult to fool a man when he knows what is going on."

"This isa good," he agreed.

"So you have already begun learning some words," she said.

"Ia listen," he said slowly, pointing to his ear.

From then on when the two spoke in the evening, Mrs. Veltri would talk for a while in English and Vicenzo would listen and ask questions. The more he did, the more he learned of the camps and what had taken place between the miners and the compainies. "You know a great deal about this place," he told her one night.

"I used to teach here," she answered.

"Why did you give up teaching?" Vicenzo asked.

"In English!" came the reply.

"Whya dida you geev upa school?"

"The camp where I taught had only two teachers. The superintendent of the mine had a niece who needed a job so I was let go."

"Thatsa no fair."

"There are many things that are not fair here. I have been to some other parts of the country and things are much the same there. I like working here in the boarding house—cooking—and when someone like you comes along it helps me remember the old country. It has been many, many years since I have been there," she said with a faraway look.

"Sometimes I wonder if leaving the old country was worth it. Things were bad there but at least we knew who we were. Here we are just someone who does work that no one else will," she said.

"You mean like coal miners?"

"Like coal miners. There are others who share this, but something is wrong. This country is like making a stew; you pour in all the ingredients and hope it comes out all right. Only if you put in too much of one thing or another, it will leave a very bad taste in the mouth. It's like putting oregano and garlic together. One is going to dominate the other and the final taste is bad. You know what I mean?"

Mrs. Veltri left the room and headed for the kitchen. "Come in here," she said. She limped badly. Vicenzo had seen the limp before but it was not always as noticeable.

"You hurt your leg," he said.

"It was quite a few years ago."

"What happened?"

"When I was teaching school I used to have to cut the wood for the stove. One morning it snowed eight or nine inches, so I went early to fire up the stove. While I was cutting I slipped and the bone in my leg cracked." She stopped talking.

"There was nobody to take care of it?" Vicenzo asked.

"It was cold lying there in the snow. Then the students began to show up. One of them heard me calling and came. By the time they got me inside, my face and hands were numb, I think maybe it was a good thing that it was so cold or the pain would have been worse." Again she stopped talking.

Vicenzo could sense that she did not want to talk more about the leg. "I hear strange stories about the river bottom," he said, trying to change the conversation.

"What have you heard?"

"Why do they call the river *Purgatory?*"

"Have you ever seen the sun set over the mountain range to the west?"

"Yes. It is beautiful, like the whole sky is glowing from the mountains to the sky."

"They are called the Sangre de Cristo, the blood of Christ. There is a legend that long ago the first white men to come into the area were a band of Coronado's men."

"Who was Coronado?"

"He was a Spanish *conquistadore.* The men came up over Raton Pass, the pass that leads over Fisher's Peak. They set up camp along the flood plain. That night they were watched by a group of Indians who roamed the hills following the buffalo."

"Have you ever seen these Indians?" he interrupted.

"I saw them when I first got here, but they have disappeared in the last years. At dawn they attacked." She continued her story. "When the main body of men found them, all that was left were their bodies rotting in the sun, their scalps removed from their heads. There was no priest with the men, so that when they were buried there were no last rites said for them. Because of this, it is said, their souls were not allowed to enter heaven, nor could they be condemned to hell. And thus they have to stay here along the flood plain and the hills and wander forever.

"That is why they call it the Purgatory River, because the souls are as though they are in purgatory. They can neither go up nor down," she added.

"I don't know if this can be," he said when she was finished.

"You listen," she said, "some night when you are near the river and you will hear them wandering."

She finished in the kitchen and Vicenzo thought for a while.

"There is something that bothers you," she said.

"Yes, there is something that I think is more serious than the sound that roams the river bottom, but I do not know if it is good to talk about."

"If it bothers you it is best to talk about it."

"The other night when I was on my way home, I was stopped by a man. He said that I should meet him in the hills behind the coke ovens.

When I asked him why, he said that it was important and that I should be there. So I agreed to go and I met him there at ten o'clock that night. When I got there, he was with two other men."

Mrs. Veltri stopped what she was doing and sat down close to Vicenzo.

"One of the men said to me, 'You come here from Italy.' I said, 'Yes'.

"Then he said, 'I have seen you with Frank Naccarato.'

"He is a good friend of mine, I told him.

" 'Has he told you of the miners' union?' the man asked."

Vicenzo had recalled what Frank had told him about joining any organization. He could barely see the men's faces in the darkness, he told Mrs. Veltri. The moon was on the last quarter and they appeared almost as shadows.

" 'What is this organization for?' I asked.

" 'To take care of the men. Without it the company will make things so bad that soon we will all be dead.'

" 'My brother belonged to a union when he lived here.'

" 'He does not belong any more?'

" 'No, he does not belong any more. He is dead.'

" 'That is why we are in the union. To stop men from dying. You have not lived here long," the man continued. 'Look and see what the company is doing to the men. And when you are as sick of it as we are, you will want to join with us.'

"Then they returned to the camp," Vicenzo concluded.

Mrs. Veltri looked at Vicenzo and said, "Why does this bother you?"

"They will want to know soon if I will join. I know that it will be very difficult not to take the side of the company or the union. To do so would leave me without friends."

"It is a difficult thing to decide," Mrs. Veltri agreed. "You will have to decide what is best, but remember where your loyalties should serve you best, then decide."

"I have only been here *nove* months," he said.

"Nine months," she interrupted, "say it in English."

"I hava been here nina months, anna I donna think everythinga isa good here."

Vicenzo took Mrs. Veltri's advice and soon had his first lesson in the methods of the mining operators. The occasion was the election of the mayor of the city of Trinidad. The town was the largest in the area and was the hub of the surrounding camps. Vicenzo was called away from the ovens along with the other men one morning and given a paper on which were the names of several men. He was told to mark an $X$ next to the man he thought best for the mayor of the town. Vicenzo's first reaction was that he did not think it best for him to interfere in the business of the town.

"I do not know these men," he said to the man who was telling them what to do in Italian.

"It does not matter. Just put an $X$ for the man you think is best."

"This man that I am voting for, he is very important?"

"If you mean the position he is being elected for, yes. With the city council set up the way it is, he has the power to stop any legislation that passes them, so it is important that you vote for one of them."

"But I do not understand. I have never seen either of these men. How would I know who is the best one?"

"Here, put the $X$ here in this space."

Vicenzo hesitated for a moment when Mario, who was waiting his turn to vote, interrupted. "Go ahead and put the mark where he tells you. It is for the best."

"You are in America now," the mining official continued. "You should always exercise this right. It is the most important one you have."

"If it is so important, I should be able to do it in a better way." Vicenzo put the mark on the paper, then returned to work. At dinner break he sat talking to Mario about the election and the man he had voted for.

"I think maybe my father would be proud of me. We are not given the right to choose who is to govern us in Italy."

"Do not be too proud just yet," Mario answered.

"I did not vote for the right man?"

"There was no right or wrong man, there is just the man who will win. He is the man for whom you voted the same as me."

"I don't know what you mean. There were the two names on the paper."

"So you know enough English to know that there were two different names?"

"I do not know enough to know what went on today."

"It is just as well. The man that you voted for is guaranteed to win because the company wants him in office. It is not just the company here in this camp, but all the owners in every camp in this county and the next."

"If these owners are so sure that this man is going to win, why is it so important that I vote?"

"Because these men use the number of votes that their man gets to prove to the people in Denver that the men are satisfied with the conditions here. You know what the man said about this great American right to vote?"

"Yes, when I said that in Italy we did not have this right."

"Well, it is not such a great honor here, either. You see the mules over by the barn? They have the same right as you."

"How can they get these animals to vote?"

"You have heard the owners call them by name, haven't you?"

"When they bring them to the entrance of the mine."

"They use the names to register them so that they can vote. They mark the papers for them."

Vicenzo stared at Mario. The emotion that he felt within him for having voted changed to shame. "I think my father would not be so proud of me after all. Maybe he would think I was very foolish. I have not done many things here that I would be proud to show him."

In the distance the loud cry of the mules in the corral caught Vicenzo's attention. "Laugh, you son-of-a-bitches," he muttered under his breath.

"Frank told me that this camp was different. I cannot believe that anyone who treats men as he does his animals, is showing justice to the men." he said to Mario who laughed at his first comment.

"Frank was right. The boarding house where you live is the best, thanks to Mrs. Veltri. In the other camps they do not provide the electricity that you enjoy or the inside toilet. And at least the sewer does not run into the drinking water here. As long as the conditions here are not like the rest of the other camps, you should not complain. It does not matter who is in office in Trinidad. The companies would control him anyway."

It was time to go back to work. The rest of the afternoon Vicenzo could not help but think about what had happened that afternoon. In the evening he went to Mrs. Veltri with many questions.

"The men in the ovens made a fool of me today," he told her.

"What do you mean?"

"This election that they are having is nothing but a mockery."

"You voted today?"

"Yes, along with the rest of the mules. 'Come vote, it is your right as an American,' they told me. Well, they can have their rights."

"Do not be so upset. You are not the first to vote like an ass or the first to vote for a man who had already won. Where did you get all this fire?" she said, seeing the color of his face.

"From my father. He did not care for such injustice either, and he passed it down to me."

"So you got it from your father. What makes you think that he was so interested in justice?"

"Many years ago when I was small, there was a landlord who used to feed off of the people. Then one day he disappeared. Many thought that he was killed and buried somewhere, and that the men of the town were responsible."

"And your father was one of the men?"

"I remember him watching me as I played. I remember him waiting as a lion does for his prey to be off guard."

"Were they ever arrested?"

"They were never caught."

"Well then, Vicenzo, you should not be surprised. It is much the same here. The legality of things depends upon whether or not you are caught. Unfortunately there is always a gap between those who make the laws and those who have to obey them."

"There must be someone who is trying to change this."

"There are many who are for the union."

"What is this union?"

"It is an organization that tries to see that the men are treated like men."

"This is the type of organization that I would like to be a part of. Who are these men? I would like to talk with them."

"It is not that easy. The dues are sometimes very high."

"What is dignity worth in these camps? It cannot be that much."

"The price is often life. Many have died because they belonged to this union of workers."

Vicenzo had heard this before. Somewhere in the past was the time when his father was here in America. For a moment he drew close to his brother. His father's words brought him from the past. The words that he did not understand became clear . . . *He died with dignity, Maria, for what he thought was right.*

The dignity of the men, Vicenzo thought, we are not beasts.

*I do not care what is right, I want my son. . . .*

She did not understand what it feels like inside if we are treated like animals. And if we accept it then we are no better than they are.

*He was a man, Maria, and he had to do what was in his heart. No cause was worth his life to me. I cared for him when he was sick, and nursed him from my breast to give him life. I do not care what is going on in America, I want him back. . . .*

"I think I understand," Vicenzo said.

"Then I can tell you who they are, but remember, once the decision is made you must accept the responsibility."

"Some causes are worth dying for. If the men do the work, then they are entitled to what they have earned. Tell me something else. The men at work have told me that the other camps have it much worse than this one. Is it true?"

"The people who own this mine are not stupid. They know that if the men are happy here, they have no reason to join the union which causes much trouble in the other camps. They do not know that many men have joined this union anyway. You see the membership is kept a secret to protect those who have joined."

"Then it is best not to say anything about this union at work?"

"You learn quickly. It is best. Sometimes one mistake is all you are allowed. I will give you the name of the man to see."

The next night Vicenzo spoke with Frank. "I have heard many things about the union that many of the men belong to," he told him.

"A man cannot live in the camps long without hearing of them," Frank said.

"I have thought of joining with them."

Frank thought of Augusto when he heard what Vicenzo said. "It can be very dangerous to belong to the union," he told Vicenzo. "It can even mean death."

"I am aware of this," Vicenzo answered.

"Are you?" Frank asked. "Think of the letter that was sent to your mother and father before you came to America. That's the kind of risk that you will be taking."

Again Vicenzo felt close to his brother. "It is easy to talk of integrity," he said, "but difficult to act with it."

"Then it is a good decision," Frank said.

Even before Vicenzo could meet with the men from the union again, the earth trembled and fear spread throughout the canyons.

Deep in the earth, several hundred men labored toward their death. They were "pick and shovel men," making their living by railroad carts. Each time a miner brought down his pick into the wall of coal, fine dust particles scattered into the air. The fine dust was mixed with an explosive gas. The mixture became a time bomb. Each day every man contributed to the fusing of the bomb.

Within the vein of coal there were pieces of shale and sandstone. When the steel of the pick struck one of these there was a small flash of light. Many men worked down in the narrow tunnels. The men dug coal because, for them, there was no other work and so they played the odds against time.

Laws had been passed in the state several years before, requiring that the tunnels be sprayed with water to hold down the dust. But rationality gave way to money as it often did in the camps and the law was never enforced, for water was scarce and bringing it to the mine was expensive. If the operators could not make a profit the mine would close. Then there would be no jobs. But there were the men. Industry needed the coal, the coal needed to be mined, mining makes money and money buys souls. The men worked on.

The blast that came was like an animal so strong that no cage could contain it. It ripped through the tunnels, searching for the entrance of the mine and along its path it left the mangled bodies of men. One man had caused the fire that all the men feared. The flame from a safety lamp had been relit in a tunnel that was too gaseous to work in. The man did not intend to kill his friends or himself. He was unknown as the striker of the fuse. He was the first to die.

Across the arroyo, the children in the schoolhouse felt the earth rumble and heard the explosion. From the mouth of the mine came forth smoke and fire and pieces of timber. Then the low and final rumble from down deep, and the mountain sealed its treasure with the reverence of an Egyptian tomb.

The men who had died in the blast did not have time for fear or hate. The explosion was swift.

But there were the others who waited each day for the men to come out of the mine.

# CHAPTER

## 7

The season of the year began to change. No longer did the nights have the coldness of the winter months.

Vicenzo felt a certain alienation from the struggle that he found himself a part of. The company thought of him as little more than an animal and this caused a deadening anger within him—the kind one has for a dog that has bitten a child.

He watched as the men of the camp stored guns and ammunition in various places. There are many men who took it upon themselves to ready for a battle, he thought. The company does not know how strong these men are in numbers. But more important, they have something to fight for. They gain in the strength that they get from their families and friends. The others only have money for which to fight. Yet his family was not here. His actions would not affect them. Yet there was dignity, and always the thought of his brother.

The job was beginning to be routine for Vicenzo. The long iron rod he used to level the coal after it had been dumped was not nearly as difficult to handle now, and the heat that he had thought as hot as hell became almost comfortable on the colder days. The soot that he breathed into his lungs he hated and he doubted that he would ever become used to it. The whiskey he drank did not clean his inside like some of the miners told him, and he doubted if they believed it either. Yet he still drank.

Each day Vicenzo took the lunch that Mrs. Veltri made and sat on the side of the hill overlooking the ovens. As he unwrapped it he thought that the old lady had adopted him. It felt good to have family so near. The goat cheese was fresh and it made a squeaking sound as it rubbed against his teeth. The bread was also fresh and he knew that he could warm it easily by putting it on the oven lip. It felt good to sit for the short time.

One day before he returned to work he heard the sound of a horse running hard across the wooden bridge that crossed over the arroyo. Few noticed the rider but by nightfall all had heard of his mission. The largest mine in the Delagua canyon had exploded. The night crew from the Cokedale gathered around the entrance of the mine and met the day crew as they came out. Work was stopped while the men talked of it. Vicenzo heard of these explosions and how they were feared by the men who worked in the ground. That night in Trinidad he told Frank, "I would like to go to Hastings with you."

"This will not be a very pleasant sight."

"They need volunteers to help dig the bodies out. I would like to help."

"What about your job?"

"The men in Cokedale will not work until the buried men are cared for."

"There will be a great deal of work that will have to be done. We will need all the help that will come."

Frank and Vicenzo left for Hastings the next morning. The sky had began to cloud as the late winter storm moved into the area. It is cold, Vicenzo said to himself, and I am not near the ovens where I can be warmed. Sometimes it is not such a bad thing to be at work on such a day as this. On the way Frank spoke little, and all he did say were words of warning.

"There will be many men who try to cause trouble in the camp. Some will be miners and others will be company guards. If anyone asks why you are there, tell them where you are from and why you are there and nothing else."

"I will say nothing of the union" Vicenzo answered.

"Be careful also of what you hear. There will be many lies about what happened. Some will blame the men and others will blame the company, so do not jump to conclusions. You will see many things in the camp that will bother you. It is most important that you do not let your emotions get away from you. You must keep your head at all times."

Frank turned the carriage onto the narrow dirt road that led up to Delagua Canyon. The first camp seemed deserted except for small groups of women standing near the entrances of the company stores. The sun had broken through the clouds and quickly melted the thin layer of snow that covered the ground, but the clouds in the western sky told of a storm yet to come. From the Hastings camp came the cry of a small child that echoed in every coal camp in the hills of Trinidad.

"I feel cold," Vicenzo said.

"Cover yourself with one of the blankets I brought," Frank said.

"It is not that kind of cold. There is an emptiness here. Where are the people?"

"They are probably at Hastings by now, beginning the rescue operations in the mine."

When they neared the camp, they were detoured from the main road and onto the side of the hill near the schoolhouse. From there they could see that a large circle of men spaced at regular intervals prevented anyone from getting too close to the entrance of the mine.

"What is going on?" Frank asked one of the men who had gathered around the circle of guards.

"The men want to begin taking the bodies of the miners from the mine, and the guards have stopped them."

"Who gave such an order?"

"The man in the railroad car, there across the arroyo," the man answered, pointing to a hill opposite them.

Frank walked across the arroyo to the car and demanded to see the person who had given the order to halt the rescue.

"Who is in charge?" he asked one of the guards outside the car.

"No one is to see Mr. Wetzel without his direct orders," one of the men with a rifle answered.

"Tell him that Frank Naccarato wants to talk to him."

"He gave orders that no one be allowed in the car unless he asks to see them," the man said. Frank reached up to the small balcony the man was standing on, and grabbed him by the shirt. "You tell him to get the hell out here *now*, before someone is killed."

The man disappeared into the car and soon came out with another man dressed in a grey suit and tie.

"What seems to be the problem?"

"The problem is the miners. They may still be alive in there but they're going to die unless you start a rescue party as quickly as possible," Frank replied, his voice rising.

"Mr. Naccarato, we have dealt with many explosions. Right now we have no idea what condition the mine is in, or any indication that there are any survivors. Until we have information, any attempt to go in there would be suicide," the man said calmly.

"Any if there *are* survivors? What do you think they are doing right now?" Frank asked.

"I have been in rescue parties before. You know as well as I do that when the men are brought out it is not a very pretty sight. You know that some of them will come out in pieces."

"You're afraid that the people will see what it is like to have to work in one of those damned holes! Panic or not, there are men down there who still might be alive. And those people are not going to wait very long before they take this into their own hands. The guards are not going to be able to stop them."

"Those men have dealt with this sort of thing before. They know how to handle mobs."

"The mobs you talk about are wives and brothers and fathers, who want to know if the men are still alive—a hope that you are taking away from them every minute that you stand here talking. You better do something, and fast, or you're going to have blood all over this canyon."

The conversation was broken off by the low hum of many voices coming from one section of the circle of men. The sound grew louder and as Frank turned to see what was happening, a fight broke out and several shots rang through the air. Frank spoke quickly to the man in the suit. "It may be too late, damn you!" Then he rushed down the side of the hill to the scene of the action.

When the shots rang out the crowd around the men broke for cover. Screams rose from many of the women. Frank ran over to a group of men who stood in a circle around another man. He broke through, fearing that one of the people from the camp had been shot. He found a man kneeling over a camera with blood running from his mouth.

"What happened?" he asked the man who was wiping blood from his face.

"Those lousy bastards ruined my camera. They smashed it with their rifle butts."

"What were you trying to do?"

"Get a few pictures for the Pueblo paper. They don't want pictures because they don't want people to know what really happens in these camps."

Frank helped the man to his feet and picked up what was left of the camera. The two men went over to Frank's cart.

"You could have given those guards a reason to fire upon the people," Frank told the man.

"Someone has to let the people of this state know what is going on down here, or they're going to keep getting worse," the man answered.

"And you are going to tell them."

"I will tell anyone who will listen."

"Then you will accomplish more than any one of us has. I do not think you realize what you have taken upon yourself. What is your name?" Frank asked.

"Carl Rayon. I write for the *Pueblo Chieftan.*"

"You stay around, Mr. Rayon, you might have your story yet. The men have needed someone in the press for a long time. The newspaper in Trinidad will only print what's told to them by the company. We'll get you another camera, but you will have to be more careful or you'll get hurt."

When Frank returned to Vicenzo, a deadly silence had come over the camp.

"The people are not going to give up trying to get to the men?" Vicenzo asked Frank.

"No, but there is little they can do until help arrives. Look around, do you see many men?" Vicenzo shook his head. "That is because they are trapped down there, and they are the ones who would take action. It would be difficult for the others."

"That is why I came," Vicenzo answered.

"And soon there will be others. I only hope that it will not be too late."

And then there was waiting. Each minute brought new fears to those who had family and friends in the mine. It was nearing mid-afternoon when men from the upper part of the canyon began to arrive. At first they went unnoticed, but their numbers could not be concealed for long. Inside the company car reports began arriving that guns were being brought in from the surrounding camps. The guards on the outside of the train told the officials inside of the increased movement in the camp. Around four o'clock the man in the suit came out.

"It will be dark soon," he told the others with him, "By the time they reach any of the miners it will be dark. Have them start into the mine."

He began walking toward the main porthole when he saw a group of men going toward the entrance of the mine. "Bastards," he said out loud. "I told him to send the guard in! Hurry and tell the guards that we are organizing the rescue party and see to it that the word is passed among the people."

The men took with them shovels and picks. Strapped to each man's belt was a sack. The first hundred feet into the entrance of the porthole had not collapsed and as they walked through the narrow passageway Vicenzo became weak and light in the head. He pulled the mask that he had strapped on his head over his face to protect him from afterdamp, the poisonous gas that fills a mine after an explosion. It was because of this gas that the company said there would be no survivors and the men were told they must accept this when they went to work for the company. There was a thick haze of coal dust and dirt in the air, making the men appear as images rather than as real people. Soon they came to the place where the earth had caved in. One man started digging into the slide and then they all were digging. The picks and shovels added to the coal and dirt haze. They dug for over two hours when they were stopped suddenly by one of the experienced men. He fell to his knees and began digging with his hands, then he pulled at what looked like a man's arm. He was aided by others and soon the first victim was removed from the mine. Vicenzo had not seen the man's face clearly, but he could tell that he had been crushed by the rocks that had fallen from the roof of the shaft. Then they began to find others who had been buried in the main shaft and the pig engine was found near them.

When Vicenzo was relieved for rest he left the mine. Upon entering the outside world he found that night had fallen and the sky was as dark as the inside of the mine. He did not think of anything but how tired he was and that there was nothing more he wanted than sleep. Snow began to fall and the white flakes stuck to his eyelids. The sweat had frozen on his shirt but the cold could not affect him more than his fatigue. At home, Frank helped him remove his clothes and he was soon asleep.

"They knew it was unsafe," one of the men said, "and they would not stop digging. Mike Ferraro told them it was so bad in there that he refused to work."

Vicenzo awoke to the sound of men talking in the boarding house.

"He was not killed in the explosion?" another asked.

"No, he told them that if they would not clear the mine of the gas that he would quit. They told him to pick up his check and get the hell out."

"He knows how lucky he was," another man said.

"You know who they're going to blame for this? The foreigners. Every time something like this happens it's easier to blame them."

"The last explosion was blamed on the carelessness of the miners. Last night one of the men taken out of the mine had matches in his pocket." The men were speechless. All of them knew how dangerous it was down there. They all knew the rules about matches."

"This will give the company a reason to blame the workers," one man finally said.

By this time Frank had arrived. Vicenzo was washing when Frank asked him how he was.

"I feela fina," he answered in broken English, "justa tired."

"Do you want to continue the rescue?"

"I willa go back."

There was a sharp pain through Vicenzo's back and forearms. This pick is not kind to the body, he thought. If it continues to be such an enemy I shall have to think of ways of becoming strong so that it will no longer bother me. The sun was no kinder. The rays pierced his eyes and the numbess in his head turned to pain. "I feel like I shall throw up," he said in Italian in a low voice so that Frank could barely hear him.

"It is the gas in the mine that you are not used to. Are you sure that you want to go back in?"

"I have to. Yesterday I had a strange feeling when we found the bodies of the men. It was like I was searching for someone. But we never found him. Perhaps today."

The two walked through the slush in the streets. As they moved slowly they heard crying from the gate of one of the small mining houses. They slowed their pace and neared a small girl clinging to the iron spokes of the gate. Her fists were clenched tightly around the iron and her forehead was pressed against the cold bars. When she saw them she said, as though out of breath, "I want my papa."

"She cries for her father."

"Yes, I know." Vicenzo said.

Vicenzo said softly, "Donta cry, little girla, we will doa whatta isa pozzable to bring outa you' daddy."

The little girl could only whimper in reply.

"I don't like this business," Vicenzo said to Frank. "There is something wrong here."

Before he could continue, a woman's voice broke in. "You sona bitch Americanos, you taka our men and putta them ina that stinking hole and then expect us to live lika animals. *Povera* America. Soma day you all gonna burna ina hell!" The woman bit her forefinger, then led the little girl into the house.

"Americano. I didn't do this thing to these people. I came here to help."

"Don't pay any mind to her, she is upset. They have to blame somebody, it makes it easier."

"The little girl spoke in Sicilian."

"They are here too. Along with Greeks and Slavs and Austrians and many others. They will all blame someone. Do not take it personally."

When they reached the mine smoke was coming out of the entrance. "What now?" Frank asked one of the men who was covered with dingy gray and black from the mine.

"We had to stop about 8,000 feet down. There's a fire in there. When we broke through the slide, we started bringing out bodies. Then it flared up. It must have been oxygen from one of the air vents that kept it going until we broke through." The man paused for a moment and then added, "I think I have just seen hell. We took out two that could not even be recognized, they were burned so badly."

"Perhaps it is best we do not know who they are," Frank answered, as though trying to convince himself. "Has the coroner arrived from Trinidad yet?"

"He is over in the machine shop," the man answered.

The path to the machine shop was filled by women who were trying to see if their husbands were among the bodies that had been brought out. One of the men who stood outside the entrance recognized Frank and allowed him to enter the building. Inside, all the machines and conveyor belts stood silent. A man, his shirt sleeves rolled back, worked intently on a body on the table before him.

"Dr. Donalson," Frank said.

The man turned. "Hello, Frank."

"It is bad?" Frank asked.

"It is very bad. There are those here so badly burned that the only way they can be identified is by their mining check. Others are crushed beyond recognition. They are little more than chunks of meat." The doctor paused. "How could they allow this to happen, Frank? The worst ones have been blown to pieces by the explosion. They were brought out in gunny sacks, piece by piece. I can cure no one of this plague. No one is going to come out of there alive."

"Do what you can for those who are left. If there is anything I can do to help, let me know."

"There is nothing anyone can do for these poor souls. But there are their families. If there is anything that can be done for them, that will be best. They are out there now."

While the two men were talking, Vicenzo looked about the shop. He could see the outlines of faces straining to see into the clouded glass windows and through the blankets which covered other windows. In the corner of one window he could see the eye of a woman who had found a small crack and now looked at him, hoping that he would give her some sign of hope.

If I recognized her husband, could I tell her that he was here, or would she prefer I told her that he was still inside the mine? What do you want me to say? Vicenzo thought. That your husband has been blown apart? That he will always be lost? What is best, to know or to remain ignorant?

Vicenzo turned away from the eye and again looked about the shop. The bodies of the men had no more life than the cold pieces of machinery. It is so easy to die, Vicenzo realized. Frank's voice broke into his thoughts.

"The important thing is to prevent more violence in the camp. Many of the people are ready to blame the company and to take revenge for their sorrow."

Vicenzo moved slowly about the tables where the bodies were laid in rows. His shoe began sticking to the floor. It was blood that was causing it to stick. The red substance had formed a small pool around the legs of the table where the dead men were laid. From the small pool to the table leg, Vicenzo's eyes traced the liquid to the bodies.

"Come, Vicenzo, there is nothing that we can do here now. We will be needed elsewhere."

When the two were walking back to the boarding house, the woman who had seen Vicenzo through the window grabbed his arm and began speaking in a language that he did not understand. Out of desperation he turned to Frank and cried in Italian, "What does she want of me?"

"She wants to know what has become of her husband."

She continued pleading, repeating the same words over and over again. Frank positioned his body between hers and Vicenzo's. Others joined in her pleas. Voices came at them in languages neither understood, mixed together in a mass of confusion. Bodies surrounded Vicenzo and he could again feel tugging, but on both arms this time. Losing sight of Frank, he tried to make his way down the hill but could not get away.

Then a loud voice quieted the women. The doctor had come from the machine shop holding a handful of mining checks. "I am going to put the numbers on the wall," he said. "Find someone who can read the numbers and they will let you know if one of them was related to you."

The voices started again, but this time not as loud. The women began to move slowly toward the machine shop.

"Vicenzo!" Frank called.

"This will be very difficult for them," Vicenzo said.

"Remember," Frank said, "you must keep steady here. Try and be a source of strength for those that need it."

It was difficult for Vicenzo to understand. Frank looked into Vicenzo's eyes and saw that he was in anguish, his soul ill at ease. He put his hand on the back of Vicenzo's neck and said softly, "Be strong. Your father would be proud of you."

"These people suffer. Why?"

"Because there are those who have, and those who do not, and that is the difference. Those who do not, must be strong for each other or they have nothing. Sometimes it gives them more than those who have everything, so be strong."

The next shift to go into the mine descended early in the afternoon. Vicenzo was not among them. He sat upon a hill directly opposite the porthole, watching the men come and go about the rescue operations. From there he could hear the wailing of the women. Ministers of different faiths had come to the camp to comfort the living.

Two hours after the men descended into the mine they were forced out by smoke. Many talked of closing the mine but they were stopped by others who imagined themselves down there being given up for dead. And so the operations continued into late afternoon. Soon there was a procession of bodies being taken from the mine to the machine shop.

Tension began to build as the men continued bringing out the mangled bodies. The company knew that it would be best to work at night, but the fears within the imaginations of the people became worse than the reality. Frank saw that the company was ready to deal with a riot.

"Have you seen the guards?" he asked Vicenzo.

"There are very many," Vicenzo answered, "they are everywhere like rats in a sewer."

"We must be careful that emotions do not cover our thinking."

"I do not think that the men will start trouble with so many women in the open. I am going into the mine again tonight," Vicenzo said.

"Be careful when you are in there. Watch behind you and make sure that no one destroys the rest of the mine," Frank cautioned.

"Why would they do that?"

"It would be the quickest way of getting this over with," Frank answered grimly.

Vicenzo joined the next shift to enter the mine. This trip was much longer than the first time he had gone down. The men had already dug down to about eight hundred feet. Vicenzo became apprehensive at the many turns that were taken in the descent. The blackness gave way only briefly as the light from the caps illuminated a small portion of ground immediately in front of the men. Vicenzo turned to see the blackness close in around them. Nothing could be so empty, he thought. The light creates, and when it is gone there is nothing again.

The men passed through a small archway where the roof had been timbered, and into a long, narrow passageway. They moved cautiously, fearing that another slide would trap them also. Through the tunnel there were two passages that formed a V and the miners hesitated before going down either. Then one pointed to a faint light in one of the passages and the men hastened to what they hoped was life.

They found a man neither blown to pieces nor burned, but waiting for rescuers. He sat with his hands dangling from his legs, his arms resting upon his thighs, his head slumped forward to his chest. His head was raised by the leader of the expedition and the man's mouth opened as if he were about to speak, but his eyes remained closed. Vicenzo took him by the arm and shook it, but he was stopped by one of the other men who shook his head. The others had started in the direction of the room where the men had been working. There, like a wax museum, were other miners still and lifeless, their cold faces giving testimony to their fate. There, like Pharaohs of ancient Egypt, the men were preserved, waiting for their rescuers, and no pyramid contained a greater treasure than this deadly cave.

The members of the party were at first afraid to touch them. One victim knelt, his hands still folded and a prayer on his lips. Another had bloodied hands and fingers, as though he had forsaken the pick and shovel for his bare hands. One was wrapped in canvas as though he could hide from the death that came so quietly; another, still clutching his pick, lay face down in the coal. And there were the others who were resting from trying to dig their way out. They lay in various positions, one with his head on his arm, another curled up, his arms folded about his chest. All had hoped that in some way they could work free from the tomb.

The rescuers worked swiftly and quietly, communicating by gesture, the gas masks pulled over their faces as they dug. A gentle breeze went unnoticed, pushing its way past the men to the entrance of the cave. One by one, the miners were laid in a cart that had been brought to serve as a hearse for the dead men. Empty lunch boxes added to the horror of what had taken place there. The food was all gone, the bottles empty.

Then a cry stirred the men out of their mechanical movements and they ran in the direction of the sound. They ran almost blindly with the hope that it was from some miner who had lived through the explosion, but their hopes were short-lived. When they got to the source of the cry they found one of the rescuers kneeling over a man who had a pick stuck in his chest, and another with the side of his head smashed in. The man who had cried out knelt gripping his mask, and in a quivering voice said, "This is insanity!"

The leader of the expedition quickly took him by the shoulders and directed one of the other men to take him from the mine. When this was done the man began getting the bodies ready to be taken from the room. Vicenzo stood quietly near one of the pillars of coal, waiting for some reason to continue. When the leader saw the look of anguish on his face, he went over to him.

"What is the matter?"

Vicenzo returned a blank look.

This time he asked in Italian, "What is the matter?"

"Why are these men here?"

The man hesitated a moment. "Because it is their work."

"To die like this."

"No. Not to die, to live."

The men continued moving the bodies from the room. Another man entered and began checking the air with a safety lamp. When he was finished he took off his mask and said to the others, "It's all right, the air is good enough to breath." The other men began removing their masks, as did Vicenzo.

"There must be something better than this," he muttered.

"They take no shame in their work. They do it well, better than anyone ever has. They are proud that they can do a job so well."

"But it is their job that kills them," Vicenzo answered.

"It is not their job that kills them."

"Then what?"

"It is that they must live. When they came here, they were strangers. They knew nothing of this place. But in many ways it is like everywhere else. Nothing comes easy. Because they were different from those who were already here, they had to prove themselves. Pay their dues."

"But they are dying!"

"For every one that dies another grows strong. The man who cried out when he found the dead man with the pick in him—the dead man was his uncle. His father has not yet been found. Maybe one day he will be able to get the hell out of the camps, but we pay our dues first. We have been doing it for a long time, it seems like forever sometimes, but we endure. Capisci? Now come, let us finish our work."

Vicenzo began helping with the man who had died from a head wound. When he turned the body a pocket watch slipped out. Vicenzo picked it up. The hands had stopped.

"It's only a matter of time for us all," the leader said to him. "Remember this when you are out of this hole. Be kind to those who ask what you have found here. Tell them nothing of how these two died when you give his wife the watch."

"These men, they were friends?"

"They were friends. It is hard to imagine the kind of madness that one might get down here. Survival drives like nothing else inside us. I will remember them as friends, as I saw them many times drinking and playing *Briscola* together."

Some of the men had already taken the dead to the surface. Now there were only about half as many rescuers as had originally started into the mine. Those that were left continued downward. Soon they began to notice a dampness about 8,000 feet into the mine and before they could go another hundred feet, their shoes became wet.

"Soon we will have to surface," the leader said. "The pump must have been broken in the explosion and the water will soon fill the room. We must hurry."

The last body to be found already had begun to float in the water that seeped from the walls. Pieces of ties and other debris made it difficult to move about. The men did what was possible to separate the bodies. They pushed their way through the water and groped for as much as they could find. The light from their caps made the water glisten as though it were filled with diamonds. An oily substance clung to their clothes. Their faces were black with coal dust and breathing became increasingly difficult. The air shaft that brought fresh air in would soon be clogged by the floating debris in the lower depths. When all that could be done was finished, the men began their ascent. It did not seem as far going up. The anxiety of hoping to find life was gone, and the men realized that no one would be able to enter the mine until the water was pumped out. By then, no one would still hope that his son or father was alive.

When they reached the surface, Vicenzo saw Frank. He went over to him and said, "I am going down to the arroyo and wash. I feel dirty."

In the arroyo Vicenzo removed his clothes and laid them near the bank. The water was cold as snow but he dove in, his entire body entering all at once. The coldness was soon gone and he scrubbed at the black spots upon his body. His hands no longer had the greasy feeling that they had in the mine. The burning that he had felt in his lungs was also gone.

Vicenzo left the river and lay down on the young grass that had been three weeks in growing and was hardly tall enough to sway in the wind. A cool, gentle breeze dried his body. As his mind cleared, he thought, I fear these things that I do not understand. I would be ashamed for my father to hear my thoughts, but this is something I do not understand. I did not understand my father when he told me of these things, but now it is even more difficult. The things that my mother taught me do not fit here. There are no laws of decency. These people cry out in tongues I do not understand. If I could see and touch this thing that takes men's lives, it would be easier to understand.

Those who manage this place have become the proprietors of hell. The fires that burn from this coal are no less hot than those of the inferno of Satan. They are the color of blood and burn hotter than any mineral could ever burn. They burn with the tears of small children and the despair of women. My mother taught me no prayers for those who burn in hell on earth. And yet to run would be cowardly. My brother did not run. His head became clouded with emotion. The sun began to set upon the Sangre di Cristo mountains and the red fury that burned in Vicenzo's head colored the sky.

He awoke next morning to the roosters' crowing. He had slept on the grass and it left creases upon his face and arms. Sand clung to him as he got up. He returned to the river to wash his face. After he had dressed, Vicenzo heard the watch ticking in his pocket and remembered the chore that he had for that day.

On his way to the woman's house, many things passed through Vicenzo's head. He tried to push them out so that he could think of what he was to tell the woman. What if she had a little girl like the other woman he had seen? What if she blamed him for what had happened to her husband? Still other things crept into his mind. When he had come out of the mine, one of the men had thrown his helmet into the pile of rubbish and cried out, "I quit! I have worked here a long time, but enough is enough. I'm going to tell them to pay me what they owe me and then I'm getting the hell out of here."

It would be so easy to quit now. To go where, to what? Back to the old country? "It would be so easy to quit," Vicenzo said aloud. "To quit." He did not like the sound of the words. There is always a home in Italy. My mother and father.

The squeaking of railroad car brakes shattered his concentration. He looked up to see a carload of caskets arriving in the camp.

Again he remembered the watch. The woman must be told. She would not have to go to the machine shop. The thought burned in his head and the watch burned in his pocket.

He walked rapidly to the house he had been directed to. He passed through the gate, hoping that no one was home. He rapped lightly on the screen door. A strong aroma came from the kitchen as if someone had been baking an apple pie. Then he heard the sound of feet and his heart began to pound in his chest. A tall woman in her thirties approached the door. In an Austrian dialect, she asked who was at the door.

Vicenzo felt the blood rush to his head and answered in Italian, "I am from the rescue party that went into the mine."

The woman looked at him in confusion. Vicenzo thought hurriedly and again tried to communicate with her. "I am from the mine." He pointed toward the hills. Vicenzo looked at her and felt like a stranger to the human race. Her eyes were swollen and red. Her hair was pushed back and tied into a bun. Her dress was long, nearly to the floor.

She looked at the man who stood at her door, half-afraid of the news he might bring, then said very calmly in English. "You have news of my husband?" Vicenzo remembered the watch. He took it from his pocket and held it out to her. She pushed the screen door open and gestured for him to go in. He took his hat off and entered.

The woman went into the next room, the kitchen. Vicenzo stood quietly, not moving. She soon reappeared and said, "Please come here. I have work to finish." He went into the kitchen were he saw that the woman had been baking the day before, for there were pies along both sides of the kitchen. She moved about like a machine, preparing two more pies and placing them very carefully in the oven. Then she turned to Vicenzo again. "My husband will be hungry when he comes from the mine. This is his favorite."

Vicenzo again held out the watch. "Thisa isa you husb. . . .

She shook her head and said softly, "Tomorrow. Tomorrow. You will have some pie?" She began preparing him a dish before he could answer. When she turned to put the dish on the table, Vicenzo could see tears in her eyes. "You are young," she said. "How long have you been in this country?"

"Only a shorta time."

"I have not been here too long, or maybe," she hesitated, "it has been too long. How is Europe? When I left six years ago things were not good. America seemed like such a great country to escape the politics. But here it is a different kind of war. Often bullets do not do the killing." She almost seemed lost for a moment. "How did he die?"

"He wasa killed by the . . . the . . . gasa . . . the gasa after the explosion."

"Then he was not in pain." The woman's head dropped to rest on her fist which she held between her eyes. "The people," she began again, "are blaming us for this killing. We suffer like they do, yet they say we did it because of what is happening in Europe."

"They have no heart," Vicenzo said, "or worse, they have no head."

"And I have no husband."

The woman left her chair and went to Vicenzo and looked into his eyes. He took from his pocket the watch and placed it on the table and rose slowly.

"What am I to do alone?" she asked.

"I ama very sorry for you' husband. I ama new here, I do notta know whata will helpa you. I wisha I could. There are many here thata I see, but I worka for the same people as you' husband. Only Goda knows whata isa best for them now."

"Life is not life here. It stinks of the black earth. Have you ever had to work down there? Every night my husband would come home covered black. And now it has taken him. They take him from the earth only to put him back." She broke down crying.

Vicenzo said, "I ama very sorry. I dida my best to find him. I hoped ita would help." Vicenzo left the woman sitting at the table, her face buried in her hands. He began searching for Frank.

Frank had returned to the machine shop where many of the widows had broken in and removed their husband's bodies. Frank had tried to help some of the women but hysteria ruled their minds. When Vicenzo found him he told Frank what had happened with the woman.

"I do not think I can take hearing the women cry for another night," he said to Frank.

"The mine in Cokedale will start again soon. It is best that you return."

"I do not think that I was much help to her," he finally said. "When I left she was crying very bitterly."

"You have done all that was possible. Return to the camp."

"What will you do?"

"Do not worry, I will get a ride back."

"I do not mean that. What will you do here?"

"The worst is yet to come. This is not the first time that such a thing has happened in this canyon. I have seen it once before. There will be a long funeral procession. And after that, a hearing on what happened inside the mine to cause the explosion. The people will be very emotional but the owners will be strong. I will stay to try and see what I can do."

"And what about the men with the rifles?" Vicenzo asked.

"For the past years this place has been like a powder keg. Perhaps this will be the match that will light it. Many will suffer. This will not go unanswered. There is too much hatred here. Now go back to Cokedale. You have work to do there."

Vicenzo left the camp that morning. He had done what he thought was right, yet he knew that the people there needed more help than he could give them. There was nothing, he knew, that he could do for the men in the mine. He thought of them and their faces floated through his mind, showing expressions of despair and hate. They had been betrayed by humanity, he thought. They had to pay too high a price for the right to make a living. Then there were those who were left behind—the wives and the children. They must take what is left and start again, and in so many years they will be little more than a memory.

As Vicenzo approached the exit to the canyon, he was stopped by two guards with guns. One walked in front of his carriage and stopped the horse.

"Where do you think you're going?"

"Back to Cokedale, where I live," Vicenzo answered.

"What's the matter, don't you speak English?"

"Of course he can't," the other man answered before Vicenzo could say anything. "You can't expect these dumb foreigners to be able to speak anything but that gibberish they use."

"This gibberish ruled the world at one time, and if you want to find out how, keep your smart tongue," Vicenzo said.

"Don't give me that talk. Just what the hell are you carrying in this wagon?" Vicenzo watched the barrel of the gun move upward as the man used his other arm to look through the back of the wagon. Then he swung his whip at the man's face and pulled the reins of the horses at the same time. The whip hit the man's face, knocking him to the ground. The other man was pushed by the horses to the side of the road. The men immediately got up and began firing at Vicenzo as he moved away from them. Three miles down the road, Vicenzo slowed the horses. He felt dizzy and sick to his stomach. Blood was running down the side of his face.

"Bastards!" he said out loud. "There will be more blood shed than this before this is over. If those people want to crucify us they can expect more hell than they ever thought possible," he said in Italian. Then in English, "I cana speeka your damna language, you somma na bitches. We doa you' dirty worka and you treat us like animals. This willa nota be the enda ofa thisa."

# CHAPTER

# 8

Vicenzo awoke late in the afternoon. He opened his eyes. The room appeared hazy. The sheet felt damp upon his face and he realized that he had passed out. I must take care of my head before the others come back to their rooms or there will be more trouble, he thought. He rose slowly and went to the dresser where he could see himself in the mirror. The wound had bled profusely and the blood had dried so that his hair looked as though it had been pasted to his head. He brought some warm water from the bathroom and began breaking the blood apart from his hair with a damp washcloth. The wound was covered with dried blood and when he dampened it with the cloth sharp pains shot through his head and into his eye.

When he was finished cleaning the wound, he took the sheet from the bed and put it with his shirt, rolled up, into a sack. Then he lay back upon the bed and rested until a knock came on the door. He did not answer until he heard, "Vicenzo, Vicenzo, are you in there?" He recognized Mrs. Veltri's voice.

"*Avanti,*" he answered.

"The ovens have started working again," she said as she came into the room. Vicenzo did not respond. "You do not look so good," she said, "you look pale. How do you feel?"

"I feel all right," he answered, not moving.

"It will be best for you to return to work as soon as possible," she said. Then she saw the wash basin with the bloody water in it.

"What has happened?" she asked. "Have you been hurt?"

"No," he said turning his head. "I will get ready to go to work"

"Not before you tell me what has happened," she said.

Vicenzo sat up. "It is just a small cut. I will get ready for work." Mrs. Veltri could see that his hair was wet and that it had been pushed down on one side of his head. She walked over to him and took hold of his arm.

"What has happened to your head?"

"It is all right," he answered.

"I will decide that for myself. Now sit down and let me see." Vicenzo sat down and she began to move the hair away from the wound.

"How did this happen?"

"When I was in the mine, taking bodies out," he answered, "I struck it on a beam."

"Why did they not care for it in Hastings?" Vicenzo did not answer. "I ask you again, how did it happen? And do not lie!" she said.

"It is not important," he said.

"I am going to get some bandages. When I come back I want to know what happened." Her face grew stern. "It is important to me." Then she left. Vicenzo got a clean shirt from his drawer and put it on.

Mrs. Veltri returned and began to dress the wound. She said nothing but Vicenzo could feel that she was waiting for him to talk.

"When I was leaving the camp I was stopped by two men who wanted to look through the wagon. I did not let them," he said.

"Did you fight them?"

"No. They had guns."

"And they shot you?"

"When I drove through them, they shot."

"You were lucky their aim was not so good."

"It was good enough," he answered.

Mrs. Veltri rubbed ointment on the wound and Vicenzo winced in pain. "You should see a doctor," she said. "The wound is bad."

"I do not need a doctor," he answered. "Right now they are busy in Hastings." His voice dropped off as he spoke.

"It was bad in Hastings?"

"You could not believe how the men were when we took them out." He stopped talking and silence hung over the room. He waited for her to say something but she did not. "You have seen what an explosion can do?" he finally asked.

"I have waited on the outside," she answered.

"I am very thirsty," he said, feeling as though he had to say something.

"You have lost a lot of blood. It is good to drink water. Many men have not yet returned to Cokedale. You should be able to work the entire night shift."

"I will hurry down," Vicenzo answered, placing a cap upon his head and opening the door.

"Watch yourself," Mrs. Veltri said.

I have seen bodies when they have come out of the mine, she said to herself, and I have seen the explosion many times in my nightmares. That is the curse the earth gives us for raping her, that is the price we pay. They will take the bodies out of the earth today, and tomorrow they will put them back.

In Hastings, the situation steadily worsened. Venturing back into the mine would be suicide because water had saturated the timbers that supported the roof and soon would weaken them. The entrance to the mine was sealed. The cost of repair was too great and it was beyond reason to expect the men to descend under those conditions. Hope that anyone had survived the explosion dwindled among the relatives and for one last time they went through the articles that had been brought out: the remnants of a lunchbox, a pair of broken glasses, a half-burned mining cap . . . .

Some said that sixteen men were left in the mine, others said nine. Many had not been identified and there was arguing as to who some of the burned or dismembered bodies were. On these not even the mining checks had been found. The bodies that were so badly maimed were placed into the caskets and the tops were closed. Some people attended more than one funeral so that they could feel that they were with their loved ones while the mass was being said. Others who had many friends in the mine stayed in the church most of the day. For them it seemed an endless procession from the church to the cemetery.

When the priests and ministers finished the prayers for the dead and the consolation of the living, a strange quiet came over the southern Colorado camps. The memory of the men produced bitterness and hatred toward the company. The workers talked among themselves of those who had died of afterdamp. Fear made them cautious when they again entered the other mines; not of dying but of being trapped alive.

In Trinidad preparations for the trial to determine the cause of the explosion got underway. Here in the granite courthouse, all the bitterness, hatred, and fear would manifest itself during the hearing. The tension of the coming battle affected everyone in the town and it seemed as though the town was holding its breath, waiting for the inquiry to begin.

Osborn watched the front of the opera house from a window of the Columbian Hotel.

"If the union has brought anyone into town they have not met with them here," he told another man who sat looking over a bunch of newspapers.

"Who owns the *Morning Sun?*" the other man asked, holding up one of the papers.

"A man named Maio," Osborn answered.

"I thought you said that company controlled the papers here?"

"Two of them. This one is not important. It's a small paper."

"It says in this not-so-important paper that less than month ago the mine was declared unsafe because of the amount of coal dust suspended in the air. Where the hell did they get that information?"

"Reports like that are common around here. They don't mean much," Osborn answered.

"It goes on to say that there was a recommendation that the mine be watered to hold down the dust but it was never done."

"Water is scarce around here. It's not only difficult to find, it's difficult to transport. It would have cost over ten thousand dollars to set up the system to bring water to that mine," Osborn explained.

"Then there was no attempt to spray the mine?"

"I don't know what things are like in Canada or in New York, but out here you do what's possible with what you've got," Osborn raised his voice as he spoke.

"Let me explain something," the other man said, putting the paper aside. "Last year Mr. Rockman spent three hundred thousand dollars on a bird sanctuary in New York. If this paper is right, he spent thirty times more on keeping birds alive than he spent to keep these men alive. If one of the large newspapers prints this it will burn a path a mile wide from here to Washington."

"When Mr. Rockman got in touch with me in Montreal, he said that he didn't know what was going on out here, that he had never been here.

I didn't think it possible for an operation this large to escape his attention, but after seeing the mines I know he was right. Those men in New York have no idea what's out here. And I'll tell you something else. You have no idea what's going on back there either. Public sentiment is our worst enemy. It makes the politicians turn tail and hide behind their electorate. That's why it's important that we don't lose control of the situation."

"Don't worry. We have handled situations like this before," Osborn answered.

"We don't want a great deal of trouble from Lewis and the union."

"The union is not as strong as Lewis thinks. We have many informers in their union. We'll know well in advance if they plan on doing anything."

"You mean like strike?"

Osborn became nervous at the question. "There's no indication that they have considered calling a strike. If they do, we'll know about it."

"So you keep saying. Just be sure you don't let things get out of hand."

Osborn continued watching the opera house. He did not like having to take anything from the Canadian. He was not used to anyone telling him what should be done, or how things were to be run. Rockman had no interest in the mines other than the money they made and Osborn knew it. That was why he never interfered in the internal affairs of the mines. But now he could feel something different. There was more tension in the front office, more than there ever had been before. Osborn didn't like having to go through channels to get things done and the more he had to do with politics the less he liked it. His tactics had made him the ruler of the coal empire in Colorado and he wanted a quick return to normal operations.

"When is the trial?" the Canadian asked.

"In two weeks." Osborn answered.

"It would be better if you had the date moved back a couple of weeks to give the people a chance to cool down."

"I don't know if we can,"

"Who's the judge?" the man asked.

"Faris."

"He's on the payroll, isn't he?"

"Yes."

"Then what's the problem?"

"I think the sooner we get this over the better. If we delay, it will give the union a chance to bring in help."

"I thought you said you had everything under control."

"I do, but you don't know these camps. Sometimes the harder you squeeze the more things get away from you. You never know how these people will react. They come from thirty different places. Most of them don't even speak English. You never know what they're thinking. The sooner we get this over with the better." Osborn walked away from the window, hands in his pockets, his head turned away from the other man.

"How strong is the union here?"

"Not very."

"In numbers."

"They couldn't have more than . . . ," Osborn said slowly and then he hesitated.

"You don't know?"

"They don't volunteer much information. We have informers, but they're not always reliable."

"What have you done to stop men from joining this union?"

"You sound like I let the union big shots do what they want around here," Osborn snorted.

"I know what these papers say and I know the governor isn't very happy with what's going on down here. He's been telling everyone that you want the Guard sent in. Do you know what that will do to him politically? All we need is to lose that office and we'll really have trouble." Osborn began pacing back and forth, his face flushed.

"Governor Tillis says that you can't handle it any more," the Canadian pressed.

"I keep these camps running! Nobody shits around here without me knowing about it."

"Then we shouldn't have anything to worry about."

"I'll cover my end. You just be sure and cover yours," Osborn said.

"What do you mean?"

"I don't want any national people brought in by the union. I'm not in any position to stop them. You'll have to do it."

"You mean that old woman."

"Yeah, I mean her. I don't want her here. You keep her out of the state, as far from here as you can." Osborn walked back over to the window. "Those sons-of-bitches think she's their mother," he said half under his breath.

"What's that?"

"Nothing. That goddamn woman causes more trouble around here than the union leaders. They react to her like crazy men. As soon as she starts talking, they go wild. She curses like a mule skinner, even worse than the men do in the mine, and they listen to her."

"Don't worry, we'll stop her even if we have to have her jailed," the Canadian answered.

"It won't be that simple. I've had to deal with her before. She's real tricky, and she has more guts than I've ever seen in a woman. One time I saw her light up a big cigar in front of a group of men. Then she starts puffing and strutting back and forth across the stage and starts telling them that nothing can stop the working man. If they had anything in them at all they wouldn't let skinny little runts like us stop them."

The Canadian became more serious. "Then she'll have to be stopped from coming here, at least until things have time to cool off. What have you done about legal representation for the trial?"

"We've got the best lawyers money can buy. I don't think that the union will be able to prove the explosion was the company's fault. We still don't know what caused the blast." Osborn continued to watch out the window. Two men entered the opera house, but there was still no sign that anything was going on there.

"I thought you said that the mine had not been sprayed," the Candian said.

"It hadn't, but they still can't say for sure that it was the cause of the explosion. They can't even say that particles can ignite. It's never been proven."

The Canadian hesitated for a moment and then said, "Who is going to represent the men?"

"We're going to have problems there. Hendrekson is in town."

"Who is he?"

"We've had trouble with him before. He's a pompous bastard who uses words like fire."·

"What can he prove if there's no evidence?"

"He's too smart to try and prove anything. He'll be out to make us look bad in front of the miners. He makes us look weak and when that happens the men lose their fear."

The man got up and collected the papers from the couch. "I'm going back to Denver this afternoon. I'll be back the day of the trial. I'm also going to send a telegram to Mr. Rockman to send out one of his legal advisors. Keep things together until I get back."

"You just let me handle things my way. I know what these men understand," Osborn answered.

"We don't want any more publicity, so play the rough stuff down. I'll try and see what can be done about keeping Mrs. Jackson out of the area."

He left and Osborn continued to watch the opera house. There were few people on the street. Something is going on, he thought. The street is too quiet.

For days the company lawyers gathered information on what had happened the day of the explosion. They talked with the company men who were working outside the mine as well as those who worked the tipple. They talked with the men who were working in the machine shop and those who were in the mule barn. They talked with the men who were pulling ovens and those who had worked the night before. Most important, they talked with the men who had gone into the mine during the rescue operations. Every detail that these men gave them was carefully gone over with the hope that they could use something to prove the men were at fault.

The other side also prepared for the battle, but theirs was a more difficult task for they were known losers. Their record was a constant reminder of their embarrassing position. The union called upon a man who had some success in dealing with big business to represent them. Even more, he knew what it was like to come from a coal camp, to have the cards stacked against you. The days between the closing of the mine and the trial passed quickly.

Frank Naccarato left the opera house early that morning with several men. The tension between them and the company had been building since the day of the explosion and Frank knew that this time something had to give, or like an overfilled balloon, it would explode. The men headed for the courthouse which was several streets away from the opera house. It was one of the first structures built in the town and it sat upon the side of the second hill, away from the main street. The street leading to it ran like giant steps, reminding Frank of the hills around his home in Italy.

As he and the others neared the courthouse they could see the large granite blocks that made up the building. The courthouse held a kind of mystique for the immigrants who came from Europe. Throughout the continent were reminders of the days of the early Romans. Here, thousands of miles away, were the same large columns with hand-cut caps, rising above the other buildings of the city, a memorial to the ideals of democracy. Fourteen columns lined the front of the second and third floors of the outside of the building. Above the entrance were three large arch-shaped windows that looked like the triumphal arch built by Trajan two thousand years before.

When the men arrived they sat in the back of the courtroom discussing the trial.

"Perhaps today we will be able to prove how careless the company has been," one of them said, "then the state will force them to obey the laws.

"Who will be the judge?" another asked.

"Someone picked by the company," Frank answered. "They will try to set us up again. They will try to have the decision made before it is even started."

"This trial will not be any different from the others," one of the men said.

"They never are," another answered.

"That is not what is important," Frank said. "We cannot stop trying to change what is happening to us. The men who were destroyed in the mine will not let us give up. If we do, then we have lost something even more than life."

Voices came from outside the courtroom and the men became quiet. Several people entered the room, one of them a tall, lean man with dark hair and a mustache.

"I have not seen this man before," one of the men with Frank said.

"That is John Hendrekson," Frank answered. "He is the one who got the union leaders out of jail when the northern fields went on strike two years ago. He has been here since the day of the explosion."

The men who had come from the hall went to the front of the room and began preparing papers on a large desk. Then others began to come into the room.

Many of the people were women and children and older men. The company continued work at the mine so that it was impossible for many of the workers to attend. Those who were there were members of the night crew. Then the room grew silent. Frank turned to see two older men escorting an older woman through the door. They passed down the aisle to a row near the front of the room.

"Is she one of the widows from the explosion?" one of the men asked.

"Her husband was killed several years ago in a mining accident. When she tried to collect enough money for a decent burial, there was a long battle between the company and the union. The union tried to break the company's practice of only paying twenty-five dollars for the casket. They tried to get more, but sometime during the legal struggle her mind snapped and that ended the case. I have not seen her in a long time."

Hendrekson left the front table and approached the woman. "He is planning something," Frank whispered.

In a short time the small courtroom was full, with many waiting outside. When the judge arrived everyone rose except the woman. She sat staring into one of the corners of the room. The judge was heavy-set, with broad shoulders and a thick neck. His small round eyes peered over the wrinkles of flesh on his face, out over the courtroom.

"Bring me some water," he ordered one of the men who was standing near the bench, "and make sure that it's cold." When the water came, he took off his black gown and laid it across the top of the bench. "Bring the fan," he told the man who had brought the water. "Don't turn it on yet, just bring it and put it over in the corner." Then he took his gavel and pounded the desk with it three times. "I want quiet in here," he said, loudly enough for the people in the hall to hear him.

"Your honor," Hendrekson said, standing up. The judge acknowledged him.

"Before we begin, may I ask who has been appointed foreman of the jury?"

"Why?"

"I would like it to go into the official record."

"I want you to understand something from the beginning of this trial, Mr. Hendrekson. I am familiar with your reputation in court and what happened two years ago in Denver. This trial has nothing to do with the union. It's to determine what caused the explosion of the Hastings mine and anything else is irrelevent."

"Your honor," Hendrekson said, "because of the nature of this trial and because of the great deal that is at stake to the people of the community, I feel that it is necessary to determine this man's relationship to the other members of the community."

"I won't have you intimidating members of the jury!" the judge snapped.

"I am simply trying to determine who the man is, your honor."

"He's not on trial here," the judge came back.

"I have seen this man's name in the records of hearings similar to these. If so many people are affected by the decisions that he helps make in this county, then the people have the right to know who he is."

The judge looked around the courtroom. In the front row to his right were several men taking notes. The press, he thought.

"What is your name, sir?" Hendrekson asked.

"Aaron Johnson," the man replied.

"Mr. Johnson, is it not true that you are a bar owner in Trinidad?" Hendrekson continued.

"Yes."

"As a business owner, you exert a certain amount of influence in the town."

"I know some people."

"Is it also not true that you serve as the secretary of the Republican county committee?"

"A man's politics is his own business, Mr. Hendrekson. Now take your seat and save your questions for the others," the judge said. "That will be all the questions you'll have to answer, Mr. Johnson."

Hendrekson saw his first move stopped by the machinery that had been in operation since Colorado Coal had taken control of the mine. He returned to the desk and began to organize his papers. The lawyer for the company began his argument by stating the past cases against the compnay. The argument had been used successfully many times before.

"I would like to call the committee's attention to the past record of the company. I have here the documents of these hearings and I would like to read some of these to you," he said.

"What do these have to do with the explosion of the Hastings mine?" Hendrekson interrupted.

"Mr. Hendrekson, I will not tolerate your belligerence again. If you cannot control yourself I will have to ask that another lawyer replace you. Do you understand?"

"I understand," Hendrekson said, sitting down.

"In 1905," the company lawyer continued, "a man named Larsen was killed by a rock fall that was due to his own carelessness because he did not remove the rock upon timbering. In 1906, another man was killed due to the same circumstances . . . ." The lawyer continued for some time, the message always the same—accident was avoidable . . . rock fall due to negligence of the miner . . . accident causing broken neck . . . fallen rock . . . due to his own negligence . . . death by neglect on his part and no other . . . death due to the negligence of the deceased . . . run over by an electric car because of his own carelessness . . . "And those who died in the Hastings mine did so because of the neglect of their fellow miners and were solely responsible for their actions. Therefore, let the decision stand. We hereby exonerate the company."

Hendrekson sat listening as the major part of the morning was taken up by past cases that had been decided in favor of the company. As the hearing continued he began to get nervous. There seemed no end to the words of the company lawyer. It was not that he was not used to the rhetoric of the courtroom, but he had seen too much of the coal camps and he knew that words were not enough.

When the lawyer was finished, a number of names were read off by the judge. These men were brought in by the court, or by the company, Hendrekson thought, to give the known facts of the explosion. Numbers were presented by the first man, documenting the men who were at work the morning of the explosion. Confusion began to surface when the second man to take the chair gave the number of bodies that had been taken from the mine. This number did not match the figure given by the first. Then a map of the mine was brought in and one of the company engineers explained the workings of the Hastings mine and pointed to where the cave-ins had occurred. Facts and figures poured from the man's mouth continuously.

Hendrekson heard a low cry come from behind him. When he turned he saw the widow with her face buried in her hands. Mrs. Velardi sat weeping as the men who had escorted her tried to quiet her. When she stopped, the company lawyer began quickly to bury the woman's outburst with words.

"The company spent four thousand dollars on the ventilation system just three years ago, and another two thousand dollars making sure that the electrical connections were safe so that no sparks would come from the connection," he said. "The company has always had strict rules about timbering and other mining safety, but the men too often disregarded the rules so that they could dig a little extra coal," he finished.

The reaction by the jury to his speech was an expected one. With luck they would be able to finish by late that afternoon and have their decision by morning. Then it would be forgotten until the next time they needed to be hauled out to render a decision.

"Your honor," Hendrekson began, "the company's record concerning mining accidents is impressive. However, I think that counsel left one name out. For the record I think that the name of Henry Velardi should also be included."

A cry came again from the widow and this time the jury heard her and turned to see her faint. Hendrekson left the front of the room to go to her but she was quickly lifted by one of the men who had come into the room with her and carried from the courtroom.

"The court will take a fifteen-minute break," the judge announced, leaving the courtroom.

Outside the air was beginning to warm. "Is she all right?" Hendrekson asked when he got outside.

"She was taken to the home of a friend," one of the men answered. "It is better if she stays there the rest of the day."

"They would like to finish the hearing today," Frank said, standing behind Hendrekson.

"The way it looks now, Faris is going to end it this morning," Hendrekson answered.

"There is no way of forcing the company to stick to what was found at the mine after the explosion?" Frank asked.

"Not unless I can get all of the witnesses to the stand. The company's lawyer has had a great deal of practice wasting time."

Frank saw several men coming up the hill. The Greeks, he thought. He turned to see several more coming from the top of the hill. Hendrekson turned to go inside. "Take what time you need," Frank said. Hendrekson stopped. "The company will not give you any trouble. Just take what time you need."

When the hearing started again the company lawyer continued the precautions the company had taken to prevent explosions. If the company had done half of these things, Hendrekson thought, the mine could not have exploded. And now, to prove that the company had never done what it said it had, we would have to dig out the mine, something that could not be done. When the lawyer finished, Hendrekson acted quickly.

"I would like to call Mr. Tamburelli to the stand." A short, dark-haired man came forward and sat down. "Mr. Tamburelli, will you tell the court what happened on the morning of the Hastings explosions."

"I went to work that morning like I always do. But that whole week I could tell that something was wrong."

"What do you mean, something was wrong?"

"The air was not good."

"Your honor, the court cannot accept the testimony of this man. He is just a worker not a trained mining inspector," the company lawyer said, rising to his feet.

"Your honor," Hendrekson said, "this man has had considerable experience working in the mines in southern Colorado. He is respected by the other men as having an excellent safety record. Therefore, his opinion concerning the condition of the mine should be given."

"Very well. The court will recognize his testimony while realizing that his capacity in the mine is that of a worker and not a mining inspector."

"Thank you, your honor. Now, Mr. Tamburelli, you stated that you believed that something was wrong with the air in the mine. Can you tell us what specifically was wrong?"

"As I said, the air had not been good for a week. On the morning of the explosion, I went in maybe two hundred feet. The air was worse than it had been all week so I left."

"Where did you go when you left the mine?"

"I went to the company office."

"For what reason?"

"I went to report that the air in the mine was bad and I said that I would not work until they did something about it."

"Then you were going to quit unless the air was cleared of the gas?"

"Your honor, it has not been established that the mine exploded because of gas, or that the gas content exceeded the safe limit on the morning of the explosion," the company lawyer interrupted.

"I said that I would hear the man's testimony," the judge said. "If you have questions for him, wait until Mr. Hendrekson is finished. Mr. Hendrekson, don't put words in this man's mouth. Mr. Tamburelli, what was your reason for leaving the mine."

"The air was bad," the man answered."

"What do you mean by bad?" the judge asked.

"There was too much gas. When the air is like that, it is easy to set off an explosion."

"Would you tell the court what happened at the company office?" Hendrekson continued.

"He said that if I didn't want to work to get the hell out of camp."

"He said nothing of the condition of the mine?"

"He said that if it was good enough for the other workers, it was good enough for me."

"What did you do then?"

"I went to pick up the money that the company owed me."

"You weren't going back into the mine?"

"Hell no! I have seen what explosions do to a man, and even worse, to his family. The hell with them"

"That is all I have to ask this witness, your honor," Hendrekson said.

"I have a few things I would like to ask the witness, your honor," the company lawyer said. "What was your job at the Hastings mine Mr. Tamburelli?"

"I dug coal with a pick and shovel."

"Then you had no experience with instruments that measured the amount of gas within the mine?"

"I've had twenty years experience digging in the mine. This is the only instrument that I need." Tamburelli said, pointing to his nose."

"Do you know what this is?" The company lawyer picked up a lamp from his desk.

"It's a gas lamp."

"Do you know what it is used for?"

"To measure the gas in the mine."

"During the week before the explosion, as well as the morning of the explosion, these lamps were in constant use. They showed that the gas level was safe."

"Then why did it explode?" Tamburelli asked.

"Someone in the mine was the cause. Someone down there broke the rules that every miner knows must be followed. Someone down there was responsible for his fellow workers' lives."

"Your honor, I object to those remarks. They are nothing more than slanderous statements prepared for the press," Hendrekson interjected.

"I warn you that I will not have you making a decision for this court," the judge said to the company lawyer. "The last remarks made will be taken from the record. "If there are no other questions for this man, he is excused."

The room became silent. "I would like to present to the court this official document, your honor," the company lawyer said, handing it to the judge.

"I would like to see that," Hendrekson said, approaching the bench. The judge finished reading it and then handed it to Hendrekson.

As he was reading it, the judge said, "The court will recess for dinner and begin again at one o'clock." He slapped his gavel again upon the desk.

"I would like to look over this document," Hendrekson said.

"After lunch, Mr. Hendrekson," the judge answered, "after lunch," and he extended his hand for the document.

The courtroom emptied except for Hendrekson who sat at the desk going through papers. Frank saw him and walked to the front of the room.

"You'll need something to eat," Frank said.

Hendrekson looked up at him saying, "I've seen you some place before."

"At Hastings, the day after the explosion. I saw you many times that day. My name is Frank Naccarato."

"It's good to meet you, Mr. Naccarato. I understand that you did quite a lot for many of the families who were affected by the explosion."

"Not so much, I am afraid," Frank said.

"I know how you feel. Is it possible to do anything here that isn't predetermined?"

"You are doing what you can. No one can expect more."

"I haven't done anything but listen to how much the company has done and how careless the workers are, but it's not like that down there in the mine, is it?"

"No. It's not like that. You have to go down there day after day to know what it is like, but you don't think about it, you just do it."

"The justice to these men is no justice. The blindfold is on too tight and the scales weighted too heavily," Hendrekson said.

"Justice isn't blind here," Frank said, "she's fat from all the men she has devoured." Hendrekson returned to his papers, looking for the document that he had concerning the condition of the mine.

"Don't be too surprised if they come up with more that you expect, Mr. Hendrekson. We are used to this kind of justice. She is on the payroll too."

"Then we'll come up with our own justice. Have you had experience in the mine?" Hendrekson asked.

"I worked down there for seven years," Frank answered.

"I have some information that says that some of the mines in this area were not gaseous but there was the possibility that they could explode because of the amount of coal dust suspended in the air."

"I have heard this."

"The information goes on to say that the Colorado Coal Company was ordered by the state to spray the mines to hold down the dust. Do you know if the order was ever carried out?"

"There was no sprinkling of the mines. There was no sprinkling of the Hastings mine. The area is too dry and it would have cost a great deal of money to put such an operation into effect."

"That's what the information I have says. Then it is true."

"Bring the papers with you, and while we get something to eat we can talk to some men who worked at Hastings. They will know for sure."

Hendrekson went with Frank, leaving the courtroom deserted.

When the people returned to the courtroom it was hot. Several of the men carried large red handkerchiefs that they used when they were in the mine and they used them now to wipe off the sweat as they waited for the judge. One of the men opened the windows and another braced the doors open, but there was no breeze to relieve the heat from the sun. The people suffered in the heat but remembered the snow that fell just two weeks ago on the night before the explosion.

Frank and Hendrekson moved quickly up the brick street that led to the courthouse. Hendrekson held on to several pieces of paper and as they approached the courthouse he chewed the remainder of a sandwich. The judge had still not arrived. Frank took his seat with the other men while Hendrekson returned to his desk. In about forty-five minutes the judge returned. Again he placed his robe across the bench and began giving orders.

"Turn on that fan," he instructed one man, "and bring more water, with ice in it this time."

"Your honor," Hendrekson said, "may I see the document that was introduced before the court recessed for lunch?"

"In due time, Mr. Hendrekson, in due time."

The judge seated himself and took from his back pocket a white handkerchief. He wiped his forehead and neck. Then he started going through the papers on his desk. He took one and handed it to one of the men standing near his desk. The man brought it to Hendrekson.

"While you're looking over the document, the counsel for the company can present his next witness," the judge said.

The company lawyer began. "I would like to enter this magazine as testimony to the conditions of the mine and the camp in general. In it you will find an accurate description of what the company has been doing for their camps. They have been improving the conditions for ten years now. They provide clean, spacious homes with indoor bathrooms and landscapes; they provide entertainment, dances and ballgames and fair grounds where boxing matches are held frequently."

In disbelief of what the man had just said, Hendrekson stopped looking at the document.

"The attitude toward the men had always been good and precautions in the mine are the best that anyone can find in the mining business," the company lawyer continued.

"I cannot believe that you can accept this as part of this hearing," Hendrekson shouted, rising to his feet. "Anyone who has been in the camps knows that these are nothing but lies!"

"Mr. Hendrekson, that will be enough!" the judge bellowed.

"No, it's not enough! You may make the people in Denver believe these lies, or people in New York, but to enter them here, with the camps around you, makes a mockery of this court."

Two men moved toward him. As they did, several of the Greeks also moved.

"That's all right!" the judge shouted and the men stopped. "If you wish to protest the entry of this magazine then it will be recorded. But I will have no violence in this courtroom. You will have to follow procedures, Mr. Hendrekson, or you will be escorted out. Do you understand?"

"I understand," Hendrekson said, trying to quell his emotions.

"You may proceed," the judge said to the company lawyer.

"I would like to call Mr. Edward Jenson to the stand." A tall man approached and was seated on the stand.

"Mr. Jenson, were you in the machine shop the day after the explosion?" the company lawyer asked.

"Yes, I was."

"I would like to call the court's attention to these articles and ask you to identify them for us." The lawyer went to his desk and picked up several items, showing them to Jenson.

"They're wooden matches and a pipe," Jenson said.

"Will you tell the court where they were found?"

"They were taken out of the pockets of one of the miners who come out of the Hastings mine."

"Isn't this in direct violation to mining regulations?"

"Yes, it is."

"Will you tell the court why?"

"Any fool knows that when you take matches into the mine you're asking for trouble. Even if the gas content is at a safe level a man would have to be a damn fool to light a match down there."

"Were violations such as this one common in the mine, Mr. Jenson?"

"They were too common. Sometimes I wonder if some of the men knew the risks when they did something like this."

"Is it your opinion that the mine was safe?"

"The mine was safe enough," Jenson agreed.

"Safe enough for work to continue, but not safe enough for carelessness such as this," the lawyer said, holding out the matches and pipe so that everyone could see them. Then he put them on the judge's desk. "I would like to enter these as part of the evidence, your honor."

The judge looked at Hendrekson.

"Would you like to inspect these before I enter them as part of the evidence, Mr. Hendrekson?" he asked.

"No, your honor, but I would like to ask the witness a couple of questions."

"Proceed."

"Mr. Jenson, what was your position at the Hastings mine?" Hendrekson asked, as he walked around the desk. Jenson followed him with his eyes, thinking of what he had been told about this man by Osborn.

"You mean, what was my job?"

"Yes, what was your job? What did you do?"

"I was the night foreman."

"Were you involved with the rescue operations?" Hendrekson asked.

"I was," Jenson answered.

"Was there any indication that the man who was found with the matches was responsible for the explosion?"

"No, I can't say that he was responsible, but he could have been."

"But you don't know for sure."

"No."

"Was there an indication that any other miners had brought matches into the mine?"

"Not that I know of, but on many of the men we couldn't tell. Some of them were burned pretty bad."

"Mr. Jenson, as foreman, you must be familiar with the various machines that are used in mining, are you not?"

"Yeah, I know what we use in the mine."

"Are you familiar with a machine that is used to cut coal?"

"We don't produce during the night shift. That's when the blasting is done so I haven't seen it used much."

"Why was it brought into the mine?"

"The company is trying to modernize the mines."

"And this machine replaces men?" Hendrekson asked.

"If the machine does the cutting, fewer men are needed."

"How long would you say the machine had been used in the Hastings mine?"

"Three or four months."

"Isn't it a fact that although the machine had been in the Hastings mine three or four months, it had been used only a few times?"

"Well, there had been problems with it."

"What sort of problems?"

"With the wiring."

"Could you be a little more specific?"

Jenson hesitated and shifted uncomfortably in the chair. The courtroom grew still. The constant hum of the fan filled the room. Jenson took his white handkerchief from his pocket and wiped his face. He had not expected questions concerning the coal cutter.

"Do you know what kind of problems the company was having with the cutting machine?"

"There were too many sparks." Jenson finally answered.

"What kind of sparks?"

"From the machine! Haven't you ever seen sparks before?" Jenson answered.

"I have never seen this machine operate before. Do you mean that it made sparks as it cut through the coal?"

"No. They were electrical sparks. The machine came all the way from England. When we set it up it started giving off electrical sparks so we had the wiring checked."

"Couldn't electrical sparks cause an explosion?"

"They could."

"Then why was this machine not taken out of the mine to be checked?"

"It had to be assembled *inside* the mine, and once it was, it was never taken out." Sweat began running down Jenson's face.

"Was the machine in operation on the day of the explosion?"

"I don't know."

"Was it in use that night during your shift?"

"We tried it for about an hour."

"Then there is a good chance that it was used that morning?"

"I don't know."

"Did the machine operate properly during the night shift?"

"We didn't have any problems for a while, then she started acting up so we shut her down. There were men working on her when the night shift was over."

"Then it could have been started again?"

"I don't see why not. The mine was safe. The inspectors had given us the OK, and we didn't have any problems with the birds." Jenson said.

"What birds, Mr. Jenson?"

"The birds that some of the men take with them into the mine. If the air is bad the birds die," he said.

"Don't you think that a company that grossed over one and a half million dollars last year would take the time to check on the safety of the air, before operating a machine that they knew didn't function properly?"

"Objection!" the company lawyer cried out. "He's asking the witness to make a judgment that is not his to make."

"Sustained. Mr. Hendrekson, don't forget that no one is on trial here. We're simply trying to determine what caused the explosion."

"Your honor, the decision of this court will affect many people. They have a right to know what happened down there."

"Then get at them without badgering the witness."

Hendrekson returned to his desk and started going through his papers again.

"The witness can return to his seat," the judge said.

"One minute please, your honor, I'd like to ask him another question."

"Take the stand again, Mr. Jenson. You remember what I told you, Hendrekson," the judge said.

"According to the reports that I have, the explosion started somewhere in the sixth or seventh entry. Is this true?"

"It looked that way but it's hard to say. Many believe that the point of the explosion is the least damaged."

"Where was the machine when the explosion took place?"

"It was in the sixth entry."

"And was it damaged by the explosion?"

"It was damaged all right."

"How badly damaged?"

"It's hard to say. We weren't down there that long and the time we were there we were too busy looking for survivors," Jenson said.

"Would you tell the court what you did find in the sixth entry?"

"There was a great deal of debris. An explosion will try and find its way out of the mine to one of the entrances. If the cutter had caused the explosion there would have been a great deal of damage from that point to the entrance."

"Was there great damage in these entries?"

"There sure was!"

"Can we assume that if the machine was the cause, then there wouldn't have been much damage to the sixth entry?"

"Not necessarily. You see, things are not always as cut-and-dried as that when you're dealing with a mine explosion. When a blast starts ripping through the tunnels, it's difficult to say what it's going to do. I've heard that sometimes two blasts start from one explosion, each going off in a different direction. The only thing that is left are bits and pieces."

"I see," Hendrekson said. "That will be all for this witness."

By midafternoon there was still no breeze, and the fan seemed useless except to make noise. The people inside the courtroom grew more uncomfortable as their shirts became as soaked as their handkerchiefs. Hendrekson unbuttoned his shirt as did the other lawyer. The judge finished the water and ordered more.

"Your honor, I would like to call Mr. John Carmicle to the stand," Hendrekson said after Jenson sat down. The man's name was familiar to Frank, as it was to many of the men present. Why does he call this man? Frank thought. He will say what the company wants him to.

"Mr. Carmicle," Hendrekson began, "you are the superintendent of the Hastings mine."

"Yes."

"And you have been in charge of several other mines for Colorado Coal and Fuel?" Carmicle nodded. "Then we can assume that you have had a good deal of experience in the coal mining business?" Hendrekson said.

"About thirty-five years," Carmicle answered.

"Were you in Hastings the day of the explosion?"

"Yes, I was one of the first men to enter the mine after the explosion."

"What time was this?"

"The first party entered the mine about seven o'clock."

"At night?"

Carmicle nodded.

"According to the information that I have, the mine exploded a short time after the morning shift entered."

"We don't know exactly what time she blew. It could have been as long as two hours after they arrived for work," Carmicle said.

"But this was the morning crew, wasn't it?"

"Yes."

"If the mine blew, say, no later than 9:30 in the morning, why did the rescue party not begin operations until seven that night?"

"There were several reasons for the delay," Carmicle said mechanically. "First, the mining office heard that there had been trouble from one of the miners. He had started into the mine, got about two thousand feet in, and was forced out.

"You did not hear the explosion?"

"We had been using dynamite in the area. It was common to hear blasts."

"And the blast caused by the explosion in the mine was no different from these blasts?"

"The explosion blew most of the brattices out, so much of the sound was absorbed by them," Carmicle said.

"Would you tell the court what a brattice is?"

"Sure. They're air ducts used to bring fresh air into the mine."

"How long was it before you realized that the mine had exploded?"

"Well, it's like I said, one of the men came and told us what had happened. At first it sounded like there was a fire. If we started digging we would let oxygen into the mine and it would fuel the fire."

"And this was the sole reason for the delay?"

"There were many things that we had to consider before we started into the mine," Carmicle said.

"Like the reaction of the people when they saw the men coming out in pieces?" Hendrekson said.

"That has nothing to do with this trial, your honor," the company lawyer said, rising again. "We're here to determine the cause of the explosion and not what went on afterwards."

"You are out of line, Mr. Hendrekson," the judge said.

"Your honor, if the delay in the rescue operations was an attempt to cover up what happened in the mine, then it is very much a part of this trial." Hendrekson said.

"I'll determine what is and isn't pertinent to this trial. I'll remind you again to watch your questions or I'll dimiss the witness," the judge warned.

Hendrekson returned to his desk. He saw the newspapermen in the first row of the courtroom busily writing. He wiped his brow and picked up several papers from his desk. The heat of the day was taking much of his energy, and he knew the judge would soon dismiss the court for the day.

"Mr. Carmicle," he said, returning to the front of the room, "were you aware that there might be many men trapped alive down there?"

"The men know the risks when they go to work in the mine. If they don't want the work, there are many others who do."

"Then you were not so concerned with the possibility that there might be survivors?"

"Of course we were, but we didn't know what we would find when we entered the mine. It could have been a trap. There are hundreds of Austrians who could have blown that mine on purpose, because of the war in Europe. Hundreds more could have been killed," Carmicle said, becoming flustered. "That mine was the primary producer of coal in the canyon. The company will lose a lot of money because of this explosion," he finished.

"Was there any consideration as to how the people would react when the men started coming out of the mine?"

"There were company men in there too, twenty-five of them, so it wasn't only foreigners. You forget that if it weren't for the mine those men couldn't find work to feed themselves or their families."

"These *foreigners* were working in an American mine, doing work Americans wouldn't do, and they were paying their dues which got a little too high," Hendrekson said.

"The company did all it could. We used electric lights to mark the timbering. The inspectors were sent in every month. Everything possible to prevent an explosion was done."

"Tell that to the sixty-two widows and their children when you bring them the twenty-five dollars for the caskets. That's all, your honor, I have nothing more to ask the witness."

The judge slammed his gavel against the desk and intoned, "The court will be dismissed for today and will begin promptly at eight o'clock in the morning."

As the courtroom emptied, the Canadian watched from a seat in the back of the room. This is not going to be as easy as Osborn thought, he said, half to himself. The newspapermen were the last to leave the room. Osborn better have more control over them than he does over the hearings, he thought. It should have been completed today. Then he left.

Outside the courthouse, Frank met with Hendrekson.

"The judge left in a hurry," he said.

"It is a good time to regroup," Hendrekson said. "I hope I gave the newsmen something to put in the papers. We'll need it if the state is going to do anything to help these people, or they'll get nothing just as they have in the past. I need a shower," he said walking away from the courthouse.

That night, in his room at the Toltec Hotel, Hendrekson went over his information carefully. The air cooled quickly when the sun was gone and a faint breeze stirred the curtain in the open window. Tomorrow I will act quickly, he thought. I am lucky there is a tomorrow. If there were only some way to get these people what is rightly theirs, some law that could produce justice for them. He stood looking out over the empty brick street. I would trade all of the laws for the right sword.

In the camps the work continued.

# CHAPTER

# 9

Hendrekson passed the night in restless hours of half-sleep and incomplete dreams. When morning came he was sitting in the wooden chair with several law books on the table next to him. He searched intently through one of them. Then he heard a whistle from the street and put the book down and went to the window. The paper boy had passed and a bundle of newspapers lay on the sidewalk outside the hotel. He put the book with the others and went quickly to the stairs and out through the lobby. He knelt over the papers and untied the thick twine that bundled them. We are drawing nearer to war, he said to himself as he read the headlines. Then he passed quickly over the heavy black print of each article. In the bottom corner of the paper he began reading:

## CONDITION OF MINE REPORTED GOOD
## DAY OF EXPLOSION IS TESTIMONY
## OF SUPT. CARMICLE AT TRIAL

The trial that stems from the April 17th explosion at the Hastings mine got underway at 8:00 o'clock yesterday morning at the county courthouse. The survivors of the mines who died in the explosion have brought suit against the Colorado Coal and Fuel Company, claiming that the explosion occurred because of negligence on the part of the company.

Although the company does not recognize the United Mine Workers' Union, it is believed that legal representation for the people is being provided by this union. The Colorado Coal and Fuel Company is the leading producer of coal in Southern Colorado and is owned by Mr. John Rockman of New York City.

Various rumors have been afloat in the area since the day of the explosion and compensation to the families for their loss will hinge on the determination of the cause of the explosion. One rumor, considered to be a far-fetched theory, is that war-crazed Austrians caused the explosion. Other causes suggested concern the fact that the Hastings mine was considered to be a highly gaseous mine, almost impossible to keep free of gas. Another suggests that coal dust was the cause.

The first witness called was W.J. McNeil, traveling auditor, who presented a list of names of those who had checked into the mine that morning. He testified that of the 121 men who were in the mine on the morning of the explosion, 96 were miners and 25 were company men. He testified that these numbers had been taken from the records at the lamp station.

The second witness was P.R. Langly, employment agent, who arrived at the scene the morning after the explosion and made a check of the bodies as they were brought out of the mine. He testified that 86 of the bodies had been identified.

W.F. Blackburn of Denver, chief engineer, then identified a map of the Hastings mine, showing the slope and the workings of the mine. He explained the operation of the mine in detail, including the latest safety features in use in the mine. He pointed out several sections of the mine as possible areas where the explosions originated.

Hendrekson read the article quickly and soon came to the bottom of the page. He became aware of a man standing over him and looked up.

"The papers," the man said.

"What?" Hendrekson said.

"The papers," the man repeated. Hendrekson looked at the bundle.

"Of course," Hendrekson said, standing and reaching into his pocket for some change and handing it to the man. The man picked up the bundle and turned to go back into the hotel.

"Excuse me," Hendrekson said. "Is this the only paper delivered to the hotel?"

"No," the man answered. "The *Morning Star* should be here at any minute."

"Thank you."

Hendrekson waited outside the hotel until the other paper arrived. He took one, put the change on top of the bundle, and went into the hotel lobby. He read the article while sitting in a large leather chair. When he was finished, an ironic feeling of stupidity came over him. The fact and the law, the thought, these are as useless as the law books in my room. The fact and the law mean little here, there is only the sword.

He returned to his room, tossed the papers on the table with the books, and washed in preparation for the second day of the hearing.

He was the first to arrive at the courthouse and sat at the desk again, going over the papers he had prepared. The morning sun began to penetrate the stained glass windows that lined the upper part of the walls of the room. Each window was composed of blue and gold glass with a red torch in the middle, and as the rays passed through them a montage of color was projected upon the white walls of the room. Between the frames were long pillers with Ionic caps reaching nearly to the ceiling. Someone passed by the outside of the room and footsteps echoed from the marble floor. Hendrekson turned but saw no one. He had not realized the size of the room before. There must have been three hundred people here yesterday, he thought.

He heard voices coming from the chambers. The jury, he guessed. There were two large jury boxes, but only one was filled. Who fills the other one while we conduct this trial? He wondered. And who will sit in judgment when it is over? He looked at the large wooden desk that elevated the judge above the rest of the court. The power above us all but not without the responsibility.

People began coming down the aisle. The company lawyer came through the wooden gates, the only break in the railing that separated the spectators from the arena. The room filled quickly. The jury entered, and the judge came in and sat down.

"I call this court to order," the judge said, pounding the gavel upon the desk. "You may begin, Mr. Hendrekson."

"Your honor, I would like to submit this list to the court in regard to the record of mining explosions. On August 7, 1902, the Berwin mine exploded. Thirteen men were killed. On October 28, 1904, the Tercio mine exploded. Nineteen men were killed. On February 19, 1906, the Maitland mine exploded. Fourteen were killed. On January 23, 1907, the mine at Primero exploded. Twenty-two were killed. On May 5, 1907, the Eagleville mine exploded. Forty-two were killed. On July 6, 1909, the

Todler mine exploded. Seventy-two were killed. On January 31, 1910, another of the Primero mines exploded. This time seventy-six were killed. On October 8, 1910, the Starkville mine exploded. Fifty-six were killed. On November 8, 1911, the Delagua mine exploded. Sixty-nine were killed."

Before he was finished, memories of explosions had been brought from the past like skeletons of death that had been buried in the minds of those who had worked in mines, or had read in the papers of the disasters, or had tried to justify to themselves why so many had died. The explosions had worked their way into their lives and created a living death in the camps.

Hendrekson handed the list to the judge. The judge looked at the list and submitted it to the court. "You may call your first witness," he said to the company lawyer.

"I would like to recall Mr. Carmicle to the witness stand, your honor," the lawyer said. The man came from the back of the room, was seated, and took the customary oath. The lawyer began.

"For the sake of clarification, I would like to begin with the events on the morning of the explosion. It has been suggested that rescue operations were delayed beyond a reasonable time. Mr. Carmicle was not given ample time to explain what procedure was followed on the morning of the explosion. Mr. Carmicle, would you tell the court what first attempt was made into the mine?"

"The first men that entered the mine were what we call helmeted men. They were sent in to check the conditions of the mine.

"What time were they sent in?"

"It must have been about ten-thirty."

"In the morning?"

"Yes."

"And what did these men find?"

"At that time the mine was not accessible beyond 1,200 feet. Later that afternoon another attempt was made into the mine."

"What time was this?"

"Three o'clock."

"Were you a member of this party?"

"Yes, I was."

"Would you tell the court what that party found?"

"We went in about 1,200 feet when we reached the first workings. We figured the nearest workers who were trapped were 2,000 feet beyond that. We knew that the only hope they had was if they were getting air from the main shaft."

"What were the conditions this far into the mine?"

"We couldn't stay in there very long. The smoke came in thick black clouds from below. We would have all died if we had stayed."

"Didn't one man in fact die while attempting rescue operations?"

"Yes. I don't think the cause of death was ever determined, but he just dropped while he was in the mine and when we brought him out he was dead."

"What was the general attitude of the rescue party, Mr. Carmicle?"

"Our first thought was to get to the men who might still be alive. Of course we had to consider the safety of those in the rescue party too."

"Was anything else being done for safety during this time?"

"We had men taking water to the mine in case there was a fire."

"Thank you, Mr. Carmicle. That will be all, your honor."

"Mr. Hendrekson, is there anything that you would like to ask the witness before I dismiss him?" the judge asked.

"Yes, your honor," Hendrekson replied. "Mr. Carmicle, you stated earlier that one member of the rescue operation died suddenly inside the mine?"

"Yes," Carmicle answered.

"What were the circumstances of his death?"

"Do you mean why he died?"

"What was he doing when he fell?"

"Well, the men were trying to repair some of the damage to the main slope so that they could continue into the mine. They were removing rocks and timbers, anything that would prevent entry," Carmicle explained.

"Then this didn't take place during the first entry into the mine, did it?"

"No."

"In fact, this particular death didn't take place until the *second day* of rescue operations."

"Yeah, I guess it was the second day."

"Mr. Carmicle, when was the last time the mine had been inspected?"

"A couple of days before the explosion."

"Even though the mine had been inspected just two days before, it exploded. Can you give any possible explanation for this fact?" Carmicle hesitated.

"Is it possible that there was an oversight during the inspection?" Hendrekson asked.

"The mine was inspected twice a week. The gas content was checked on the twenty-third, so were the fans. At the time of the inspection, the fans were pushing in 26,000 cubic feet of air which is above state regulations. I don't believe that there was any oversight."

"Mr. Carmicle, is there any reason why the rescue operations would be carried out in secrecy?"

"They were not a secret. Everybody knew about them," Carmicle answered.

"There was nothing that the company was doing that they did not want the people to know about?"

"There was no reason for secrecy," Carmicle said sternly.

"Then why were guards posted around the mine?"

"They were put there for security. We knew that when word got out that there had been an explosion, people would come to the mine. It was a very dangerous place to be and many of the people would be hysterical."

"And it was necessary to put armed guards around the mine? Wasn't this dangerous?"

"You control the situation the best way that you can. You realize this when you have worked in these mines as long as I have."

"Was it also necessary to prevent the newspapers from covering the explosion?"

"We didn't *prevent* them from covering the explosion. We gave them all the information they wanted," Carmicle answered, motioning to the men in the front row of the courtroom.

"Are you aware that while Mr. Rayon was attempting to take pictures of the mine, his equipment was destroyed?"

"I do not know Mr. Rayon," Carmicle answered.

"He is a reporter for the Pueblo paper. He's not here today. For some reason the paper sent someone else." Hendrekson walked over to his desk and took from it a broken camera. "However, he did manage to send the camera that was broken. Your honor, I would like to submit this to the court as evidence."

"I didn't know anything like this took place," Carmicle said, "If it did," he finished.

"That will be all," Hendrekson said.

"You are excused." The judge motioned Carmicle off the stand.

The courtroom grew restless. People began to talk to each other. Many of them had been there the day of the explosion. They knew the violence that had gone on and the words of the superintendent renewed the bitternes they had felt that day.

"I would like to call Mr. Charles Vecillio to the witness stand," Hendrekson said. Vecillio came from his seat, passed through the wooden gates and took the witness chair. The oath was given and Hendrekson began.

"Mr. Vecillio, what was your job at the Hastings mine?"

"I was a rope rider on the day shift."

Is it true you are the only survivor of the explosion?"

"Yes," the man answered in a low voice.

"Can you tell us why you were not killed with the others?"

"I had made two entries into the mine that morning, but was not far enough inside to be killed."

"Were you also one of the rescue workers?"

"Yes."

"Would you tell us what you found when you went into the mine?"

"Everything was a mess. The timbering had been smashed into toothpicks. The carts and tracks were mangled into hunks of tangled metal. The air was bad. At times we could hardly see what was in front of us," Vecillio answered.

"How did the men react, having to work under these conditions?"

"There is a close relationship between miners. Mr. Hendrekson. And some of the men had blood relatives in there. But for all of us, it was important that we find any survivors as soon as possible," Vecillio answered.

"Mr. Vecillio, you mentioned a strong relationship between miners. Would you explain that statement?"

"Sure, I'll explain. We work down there together. Today, tomorrow, the next day the same thing might happen, and down inside we have to know that if another mine goes, one that we're working in, that they'll come after us as soon as possible. We don't talk about it but we have to know it. In that way we're all related."

"How long was it before you encountered any of the men?" Hendrekson asked.

"We worked through two shifts before we found anyone. Like I said, the debris was unbelievable. When we did start finding bodies we knew that some would never be found because of the way the steel and rock had been mangled together. We knew that we would never find them"

A strange note came into Vecillio's voice. He talked unemotionally, his eyes fixed in front of him. The other people in the courtroom looked at him as though he were one of the dead come back to speak for the others.

"It was hard to see down there," Vecillio went on. "It was like a monster had torn through the tunnels, destroying everything and taking life like the devil himself turned loose, leaving the men no way of escaping him. The timbering could not have withstood the pressure that came through there. In some places the whole mountain came down.

"The third party to enter the mine broke into the tunnels. We passed the second north entry and began putting up timbering in the third, some distance from the fork. That's when started finding them."

"Do you mean the dead men?" Hendrekson asked when Vecillio paused.

"I won't say we found three men," Vecillio continued. "We found parts of three men—half of one we found on a brace and the other half on the floor of the slope some distance away. We did not find all of the second one. The third was a boy, his name was Herrera, he had gone down to bring his brother a helmet. We found him buried from the shoulders up by a huge rock." Again he stopped. The feeling that had come over the camps, like the dark cloud that moved inside the mine, now covered the courtroom.

"Were all the bodies in this condition, Mr. Vecillio?"

"Not all of them were in pieces. Some had been burned, their faces, their hands, their clothes. You didn't even know who some of these men were, they were burned so bad. We had to use their mining checks to identify them . . ."

"Mr. Vecillio," Hendrekson said gently, "were any men found who had not been killed directly by the explosion?"

"The fourth and fifth entries had been closed off by cave-ins. We found men there. They were easy to identify."

"Why wasn't there any problem identifying these men?"

"They had died of afterdamp. When the timbering gave way, they were trapped with only so much time before the gas killed them."

"Was there any thought that there might be men such as these, trapped and still alive?" Hendrekson went on.

"Those were the men that we went in there to save. The others were in God's hands."

"Then there was hope that you could reach them in time?"

"For miners there is always hope, until they are found."

Hendrekson went behind the witness chair to a map which had been placed in the corner. He picked it up and moved it so Vecillio and the jury could see it.

"Mr. Vecillio, would you identify this map for the court?"

"It's a map of the Hastings mine," Vecillio said.

"Would you tell the court what procedure was followed when rescue operations began?"

Vecillio got up from the witness chair and went to the map.

"We entered the mine here," he said, pointing to the entrance of the mine, "and we came to the first cave-in here. Then we worked toward the sixth and seventh entries, here."

"What did you find at the fork of these two entries?"

"We found the body of Dale Rowley, a mining inspector."

"What was unusual about his body?"

"There was no damage beyond it. His lamp was on the floor in two pieces, and there were matches with it."

"If the point of the explosion is the least damaged, is it not possible that the explosion originated at this point?"

"Many of the men believed that the explosion came from here," Vecillio said, pointing to the point where they had found the body, "and spread down the sixth and seventh entries here and here."

"Objection, your honor!" the company lawyer shouted. "The witness is being lead."

"Sustained. What the witness has said is conjecture. It has not been determined that the point of the explosion was the sixth entry and therefore, the testimony must be viewed in this light."

Hendrekson felt frustration again. The law books and the newspapers flashed back to him.

"That's all I have to ask this witness," he said, sitting down. The Canadian, who had taken the same seat as the day before, got up and walked toward the door of the courtroom. Then he stopped and looked directly at the judge. The judge watched him and became uneasy.

"Do you have anything you want to ask the witness?" he asked the company lawyer.

"Yes, your honor," he said. "Isn't it true that there is no real proof that the point of an explosion is always the least damaged, Mr. Vecillio?"

"That's what many miners believe."

"Isn't it also a belief that the birds that some of the men take with them show if the mine is free of gas or not?"

"It's true. Many of them believe that."

"Yet there is no evidence that any of the birds died of gas on the morning the mine exploded, is there?"

"No."

"This belief isn't necessarily true, is it?"

"I guess not."

"Your honor, if you would call Dr. Donaldson to the witness stand, Mr. Vecillio can be excused. I have no other questions for him."

Dr. Donaldson took the witness stand. His face was worn and unshaven. His hair was unkept. As he sat upon the stand he knew that he would be expected to recount the days after the explosion. He detested having to go over the facts, facts that would bring the bodies back into his conscious mind; facts that caused him to hear the voices of the women and children outside the machine shop door; facts that recalled the smell of burned flesh; facts that reminded him of the taste of blood when he wiped his mouth with his shirtsleeve and the blood that would stick to his hands.

"Dr. Donaldson, what did you find on the bodies when they were brought out of the mine?" the lawyer asked.

"I found many things."

"Would you be more specific?"

"I found a great deal of money—seven hundred dollars on one. Another had hidden a box with three hundred dollars in it."

"Isn't it unusual that these men had taken so much money with them into the mine?"

"I don't know."

"Do you have any idea what they were going to do with it, or where they had gotten the money?"

"Many don't trust banks."

"Isn't it possible that they could have been sent in there with the money to purchase something, like explosives?"

"Objection, your honor! The witness is being asked to speculate," Hendrekson said.

"Sustained."

"What else was found on the bodies, Dr. Donaldson?"

"Just things that men carry with them, watches, wallets, anything and nothing."

"Was there anything else, like things used for smoking?" the lawyer pressed.

"Someone has already testified that matches were found, matches and a pipe," the doctor said.

"Wasn't it a fact that matches were found on several of the dead miners?"

"Two, to be exact, I found matches on two of them."

"Isn't it possible that many more carried them, and that the matches were destroyed?"

"Anything is possible," Donaldson said drily.

"Would you tell us the official count of bodies to come out the mine?"

"There were 121 men inside when the mine blew. They brought me 101. I could identify 93."

"That leaves twenty-four men who could not be identified nor found. Any of them could have been responsible for the explosion." Donaldson did not answer. "That's all I have to ask this witness. Your honor."

"Mr. Hendrekson, your witness," the judge said.

"Dr. Donaldson," Hendrekson began, "were all the bodies that were brought out in the same condition that you described to us?"

"Not all of them. Twenty-eight were not."

"What was the cause of death of these men?"

"They died from afterdamp."

"Would you tell us what this is?"

"It's a poisonous gas that forms when methane gas explodes."

"Is this a common cause of death in an explosion such as this?"

"Yes."

"Then the company would have been aware that this gas had formed within the mine?"

"It's generally known, regardless of the cause of the explosion, that poisonous gas forms in such a case."

"Dr. Donaldson, what indication was there that these men died *after* the explosion?"

"The men who brought them out said that their lunch boxes were empty and that the water had been drunk. They couldn't have been killed by the explosion itself. There were no marks on them," Donaldson said.

"How long after the explosion did the men die?" Hendrekson asked.

"They had time to eat. They could not have lived too long after that. The food hadn't been digested so it depends on how long they waited to eat. I didn't perform the autopsies until the day after the explosion. They weren't found until early the morning after."

"Is it your professional opinion that, had rescue operations been started immediately, these men could have been saved?"

The doctor looked at Hendrekson and then at the judge. "That's an absurd question," he said, turning back to Hendrekson. "It does not matter if they could have or not. They *weren't!* The men are dead, and delaying getting them out was a crime against mankind. Those men needed help down there, and there is no reason that they should not have gotten it as soon as possible." The doctor's voice dropped off in despair.

"For those men it does not matter," he continued. "They are dead. But there are thousands around here who are in mines just like the Hastings. It could happen again while we sit here talking . . ."

"Dr. Donaldson," the judge interrupted, "I'll have to ask you to just answer the questions. All we are interested in here are the facts."

"The facts?" the doctor cried out. "I'll give you the facts and they're not the facts that you have in front of you on pieces of paper. Were you there? Did you see 121 men destroyed? I don't give a damn if they were workers or inspectors or bosses. They were men. But they weren't the worst victims of that explosion. There are others who live, day after day, with the fear of the same thing happening. Were you there to hear them over and over again—voices every time a body was brought out of the mine?" the doctor asked. "The women would cry out, 'Were you in there? Were you in there?' They'd ask everyone who came out. Many of them repeated the words in English that they didn't even understand. Then they would leave and come back in a little while and ask again. 'Where you in there?' One poor woman pounded on the door until the hinges came loose and the door fell. She came into the room carrying a baby. I don't know what will happen to them now . . . .." the doctor's voice trailed off.

He appeared exhausted. The judge slammed his gavel. Two men approached the doctor and escorted him out of the courtroom.

"The jury will consider the facts as they have been presented and will return this afternoon with their decision," the judge ordered, and then left the room. The courtroom began to empty. Hendrekson sat at his desk for a few moments, then he began to collect his papers. Frank went to the front of the room and stood behind the wooden railing.

"It has been a difficult trial," Frank said. Hendrekson turned to see who had spoken.

"It is an effective machine they have here, well oiled with money," he answered, "and the blood of the miners will not slow it down."

"You know what the verdict will be."

"Let's get out of here," Hendrekson said.

The word passed quickly on the streets of Trinidad that the trial was over and the verdict was being decided. It moved to the canyons where the families of the dead men waited for justice. The interlude between the end of the testimony and the verdict had begun, and the union men prepared for the decision.

Telegraph messages began arriving in Trinidad and soon Frank was notified that Lewis would be returning to Trinidad with several other union officials. When he received the messages he hurried down to the Toltec Hotel to talk to Hendrekson. He found him in his room preparing to leave.

"You are going back to Denver?" Frank asked when he saw the suitcases.

"After the verdict is given," Hendrekson said, continuing to pack.

"I have a message from the union officials in Denver. They are coming to Trinidad. There is going to be trouble."

Hendrekson stopped his packing. "What kind of trouble?" he asked.

"They think that it is the best time to call the stike."

Hendrekson said, "Many people will suffer."

"If the verdict is what we expect, nothing will change. We will go back to the same existence we had before," Frank said.

"Until the next explosion."

"The explosion is only a part of the problem. The way these people are forced to live is equally bad."

"So I have seen. How strong is the union?"

"Only a strike will tell. The company has done many things to prevent the men from joining, but neither side can be sure how many will walk. You should stay for a while longer. You will see that all the laws in the world mean nothing when all you have is a shovel, and your enemy has a gun."

"The company has a great deal of money. They've bought themselves a governor and who knows how many politicians in Washington. If the union calls a strike they will have to fight alone," Hendrekson said.

"The politicians in Washington have their own war to fight. They are not concerned with the people here. These men are trying to protect their families. If the government was concerned, they would have come here years ago. We are used to taking care of ourselves. The rest will be in God's hands."

"We cannot blame God for what is happening here, my friend." responded Hendrekson. He paused and looked directly at Frank. "It has been a long two days," he said. "It is almost time for the jury to return. Let's go back to the courtroom to hear them out."

They left the room for the courthouse. Small groups of men had begun to gather on the corners of the town. Others gathered around the courthouse. Inside, the room was again full. Hendrekson was at his desk when the jury entered and the verdict was handed to the judge.

"The jury has determined that, due to the evidence, the explosion started at the fork of the sixth and seventh entries and proceeded to the main entrance," the judge announced. "Because of the safety precautions taken by the company, it was found that they were not directly to blame for the explosion. Because evidence has shown that both the miners and the inspector carried matches into the mine, and since this is direct violation to the rules that govern the safe operation of it, both are guilty of contributory negligence."

The judge looked out over the gathering. "The company is so ordered to pay the normal burial fee." He slammed down his gavel and left.

"What is this contributory negligence?" Frank asked Hendrekson.

"It means that neither side is to blame."

"Then the company will pay the twenty-five dollars for the casket and that is all?"

"That's what it means," Hendrekson answered grimly. "Nothing will change."

He left for Denver late that afternoon. He told Frank that he would do what he could for them while he was there to stop the impending violence. Frank did not know what that could be.

An eerie state of fear settled over the camps. The next day, the union bosses arrived from Denver and the strike call went out. Very little happened that first day. Few men walked out and the company breathed a premature sigh of relief. The men looked with suspicion upon things that had formerly been routine. When trains arrived they watched carefully to see who or what was being brought into town. More guards were sent to the camps to protect company property. Then, as though the strike call had been rescinded, all the men who had left work returned, and a meeting was called for the workers. A false sense of security was felt by the company and they took what they considered as their advantage by putting a tighter hold on the camps.

Vicenzo heard of the verdict while he was at work. He had started working the day shift and he could feel the tension between the workers and the guards on the day that he heard the strike call go out. But many of the workers did not believe that the order had come from the union. They thought that the company was trying to fool them to find out who belonged to the union. When the union learned of this they revoked the order until they could better organize the strike. That night Vicenzo left for Trinidad. He believed that if anything was going to happen, Frank would know about it.

Frank had stayed in town the entire day, meeting with the union bosses and with groups of men outside the opera house, and that was where Vicenzo found him.

"What brings you to town?" Frank asked.

"I come to find out what is going on. Some believe that there is going to be a strike. I have missed much work already, and when there is no pay, there is nothing to eat."

"Don't worry, Vicenzo," Frank said, "there will always be something to eat. We have learned to live in bad times and if it is necessary we will do so again."

Vicenzo reached into his pocket and took out several newspaper clippings. He asked Frank to read them. After Frank read the last one, Vicenzo said, "Mrs. Veltri cut these out of the paper. At night she looks at them and sometimes she begins to cry. They must be very important to her."

Frank looked at them again. "These are the accounts of the last two weeks, after the explosion. This large one says that the mine is on fire and that the men will soon be rescued. It is dated the day after the explosion. This one says," Frank held the article out so that Vicenzo could see it, "the first bodies were brought out of the mine and it gives the names. It also says that there is hope that there are men who are still alive. By the time this one came out, there was no longer any hope of survivors. The rest are much the same. Each gives a number and then the names. Of these names that she has underlined," Frank said, pointing to two, "this one is her sister's husband. This one was her hephew."

"The explosion was very close to her," Vicenzo said.

"It was close to many. There have always been great differences in the camps. We brought them with us when we came from Europe, but now we are all dying together. These men were from Tirole, they were Slavs. But it does not matter any more what nationality we are. We are all in this togther."

"I shall put these back," Vicenzo said. "Perhaps I can help her. She has done so much for me." Vicenzo folded the papers carefully and put them back into his pocket.

"On your way into town were you stopped?" Frank asked.

"At the gate to the camp."

"Did you have your union card with you?"

"I put it here in the brim on my hat."

"It is best to leave it in Cokedale."

"I understand," Vicenzo said.

"You must be very careful now. Things are going to get worse and there will be shooting. Many of the men are beginning to get edgy."

"Yes. I know."

"Meet me at my house in about an hour," Frank told him. "We will forget about this thing long enough to eat a good dinner."

Frank went into the opera house and Vicenzo headed for the other side of town where the red lights glowed brightly in the night air. There, he thought, will be the best way to forget about the explosion, and the men in uniforms, and the ovens, but most of all the dreams.

Later that night, he ate with Frank and his family. They talked and laughed. Marietta's questions about the old country seemed endless. At times it was hard for Vicenzo to remember the old country and some of the people there. On his way back to Cokedale the night air was cool but Vicenzo's head throbbed at the temples and he began to think that something was wrong with his head. He hated the men who had nearly destroyed him. Perhaps tonight will be different, he thought. Sleep will come and there will be only darkness.

# CHAPTER

# 10

When Vicenzo returned to work he felt a tension among the workers greater than had existed immediately after the explosion at Hastings. He knew that, out of respect, there would be no violence while the men were being buried. But as time passed and sorrow became memories, bitterness and hatred grew in the camps.

The company sent more guards into the camp and with them came barbed wire and searchlights. Each night he watched shadows cross the wall of his room as the lights sought groups of men who might gather to talk of organizing. He heard of union leaders who had come to Trinidad to get men to rally to their cause.

Vicenzo disliked the word *cause*.

"When people have nothing to do with their lives they look for some *cause* to make them feel important," he told Mrs. Veltri. "In Italy we take care of ourselves and our families and we did not make it other people's business to give us purpose. But here in America, there are so many strangers with so many tongues. In Italy the family sealed us together like iron, no matter what happened." Then he thought of his family and how the war must be hurting them. And he thought of Carmela.

Vicenzo lay upon his bed, unable to sleep. His head ached and he turned often, trying to relieve the pressure. He heard voices from outside the room and tried to listen for words that he understood.

"It is time for change," one voice said. "In this land of freedom, everywhere we are chained by its laws."

"It is difficult to see your family living in the filth of these camps, to see your children playing in the arroyo where people throw their trash, and to see the women hang clothes on the line only to have them soiled grey before they're dry."

"Justice will rule over those who have made this hell."

"It is past the time for justice. Reason has no part here."

"Revenge has no purpose but to destroy the flesh. There is a greater justice that shall rule over those who go without punishment here."

"There is the catch! We shall only know by joining the past. We can believe, but we shall never know . . ."

"In believing we shall know, for without eternal justice there is no right or wrong, and it is to each to obey or disobey according to his good reason, for law is based upon justice."

Vicenzo began to fade into half-consciousness. I would like for Carmela to be here, he thought. I am close to Frank and his family but he cannot make up the core of my family. Only Carmela and children that are ours can do that. It is very difficult to live for oneself. Then he thought of the families that had been torn apart in Hastings and of his own family in Italy. A cold fear came over him, but then, a strong surge of survival took over. He thought of his brother and of the mine. The memory of his brother was vague but he remembered his voice. He knew these camps, Vicenzo thought. They were like this while he was here. Then he remembered the voices on the day of the explosion and the mine that had been sealed. He saw himself standing before it, the piles of debris around him. The camp was silent. All the women and children were gone. Then he passed into sleep . . . .

The entrance had been sealed to the flesh, yet a voice called to him from within to enter. "It is not possible," he answered.

Vicenzo saw clearly the mine that had caused so much sorrow and heard the voices of the dead coming from the sealed entrance. One voice was clearer and louder than the others.

"Enter," the voice commanded.

"But there is no way," he answered.

"You cannot enter as the others have. Your flesh still lives. You can only come without the use of your eyes. Turn your face from the sun and enter."

As he drew nearer to the entrance he could hear the mourning of women and children who cried out for protection for centuries upon the battlefields of Europe, and now cried out from this strange new battlefield. The same blood that covered the ancient plains with honor ran through his veins and it became hot when he heard their cries. Their voices came from the entrance and moved within him emotions that had been sleeping for centuries.

Then he saw the spirit that had spoken to him and he recognized it as that of his eldest brother.

"This is where you must descend," it said, pointing to the entrance, "but look there before you go."

The spirit looked to the western sky where the moon was among the clouds in the blue sky. "There is the mystery of life, of your beginning. It is that world the flesh does not allow the mind to perceive."

Then the spirit looked to the eastern sky where the sun was blocked by clouds that stood like marble columns capped by hands of the great sculptor. "And that is where you are to go," the spirit said. "where the mysteries of past and future are one." The rays of the sun shot over the top of the facade of the mine. Engraved above the entrance were the words: HERE LIES THE JOURNEY FROM DARKNESS TO LIGHT. GO WITH COURAGE AND WISDOM TO THE END

"This is your path," the spirit said. "Learn the ways of the earth. The chisel and brush are no good here. Only the pick and shovel are of use. They are the tools that must begin civilization. Enter, and remember, you can die only if you allow your spirit to surrender to those who would degrade you. There is no honor in the defeat of the spirit. While you are there nothing will be easy. But remember that the flesh will pass but the spirit will not."

The two passed from the sunlight through the entrance of the mine and into the world of shadows. There they boarded a cart that had been set upon rails and was pulled by an ass. The cart began moving slowly and then began a greater descent and moved faster. Voices of mourning came from the walls of black rock.

Vicenzo became afraid and fell to the bottom of the cart, his hands covering his eyes.

"Why do you fear?" the spirit said.

"I cannot see."

"Courage and wisdom," the spirit said. "Close your eyes and see with the soul. Here you will live much of your life. With this work you will feed your family. You will take from the earth the energy that is life."

The darkness was cut by a glowing red light that emanated from the walls. He could see the layers of granite and between them the veins of coal. They passed a cross-cut where coal was dug, and there stood the rooms where the men worked, pillars of coal marking each room. A deep, low rumble came from beneath them.

"The explosion," he said.

"Do not fear," the spirit said. "There are many dangers here but wisdom will dispel your fears. Timber carefully and listen, for the hollow roof for the earth is not solid." The cart turned sharply and the ass marked the turn with a loud guttered cry that echoed through the tunnel.

"Beware of the tracks," the spirit said. "Many have suffered because of the flesh that has been destroyed upon them." The ass cried out again. "And beware of this ass who is known for his lack of reason but has been given a value greater than yours by those who employ it, for it will not always act as you command it."

Again the tunnel turned and the beast followed it. The tunnel became hot and the air stale. A low hiss came from the path ahead, like water that has been poured on hot rocks.

"It is hot," he said to the spirit.

"You can endure it," the spirit said.

"Yes, but there is no relief."

"When the flesh is misused until it can no longer endure, the spirit must elevate the body above that of the animal. Ahead of us are those who have caused their spirit to abandon their bodies because they refused to allow others to live with dignity, and in doing so have forced them to live eternally with the flesh. *They cannot die because they have never lived.*"

Ahead, the tunnel was long and narrow. The speed of the cart seemed greatly increased until the air was hot and heavy. On either side of the cart the earth was cracked as if by some great quake, and from the cracks came the hissing of escaping gas.

The tunnel grew dark and ahead of them there was another entrance. As they neared, flames came from it. "The fires cannot harm you," the spirit said. "They are here to torment the guilty."

A cold sweat began to cover his body. He turned again and again as his heart beat faster. Clouds of moisture surrounded him. Noises came from the outside. He slipped from the shadows of the mine. Abruptly he awoke. The room was dark but he could sleep no longer. He cleaned his body of the sweat and dressed.

Vicenzo sat upon a hill that over looked the river bottom. The lower steps of the plateau led to the top and were still covered with snow. A cool breeze that came from there carried moisture that felt cold on his skin. It was nearly dawn and Vicenzo felt tired. Mountains outlined the horizon, forming an uneven line across the sky. Soon it will be time for work, he thought.

When dawn came long shadows formed across the hills. When the sun had lit the sky, Vicenzo left the hills and prepared for work. The sun was hot that day and the ovens filled the air with smoke but Vicenzo took no notice of it.

"Vicenzo is at work?" Frank asked Mrs. Veltri as they stood outside the boarding house.

"Yes," she answered. "He did not sleep well last night. I think his head was bothering him but he would not say."

"I got a letter from his father yesterday. He wants to know how things are here in the camp. Carmela wishes to come to America."

"It is not a good time."

"It is very bad in Italy too," Frank said. "The boats have been stopped from coming here for now, but Santino says that when they are allowed again Carmela wishes to come."

"I will talk to Vicenzo," Mrs. Veltri said.

# CHAPTER

# 11

In the weeks that followed the hearing, business continued in the granite and glass buildings of New York. The demand for coal increased and the cry from industry to the Colorado coal fields resounded through the canyons. The year before the explosion had produced record profits and to offset the closing of the Hastings mine, other openings in the earth were planned and production in existing mines increased. More men were sent to Colorado and in the Valdez mine alone, eight hundred men worked three shifts a day. Many knew that this mine was highly gaseous but it had never blown. To the men the coal seemed endless. Tunnels ran under the state line and into New Mexico, as well as miles to the north. The bars and whorehouses were kept open continuously and the talk of strike seemed to be drowned out by the hustle wthin the camps. Some of the families who had suffered after the explosion left the camp, but many more remained.

Vicenzo became accustomed to working twelve hours a day, six days a week. He did his work well, pulling as many ovens in an hour as men who had worked there many years. His arms and shoulders became firm, and dark hair began to cover his back and chest. His hands grew powerful and each time he took hold of the scraper to pull the coke from the ovens, the veins in his arms bulged as though they would burst. He spent any spare time he had drinking and playing cards and he thought that his father would be proud if he saw him compete with the older Italians at *bocce*.

With one sport that was popular in the camps he became fascinated. On Sundays, fights were held. The company seldom interfered and then only to promote them or to act as a go-between in the betting. The men fought for little more than the prestige they gained. Although Vicenzo never entered the ring, many times the night after a fight he fought in the bars. The ring held the fascination of the Coliseum he had seen in Rome, and when the men came together in the ring, he remembered the stories of the gladiators that his uncle had told him.

Vicenzo heard of one fighter who had not been beaten, a young man from Rome who was being talked about in all of the camps. He waited until the man fought on a Sunday that he did not have to work, and when the day came he rose early and left Cokedale and took the winding dirt road through the hills to the Delagua canyon.

The first camp he passed was Tobasco with boxed-shaped houses dotting the hillsides. Above the crooked rows of hastily built houses were shanties, small, ugly dwellings. Some had three sides, others were little more than canvas stretched over rope tied to trees. Women moved about, preparing food over open fires. Some of the men sat on trunks and crates, cleaning their tools. Those who worked the night shift slept, half hidden in the tents.

He moved ahead quickly and soon came to Berwin where the houses cluttered the hills. There appeared to be no break separating it from the next camp, Hastings, where the fight was to be held. He passed the Hastings' number one mine. "Excusa," he said to the first person he saw.

"You tell me wheresa the fight?"

The man looked puzzled.

"The fight," Vicenzo repeated, clenching his fist. The man backed away. "Imma no fighta you. Imma looka for the fight."

"You passed it as you came down the road," another man answered, continuing to work.

"Thatta way?" Vicenzo pointed back toward the road he had taken.

"Ya. Go back to the old mule barn. The fights are held there."

"Grazie." Vicenzo hurried back along the road until he came to the barn. A small group of men were gathered there and one man stood in the middle.

"You guys get the hell out of the way," the man told them. "I've got to get the ring made. Take your bets over there." The men moved out of the way and Vicenzo watched as a short, dumpy man marked a large circle on the ground with a stick.

"That should do it," he said when he finished. "That should give them plenty of room." The men continued to haggle outside the circle.

"I won't give no two to one, I don't care how young the kid is," one said.

"He ain't been beat yet, another answered.

"It don't make a damn bit of difference how old he is," the first replied.

Vicenzo took a plug of tobacco from his pocket and bit off the chunk. He rolled it until it was settled between his lower lip and his teeth and then positioned it to one side of his mouth. The juice oozed into his mouth and he spit it to the ground.

"You gonna bet?" The words came from the direction of the men. Vicenzo nodded slowly.

"Well, you better do it now before the fighters arrive. Nobody'll give you any kind of odds once the fight starts."

"You know whosa fight?"

"One is from Hastings. His name is Bonacquista. He's the Italian kid that hasn't been beat yet. The other one's Johnson from Valdez. A lot of people call him the champ."

"Theysa both miners?"

"Johnson is. I don't know if Bonacquista is. He hasn't been here very long. If he isn't he will be," the man said with a half-smile.

"Look, you wanna bet or not? I ain't got all day."

"Whenna they come I bet," Vicenzo said. The man walked away and Vicenzo felt in his pocket. He took out three bills. Two of the bills, he knew by the paper they were printed on, were company script. They were worthless everywhere except in the company store. The third he unraveled and looked at. Ten dollars. Then he thought that it would be a while before payday. The sun burned down as the men waited for the fighters, and Vicenzo contemplated betting.

Tension had eased at Hastings but not far from where he sat the mine had exploded. He knew the faces of the men and women here during that time of trial. The hatred in the Valdez Canyon did not need much more festering to ignite.

The camps he had passed on his way to Hastings were so similiar to the camps up the river from Cokedale. Like Old Town, where the water tasted like sulphur. He had seen people dump garbage into the arroyo above where it would be washed down to their drinking water. He thought of how the blacks lived in a run down hole where rats crawled everywhere. Hells Half Acre, sat next to the railroad tracks where the coke was loaded, blanketing the houses with soot.

Johnson arrived first. He was a large black man whose body had been hardened in youth by the use of a pick and shovel. Not long ago he had reached that peak where the body stops building and levels off before continued digging weakens it.

"Hey, there's my man!" one of the men who was busy with the bets called out when he saw Johnson. "You ready to give us a knock out?"

"I'se always ready," Johnson said.

"You ready to bet?" Vicenzo turned to see the man who was taking bets.

"Thisa man, he has fought many times?"

"Hell, there ain't a man who has lived here very long that hasn't seen him in one camp or another. I'll give you some advice, he don't lose too often."

"The other fighter, he'sa no come yet?"

"That's him coming up the road." Vicenzo looked toward the road and saw a young man coming toward the barn.

"He'sa young," Vicenzo said half-aloud.

"Maybe a little too young. They say he started fighting in the schoolyard. The other kids would make fun of him and he couldn't take it, so he started taking them on, one by one."

"Hey, Bonacquista!" one of the men called. "Did you bring a stool to stand on? You might not be able to reach him if you didn't." Bonacquista glanced toward the men and kept walking.

"I'ma bet on him," Vicenzo said, handing the man the ten-dollar bill.

"You think he's gonna win?" the man said, writing the bet down on a piece of paper.

"I think so,"

"Shit, he can't be more than fifteen or sixteen. You dumb wops think that because he's Italian he can't be beat."

Vicenzo leaned over and grabbed the man by the shoulder. "Maybe whenna it's over, me anda you fight?" The man pulled his arm back and walked away.

The two fighters entered the ring and sat at opposite ends. Their hands were taped and the gloves put on. The other men went to the crude wooden bleachers that had been made for the event and waited for the fight to start. Others began to arrive and soon the bleachers were full. The two men were brought to the center of the ring by the referee.

"I want a clean fight," he began. "No butting and no rabbit-punching. When one man goes down there's no punching until he gets up, understand?"

Both men nodded, went back to their stools, and waited for the bell. The hammer struck the anvil and they approached each other, then began moving slowly around the ring.

Johnson stood a full six inches over Bonacquista. His large fists nearly covered his face. His eyes peered between them. He threw two quick jabs with his left. One caught Bonacquista on the upper forearm, the other was blocked by his right hand. Bonacquista swung widly at Johnson, forcing him back until a right uppercut landed on his jaw and knocked him backwards. He buckled at the knees but caught the ground with his right hand, breaking his fall, and spun his body away from Johnson who quickly came after him. Johnson knew the mistake that Bonacquista made in coming at him, and thought that if he could tag him again he would go down. Bonacquista covered his face with his gloves and Johnson landed a hard blow to the side of his head, making his ear ring.

"Hit the son of a bitch," the cry came from the crowd. Most of the men were hollering for the black man to finish the fight in the first round. Bonacquista staggered back to his corner.

Vicenzo sat down, his own fists clenched and sweat running down his forehead. He looked at the man who had taken the bet. A big smile had come over his face.

"Bastard!" Vicenzo muttered. The hammer came down upon the anvil and the two men again approached each other. Bonacquista crouched, making the distance between the two men farther apart. Johnson swung down, missing. Bonacquista began hitting his opponent in the forearms. Johnson went after him but Bonacquista drew back again and again, swinging at the lower part of his rib cage. The round ended quickly and the men booed when the boxers returned to their stools.

"He's afraid of him," the man next to Vicenzo said. "He don't fight him."

"He'sa do all right, donna worry, he'sa do all right."

The third round started and again Bonacquista crouched, punched into the other man's ribs, and backed away before the counterpunches could reach his face. Twice Bonacquista backed out of the circle and the fight was stopped as the referee brought him back. The two men circled each other and Bonacquista caught Johnson below the right eye. Johnson countered with a left hook to the face. Blood began coming from Bonacquista's nose. The two men stood pounding at each other's faces until the bell rang. The referee separated them and they walked slowly to their stools.

"He won't last another round," said the man sitting next to Vicenzo. Vicenzo looked at Bonacquista who was wiping his face with a towel. The front of his bib-overalls were wet with sweat, as were his shoulders, and he was breathing hard. In the other corner Johnson sat rinsing his mouth with water and spitting each time he drank.

The bell sounded and the two approached each other again. Bonacquista kept moving, trying to avoid another all-out battle. Two more rounds went by and the men outside the ring became impatient.

"Shit, he don't want to fight!" one of them yelled.

"Yeah, make them fight! We didn't come here to watch them dance."

Again and again Bonacquista went to the bigger man's arms and ribs. Again and again he had to protect himself when he did. Then one of Johnson's blows got through his defense and Bonacquista went to the ground.

"That's the first time for him," one of the men said. "He ain't going to get up."

Johnson stood over him waiting, but Bonacquista grabbed him as he got up so that he wouldn't have a chance to hit him again. He tied up Johnson's arms and they had to be separated by the referee as the bell rang.

Bonacquista's face was beginning to swell and blood flowed from his lower lip. Only youth was on his side now. The other man had shown little sign of slowing up. The bell sounded and Bonacquista stood up quickly and went to the center of the ring.

"Come on, do some fighting this time," a voice came from the crowd.

"Let's go, you guys. How about some action?"

Neither fighter heard anything except their own breathing. Bonacquista again went to the rib cage and Johnson countered, again swinging down at his opponent. Sweat burned in both men's eyes so that they tried in desperation to wipe them with their gloves. The sun would let neither succeed. Bonacquista swung again and again until both fighters clinched and seemed to be holding each other up.

"If you guys wanna dance, we'll hire a band," a voice came again followed by laughter. The two men broke apart when the referee shoved his arms between them and pushed. Several punches glanced off each fighter and the round was over.

Time seemed to pass quickly for the fighters but the crowd grew more impatient between rounds. Before either man was rested, the bell brought them to the center of the ring. The left side of Bonacquista's face continued to swell. It was obvious to Johnson that he would be most vulnerable there. He came at him, swinging with his right. Before Bonacquista could react, he felt himself falling to all fours. The ringing in his ears started again but did not fade this time and he hesitated on the ground, a lightness in his head, his stomach pushing its way into his throat.

"Three, four, five, six." The blood dripped from his lower lip to the ground. Bonacquista took two crawl steps and got up, hiding his face from the knockout blows that Johnson delivered. But Johnson had spent too much energy in the flurry and could not put Bonacquista down again. When the two men again approached each other, Johnson's arms seemed heavy. He held his large fists as though they were weighted. Bonacquista again began pounding. The counter-punches came, but were too slow to do any damage. The crowd roared louder and louder, with breaks of laughter. The ringing and numbness in Bonacquista's head were replaced by the laughter. He reached back into hell and swung with the energy that could only come from anger and hatred.

Johnson fell backwards to the ground. Bonacquista backed slowly away as his opponent's shattered nose bled down the side of his face and to the ground. He knew the man would not get up. He flashed his eyes, cold and hard, at the crowd who stood cheering and screaming for the other man to get up. He did not. A bucket of water was brought from the barn and thrown on him. When Johnson woke up, he saw the blurred figure of Bonacquista kneeling over him.

"You all right?" Bonacquista asked.

"You threw a hell of a punch, kid," Johnson said.

"Imma glad isa over. I donna think I coulda stand too much more." Johnson wiped his face with his arms and was helped up by Bonacquista.

"Gooda fight," Bonacquista said, extending his hand.

"Ya, kid, keeping throwing those punches and you'll do all right," Johnson said, extending his hand with the glove still on. The two men shook hands and parted.

Bonacquista walked quickly down the road away from the company-owned buildings. Vicenzo followed a short distance behind. Bonacquista reached a well that was near the side of the hill. From the well he drew a bucket of water and began washing his face. Vicenzo waited a few feet away. When Bonacquista finished washing his face, he dumped the rest of the water on his head.

"Why do you do this?" Vicenzo asked.

Bonacquista had not realized that he had been followed. As he turned, his face grew stern.

"Whatsa you' business?" Bonacquista growled.

"Ima hava no business. I justa saw the fight."

"You makea fun of the way I talk?"

"*Parla Italiano?*"

"Si," Bonacquista said, returning the bucket to the bottom of the well.

"Why do you fight in the ring?" Vicenzo asked in Italian.

"If you want to live here you fight. What the hell does it matter if it is in the ring or not." Bonacquista said, also in his native tongue.

"You fight like you have been in the ring many times, but you could not have been here such a long time," Vicenzo said.

"You don't have to be here such a long time to learn how to fight. When we got here my father said I had to go to school to learn to speak English. He said that it would be easier for us if we could understand the language of the people here. The other kids made fun of the way I talk, but they don't laught no more," Bonacquista said.

"The school is in the camp, not in the schoolhouse. Since I have been here I have heard more people speak other languages than I have heard them speak English."

Bonacquista drew another bucket of water. Cupping his hands, he filled them with water and drank slowly. "It took me a while to realize why they were laughing. I'd try tó say something and it wouldn't come out right, or sometimes they would laugh because I was bigger than the rest. Nobody laughs now. In these camps if you don't give the beatings, you take them."

"You have fought well. Come. I will buy you something to drink. You have earned it."

"What's your name?"

"Vicenzo Caputo. The men called you Bonacquista."

"Joseph Bonacquista. Where do you come from?"

"Aiello, in Calabria. And yourself?"

"I am from Rome."

"I have been there," Vicenzo said with pride.

The two began walking and soon talked of their homeland. They drank together as though they had met in some remote village in Calabria and planned to go fishing the following Sunday. Each felt he had found a friend. The two would soon learn that hate would draw them even closer together, for even as they became friends, they found that they both had the same enemies, just as their fathers had.

Night came before they parted. They would see each other many times in the future, but this first time would always remain special.

Vicenzo hurried back through the canyons, knowing that the next day was a work day and the cold air would come quickly in the hills.

The days after the fight passed quickly into the routine of work and sleep. Production began to rise with the fourteen-hour work day and the men functioned as machines.

On the Saturday evening before Easter Sunday, Vicenzo sat on the stone steps that led to the boarding house. It was after nine o'clock and he was very tired. Frank and his family expected him but he knew that Frank would understand why he was so late.

"Hey, Vicenzo, what the hell are you doing?" A voice came from the night. Vicenzo recognized it as the voice of one of the men he worked with.

"What the hell am I doing?" he said. "When I'ma not working I"ma sleeping."

"It's Saturday night. Aren't you going to the Piedmont?" the voice came back.

"No, I'ma going to Trinidad."

"That's too bad. They're going to have a helluva blow-out tonight."

"You can have this one without me," Vicenzo said in Italian while he took off his shoes. The man left and Vicenzo sat rubbing the back of his neck. He heard someone coming and looked in the direction of the sound, expecting to see the man who had called out to him. But when the steps neared, Vicenzo recognized the uniform of one of the guards.

"I thought all of you would be drunk already," the guard said.

"Why don't you go guard the gates of hell?" Vicenzo said in Italian.

"You're too stupid to even understand what I'm saying," the guard came back, hoping to provoke a fight.

"No, friend, it is you who does not understand," Vicenzo said in Italian, then got up and went inside.

In Trinidad, Frank prepared for Vicenzo's arrival. He knew the turmoil that had beset him since the explosion, and he hoped that by celebrating the holidays as in their homeland, Vicenzo would find peace. Soon the two men stood talking on Frank's porch.

"This will be like in Italy, Vicenzo," Frank said. "Tonight we pray, tomorrow we have the feast."

"You killa the pig?"

"We killed the pig just like at home," Frank said, opening a bottle of beer. "You have done this before?"

"Many times ina Italy. You gotta the pig here?"

"He's in the back yard. Come, we'll take a look."

They left t the front porch and went around the side of the house. Inside, Frank's wife had begun preparing the food for Easter Sunday. Then the bell rang in the church steeple. Vicenzo hesitated for a moment and turned to look at the church that sat on the small hill overlooking the neighborhood.

"What's today?" he asked.

"Saturday. Holy Saturday," Frank answered.

"Yesterday was Friday. It was Good Friday." He turned to Frank. "It was Good Friday and I worked like any other day. It was as though there was nothing different. I just worked."

"That is why you are here. To work. In Italy, what did you do on Good Friday?"

"It was a time for prayer."

"And yesterday you prayed to the ovens, the ovens that feed you. And that is life. Sunday we will celebrate life, so don't be so upset."

"My mother would not see it that way. It does not matter how old I am or she is, she would not agree."

"Neither would Marietta, but nonetheless, it is what we do to stay alive."

"You will go to church tomorrow?" Vicenzo asked.

"Yes, of course. We will all go to church tomorrow. At Mount Carmel there is a new priest who will say mass. Marietta has invited him to have Easter dinner with us."

"She has already met him?"

"The day he arrived. She said that he was looking forward to meeting all the people in church, and that it was our job as Italians to see to it that the church is full on Easter because it was during the time of Rome that Christ was crucified."

"Sometimes I think that Italy has been paying for it ever since."

The walnut trees that grew alongside the barn were blooming and the strong smell was heavy in the air. There were several shacks in the back yard, all made by Frank out of old wood. In them were animals that Frank depended on for food, for it was not his way to depend upon other people to feed himself and his family. Frank's garden had been planted in neat rows and was carefully tended. For Vicenzo this was home. Getting life from the soil with his own hands was as natural to him as breathing.

"Things will not grow in the ashes that I pull from the ovens," he told Frank, "and all the land is owned by the company. They know their business well. They like to have you tied as close to them as possible. They want to be sure that the clothes you wear and the food you eat you owe to them. The buildings are theirs and even the air is theirs because it has more of their coal in it than anything else."

They had reached the back part of the year. In the large pen in one corner was a pig.

"This is quite a pig," Vicenzo said. "He will feed you for some time."

"Tomorrow we skin him. You will help?" Frank asked.

"Sure. It will feel good to prepare with my own hands the food that God has given us. I think that it has been too long since I have done so."

The two leaned on the fence while the pig pushed his snout through the slop.

"He weighs about five-hundred pounds."

"You will make the sausage tomorrow."

"Yes. Everything we will make with this one."

It was dark now and the two men talked idly for a while, and walked through the chicken coop and past the rabbits.

"Where do you keep the goats?" Vicenzo asked.

"I used to keep them in the lots below the house, but the smell was too bad so I got rid of them. They are better off in the hills than here. I have planted many fruit trees there now. Tomorrow we will go look at them. Some have been there for a long time and will bear much fruit."

"The vines are there too?"

"No. Here you have to buy the grapes. They will not grow with the winters so cold. But don't worry, the press is not kept idle. The grapes come from the old country."

The words *old country* sounded strange to Vicenzo. He had not been away from his home long enough to realize that he would never return. It was not like leaving a town or province, or even like going to another European country. *Old country* sounded like something from the past and even though the memory of it often was vague, he still thought of it as home. It bothered him at night, when his brain was clear of the smoke from the ovens. He would think of his mother and father, and their images and words would fade. And when he tried harder to think of them, the words he heard sounded more and more like his own. He had only the letters they sent. Too often he left out of his own letters many things that happened and he wondered if they did not do the same.

Inside, the house smelled of Easter. The bread sat in one corner of the kitchen, rising slowly in a large speckled blue tub with a towel draped over it. The sauce for the ravioli simmered upon the stove with aromas of onion, garlic, peppers and oregano. When the bubbles rose from the bottom of the pot they popped and small drops splashed upon the stove. Mrs. Naccarato was on the back porch, talking with Mrs. De Cicco about the new priest, and waiting to roll the Easter bread and the eggs. Frank and Vicenzo sat in the front room, playing cards. "Tonight there will be some good wine. I will bring it from the cellar where it has been for four years without being disturbed, but tonight we'll drink it."

"Dinner is the best time for wine," Vicenzo said, watching Frank's movements. There was a youthfulness in him that he had not seen before.

"How old are you?" Vicenzo asked.

The question came from nowhere. Frank looked over his glasses that he had put on before they had started playing cards. Vicenzo had changed from the first time Frank had seen him. The heat from the ovens had matured his face and his hands had become visibly hardened.

"I think that I am older than you expect. Before I worked in town, for about five years when I first came here, I worked at the mine. My father worked inside, but he would not stay and he found ways for both of us to get out. Those five years were like twenty."

"Your eyes give you away," Vicenzo said.

"A man's hands harden before his heart does. His hands are made to work. They can be calloused and blistered. But his spirit must never be broken. This you will see in the eyes."

"So you are not so old as I first thought. And Marietta?"

"She is still a babe herself, like the one that she has borne."

"She does not sound like she lived here a long time."

"She was taught English before she came. She is younger than you are.

"It is not how long you have lived but the things you have done that make you age. When Marietta arrived, she had beautiful blonde hair that flowed to the bottom of her back. It was all rolled up in a bun and held with a knot. I did not see it down until we were married. I'll never forget the day she got off the train."

Marietta entered the room and Frank abruptly changed the subject. "So the men have been working fourteen hours a day," he said.

Vicenzo looked at Frank who was busily studying his cards. "Yeah," he answered, "fourteen."

Marietta placed a bowl of fruit on the table. "Would you like some fruit?" she asked with a smile.

"Thank you," Vicenzo answered, taking an apple from the bowl.

"Marietta does not like to talk about herself," Frank said when she returned to the kitchen, "and she likes it even less when I do."

"Why? What happened when she came here?"

"She got lost in Chicago. If she hadn't met three nuns who were on their way here, she might still be riding on the train. It made me feel funny when I saw her get off the train with three sisters. I thought that maybe they would chaperone her until she was thirty!"

"It would not be the first time that a young Italian girl was chaperoned for such a long time. Even now I know Carmela's mother better than I know her. Every time I talked with her, her mother answered."

Marietta returned with a tablecloth and the men resumed their card game. Vicenzo looked at her youthful face and thought of his own Carmela.

Carmela was one to be missed for she was a tall woman with northern features. Vicenzo had been taken with her the first time he saw her. Now he thought of how hard it was for him to picture her clearly, even though he felt strongly for her. The damn smoke, he thought. That damn smoke from the ovens makes you see everything as though there is a haze over it.

"When you're ready to roll the bread, let me know," Frank said, untying the bow in the back of Marietta's apron.

"The bread won't be ready to roll for an hour."

"Then maybe you can play some cards while you are waiting. Vicenzo has not had a chance to play *Briscula*.

"I think that would be nice, but only a few hands." Marietta called her friend Mrs. DeCicco in to join them.

When the game was over Marietta counted their points. "Eighty-one," she said. "We won!"

"Never mind," Frank said. "I'm going down to the basement to get the wine."

"I'll come with you," said Vicenzo.

The walls and floor of the basement were made of cement. Vicenzo had never seen a basement made with such care.

"You do this work?" he asked.

"I helped. My father and uncle did much of the work. They will be here tonight. Come back here. Here is where the air is the coolest."

In one side of the room the wall had been cut away and wooden barrels were stacked in the cool earth. Two had taps in them and around all of them there was a dark violet color where the wine had bled through the wood.

Frank took a couple of glasses from behind one of the barrels and they sat and drank.

"It is not so much to be alive as to live," Frank said, sipping the wine.

"It is enough to live one day at a time here. Tomorrow the glass might be empty," Vicenzo answered.

Before long they could hear voices coming from upstairs. Frank's father and uncle joined them in the basement. They laughed and drank until the sound of Marietta's voice interrupted them.

"Frank!" she called from the cellar door.

"Yes, Marietta."

"Come, there is someone here to see you."

"Yes, I will be there in a minute."

"No, Frank, I think you should come now."

Her voioe sounded as though she were frightened and Frank put down his glass and hurried toward the door. The other men sat and listened. They could only hear a murmur through the open door so they went quietly up the stairs. From the kitchen Vicenzo could see that Frank had become serious but he could not hear what the man who was talking to him was saying. He went into one of the side bedrooms directly across from where the stranger was standing.

"You know how the Italians think," the stranger said, "and you know what kind of trouble this sort of thing can lead to. The company knows that the union officials rely upon men like you to lead your own people. That's why I came here tonight. If you can talk the Italian miners out of associating with the others, it would be much better for them."

"The others? Who do you mean?"

"The other workers."

"There are many other workers. Some Slavs and some Poles and Mexicans. There must be at least twenty others. You mean that they should not work with these men?"

"I did not mean these."

"Then who? Maybe the Greeks?"

"These men have fought before. Many believe they are mercenaries and have come here to fight another war."

"They did not bring death into the mines. It was there long before they came."

"The mines are being improved all the time, and so are the wages.'

"The mine is being improved?"

"The company is making them as safe as possi . . ."

The man was cut off by Frank who placed his first finger over his lips.

"I was at Hastings," Frank said.

"That was an unfortunate accident. Even the inquiry proved that the explosion was caused by an inspector."

"I was at the inquiry also."

The men spoke in English and it became difficult for Vicenzo to understand everything. Marietta had crept slowly into the front room where the two men stood talking. When the stranger saw her he stopped talking.

"This is her house," Frank said. "Anything that is said here she can hear."

The older men had also entered the room and they too had difficulty understanding exactly what was being said.

"You gatta problem, Francisco?"

"No, Pa. There's no problem. He has come to wish us a happy holiday for Easter tomorrow."

"You comma as a friend?" the older man said. "I offer you a glass of wine. You comma to make trouble, I throw you the hell out!"

"I didn't come to cause trouble," the stranger said.

"Then why you come wearing thata thing?" he asked, pointing to the badge that was half-hidden by the stranger's jacket.

"It's my job."

"On Holy Saturday itsa you' job to comma here anda tella my son to hava the Italian people that trusta him to sella them down the river?"

"This is for their own good. Tomorrow most of the men will be together to celebrate the holidays. It will be a good time to talk to them," the stranger said, turning to Frank. "Make them realize what is at stake. The company is not going to back down. I know what happened fifteen years ago and I don't want it to happen again."

"Thisa badge, it say *company* ona it?" Frank's father insisted.

"This is a deputy sheriff's badge from Las Animas County."

"Then why you talk for the company?"

"It doesn't matter what you think the badge stands for, the laws aren't going to be of much help to you or anyone else when the shooting starts. You still have a chance to stop it before anything else happens." The man hesitated. "You still have the choice to talk to the men tomorrow."

"Whatta choice!" Frank's father broke in again. "Are you blind? Do you go through the camps witha you' eyes closed? We do nothing now anda year from now another hundred men willa be dead. Maybe two or three hundred. Isa thata you' choice?"

Frustrated, the stranger said to Frank, "Do you think that I could talk to you?"

"This is my father's house also. You talk to me, you talk to him too."

Frank's father looked taller than his five feet.

"You see thesea hands?" he said showing both his hands. "They worka down the mine. They take the coal out a piece at a time. That'sa what I do for this company for many years, even before Frank comma here when he's just a smalla baby. What kinda work you do? You think that you' company last long with what you do?"

There was no answer and the older man left the room.

"I don't want to see violence come back into the camps. There are others that don't give a damn whether you people live or die. They have all the guns that money can buy."

"I have seen many," Frank agreed.

"Not like those that I have seen, and they're planning to bring guns like you have never seen before."

"All guns can do is destroy us, but there are things that will never change."

"Then you can expect the worst."

"We have known the worst for many years. You know how the people live in the camps up the river. You know that the water they drink is poison. Where they live is not fit for animals. And you know that if they do not work they starve. This country is strange to them and they know nothing else. But if you think I can tell them to betray the men they work with and that they will listen, then you are not as smart as you think. I cannot tell them this and I would not."

The house was quiet. The stranger nervously ran his hand across his mouth. He felt the the futility of his mission.

"Then they will have to fight the law," he said.

"Which law do you talk about?" Frank asked. "The law of the badge or the law of the gun?"

"They are the same thing. What is one without the other?"

"There is yet another law. It is here," Frank said, pointing to his heart. "It has been given to us and it cannot be changed."

"That kind of thinking isn't going to feed the people in the camps. And it isn't going to keep the snow and wind out.

"I'm giving you a chance to try and convince the people that you have influence. You can tell them to stay away from the troublemakers. The only place that they'll lead you is to the graveyard."

"I think that you have overestimated what I can and cannot do," responded Frank. "These men have minds of their own. Do you think that I could convince my father that he should give up what he thinks is right? There are many men who are older than I am who feel the same way. I could not tell them what to do and I would not, even if I could."

"I don't think even you realize how powerful these men from the company are."

"There are men such as this everywhere. At one time they were called by titles and thought themselves to be royalty," Frank shook his head and looked directly at the stranger. "And many have died before."

"Then you better get ready for another kind of man, because this one does not even know that you exist. He doesn't have to look you in the eye to have you destroyed. And if a thousand of you are destroyed, he would not even know about it. You're not even peasants now, just a dollar sign in a bank."

Vicenzo listened to the words that Frank had said. He began to see the world as his father had seen it and the memory of his parents became stronger. He felt the fear and anxiety that had torn at them until they knew that they must let him go to America. A moment's depression swept over him. But what he had left behind with his father was here too, and he had only the experience of knowing his father to face it. And that would be enough.

"There will be benefits for those who don't strike. The company is going to give its workers a raise."

"I have heard of such raises before." Frank's father returned from the kitchen and broke into the conversation. "The company always givesa few pennies every time they thinka they have to. Why don't you go back to you' company and tell them to keepa their goddamn thumbs offa the scales when the cart comma outta the mine. Or maybe you tell them to cover the cracks in the houses so that the women and children don't freeze in the winter. Thatta raise isa bullshit, lika everything else the company does. They see you starve to death ina street before they give you something to eat."

When Frank's father finished speaking the room again became quiet. His voice had steadily risen, his face had become red, and his fists were clenched.

"Iffa you' soul coulda burn," he said slowly, "they would throw itta into the oven and sell 'um."

"Take it easy, Papa," Frank said, taking him by the shoulders and easing him to a chair.

"Then we cannot expect any cooperation from you," the stranger said as he moved toward the door.

"One minute," Frank answered him. "Come and talk with me for a minute on the poorch."

The two went out onto the porch where the night air had cooled the earth.

"When I came here tonight I did not expect to have an argument. You must be reasonable and not let the emotions of others prevent them from bringing disaster on themselves," the stranger advised.

"Disaster is a way of life for many people here. Many feel that things will never get better. They also know that much coal will be needed if America enters the war, and that it will be a good time to let the people in Washington know how serious the situation is here," Frank answered.

The stranger pulled the collar of his coat up and looked down the dirt street. "These people would have been better off if they had stayed in Europe, especially if they wanted the men in Washington to be concerned about them." The man hesitated and turned away from Frank. "There's no help for them anywhere. Osborn has seen to that. Everybody knows it and, most of all, he wants *you* to know it. You can't win."

"The people will not change. As long as the men keep dying, nothing will change."

"Then these people left one war only to come to another."

The sky was dark. A sliver of moon sent a few rays of light through the bare branches of a tree in front of Frank's house. Along the street, lights from the houses broke the pattern of black.

"If it takes a war for the government to come here and see what is happening, then there is going to be one. These men would fight for a decent life here, or in any country. A flag doesn't make an enemy. If troops are brought in, the men will fight for what they believe is right," Frank said.

"Who do you think will be sending the troops? The government? They are willing to send troops to Europe but it is going to take much for the president to send troops to fight on American soil. Even your timing is bad. The people in this country are not looking to Colorado right now. What kind of war do you think it will take to get their sympathy?"

"You do not realize the kind of men you are talking about. Sympathy is something that they do not care for, and governments they do not trust. They are used to taking care of themselves and their families. They have been like that for many years and to expect them to change now is stupid."

"I had hoped that you would be more reasonable. I was here ten years ago when the Irish tried to strike. You don't see many Irish in these camps, do you? They're scattered all over hell now."

"What makes you so concerned for the Italians?"

"The Greeks I know will not be persuaded. They have been infiltrated by professionals who fought in Europe a few years ago."

"There are many Greeks who have nothing to do with any war."

"It only takes a few to make people think that they do. That isn't the important thing. The company thinks that the union has armed its men. The Greeks have given them the excuse that they needed."

"They don't need any excuse. If they are going to do something they will do it, even if they have to bend the laws."

"They will not have to bend any laws. They have enough people upstate so that anything they do will appear legal whether the laws are broken or not. But that will not be important when the shooting starts. The type of men they bring in will kill anyone. It's important that you realize that. You have known detectives who have harassed the men right on the main streets in Trinidad. But what happens when they start shooting from behind buildings and there are women and children killed, along with the miners?"

"You have not answered my question," Frank said.

"It's not just the Italians, it's all of you. You come here expecting some sort of Garden of Eden, but fruit trees don't grow on rock. If it were just the men, then you could fight until the canyons catch fire and burn until there is no coal left. But when the gunmen are hired, there is no distinction made between the women and children and the workers. I have seen it happen before."

"The company would have to go to hell to find men like that," Frank said.

"And so they have. They do not consider you any different from the animals that haul the carts out of the mine."

Frank became silent. Then he spoke slowly. "I know that they will not give in to any kind of threat. But the men have more to lose than anyone that the company can bring in from the East. Those men have no families. They can act without discretion."

"But the miners will put their families first and this will put them at a disadvantage. Don't think that the company doesn't know this and that they will not use it to their fullest advantage."

"It is best that you leave now, if you have nothing more to say."

"With stakes like this, you think that the miners will still continue with their hopes of striking?" the stranger asked in a surprised voice.

"I think that you do not understand the women who come out of these camps. Do you think they do not know what the men have to do in the mine? They go in there every morning when the men go to work. They go in there with them.

"The men will prepare the best they can. It would be a good thing to tell the company that before they bring in men to fight, they better prepare to put their own lives on the line also. If these men give in now they will forever be nothing more than the mules that the company values so highly. Now get the hell out of here."

Frank watched as the man left. Vicenzo came around the corner of the house where he had been standing.

"This man comma here to bringa fear?" he asked.

"He wants us to think of our weaknesses," Frank said in Italian. "He knows that if the workers split, they will have no chance if they strike. They know that the family is important enough so that the men will try to protect their families first if a strike begins. A man who has nothing to lose can be much more reckless with his life."

"What are you going to say to the men in the camps?"

"They already know everything that this man has said tonight. The company knows that tonight is a time of happiness for us, in preparation of the sacred holiday. They did the same to the Greeks last week when they celebrated their holiday. It is one of their many tricks.

"Your father is upset."

"It is best that we go into the house and calm him so that this night will not be ruined. Say nothing of strikes tonight so that it will be forgotten as quickly as possible, or Sunday will be a time of worry instead of happiness."

"I will get out the cards," Vicenzo said.

They went into the house and soon the four men were playing the game again. The events that had occurred earlier faded into a blur of kings and queens, but the thoughts continued.

Marietta was at work again in the kitchen, rolling the dough into strips and then wrapping them around a hard-boiled egg for the Easter bread. When baked the bread had a wonderful fragrance. Soon friends came by to wish them a happy holiday, to talk for a time, and to sit in on a round of cards.

As Vicenzo ate the bread, it gave him the feeling of home. And for a time the smoke cleared from his mind and he could hear and see his mother cooking in the kitchen. This he knew was important and his sense of what was real and necessary became strengthened. Then the new priest stopped by and the atmosphere became more formal. He blessed the home and spoke of the bread. Then he too was gone for it was late.

Vicenzo slept in the room in the basement that night. In the morning he would go to the nearby church and then spend the rest of the day with Frank's family. For that day they would be his family and he would feel closer to home.

In the morning Vicenzo was awakened by voices from the rooms upstairs. He dressed quickly in his best clothes and joined the rest of the family. When they were ready for church they met many of their neighbors in front of the house. As the church bell rang, they started in that direction.

"Good morning, Father," Frank said as he entered the church.

The priest peered at Frank through his round glasses. "Good morning," he answered, nodding to Mrs. Naccarato.

"We will be glad to have you come to dinner today, Father," Frank said.

"Thank you very much, but I have already accepted an invitation for dinner. But perhaps later we can play a little bocce if there is a court nearby."

"There is one behind my house," Frank replied.

"Then I will see you later today," The priest promised.

Mrs. Naccarato led the family as near to the front as possible. Vicenzo waited until last to enter the pew. After kneeling for a few moments he sat and looked about the church.

The familiar service started.

The Latin was easier for Vicenzo to understand than were many of the English words that he heard used in the camps. This language is made for prayer, he thought. It flows so smoothly and does not have the harsh sound of English.

Vicenzo again looked around the church while the priest moved along with the mass. His eyes focused on a statue of Mary. How it must have hurt her, he thought, as she looked upon Christ's body. She could only watch as her son died.

Vicenzo thought of his own mother's face the day he left. Was it possible that he might see her again, or would he have only the memory of her own heart crying out through her eyes as he left her? Mother of God, he thought, go to her and comfort her.

Then the priest began his sermon.

"My name is Father Zacardi," he said. "I come from St. Louis and I will be your pastor in the time to come. They will be good times if it is

God's will, but if they are not, then it will be up to us all to live in Christ's name and bear whatever is His plan for us.

"Today is Easter. Today is the culmination of all that is great in the church. Today we can rejoice because death has been conquered, but is was not an easy matter. Sometimes, when times are good and happiness is the predominant feeling, we tend to forget the times when we thought suffering would forever be with us. Let us remember that good things do not come easily. They have been paid for with pain and we should watch carefully those good things least we should take them for granted and lose them.

"Let us remember too the pain and suffering that Christ had to endure before we could rejoice at His triumph over death," the priest continued. "I know that the people here are used to living with the thought of death. I have heard much about the explosion that occurred just a short time ago, and I have talked with many who have told me of the men who are constantly being maimed in the mines up the river. I have talked with many women there who fear from day to day, not knowing whether their husbands will come home that night. It is times like these that make the good times that much greater. It is easy to say that as Christ underwent all His sufferings, He knew that He was the son of God. And do we know less? If we have faith in what He did for us, then we too know that we will rise when our time comes. But it will not come without some of the suffering that Jesus went through. Even the small sufferings that we are made to bear will bring us closer to the time when we too will rise from darkness and ascend into heaven.

"Let us recall the passion and death of Christ. Let us think of the small babe born in the stable in Jerusalem. For thirty years He worked with His Father and was known by no one until His hour had come. Then for three years he showed kindness to those who would destroy Him. Where would be the justice of His death? Not until the moment He arose from the dead could this justice be realized, for if the gates of heaven had not been opened there would be no right or wrong. How many men are never brought to justice in this life? How many men have the blood of other men upon their hands?

"How many have been responsible for the sufferings of men and women in the canyons that surround this town? Yet how many of those men who are responsible for this will ever come to justice here on earth? Those who died will rise again and the canyons of hell will be split to make room for those who murdered them.

"Remember that Jesus brought a message of love and forgiveness to the people of this earth and He proved that death can be conquered; but let us not forget that He suffered greatly before this was possible.

"Let this day be remembered then as a day when the suffering ended and new life began. Let us endure the hardships that life brings to us so that when death comes we may be welcomed into God's arms and walk with Him just as the Apostles did when He arose from the dead." The church was silent when the priest concluded. Then the organ sounded and the people began to sing. When the mass was over the new priest stood in the back of the church, meeting and talking to the members of his parish.

At dinner time, Frank's family, including Vicenzo, came together.

"There are two times of the day that a man should spend with his family," Frank had told Vicenzo. "One is when he eats. He should try to be sure and have at least one meal with his family, no matter how busy his job makes him. It is important because the family is drawn together to thank God for the good things that they have. And if a man loses everything else and still has his family, then he has much more than he has ever lost. The other time is before he goes to bed. It is the mother and father who keep the family together. If the mother and father are healthy, then the children will grow as part of the same tree."

The afternoon was spent peacefully. For a brief interval there were no mines, no ovens, and no guards. The men played bocces with all the fervor of world champions while the women watched the children as they searched for the painted Easter eggs hidden throughout the neighborhood.

The following days were peaceful in the camps. Vicenzo returned to Cokedale with a new feeling of closeness to his own family and much affection for Frank's.

Ten days after Easter, Vicenzo met the fighter from the Delagua camp in Trinidad and they talked again as friends.

"Are you going to the game today?" Bonacquista asked Vicenzo.

"You mean there is a fight today?"

"No fight," Bonacquista said. "The baseball game."

"Basaball?" Vicenzo said. "What's a basaball?"

"It's a ball, round like this."

"Like bocce," Vicenzo said.

"No, it's not wood. It's leather."

"You only play with one ball? How do you score?"

"You run around sacks, they are called bases, after you hit the ball with a stick, called a bat."

"Wait a minute. You run around in a circle after you hit the ball?"

"Yes, you have to touch the sacks before they put you out."

"Put you out of what?"

"You get three outs. If they put you out you only have two more."

"Whatta you mean, putta you out?"

"Each team gets nine players. One team puts their nine in the field. The other teams puts one out with a bat."

"A bat, you mean a stick?"

"Yes, now you are getting it. Then one of the ones in the field throws the ball and the one with the stick hits it and runs around like this, touching all the bases unless they catch the ball and put him out."

"Ifa you outside, where you gonna put him?" Vicenzo asked.

"Not outside. Back to the bench."

Bonacquista tried to explain the game while they rode along the hills. When they neared the camp, Vicenzo saw for the first time that guards had been put at the entrance. When they got close enough, one of the men called out to them. "You two work here?"

Vicenzo saw that he had a badge and a uniform like the men he had seen in Trinidad.

"I worka here," Vicenzo called out. The men walked to the middle of the road so that they could stop the cart.

"Are you bringing anything into camp?" one of the guards asked.

"This isa my friend," Vicenzo answered, motioning to Bonacquista.

"I mean goods. You got guns or bullets in the cart?"

"I buya the mining things atta the store. The clothes, the food, the gloves."

By then the other guard had walked around to the back of the cart and was searching it.

"Whatta the hell issa he think he's doing?" Vicenzo asked.

"Just checking for things that should not be brought into the camp, like guns," the guard answered.

"We donna have no guns," Bonacquista said.

"What are these?" the guard said, holding up a pair of boots.

"What the hell do you care?" Vicenzo said.

"Did you buy them in Trinidad? They look new."

"I buy 'um. I pay for 'um!" Vicenzo said.

"You bought them in Trinidad, you should have bought them in the company store."

"Your store charges us twice whatta you pay in Trinidad. I paid for those boots and I'ma keep them," Vicenzo said, getting out of the cart.

The butt end of the guard's rifle met his mouth and he fell to the earth, blood running freely to the ground. Bonacquista grabbed the other guard and wrestled him into the side of the cart. The first guard again used his rifle and Bonacquista too fell to the ground. Vicenzo tried to get up, but could get no farther than the side of the road where he lay, his lip cut to the base of his nose.

The two were finally found by some people who were traveling back to camp. Vicenzo kept his mouth covered all the way home. His face ached as though part of the rifle was still sticking in him. Mrs. Veltri looked after him and Bonacquista left for Delagua. She thought that Frank should know what had happened and sent word to him. Frank arrived with a doctor who stitched the cut.

"What the hell happened?" he asked Vicenzo.

Vicenzo turned away. "The bastard," he said slowly. "I fin' him."

"Do you remember what they looked like?"

"I fin' him."

Vicenzo nodded his head.

"Listen to me. You tell no one what has happened. If you go to the sheriff it will only mark you as a union man. Don't let them know who you are."

"I don't go to no one. I take care him."

"Listen, don't do anything stupid. You look at me," Frank ordered.

Vicenzo turned.

"We take care of our own. My grandmother used to say, 'The world is round; today may be yours, but tomorrow is mine.' You understand? We'll take care of it, you have my word."

"*I* take care of it," Vicenzo mumbled. "You donna do nothing unless I'ma there."

"You will be there. Don't worry. You take care of yourself for now. There will be another time."

Frank spoke to Mrs. Veltri. "It is difficult to leave Italy now," he said. "It may be a while before Carmela will be able to come. I will keep trying. Make sure he doesn't do anything stupid. I know how I would feel if this happened to me."

"Maybe not so much. This is not the first time for him," Mrs. Veltri said.

"What do you mean?"

"When he was coming out of the Delagua canyon one of the guards shot and creased his head."

"He didn't say anything."

"He doesn't say much."

"I hope he doesn't go looking for the men. That could cause a great deal of trouble."

"He is not going to take this so easy. He will do something."

"I know. I only hope that he waits until the time is right or it could be bad. Remember his brother. Keep one eye on him."

The next day at work was very tiring. The sun was warm and the sweat ran from Vicenzo's face freely and burned the cut. When he wiped it the pain shot through his mouth. It was difficult to eat for the next two weeks. Because he did not shave, he had for the first time a moustache.

One day, not long after the incident, he went into the company store and saw boots like the ones that had been taken from him. He looked closely at them. They were his size and the price on them was the company's price.

"Where did you get these boots?" he asked the clerk.

"The same place that we get all of the boots. They are brought in from Denver," the clerk answered.

"Thisa pair isa marked."

"Here, let me see them," the clerk said, coming over to him. "There's nothing wrong with these boots. Hell, they'll get more marks on them than that after one day's work."

"Thesea boots comma from Denver?"

"They come from the same place as the rest," the clerk said. "If you don't want the boots, don't buy them."

Vicenzo looked at the price of the boots. It was double what he had paid for them.

"You keep 'um," Vicenzo answered, then left the store.

Two months later he moved the hairs of his upper lip to expose the scar left by the blow. It was long and white but could not be seen when the hair was in place. Half for pride and half for recognition, Vicenzo did not shave.

# CHAPTER

# 12

Clouds gathered in the sky over Trinidad as Vicenzo and Frank sat in the restaurant part of the opera building across the street from the Columbian Hotel. They talked with men who had come from the northern coal fields and had already experienced the strikes there. One of the men, small and thin, spoke bitterly about the thugs who had been in the northern fields and now appeared on the streets of Trinidad.

"They're bastards," he said. "They have no mother and their father was Satan. They'll kill without the company giving any orders, sometimes for no reason other than they want to be feared."

"Where do they come from?" Frank asked.

"Virginia. They were known to be killers there too."

"They have no weakness?"

"They're smart," the man answered. "Belker wears a plate of steel under his vest. It covers both the front and back. A year ago one of the miners in the Erie camp shot hit point blank, in the heart. Belker stepped back and laughed. The man was so shocked that he hesitated. It gave Belker the chance he always seems to have. He shot the miner six times, three times after he was on the ground."

They were interrupted by the entrance of two men Frank did not know. The silence of mistrust covered the room. The hills around Trinidad had become alive since the explosion. Many strangers filled the streets and it was the careless man who talked without knowing who listened.

"Why were they brought here?" Frank asked after the strangers passed.

"They keep the men in constant fear. In the north they made a man think twice before he acted. Often it was the difference between life and death and always it was hesitation that gave them the advantage. These are careful men. They don't make mistakes."

Frank reached into his pocket and took out a telegram. He glanced at it and handed it to the man. "Do you think Belker was brought here because of this?"

The man looked at it and said, "So the union is bringing Mother Jackson here to talk to the miners. It seems to fit. The union and company are starting to play their games again. One brings in a killer and the other brings in someone who will rule the men to fight back."

"I've heard her talk before. I have seen how men react to her. She will be remembered for what she has already done, but if the men here are killed like they have been in the past, they will not be remembered," Frank said.

"The leaders have put too much faith in her," the man answered.

"And they know there are some of us who do not trust people who talk from here," Frank said, pointing to his heart. "When you are putting your life on the line, do not let the fire burn too hot or it will blind you."

"But don't forget, she can also gain support in Denver. She has influence that we don't and friends that we need," the man said mechanically.

"She won't be the one to suffer if the bullets start flying," Frank said. "If the men let themselves get carried away and start trouble, people will get hurt. Not only the men, but their families. This Mother Jackson will be in Denver and not in the tents freezing with the workers. And she won't be the one who'll be six feet in the ground."

While Frank was talking, Vicenzo saw a man enter the Columbian Hotel. For a moment he thought that the man looked familiar.

"*Scusa un momento,*" he said, leaving the table. Frank put his finger to his lips and moved it quickly to one side. Vicenzo recognized the message and nodded.

A small group had gathered in front of the hotel. Vicenzo passed through the men as they watched him carefully. The man with Frank saw him go into the hotel and motioned to Frank to look.

"Your friend knows where he is going?" he asked. "The hotel has many guards."

"He's careful. If he goes in there he has a reason," Frank said.

"I hope that his tongue knows when to speak. One slip and many will answer," the man warned.

Inside the hotel Vicenzo was stopped by a uniformed man. "What are you doing in here?" he demanded.

Vicenzo said, "I comma to getta something to eat." He pointed to the dining area.

"You got money to eat here? American money?"

"I gotta money they pay inna the camp."

"You mean script? That's no good here."

"I gotta money, no script," Vicenzo answered.

"What's the problem?" a man asked from behind the desk.

"This import thinks that his script will buy food here," the soldier said.

"If the man has the money, he can eat here or anywhere else," the man answered him. "That uniform don't mean shit in here. This is my hotel. When you leave the town, he'll still be here, so if the man wants to eat it's none of your business," he said.

Vicenzo looked at the man behind the desk. This man stands up to the armed guards, he thought.

"If you want to eat, go in there and sit down," the man told him.

The man in uniform moved toward his gun but was stopped by one of the other men. "Don't be a damn fool. You start trouble now before the others arrive and this town will be crawling with those miners."

The soldier backed off, staring at Vicenzo. "They ought to ship that scum back on the boats they came on," he said. Vicenzo turned and went over to one of the tables. He sat for a short time drinking coffee and watching men come into the hotel. Then he saw the man he had followed. He came from the stairs near the entrance and stopped to talk with the man at the desk.

While he was talking, another officer approached him. "You certainly took your time getting here this morning," he said. "You were supposed to be here two days ago."

When the man turned Vicenzo saw his face. What is he doing here? He thought.

"It is not so easy to come into this town when you have business such as mine," the man said. The two moved away from the desk and Vicenzo could no longer hear what they said.

They turned and Vicenzo looked away so that they could not see his face. When he looked up again the officer was getting into the elevator and the other man was heading out the door. Quickly Vicenzo moved to stay behind him. Outside, the man got into a cart and headed to the corner of the street. Vicenzo followed, a distance behind him. As the cart went faster Vicenzo quickened his pace. The man was going in the direction of the breweries and red-light district. The buildings were familiar to any man who worked the mines, and often courage was gained from a night's stay in one of the houses. Occasionally men disappeared for days at a time after payday. Some of the women were beginning to come out now and hang sheets on lines behind the houses. The women scurried about in undergarments that revealed enough to excite even a man who had worked himself into senseless insensitivity and Vicenzo slowed enough to watch them move about. The man stopped in front of one of the buildings and went inside. Vicenzo waited a short time and then followed him in. Inside he was met by a woman whose breasts formed a sharp curved V.

"You want a girl?" she asked. Vicenzo's blood rushed to his head and he flushed.

"There is always time for. . . ." He hesitated. He has heard the word in English many times, but here where it meant as it was said it did not seem to fit. He cupped his fist and stuck his thumb out between his first and middle fingers. He said, "There is always time for this. Righta now I wanna know where is the man who just came in."

"Who sent you here? Some wife?"

"No one. He'sa friend. Tella me where he isa, and later, me anna you. . . ." He shook his hand slowly.

"He's up there," she said, pointing to one of the doors. "But I don't want family problems here."

"Donna worry," Vicenzo answered. When she turned he gave her a pinch that he could not resist.

Vicenzo went up the stairs and stood outside the door. The smell of sweet oils came through. He rapped a couple of times upon the door and said slowly, in as good English as he could, "Open up, it's the immigration people."

There was a quick series of movements and Vicenzo ran rapidly down the stairs to the outside of the building where he saw the man running along the top of the building. He followed him along the ground. When the man got to the back of the building he jumped and tried to get up but was tackled by Vicenzo. The man made an attempt to reach into the waist of his pants but was stopped by Vicenzo who grabbed his wrist. They wrestled on the cold ground. Then the man looked at Vicenzo. "You son of a bitch. I could have killed you." And he pulled a gun out from under his belt.

"I donna ting so. I remember how you work," Vicenzo said smiling. "Come sei ritornato all' América?" Vicenzo asked.

"For a price. Everything here is for sale for a price. Sometimes it's money, sometimes it's information, and sometimes it's being a little smarter, but always a price."

"It's been a while," Vicenzo said. "I didn't think that I would ever see you again."

"And you found your relatives? It looks like they have taken good care of you."

"I found them all right. They have done much to help me."

"Including teaching you English. And now a moustache. It makes you look much older," the man said.

"I am older," Vicenzo said, pointing to his head. "You grow wiser here or you die."

"Welcome to America, friend," Vito said. "Here they call me 'Shorty' ". "Come on, let's go inside. I'll buy you a drink."

The two men brushed themselves off as they walked back to the house. Inside Vicenzo met the madam again. Her long red hair was pushed back and flowed to her buttocks.

"You didn't waste much time in coming back," she told Vicenzo.

"How coulda I resist?" he said, trying to flatter her.

"We don't have time right now," the man said. "I'll go up and get what I left and we'll go some place where we can drink and be alone."

Shorty disappeared behind the door and was gone longer than Vicenzo expected. Finally he returned.

"You've got a hell of a timing," Shorty said as they walked to a place called the Alamo. They went inside and ordered drinks.

"What the hell happened to you?" Vicenzo said. "The last time I saw you they were sending you back to Italy."

"I left a few things undone, so I came back to finish them. After a while I thought I'd come and see what was so great about Colorado that you spoke of. So here I am."

"Not so fast. I saw you today going into the hotel downtown with the men in uniform. Are you working for them?"

Shorty hesitated and then looked directly at Vicenzo. "You and me," he said slowly. "We come over to this country together a long time ago. We came as friends. But now that we are here it is not so easy to trust friends. You learn quickly that the man that works beside you day after day might turn you in to the company as a troublemaker. He is paid by this coal company and maybe you make trouble and maybe you don't but the money is more important than anything else," Shorty said. "You understand then what I am trying to say?"

"You see many things in the camps but you don't say anything. Why did you come to Trinidad?" Vicenzo asked.

"I come to find work."

"And the men I saw you with in the hotel? You work for them."

"Those men mean nothing. There are others who buy and sell them like so many pieces of meat," Shorty said.

"I know what kind of men you mean. Those who own these camps, those who pay more for mules than they pay people who work for them. Now, are you working for them?"

"They pay me, but I do not work for them. When I got back to this country I went to work in a place called Virginia. I went into the mine. You ever been down there?"

"I've been in the mine but I have not worked there," Vicenzo answered.

"It's like playing cards with your life in the pot. You don't know when the ace of spades is going to turn up. Day after day you go down, and there's the mountain on top of you and if it comes down that's it. Nothing to bury, nothing left. Finito."

"You know what the company says when they hear the miners talk like you?" Vicenzo asked. "They say, 'If you don't wanna work, starve.' That's your choice here. They think they are better, they don't like to dirty their hands. They think we are good for nothing else. These men you were with today, they will pay to find out who is in the union?"

"They will pay me more to tell them who is in the union than to bust my back in that stinking hole," Shorty said.

"And when the men die and the children cry for their fathers you will hear the names. Even when you sleep you will hear the names. I know. I have heard them call out to the men who have been killed in these mines."

"I'll tell you something. The worst for these people has not happened," Vito said.

"Death is not the worst. There are those who must live when the men have died. I know of many."

"That's not what I mean. They are planning to bring even more men. They say that if the miners try to strike they will get rid of them, just like they did ten years ago."

"You would help them destroy the miners?"

"I came here to work. I thought that if there were good people here, like those we left in Italy, I might stay. These companies are the same in Virginia as they are here. It seems there is no way out of this."

"There are men who are trying to help the workers. I know a man who will tell you how. I will give you his address and you can see him tonight. Then we will meet in Cokedale and you tell me what he says," Vicenzo said. He grabbed Vito by the wrist and continued. "Now I am going back to the camp. With what I have told you already, you can make much trouble for me. I don't want to lose my shirt again, paisan."

"I will go to this man, and I will see you in Cokedale," Vito said. Then the two departed.

It was not difficult for Frank to present to Vito the situation that existed in the Colorado coal fields. He had seen this same kind of company operation in Virginia and had decided that whatever went on was none of his business and that he had no intention of taking the trip across the ocean because of deportation again. But Frank was a good talker and soon Vito believed that Frank could provide protection from the company and guarantee that if he were found out he would be given help in another part of the country. And the prospect of being paid twice for doing the same job seemed like easy money.

"This is your job," Frank said. "When new men come into the camp we'll approach them and make them the offer of representation with the union. If they refuse, you give their names to the company officials and say that they have joined the union."

"And what if the company approaches this man and he denies having joined the union?"

"It will be a common thing because we operate on an oath of secrecy. Any one of us would deny joining the union," Frank answered. "But the important thing is that the company believes that you can be trusted."

"Don't worry, I have had to fool many to come this far."

"They will watch you for some time before they act on what you tell them. They'll probably test you with one of their men to see if what you tell them is true," Frank warned.

"Then it is up to us to see to it that what I say *is* true. I will set somebody up first. If he is sent down the canyon then we know that they believe me." Vito looked at Frank and saw a glance of mistrust. "I have been watched by the best men the government has, and they have caught me too often. But now I know how to move about without disturbing the air that I pass through. I will make sure that they think what I say is true. You make sure that I am not taken from the back."

Frank clasped Vito's forearm in a sign of agreement. He was assured by what Vito had said, for it showed him to be a hard man. And hard he must be to survive the beatings that he would receive if he should by revealed as an agent for the union.

In the months that followed, Vito worked carefully. Many names were turned in to the Columbian Hotel at Trinidad and those men who refused to join with their working brothers were soon sent down the canyon by the men that believed them to be members of that organization that they so hated.

Vicenzo came to know better the man whom he had known so briefly in New York. The tunnels of New York City seemed a distant blur, buried under new memories. Vito fitted himself into the camp, working as a pick and shovel man in the mine. He escaped his work at night when the two men played cards, drank, watched and listened.

One night the door of Vicenzo's room opened and in walked the now-familiar shape. Vicenzo was still asleep but woke quickly with a rub upon the shoulder.

"Vicenzo! Vicenzo! Wake up!"

"What the hell . . . ? What's the matter? You drunk?"

"Come with me," the voice said softly. "There are too many ears here."

Vicenzo went with him. They stood in the hall.

"Listen," Vito said, "this is important and I have to hurry."

"What the hell is so important that you get me up like a thief in the night? You still up to your old tricks? Don't tell me they're going to send you back again."

"No, this is more serious. Someone has killed one of the private dectives, one of the big money men who was brought in from the East."

"Do they know who?"

"They took in two men for conspiring together and they have them locked up in Trinidad."

"Who were they?"

"A small skinny man from one of the northern coal fields was one, and the other I do not know. They think it was a set-up. I have to go now to Trinidad. There will be questions that will need answers."

"Wait a minute. Tell me what happened. Who was killed?"

"It's best not to know anything, take my word for it."

"I want to know," Vicenzo said grabbing Vito's sleeve.

"All right. His name was Belker."

"You mean the one who wears armor plates over his front and back?"

"That's the one."

"Where did he get it, in the face or head?"

"I don't know. I have to get going."

"You have heard more! Now tell me."

"Listen, I have to talk fast. The streets were crowded, people were moving across the street alongside the trolly car. Then a few men gathered on the corner where the drugstore is, the one across the street from the bank."

"I know where you mean. Continue."

"They stayed there for a while, then Belker comes out, like a big shot, like this." Vito put his hands in the straps of his biboveralls. "Then he looks at the men and says something like, 'You try anything and I take care of you,' and he flips his cigar in the air."

"But the men were not just there talking like they usually were. When the trolly went by, they moved in behind Belker. Then one man rushed into him and the others separated the two with their bodies. Shots were fired. The men quickly dispersed before the car could move the distance of its own length. The only ones left in the street were Belker and Wesson, his partner. Belker lay in the street with a hole the size of a silver dollar in his head. Wesson picked him up and brought him to the sidewalk and stayed over him for an hour, shouting out to the streets that they would pay for it. Then the sheriff came and his men took Belker into the hotel. It was strange. The word seemed to travel faster than the wind and everybody knew that someone was going to pay for what happened."

"Did anyone see who shot him?"

"The man they arrested had been shooting his mouth off a couple of nights ago when he met Belker on the street and Belker pistol-whipped him. Belker broke his nose and split his head pretty good but it was not like the hole that was in Belker's head. Whoever did it got real close, like this," Vito said, pointing his index finger at the base of his skull, "and then, boom. They said that part of his skull was blown completely off so that you could see the insides, and there was a blood spot as big as a wine barrel in the middle of the street."

"What do they want with you?" Vicenzo asked.

"There will be questions. They'll want to know if I know of anyone who was in on the plot and then they'll make an example of some poor stupid soul who will give them the chance."

"You said they caught two men. What will they do to them?"

"They are dead men. They'll have a mock trial, probably in the morning, and then they'll kill them. Look, take this," Vito said, taking a metal star from his pocket and handing it to Vicenzo.

"What is this?"

"A badge from the sheriff's office. If anyone accuses you of knowing anything, show them this and they will think that you work for the sheriff and they will leave you alone. I better get the hell out before anyone gets suspicious of me. I will see you later in the day. Remember, watch your ass. There will be a lot of people trying to nail as many miners as possible to make up for this killing."

Then he was gone. Vicenzo returned to his room to try and make sense of what was going on. He tried to sleep but he could feel what was happening in the camp. Men moved about slowly at first, then the pace quickened. The lights from the hill began to move about the camp. Men were coming from the town and going through the camp, searching for weapons. He heard them come to his door. They they broke into the room where Vicenzo lay waiting for them.

"Do you have any guns in here?" one asked.

Vicenzo shrugged his shoulders. He thought of the gun hidden in the drawer of the small cabinet in the room.

"Guns! You got a gun?"

Another man began searching the room. He opened the chest and threw out its contents. Vicenzo crushed the badge under his pillow. Vicenzo saw the man pull the gun out of the drawer. It was then that he reached out from under his pillow with the badge still in his hand. But his hand was stopped by one of the men.

"What the hell do you think you're doing?"

"I'll show you," Vicenzo said.

"The hell you will, you crazy wop. I know how you operate! I'm not about to end up with a bullet in the back."

The man grabbed Vicenzo around the arms. The other man opened Vicenzo's hand slowly and pulled the badge from it. The words *Deputy Sheriff* were engraved on it.

"Let him go," the guard said. "He's one of Farr's plants."

"You crazy bastard," the guard said. "Why the hell didn't you show us this before? Having this gun could have gotten you killed."

"You no give me no chance," Vicenzo said.

"Come on," the other man said. "Let's get the hell out of here. We have other places to check."

"The gun," Vicenzo said. "Give it to me."

"Yeah. Just be sure you use it on the right people."

"I'ma sure," Vicenzo answered. "I'ma use 'um right." Then the men were gone.

The rest of the camp was in the same kind of turmoil. The men realized that the months of anxiety since the explosion and the years of bitterness and hatred, were coming to a head.

Word hit the camp that the two men arrested for killing Belker had been shot in jail by Wesson. The details changed as they were passed from man to man, and with each man the story became more bloody. Vicenzo heard that the two were asleep and were awakened by Wesson who held a shotgun. He made them lie on the floor and then he shot them in the back of the head in the same spot that Belker had been shot. But Vicenzo knew that the horrible words the men used to describe the killing were for the fever that they wished to stir.

He left the boarding house. When he approached the guards at the entrance of the camp, he showed them the badge. Then he disappeared around the winding road to town. The night air was cool and Vicenzo moved at a steady pace. In Trinidad, terror swept through the streets as the guards went from house to house searching for guns. Anyone associated with the miners or anyone considered a foreigner was paid a visit by the company. The air became thick with threats and it was as hard to breathe as it was when the ovens filled the air with smoke.

The company saw its chance to clean out the union members. Many found themselves thrown into the street while their houses were gone over and anything that might be used as a weapon was taken. When they resisted, they were beaten or taken to jail.

Vicenzo was stopped twice more before he reached Frank's house, but each time he showed the badge and he was left alone. This works better than a charm, he said to himself. No disrespect to you St. Christopher, but tonight I will keep this close.

All the lights in Frank's house were on and when he went in a cool draft was blowing through the house as though all of the windows were open. Vicenzo looked into the front bedroom where clothes had been thrown out of the drawers across the room. Then he went to the next room where Marietta was picking up articles from the floor and putting them into the drawers.

"Where's Frank?" Vicenzo asked.

"In the basement," she answered.

Vicenzo found Frank wading ankle deep in wine.

"What happened?" Vicenzo asked.

"The men," he said slowly, "they come here looking for guns. They think that I hid guns for the men. The bastards come into this house where my family lives and they scare the women and children. They know that we can do nothing with them here."

"Was anyone hurt?"

"No one was hurt but I would have taught those animals how to act if the women and children had not been here. These men do not think of families. They will not act like men.

"What I have dreaded for more than two years is coming," Frank continued. "The hired killers are going to be let loose like they were tonight, and many will die. What are the camps like tonight?" he asked Vicenzo.

"The company is searching for guns. How did they come into your home? It is not in the camp."

"The sheriff sent deputies to the homes of those who were believed to be helping the miners. They had badges with them so they carried authority, they claimed."

"You mean like this one?" Vicenzo said, holding out the one that Vito had given him.

"Where did you get that?"

"Vito."

"He does his job well. Keep it. It will be of much use in the days to come."

The church bell began to toll, echoing through the streets, bouncing off the houses and through the trees. The lights of the church came on and lit the small hill on which it sat. The women of the neighborhood left their houses and went to the church.

"It is a strange time for church," Vicenzo said.

"The women pray out of fear for the men," Frank answered.

"The men are strong and they will fight. The women should not fear. It will only cause them to be weak," Vicenzo said.

"I fear, Vicenzo. I fear because I have tried to help men and by my actions they have stayed here."

"If it weren't for you, many of them would have starved to death by now. You cannot judge your good intentions by the actions of these men who come from hell. If they must be sent back to hell, they will be, if we have to send them ourselves."

"These men are not whom I fear, but myself. There are many guns hidden in the hills and many more on their way here. We got word today that the company has sent a trainload."

"First they send a trainload of guns, then they will send a trainload of caskets," Vicenzo said.

"That they have experience doing."

As the two men stood on the porch, Frank could feel the two forces coming against each other. The church bell tolled and the sound passed over the town like a heavy cloud warning the men on both sides that the time had long since passed when either would give in without subjection. The toll came again, warning them that the price would be high, but neither side could stop now. Again the toll came, and the dogs howled in strange unison.

"They say that they know when death is near," Frank said.

"It is an old superstition."

"Even superstitions have some truth," Frank answered.

The toll came again. Vicenzo felt the vibrations pass through him in waves of depression.

"It makes us think," Frank said. "There will be a time for us all and sometimes it is closer that we would like it to be. Tonight may be remembered for many generations. There is no way of stopping what will happen. We can struggle all our lives as best we can, but when it comes time for the bell to toll, we stop and remember."

A figure came running up to the porch and called to Frank. "Mr. Naccarato!"

"Yes?"

"I have word from town that men have started coming from up the river to kill the soldiers in town."

"Who sent you?" Frank asked.

"Mr. Lewis. He says that you are to try and control the Italians from the Valdez camp. They will not listen to him."

"Tell him I will be there soon. Come, Vicenzo, we must go now. There is much work to be done tonight if we are to avoid a massacre."

In Trinidad, Frank tried in vain to get the men back to the Valdez camp. As he spoke, small snowflakes fell on bare metal in a train yard in Denver. The company workers there loaded a special car made for situations like the one in Trinidad.

"What the hell is this?" one of the men asked.

"A car," another answered. "It has wheels."

"It also has a gun. Where are they sending it? To the war in Europe?"

"No, south to Trinidad."

"What do you suppose they use it for?"

"Funerals probably. Lots of them."

The streets of Trinidad appeared empty when the sun broke over the hills the next morning. There was no movement at the Columbian Hotel where the company heads met with officers of the state militia. As the sun rose higher, the shapes of men hiding on tops of buildings and in alleys became visible.

On the road north of the town the strange metal contraption made its way slowly toward Trinidad. It stopped first at Ludlow, turning off the road and pulling within fifty feet of the main entrance of the building that served as the union headquarters. Three union men looked out the window at the thing outside.

"What the hell is that? one said. "There's something wrong. We didn't get any messages about this. We better have a look."

"Hold it. Something is wrong. We better stay here until we hear from Lewis."

Then a white flag appeared from a small slit in the metal.

"It's all right, it's a white flag," another said. "Maybe Lawson has come up with some tricks of his own."

One man walked out and looked at the vehicle from the side. "Hey, it's one of those new automobiles like the ones that the big shots use in New York."

The other two came out. As they gazed questioningly at the vehicle, a barrel emerged from the slot used as a window, and began to move almost without notice. The first man came closer. When he noticed that the barrel was pointing directly at him, he turned and screamed to his friends to go back. The bullets were swift. In an instant, the three lay on the ground, bleeding from the face, chest, and legs. The car then returned to the road and continued toward town.

In Trinidad, the union bosses made a last attempt to avoid violence. "You've got to get the men back into the camps before someone gets killed," Lewis told the leaders of the individual groups who met with him in the lobby of the opera house. "There are over a hundred men out there now, armed and ready to shoot at the first thing that moves."

"You don't know what is at stake here," Lawson said. "If people in this state see us as killers, we're all finished. The camps will never change."

"They will only change if *we* change them," Tikas, one of the Greeks, said. "You can not be fooled by those men in the hotel."

"That's not important now. If there's violence we will lose all the support that we have gained upstate," Lewis said.

"The company has made fools of us again. The men they brought in wear the uniforms of state militia and yet they carry guns bought by the company. They are all around the camps like a sickness that cannot be cured unless it is cut out," Tikas said.

"You don't know how many men will be killed by a direct attack upon the office at the hotel."

"How many men does the company have in town right now?" Frank asked.

"Two or three hundred right here in town, and a couple of hundred more on the outskirts. They are well armed and know how to use rifles. If we fight them openly like this it is difficult to know how many will be killed."

"Don't forget," Frank said, "we count in different terms than the company does. For every one that we lose, there is a widow and a child that has no father, or a mother that has no son. The company loses only a hired gunman and there are plenty of them for the right price. We cannot afford to be careless."

"These men that the company has brought here, they are gunmen from Virginia, aren't they?" Tikas asked.

"Many of them," Lewis answered. "They are good with a rifle, while the men are more used to a pick and shovel."

"The men will fight," the Greek broke in.

"You kill all the ones who are here in town and hundreds more will show up. Remember, it has happened here before," Lewis warned.

"What the hell do you suggest we do? Nothing? Two men were blown apart while they slept in their jail cells!" Tikas said.

"There are still better ways," Frank replied.

"Washington will have to send men here," the labor leader broke in. "When they realize that the state militia is nothing more that a bunch of thugs hired by the company, they will have to send troops here to protect the people."

"Do not expect too much from the people in Washington, my friend," Frank warned. "They have their own problems and they are not concerned with ours."

As the men talked, others began to fill the roof tops of the buildings. Many of them clutched crude guns brought or supplied by members of the union.

Inside the opera house, the union boss strengthened his appeal.

"Go to the miners out there and stop this before they are killed," he said. "It will not matter what the negotiations have done. It is not important now. Just get those men out of here before there is a massacre out there."

"I think that is best," Frank said. He drew a dirty look from the Greek. "But we will have to go out together and appeal for them to go back to the camps now." The others agreed. But before they could take any action, the distant report of a rifle made them all hurry out to the front of the building.

The street was quiet. There was no movement from the tops of the buildings or from the streets. Commercial and Main Streets intersected each other in a giant cross, with the opera house on one corner and the Columbian Hotel directly across from it. The bank sat diagonally across from the hotel. Vicenzo hid behind one of the sandstone blocks that made up its facade. From there he could see down the street that once formed the old Santa Fe trail. But it followed the trail too closely and a sharp curve in it prevented him from seeing who fired the shots.

"How far off were the shots?" Frank asked one of the men with him.

"Maybe three hundred yards, about where the Las Animas Street bridge crosses the Purgatory."

Vicenzo moved from behind the stone. Frank recognized him and spoke quickly in Italian. "Vieni, andiamo!"

"You heard the shots?"

"Yes. Do you know what made them?"

"Several of the men saw something from the roof that looked like one of the automobiles that I have seen you drive. But it was shaped like a box and shone in the sun."

"The death special," Tikas said.

Frank turned and repeated, "The death special?"

"Morte! Morte!" the Greek said. "It has been used in the east."

"What the hell is it?"

There came another outburst of fire, this time closer than the first. Frank moved toward the middle of the street to see the answer to his question. Soon it appeared, moving slowly down the brick street. Several shots from the tops of the buildings sounded out and struck the metal of the machine, but the bullets ricocheted off its side. The barrel turned in the direction of the shots and sprayed one of the buildings. Then it swept the street with bullets. Frank and the other men ran back into the opera house. The machine rambled past, its metal wheels grinding on the edges of the bricks as it passed. When it reached the front of the hotel it stopped.

"I have heard of this machine," the union organizer said.

"You are familiar with this thing?" Frank asked.

"No, not familiar, it was only what people in Denver thought was being built, but no one knew for sure if it was real. They used something like this in the East a couple of years ago."

"Well, now you know for sure what can be done about it, now that it's here."

"There's another gun mounted on the back," the Greek said. "It can be approached from the side if there is no cover from the outside carriage."

Then a voice called out from the hotel for the union boss.

"It's Cooke's voice," the boss said. "Wait here."

"You're not going out there?" the Greek asked.

"I have to, it's my job."

"To get yourself killed by that thing?"

"No. So that those men out there won't be killed."

He stepped to the window and hollered out, without exposing himself, "I can hear you, Cooke."

"You tell those men up there that they're breaking the law."

"You tell them Cooke, they can hear you."

"They won't understand, Lewis. If you don't want a blood bath here, Lewis, you better tell them to get the hell out of here and go back to the camps."

"The men that were killed in the jail, Cooke. Who killed them?"

"I wasn't there. I don't know who killed them."

"I know you better than that. They want the men, Cooke. If they don't know who it was, they'll think that anytime one of your men feels like it they'll use their guns. They'll think that you have lost control of them."

"A meeting, Lewis. Give me a meeting so that we can discuss this."

"All right, Cooke, come out in the open and we'll talk."

"Get the men back into the camps first, Lewis. They won't understand what is going on and they'll kill me the first chance they get."

Lewis stepped outside and took a few steps toward the hotel. "Cooke," he called out in full voice.

"Come out and we'll talk, Cooke. They won't hurt you as long as I'm standing out here too."

"He's insane," the Greek said to the others in the opera house. "He's got nothing out there. No guarantee that we won't shoot or they won't shoot."

"It's a chance," Frank said. "The buildings are covered with men and so are the streets. Soon there will be many more arriving from Denver. They will have uniforms on and we won't know whether they will be militia or hired killers. It's a chance to avoid an all-out war here."

"In a week we will have them wiped out," the Greek said.

"And what will be the cost? The widows have not taken off the black yet from the explosion in Hastings."

"We fight. We have never known the meaning of this kind of talk. Men are killed every day because the conditions are so bad in the mine. Yet you still can tell me that the cost is too great. If we don't do it now, how many more will be killed in the next explosion?" the Greek shouted.

Outside, Lewis tried to position himself to the side of the armed car so that the barrel that stuck out the back could not be pulled out far enough to hit him. Then the barrel began to move in his direction and fire broke out from the roof tops. The sound of the fire ended the talk and the men all positioned themselves for the fight.

The machine answered the fire from the roofs and sprayed the buildings that it could reach. Shots from the roof tops ricocheted off the metal of the machine. The bursts came again, tearing into the wooden buildings and chipping the stone of the bank. Then the shots stopped and silence covered the street.

Lewis lay hidden by the stones, waiting for the car to move. He knew that his death would cause more bitterness between the men and the company. If the men reacted violently, there could be a massacre. His death could also mean that the miners would be without leadership and it would take the union years to regain a foothold in Colorado.

General Cooke's voice broke the silence. "Lewis?" There was no answer. "Lewis, you still there?"

The silence caused the men in the opera house to begin searching the street for him.

"Is he hit?" Frank asked the Greek.

"I saw him hit the ground, but he is not where he fell," was the answer.

"Lewis!" The voice came again, this time from a window on the second floor of the hotel. From there the General could see part of Lewis's body. A shot came from the window and the body was pulled back against the building. A short silence was followed by a rash of fire from the front of the hotel. Bullets crashed through windows and poured out of the front door. The machine began to move again. The miners reacted too slowly, and by the time they were able to return the fire, the vehicle was far down the street, its guns firing continuously. Many of the men ran atop the buildings, jumping from roof to roof, trying to get a last shot. Some ran into the street where they were fired upon by men in the hotel. Then the firing stopped and the street fell silent again.

Lewis got up and approached the hotel. "The shooting is over, you inside," he said. He was joined by several from the opera house. "Why did you not answer him?" Frank asked Lewis.

"Because I thought he would want to get out of town as fast as he could if he thought I was dead. With Cooke out of town, the men will leave and go back to camp."

"But they will not forget," the Greek said.

"It's a political game he and I are playing. If the government in Washington ever gets here, we will want them to disarm both sides. If they believe that the violence is being caused by the miners, as they are being told, there will be no disarming of the militia and that will leave the miners no way of defending themselves."

"They would like that very much," the Greek said. "But there is no way that they are going to get this rifle from me while my blood is still warm."

"Tell your men to watch themselves and to avoid violence. We have to make President Wilson believe that the miners are not the ones who started these outbreaks. We already know that he is working with the company, so tell them to watch themselves and make sure it sticks."

The Greek turned away in bitterness. There shall be a better time, he thought to himself, a better time and a better place.

Lewis and Frank went to the telegraph office to get in touch with the station outside of town to see if any new troops had arrived by train to reinforce the men who had been trapped in town. The message went out several times but there were only three cold corpses to answer the message.

# CHAPTER

# 13

The men in the Trinidad coal fields could no longer bear the indignities thrust upon them by the company. It was time to leave the dark tunnels of the mine and court death in the light of the sun. For these men it was preferable to die with lead in their bodies than to die by being crushed by a ton of coal.

The union had hoped that after the killings outside of town, enough public support would bring national guard troops into the area. Instead it brought the fear the company wanted. Men began mistrusting each other, thinking that even their best friends would be paid enough to betray them as members of the union. Men began to arrive in town wearing state militia uniforms. Everyone knew who was paying them, and the fear spread when the miners saw the weapons they carried.

The other side also had its doubts. Many had been sent down the river but how many more reamined who carried the union card? The list of names was long but who could trust the foreigners, no matter how much he was paid?

The death of the three men outside of town brought many more union people into the state. Some stayed in Denver, continuing their efforts to make the state aware of what was happening in the southern coal fields. Others went south to try to solidify the men behind the union bosses. The company had acted carelessly on the occasion of the slaughter of the three men. They had failed once again to control the killers they had hired. Fear will hold a man in check but hatred will cause him to act.

The only defense the company could offer for the killings was the fact that the miners had tried to kill Cooke while he was at the Columbian Hotel.

In Trinidad, Vicenzo sat in the back of the West Side Theater, waiting to hear one of the union officials talk of what the men should do next. The word was that Mother Jackson had been sent because of her ability to arouse the men. Frank had seen her before. He knew how the men reacted to the short, stocky, white-haired woman as she appealed to their sense of manhood. He remembered seeing her on this same stage, lighting up a six-inch cigar and blowing rings out over the auidence. Her personality drew the men in like a rabbit draws a hawk, but this small woman had more than the swiftness of the rabbit. She had the claws of the mountain lion. And she had surprised more than one unsuspecting company boss with them.

There were many familiar faces, in the group in the theater, among them the Greek who commanded the olive-skinned men from the Baltic War. He could be heard above all the others. "To getta these Greeks so riled uppa, something hasa to be up."

"These Greeks have something planned?" Vicenzo asked.

"Always," Frank answered. "Always."

"When will we know what to do? Waiting is difficult for the men. Many things are going around the camp and nobody knows what is true and what isn't."

"When it is time you will know. It is not like anything that you have seen before. You will be able to see it on the faces of the men and women, and don't think that it will just be the workers. The men who are with the company will also show that the struggle has begun on another level."

"What the hell do we wait for? We wait in the camp and we come here and wait some more. Then we go back and it's the same thing," Vicenzo said, waving his hands back and forth.

"The men are not so independent that they would act on their own. They will do nothing until someone from the union says to. They have never acted on their own and I doubt that they ever will, but I think that the union is about to test their strength. Many of them are unhappy because of what has happened in the last couple of weeks," Frank said calmly.

The door in the back of the room slammed shut and Vicenzo turned quickly. All of the chairs had been filled and many stood in the aisles.

"I don't like depending upon someone else to decide things. In the old country the men did what had to be done and that was the end of it."

"This is different, Vicenzo. There are many people who are watching what happens here, and I don't mean just the company. Many of the people in Washington are keeping an eye in this direction. As of yet they have done nothing, but some time they will have to," Frank said.

"If the camps have been like this for such a long time the men should have changed it. What the hell should the government care? Now the men should take care of it."

"I'm afraid that if the men did try, troops would be sent against them. We do not want that. If they come we want them to be on our side."

"You mean they would send the military troops, not the carabiniere? Vicenzo asked, amazed.

"Yes, they are not the police, they are troops, the National Guard. It's an army that takes care of things inside the country," Frank answered.

An outbreak of laughter halted the conversation and the men focused attention on the Greeks.

"The Greeks know how to make men forget the pressure that is here," Frank said.

"They make too much noise," Vicenzo said. "Too many people look when you make too much noise."

The time was getting late and Vicenzo looked nervously around the hall. The long red velvet curtains that hung from the ceiling reminded him of the inside of the Columbian Hotel and he felt the presence of the company guards.

"There are men here that have been sent by the company," he remarked.

"They are here," Frank agreed. "This you can bet on."

Vicenzo looked at the balcony above them and saw that men had by now filled it. Voices came from behind the curtains and the theater began to quiet down. Then the curtains parted and the head of the union stood in the center of the stage. To his right was a short, stocky woman with wire-framed glasses. To the left of him stood another man Frank did not know.

"It is good to see so many men here tonight," Lewis said, his voice carrying to the back of the balcony. "Tonight we come here as one; all brothers in the same cause. And that cause has brought us now to act in defense of our dignity as men. As you know by now, the negotiations have broken off because the company refused to meet our demands or even to recognize that you men are members of an organization that represents your rights. They have refused to agree to an eight-hour work day for the men in the mine, for those who work around the mines, or for those who work the coke ovens. We have also demanded that they pay us for what they call dead work. They have refused to even consider most of what we believe are our rights as men. They think that we do not sweat down there when we timber, or when the rooms collapse, and we have to work an entire day removing the debris without pay."

As he spoke he raised his voice and quickened his pace. Excitement spread among the men in the audience.

"If this were not enough, they even refused those rights that no man who uses his labor for another should be denied. *They denied us the right to have a checkman from among our ranks,* so that you would be guaranteed pay for the work that you have done. In doing this they have even denied you your God-given right of a fair wage for a day's work, and have in many instances given you no pay for the carts you have sent out of the mine. They have also refused to allow you to shop in any store of your choice, so that an unfair portion of your wages goes for the things that you need to survive, for the things that your families need to survive, and for the things that you need to do your work."

Again he stopped. He knew that many of the men in the hall did not understand much English and it was best not to speak quickly. But he knew that the emotion of those who did understand would catch among all of the men as fire catches in dry brush.

"By not agreeing to the demands that we made, the company has, in fact, *broken the laws of the state of Colorado.* They have persisted in carrying out their guard system and have treated us like prisoners."

When Lewis finished, he raised his hands over the men like an evangelist, his voice raised to its peak. The men began cheering widly and their reaction could be heard blocks away. Several in the hall became uneasy, knowing what the company reaction would be. But the one that they had been sent to hear had not yet spoken.

A stocky woman in a long black dress came to the front of the stage. She hesitated and the hall became quiet. She looked out over their upturned faces. Her eyes met those of the leader of the Greek men. She smiled and spoke only loud enough to be heard if there was complete silence in the theatre.

"It does my heart good to see the faces of so many good, strong working men. You are the salt of the earth. I have been to every part of this country and nowhere have I seen better men than you. Men who work hard and produce a country from the bowels of the earth. But you already know what kind of men you are. I want to tell you about the kind of men who own the mines that you work in. I want to tell you about the men who sit back on their asses and eat up the things that you have produced with your labor. And I want to tell you about their damn fool lawyers with their fancy words that have taken away your right to be men! I would hate to even try to imagine what produces men such as these. It must have been some creature that had nothing between its legs but jelly!" Laughter spread over the hall.

"Any one of you could break them in half just by bending your arm, and these are the men who dictate to you what conditions you must work in and die in. But it's not only you who have to suffer. It's also your women and children. *Their* women spend the afternoon sipping tea while yours work so that you will have clothes on your back and food on the table. Your children have little or no education while theirs are sent to the finest schools around the world. They take you for a bunch of peons, worse than the peasants in Europe and less free than the Negroes in the South, and all because you work to feed your families. You have only to look around the camps, at the barbed wire fences and the search-lights and the machine guns that are pointed at your heads every day and night, to be reminded of how they treat you."

She paused. Her words were left to sink into the skulls of the men and burrow down into their brains, burning like hot coals and warming their blood until their eyes shot fire. Then she resumed.

"A thousand years ago, the women in Europe cried out to their men to return from the wars victorious so that they would not be raped and their children sold into slavery. Now your women and children cry out to you to save them from being raped of their dignity and your children from being sold into ignorance so that the company can meet a production quota." She drew a long breath and approached the front of the stage. "And I'll tell you men something. I've known more than one company man to approach a new widow with more than condolences. More than once they have tried to *buy* what they were not man enough to get any way else."

The crowd became uneasy. The woman's words played upon every instinct that these men needed to survive in the camps.

"These men here in the camps who call themselves the state militia are nothing more than pack of thugs whose guns have been bought in Virginia. They are not even paid by the state. The same company that refuses to pay a decent wage to do its dirty work in those stinking hell-holes that they try to pass off as mines is paying those killers *twice as much* as you could ever expect to make working for it. These killers are no less bandits than Black Jack Ketchum or Billy the Kid.

"If the outright killing was not enough, the company kills you every day with the disgusting conditions that it forces you to work and live under. How many of you have been laid off for days because one of the mules that you used was skinned a bit while you were trying to get it out of one of those passages? That'll tell you which is more important to the company, you or the mules. When did they ever care if *you* were injured down there? What precautions did they take after the Hastings mine exploded? *One hundred and twenty-one men died because the company doesn't give a damn about you!* Not a single thing came from that explosion. The mines are as gaseous as the day the Hastings mine blew those poor men into the next world. How much longer will it be before the next mine blows?

The woman's words sent deep currents of fear through each man present like a sickle passing through stalks of grain. The word blast brought as many images as there were men who remembered the bodies strewn around, some dismembered throughout the tunnel. Smoke, debris and blood. Vicenzo recalled a small girl clinging to a gate crying for someone who had died. A brief moment's hesitation in her pace was all that was needed for effect and the memories began again. The worst were of women who had known only one man, too soon buried.

"And I'll tell you what the worst part of your situation is. The man who denies you rights as men is nothing more than a scrawny runt who never in his life had to depend upon himself for *anything,* but inherited his wealth from his father. If he had to do for one day what you do every day of your lives, he would shrivel up and blow away. The man who owns this company uses you for his legs because he doesn't have any to stand on. This man feeds off you like one of those vultures that come down from the hills ready to feed on anything that looks dead.

"But we're going to fool him! When he comes down to feast, we're going to be ready to grab him where it hurts the most, right in his big fat money purse. Did you know that he's spent thousands of dollars for bird sanctuaries in New Jersey and but wouldn't spend so much as a dime making the mines safe? He spends thousands more for widows in foreign countries, but he wouldn't give the many widows that he created enough money to bury their dead husbands properly.

"He doesn't think of you as men but as a commodity that he can bargain for and sell. He collects, while you do the work. And nothing is going to change unless *you change it*. Just remember what kind of men you are. You have the power to change anything you have a mind to do. Don't be afraid of him! Without you, who is going to do the dirty work with picks and shovels? Do you think he'll come from New York and take up where you left off and do a good day's work? Now let me see what kind of men I have been talking to. Come on! Stand up and show me."

They reacted immediately. Cheers rose from the theatre louder than before. The Greeks waved their arms as if they were charging into the first line of the enemy. The vibrations of raw power resounded again and again.

"Tomorrow we will show them who the real men are," Mother Jackson called out. "Tomorrow we will show them what we are made of." Many did not hear her last words, but it did not matter. The men knew now what must be done. They spilled out of the theater and onto the street.

"And now they make their play," Frank said.

"You mean tomorrow?" Vicenzo asked.

"Tomorrow the strike call goes out and we will see who has the power. Now it is a matter of numbers."

"Then it is not sure how many will go out." Vicenzo asked.

"It is never sure, but soon we will know. For tonight, only He knows," Frank said, glancing upward.

Two hundred miles away, large snowflakes began falling on large metal boxcars. The yard that had been silent not an hour before became a blur of uniformed figures who crowded into cars. Soon the ground became wet and tracks were left by soldiers boots. In a short time the yard was silent again.

The snow covered the ground by midnight. Most of the people in the camps were asleep and didn't see the flakes pile up around their crude shelters. They had often looked gratefully into the skies as the snow fell, knowing that the moisture was needed and that it would clean the air tinted by the ovens.

The sun had not yet risen when the first of the miners heard that the strike call had gone out. Many of them did not understand the things that had been said about the violation of their rights by the company. They had come from places where rights were few. They knew only of how their families had suffered throughout the struggle for power.

The night shift completed its work. When they laid down their picks and shovels, there was silence in the tunnels. When they reached the porthold they saw many new guards with rifles who watched them as though they were an enemy army approaching for battle. But there was no battle. The tired men went home quickly to rest for what lay ahead.

By the time the sun was over the mountains it was apparent that the morning shift would not be going to work. Many left their houses and gathered in small groups about the camp. Some moved about, waiting for reaction from the guards who had been brought into the camp.

In the middle of the morning, a group of heavily armed men walked down the street in the Delagua camp. "You're going to have to get off company property," one of the guards told a group of men. The men did not move. The sound of a bullet entering the chamber of a rifle filled the silence that followed. The men started to move slowly when a guard fired at one of the houses. The men scattered in the direction of their homes and several shots followed.

In Trinidad, the union bosses reveled in their success. No more than a handful of men at each mine had gone to work that morning. That meant that if the other crews were to honor the strikecall, there would be more than twelve thousand men on strike.

The company reacted with bitterness and immediately sent out word that the striking men and their families were to be removed from company property. They announced that men would be brought in from Texas to replace those on strike. In several of the camps people were awakened by gunshots that chipped away at the front of their houses.

When Frank received word of what was happening, he immediately prepared to go to Delagua. "Dress warmly," he told Vicenzo, who had gone to Trinidad following the day shift. "It snowed last night and it looks like it is going to do the same today."

"We will go to Hastings?" Vicenzo asked.

"To Delagua. There have been gunshots there."

Vicenzo thought of Joe Bonacquista. "I think we should hurry," he told Frank.

"We shall, but first we must pack a few things that might be needed. The people will come from the camps and set up their things in tents that are being brought by train from Virginia. They will need food and something to make them warm."

Vicenzo and Frank packed the cart with food and blankets and soon were on their way north. Small frozen drops of water had begun to fall, making the journey difficult. Mud caked quickly around the wheels of the cart and they began to slide from side to side. Vicenzo's jacket was soon covered with ice. When they arrived at Hastings some of the tents had already been set up and others were in the process of being so. "I would like to go further up the canyon," Vicenzo told Frank, "to find Joe Bonacquista and his family."

"You go, but be careful," Frank said. "Today it will be easy to conceal a dead body."

As soon as Frank and Vicenzo finished unloading the supplies, Vicenzo took the cart and headed into the hills. In many places along the road there was a continuous line of people carrying the few items that they owned strapped to wooden carts. Most of them looked straight ahead and took no notice of Vicenzo. But he looked carefully at their faces and at the few items that they clung to. There were old, beaten straw beds and shabby wooden chairs. There were worn kitchen utensils and used mining tools. One girl clung to a ragged doll with one arm missing. Tied onto her brother's belt was an old baseball mitt. Vicenzo passed an old man sitting on a trunk on the side of the road. "You should move on," Vicenzo told him. "It is not good to sit here in the rain. It is too easy to get sick."

The old man looked up at him and said nothing.

"You understand the English?"

The old man said nothing.

"Go to the tents," Vicenzo said.

"I comma this far. The trunk slide off the cart and I cannot get it back on. Everything else is still up there. I brought this with me and this is all I have left. They destroyed everything else." The old man put his face in his hands.

"Come on, you can't stay here, you will freeze. I will put the trunk in my cart. Get a ride with someone and I will bring you the trunk later, when I return."

Vicenzo helped him onto one of the carts that was heading for the tents and then put the trunk in the back of the cart. Then he started again up the canyon. Many of the homes he passed were empty. The sound of gunfire cut through the canyon again, followed by two dynamite blasts. Vicenzo hurried but his progress was impeded by the cart sliding on the muddied road.

When he arrived at the house where the Bonacquistas lived, the door was open. He could see movement within the house. He got out and moved quickly to the door. Bonacquista's father was preparing his wife for the trip while Joe packed extra clothes in an old box.

"Help my father," he told Vicenzo. "My mother is pregnant and we must keep her as dry and warm as we can."

Vicenzo closed the door and quickly began helping Mr. Bonacquista. "We must hurry," he said. "The guards are close by."

Mr. Bonacquista wrapped a shawl around his wife. "How do you feel?" he asked.

"I'm all right," she answered.

Vicenzo picked up a box. Suddenly the door burst open and two men walked in.

"You should have been the hell out of here before you decided not to go to work this morning," the first said. The other one began throwing boxes into the mud outside. Joe acted first, hitting the one who spoke across the mouth. The other one threw a small chair at him and would have hit him across the neck had it not been partially blocked by the door frame. Vicenzo moved at him and soon the men were swinging at each other amidst the boxes. Then a shot rang out of the confusion and the fighting stopped.

"You bastards, get the hell out!" One of the guards shouted. He had a pistol in his hand, the barrel pointed at Mrs. Bonacquista. The three men froze, staring at the gun.

"Don't you bastards understand English? I said get the hell out of here before I kill all of you." Blood was running from the man's nose which had been broken by the blow that Joe had delivered. Mr. Bonacquista turned carefully but quickly, making all of his movements away from the gun. He took his wife out of the house. Vicenzo grabbed the box of clothing and followed, with Joe behind him. Vicenzo put the box he was carrying into the cart and quickly grabbed another. Joe went to the front of the house and picked up another box and ran back to the cart. More gunshots came from the house and one hit the side of the cart, splintering it.

The family was forced to leave the road. They fled into the gully that ran alongside it. Several other guards joined those who were shooting and soon other people were forced off the road. Covered with mud, Vicenzo and the Bonacquista family moved slowly down the gully, bullets passing overhead.

"You filthy bastards. Here, take your trash with you," shouted one of the guards, tossing crates over the side. There were more shots. Mr. Bonacquista covered his wife's body every time shots rang out.

After a long volley Vicenzo said, "I'm going up for the cart. She will need clean clothes when she reaches the tents. There is little there to keep her warm. It will be hours before the hospital tent is set up."

"They will kill you," Mr. Bonacquista said, grabbing him by the arm. Then more shots wizzed a short distance above their heads.

"If they have their way, they'll kill us one way or another. At least you should have the things that are in the cart. If we are in the tents long, we will need them or we will die anyway. Take her quickly. Meet me down on the road, I will bring the cart." Vicenzo started up the wall of the gully, followed by Joe. By the time they reached the top they were around a bend in the gully and out of sight.

The two men remained silent as they headed back in the direction of the carts. The guards had busied themselves throwing out the rest of the belongings they found in the houses. When the men approached the cart they hesitated, watching the house closely. It seemed empty. Joe got in his cart and Vicenzo tied Frank's to the back. Then a shot splintered wood a few inches above his hand.

"What the hell do you think you're doing there?" The voice came from one of the houses.

"We come for what we need to live. These things belonga to us," Vicenzo shouted back.

"Who says they belong to you? How do I know you're not trying to steal from these poor imports?"

"There is nothing here worth anything to you. We need it to stay alive."

"So you call what you do here living?"

A cold wave of depression ran over Vicenzo's body. He stood unable to move. There must be some way, he said to himself, as he moved toward the front of the cart, trying not to bring fire down upon himself and Joe. I do not want to die like this.

Another guard had come out of the house. He began laughing at the two men in the cold rain who were streaked with mud. "Look at these two mudballs," he said. "I can't tell if they're black or white. I'm surprised that mud would stick to grease."

Vicenzo got slowly into the cart and they began to move down the road. One of the guards fired at the cart but they kept moving slowly, sliding as they went along. Other guards came out to see them only to laugh. Still they kept silent and moved at a steady pace.

"Look at these bastards," Vicenzo said, wiping the mud from his shirt and tossing it to the side of the cart. "It cannot go on. We must do something."

"It is enough for us to survive this day," Joe answered. "The world is round. Today is theirs but tomorrow will be ours."

"My mother used to say that when my father would come home from being cheated by the landlords. Then my father decided that tomorrow will never come unless you make it," Vicenzo said.

When they had gone a distance, Joe got out of the cart and went back into the gully to find his parents. Vicenzo waited on the road. The canyon seemed quiet. The sleet lessened. Vicenzo looked back and could see the carts and abandoned furniture. He left the cart and went to the side of the ravine where the people were crouched in the mud.

"Come," he called to them. They looked up in fright.

"Come!" he called again. They did not move.

"You musta comma," he said in English. "You musta go to the tenta colony ina Ludlow." Still they did not move. Vicenzo went part of the way down the ravine and held out his hand to one of the women who stood over her child.

"You musta come now," he repeated.

"The guards," one of the people said.

"They are busy ina the houses. You musta comma now."

The woman took his hand and he began to pull her toward the top. The others moved like frightened rabbits. The ground was soft and many slipped, but soon they could get back into the carts, many looking toward the rows of houses on the side of the hill. Joe returned with his parents and they again began moving to the tents.

By midday the line coming from the canyon became a continuous string. The rain had stopped and there were periods of sunlight and clouds.

During one interval of sunlight a Polish man began to sing a song from his homeland. He was joined by the members of his family. Soon all the people who knew the song began to sing with them.

Then the song was over and there was a strange interlude. The sun had once again gone behind the clouds and the air turned chilly. But when the sun returned a man began a Slavic song and he too was joined by others who knew the song. A Greek song followed. The Greeks in the tent colony heard them. Tikas too, heard the melody. He walked away from the tents, the words of the song on his lips. He began to sing. His voice carried into the canyon as he sang louder. He turned and raised his arms and the other Greek soldiers began singing louder and louder until, at the end of the song, they were almost screaming.

"There is something that not even those demons can defeat. It is here," Tikas said, striking his breast. The songs continued until the middle of the afternoon. The sun had begun its descent and the air had turned cold when the rest of the wagons pulled into the colony.

"There were supposed to be more tents coming from Virginia but they have not arrived yet, and I have received no word as to their whereabouts. The hospital tent is already full and so is the community tent in the middle of camp," one of the men said.

"Then it will be up to us to spend the night outside," said the leader of the Greeks. "We have suffered many hardships before during war and we can suffer them again. It is nothing less than a war now. If you had listened to me a long time ago, we would be ready for war." Then he left to go to his men and prepare them for the night.

When all that could be done was finished, Frank left with Vicenzo for Trinidad. Mrs. Bonacquista was put into one of the hospital tents and Joe and his father were given a place to sleep.

That night Vicenzo lay on the bed that he had slept in the first night he was in Trinidad. Mrs. Naccarato would not let him return to Cokedale. She saw him shiver when he first came into the house and, after giving him something to eat, she made him wash and lie down. I am very glad she is here, he said to himself. She reminds me of Carmela.

"How do you feel?" Frank asked, entering the room.

"I'm all right," Vicenzo answered. "I did not think anything could be this cold."

"Yes," Frank answered. "The Mediterranean keeps Calabria warm. Here the mountains keep us cold."

"The people were forced from their homes," Vicenzo said.

"We knew that they would be."

"There were not enough tents."

"No," Frank replied. "Some of the men will have to spend the night outside."

"The sky became cloudy before the sun went down. Do you think that it will snow again?" Vicenzo asked.

"It snowed night before last and it can very easily snow again tonight."

"The people will have someone to take care of them in the tents?" Vicenzo asked.

"Yes. Was someone hurt?"

"Mrs. Bonacquista is pregnant."

"We should have brought her to town with us. We will do that tomorrow. There is no doctor there."

"What happened in the other camps?"

"In Valdez the guards tried to stop the men from leaving camp. By the time the sheriff got there the fighting had already started."

"There was much shooting?"

"Yes. Two were killed. I don't know how many were injured. Most of the women and children were brought into town before the shooting started. I think the men had planned something. That is why Lewis left the camp at Hastings."

"In Hastings we had no guns," Vicenzo said.

"There were too many women and children. The risk would have been too great and we would have given them more reason to continue shooting. Hastings has had more than its share of grief without adding the lives of women and children to it," Frank said.

"Today could have been a day of massacres."

"There were too many places to be at one time. Lewis went twice into the Primero Canyon because of shooting. The guards tried to remove the bridge that connects Madrid to this side of the canyon. One of them was shot. I don't know if he is alive."

Mrs. Naccarato came in, bringing some heated whiskey and honey. "Drink this," she said. "It will help warm you on the inside."

Vicenzo drank the whiskey slowly and warmth spread through his chest.

"There is no doctor in Hastings?" he asked.

"He was still in the Primero Canyon when we left," Frank said. Vicenzo lay back down and Frank left the room. A cold chill replaced the warmth brought by the whiskey and Vicenzo closed his eyes.

While he rested, Vito came to see Frank. "They are arresting the leaders," he said. "Mrs. Jackson is already in jail. I think that they will come for you also."

Frank sat down in the chair nearest the fireplace. "Come," he told Vito, "and sit. Marietta, bring us a glass of wine."

"I think it is best for you to leave," Vito said.

"Go where?" Frank answered. "My family is here."

"Others have died before in their stinking jail. It is best to go away for a short time until the union bosses can regain control of the situation. Vicenzo and I will stay here and see that nothing happens to your family." Marietta came into the room with the wine.

"I thank you for the concern, but I will stay. Now sit and enjoy the wine," Frank said.

"This is no fight for heroes," Vito said firmly.

"Nor for cowards," Frank answered.

Then the waiting began. Vicenzo slept for a short time, then awoke with a cough. "My chest aches," he told Marietta. She heated some water, mixed it with more whiskey and honey, and gave it to him to drink. He sat a while with Frank and Vito and then returned to lie down.

A short time later someone came to the front door. Frank awakened Vicenzo to tell him that he had to leave. Vicenzo went into the living room with him where two men with badges waited for Frank.

"They seem to know right were you live," Vicenzo told Frank in Italian. "Every time something goes wrong, they come for you. What do they say you've done wrong?"

"They don't have to say anything, just that the sheriff wants to question me."

"Is it about the guard that was killed?" Vicenzo asked.

"It will be about many things that went on today. I expected this. There will be others questioned tonight. You stay here with Vito and watch that nothing happens. In the cupboard in the porch there is a shotgun behind some rags against the wall. If necessary, use it." Then he left.

Marietta had gone through harassment many times but she could never get used to Frank leaving with the men the sheriff sent. When Frank left, she returned to the kitchen. She sat at the table crying, her face buried in her hands.

"It will be all right," Vicenzo said to her, putting his hand upon her back.

"I don't know what they want with him. The more he tries to help people the more the others crucify him." This damnable helplessness, Vicenzo thought, all day long it has haunted me.

"Frank is a strong man," Vito said. "He will be all right."

Outside Frank got into the car that had been sent by the sheriff.

"It's real nice," he told the men he rode with. "Maybe someday I'll buy me one of these."

"You might not live that long," one of the guards said.

"Sometimes I think that I have lived too long already," Frank replied and did not say any more.

The night air grew cold. The windows on the car became fogged so that it was impossible to see outside. The driver kept his window down and had his head half outside. The cold air circulated through the car. The breath of the men poured from their mouths and one said, half to himself. "You damned people could have picked a better time for this strike. I'll have to freeze my tail off more than once before this is ended."

Frank thought of the people he had left that day, shivering in the cold rain and covered with mud from the gully, and here was a well-clothed man complaining of the cold after causing so much misery.

When they arrived downtown the sheriff was waiting for him.

"Sit down," the sheriff said. "I want to ask you some questions." "Some of the men told me that many of the miners left today because they were afraid that something might happen to their families if they refused to strike. What do you know about this?"

"The men are always afraid. Afraid that the mine might explode in their faces. Afraid that a rock might crush them to the ground or afraid that they might return home and find their families sick from the trash that has been thrown in the well that they get their water from because the company won't provide clean drinking water. But out in the sunlight, away from the mine, they don't fear."

"That's not what I'm talking about, so save your pompous speeches for those ignorant peons that you help import here. I'm talking about the Black Hand."

Frank was startled by what the sheriff said. "I don't know anything about the Black Hand. What are you talking about."

"The union and the Black Hand, that's what I'm talking about. And don't try to tell me that you don't know anything about their business either. We know that they were paid by the union to come here and threaten the men into striking, that if they didn't they would be killed."

"I don't know where you got that. The union has nothing to do with the Black Hand. It might look good in the papers in Denver to say that the men have gone on strike because the Black Hand has forced them to, but you and I know better. The only men who have been paid are the guards brought here by the company.

If you did your job and protected the people, you would know that the Black Handers would not be able to threaten them."

"I'm not paid to protect these imports. Now if you don't tell me what you know about the payoff between the union and the Black Hand, then you spend the night in jail. And you might very well stay there until we can prove the union paid them to keep the men from working."

"You will never be able to prove that and you know it. If you wanted me in jail you come up with something better than that. So make your charges and finish, because if you think that I'm going to say anything that did not happen, you're crazy."

"There will be others smarter than you who will admit that they were paid off, and by morning many of the miners will know it too."

"You let that out and you think that many of the men will leave because they fear the Black Hand, and it will be easier to bring in others to take their place. But it won't work. The men know that it is the company who has bought uniforms for their killers. And sooner or later the people in Washington will know too! Then they will send their own men to see what has been going on here."

"Throw the son of a bitch in jail with the rest of them," the sheriff shouted. Two men took Frank by the arms and led him through a large wooden door to the cells in the back of the building. There he saw familiar faces. When the guards were gone, Frank spoke to his friend, the Greek. "It has not been such a good day," he said.

"For some," the Greek answered, "for others it is warm."

"Where is Lewis?" Frank said.

"He has gone for help."

"They did not try to arrest him?"

"Yes, but we were able to delay them until he could leave."

"Who else did they arrest?"

"Mrs. Jackson was taken to the jail in Aguilar."

"That is a worse hole than this one," Frank said.

"Yes," the Greek answered. "I hope that she is alive by morning. She has caused much trouble and they would very much like to get rid of her."

The cell became quiet and Frank thought of the rooms above them. One was the courtroom. The hearing had been held there after the Hastings explosion. That was one side of justice, he thought, and down here is the other side.

During the early morning hours the men were awakened by voices in the outer room.

"It sounds like Lewis," Frank said.

"It's about time he came. My men are sleeping on the frozen ground out there. Where are the tents that he promised if we went along with the strike?" Tikas answered.

"Listen," Frank said.

"You picked a hell of a time to call your strike," the sheriff said.

"Any time would be a good one for a strike that would get the men out of those strinking mines," Lewis answered bitterly.

"It's not so easy for those people to stay out there in the cold tonight. I hear that things aren't going as smoothly as they were supposed to," the sheriff said.

"Things will be all right. Especially when the company isn't making enough money to hire men like you. Then maybe you'll come out there and join us."

"You have business here?" the sheriff asked.

"You're holding several men. I want them released."

"They're not going anywhere."

"What did you charge them with?"

"That's none of your business. Now get the hell out of here before you join them."

"They have a right to be charged with something or you have to let them go, *now*."

"If you need charges, how's conspiracy, or disrupting the peace, or murder?"

"You can't prove any one of those. Those men have the right to a lawyer."

"Those foreigners don't have the right to anything and for half the notion I'd have them deported tonight. Now you get the hell out of here."

"I'm not going anywhere without the men."

"All right then, you can join them." Two men with guns came up behind Lewis and he was thrown in the cell next to the other men.

"You stupid fool," the sheriff called after Lewis. Then they heard the door lock.

"Those tents you said would be at Ludlow, Lewis," the Greek said. "They weren't there."

"I know," Lewis said, "I know."

The Greek paced back and forth like a lion in a cage. "What do we do now?" he finally said. "Without leaders the strike will fall apart."

Lewis was silent.

Frank became nervous watching him. "John," he said, "is there someone in Hastings who knows what to do?"

"It has been taken care of," Lewis answered.

The Greek stopped pacing. "Like the tents?" he asked sarcastically.

"They were on the way. The trains were stopped by the company."

"Then they knew we were going to strike?"

"It wasn't so hard to figure out, especially when you've prepared for something as long as we have," Lewis answered.

"Then we should have been preparing for war. Only a fool does not prepare for war when his enemy does."

"We can't afford a war," Lewis answered. "There are too many women and children who stand between us and the company."

The Greek threw up his hands in disgust. "You will not prevent it by ignoring them," he said.

"We will do no good arguing here," Frank broke in, hoping to stop the words between the two men.

"We will be out by tomorrow," Lewis said. "They cannot hold us here."

"And who is going to tell them this?" Tikas said. "Or is Rockman himself going to volunteer to unlock the door?"

"We will be out tomorrow," Lewis repeated, turning to Frank. "The lawyers from the union are on their way here now."

"The law," Tikas cried out. "The law is out there on the frozen ground."

The next afternoon the men were released. Frank returned home. Tikas returned to the tent colony at Ludlow and Lewis went to see Mrs. Jackson who remained in jail on the trumped-up charge of inciting a riot. Then he went to Denver.

The fall sun again turned warm and the people in the tent colony knew that it was their chance to prepare for winter. Many talked of an Indian summer but watched the sky over the hills carefully. They had lived in Colorado too long to trust a warm day in the fall.

The company posted guards in the hills. On the highest hill, a machine gun was positioned.

The stand-off had begun.

# CHAPTER

# 14

A week after the strike began the tents from Virginia arrived. During the early morning hours the train pulled into the station and sat there until the sun came up over the plain to the east. The Greeks were the first to see it arrive and already they had posted guards around it. Tikas waited until the sun came up before he told Lewis that they had arrived.

"Hey!" he said, pulling on the man's shoulder. "Santa Claus came last night and left us a present."

"What the hell is the matter with you?" Lewis growled.

"Come and look," the Greek said. The two men walked away from the tents and to the train. Tikas slid open one of the doors.

"The tents," Lewis said. "I knew the sons of bitches would get them here."

The Greeks moved slowly in the cold morning air as they unloaded the tents. They were joined by the miners who came from their crowded tents. Word spread through the camp, and soon everyone was either helping to move the tents or seting them up. Vicenzo had moved into the colony the day after Frank returned home. He and Joe also helped with the tents.

"I would like to have half of what we left in the canyon," Joe said as they worked.

Vicenzo stopped for a moment and looked toward the hills. The entrance to the camp had been closed in with barbed wire and several guards stood watch over it. "If there were some way," he said half-aloud.

"You're not getting any ideas of going up there?" Joe asked. "That could start a lot of trouble. Remember what Lewis said about giving them a reason to shoot."

"Yes, but it does not stop you from thinking," Vicenzo said.

The men continued to work. As the sun warmed the air, they moved more quickly. When Frank arrived from Trinidad, half of the tents that had come on the train were up. He talked with the union men for a short time and then went into the tents to see what the people needed most. The rays of the sun evaporated the dew from the shrub brush and the cacti on the plains east of the colony. Little grew on the barren soil but each took what it needed to survive. A small jack rabbit came up from his hole, watched by the vulture that appeared in the clear blue sky. And a coyote stood on the side of one of the hills and looked upon the invasion of his land. No one else had wanted this spot before and now he roamed near, sniffing the air. "It is good the tents have finally arrived," Frank said to Lewis, returning from the hospital tent. "The people will feel much better when they are not so crowded."

"There is still a lot that has not arrived yet," Lewis said, looking out over the growing colony.

"Nothing has come from the northern part of the state?"

"They walked out the day after we did," Lewis answered.

"But they were supposed to wait until we were ready before they went out," Frank said in surprise.

"They had no choice. The guards forced them to go out, knowing that if all the mines went out at once, we would overextend the supplies," Lewis said.

"And so we did, but the company expected the strike to last for only a few days. It will be a big surprise to them that the men will hold out as long as is necessary."

"Yes, they do not know the men very well," Lewis agreed.

"They treated them like animals. Now who will work their stinking mines?" Frank questioned.

"They are planning to bring men from Texas," Lewis said.

Frank turned and looked directly at him. "To work the mines?"

"Yes."

"When?"

"I do not know." Lewis began walking toward the train.

"You do not know?" Frank repeated, hurrying after him.

"It can be as early as next week." Lewis continued to walk.

"That will mean violence! The men will not stand by and watch as others take their jobs. It is like taking bread from their tables."

Lewis did not answer. Frank grabbed him by the arm, forcing him to stop. "Does Tikas know about this?"

"There is little that he does not know."

"And the governor is going to allow the men to enter the state?"

"He will do nothing."

"You said that there were men in Denver who would not allow this to happen. You said that once the stike was successful there would be support from the people in Denver." Frank's face grew red as the words came angrily from his mouth.

"There is little support," Lewis said calmly.

Frank had hoped that when all the mines were closed the governor would realize enough men could no longer tolerate the ways of the company and they would come and see for himself what had happened. But reality soon returned to him. "You know there will be violence," Frank said, his composure returning.

"We must try and stop it," Lewis said.

"Yes, we must try and stop it," Frank repeated, turning to walk away. He got into his cart and began searching for Vicenzo who continued to work with Joe putting up the last row of tents. When he saw him he moved the cart close to where he was working

"Vicenzo!" he called.

Vicenzo stopped working and looked up. "I am here," he answered, waving his arm.

Frank brought the cart up to the tent. "Are you about finished?" he asked.

"This is the last one." When the tent was up, he got into the cart with Frank who turned it around and headed toward the center of the colony.

"What has happened here, Frank?"

"What do you mean?"

"What has happened to these people? Look at them. Most of them came here looking for the same kind of dream that my father thought was possible in this country. Now they are so far in debt that they will never get out. Now they don't even have a place to live."

"When reality becomes too ugly, people begin to dream, Vicenzo. Do you remember the night at the theater? How the men acted?"

"Yes. They were ready to fight the devil."

"For a dream," Frank said.

"You sound like it was a mistake. What else could they have done?"

"Nothing. Not a damn thing."

Vicenzo sensed the depression in Frank's words. "What has happened?" he asked.

Frank continued to move the cart down the crooked line of tents. "They are going to bring men from Texas to work the mines."

"They cannot do this!" Vicenzo said, becoming aroused. "If the mines are allowed to be worked the strike will be for nothing."

"They will have to be stopped," Frank said.

"Then we will stop them!"

"It is not that simple. If the men try and stop them it will look like we are to blame for any violence that occurs. There will be no help from the state," Frank said, "or from the federal government."

"Then we will do it ourselves!" Vicenzo said. "The hell with the state and the rest of them."

The men arrived at the main tent that had been set up for the organization of the colony into units for protection from a surprise attack. Vicenzo was given a place to sleep in one of the new tents and the job of seeing to it that fresh water was brought from a nearby canyon that was owned by one of the local ranchers. At night he was to keep watch over the hills to the northeast and report any kind of movement. They knew that if more guards were brought in it would be during the night so that the exact number of men the company had would be unknown to the union.

The day passed quickly. By late afternoon, Vicenzo finished moving his things into one of the tents on the outermost row. Joe Bonacquista joined him there, having moved his family nearer to the hospital tent so that if his mother needed anything she would be close to it. Vicenzo was inside the tent when Joe found him. "Hey," he said, sticking his head into the tent, "you need some company?"

"Like you, always," Vicenzo answered. "You are not going to stay with your family?"

"I will do much more for them here. Besides, there is not much room with the younger ones." They began putting Joe's things on the side of the tent with Vicenzo's. There were two others also staying in the tent, and as they moved Joe's trunk in, Vicenzo thought of the room that he had stayed in in New York. There is not so much room in this country, he thought.

When they were finished they went outside. The sun was beginning to fade. Already the sides of the hills were becoming dark and the shadows of the tents were disappearing. The chill in the air ran over Vicenzo's shoulders and he pulled his jacket closer as he and Joe walked along the edge of the colony.

"I am very tired," he said. "It will be easy to sleep tonight."

"Do not sleep too soundly. It would be a good night for the company to try something," Joe said.

"Any night is good for them when they can have someone buried," Vicenzo said.

"Did you know," asked Joe, "that the Greeks left last night? Someone said that they went to stop a shipment of arms coming from Denver."

Vicenzo hesitated, remembering what Frank had said. "More like the men from Texas," he replied.

"Who are these men?" Joe asked.

"Men to work the mines."

"There are too many rumors," Joe said. "It is difficult to know what to believe. If they find the train, there will be a battle."

"That's when we'll know how experienced the Greeks are at carrying on a war. If they are good, then the company will not know who hit them. The northern fields are on strike as are those in the Primero and the Starkville canyons. In all of these places there are men capable of pulling such a raid. If the Greeks are good, the company will not know who to strike at. If they try to strike at all of us, we will have them divided enough so that we can handle them."

Darkness came quickly after the sun set. Other men began coming from the line of tents that ended the colony. They carried old guns that had been used for hunting, and guns that had been stored in basements. The guns had been cleaned and oiled and now the men put their trust in them.

"This is where the fighting goes from the paper to the field," Joe said.

"You sound like you have been sitting in the back rooms with the politicians," Vicenzo remarked. "If the Greeks are found out then it will work against us. If the the newspaper in Trinidad makes the people believe that the violence is caused by the miners and not the company, then they will be against us and the government in Washington will know this."

When he finished talking he realized that he sounded like one of the men he had heard talking at the meetings of the union officials. He had heard words like these, spoken by men who knew the business of striking, so many times that it seemed a natural reaction to what Joe had said. Then he remembered that Joe was one of the men like himself who worked from day to day with his back, and knew little of national sentiment.

"Excuse me, my friend. I do not mean to sound like someone who has authority. I have heard too many things of unions and companies and of what we should and should not do. Somewhere in the middle of all of this," Vicenzo paused and moved his hand across the colony, "are the people. When we came here we did so with honesty and sincerity and we thought that we would be treated the same way. But things are no different here, and there is no reason why they should be."

"Donna you worry, we doa all right," Joe said in English. "Comma, let's go anda getta something to eat."

They returned to the tent and, after eating, they played cards with the two others staying in the tent with them. Suddenly the sound of movement outside the tent halted the game. The men froze, waiting for some definite sound that something was wrong. The sound came again. They scrambled for their guns, moving with caution.

Vicenzo and Joe crept around the back part of the tent while the others made their way to the other men in the colony. In the quiet air Vicenzo could feel the presence of others moving about but he could not see anyone. He waited patiently, knowing that if shots were fired they must not be in the direction of the tents.

A crouched figure moved past the first line of tents. Vicenzo and Joe moved with him. They reached the outermost tent and waited again. When the figure came closer, the two moved against him. Joe took him to the ground and Vicenzo shoved a revolver into the man's face. The man struggled and then cried out, "What the hell is the matter with you?"

"You somanabitch, we shoulda killa you right here!" Joe said.

"No, don't shoot. I'm from the camp. I was with the Greeks that left last night."

"Then whata the hell you doing now?" Vicenzo demanded, still holding the gun to his face.

"We are returning to camp. There are others."

Joe let the man up and took him to the main tent where he was identified by Tikas who was already there removing the black from his face.

"Your men were supposed to be good at this," Vicenzo told him. "You should be more careful. This one almost got himself killed." Joe and Vicenzo returned to the tent and waited.

For the next hour the Greeks crept into the colony. "I don't like the men sneaking around out there," Joe said. "It gives me a funny feeling. How do we know the company isn't sneaking guards in with them to cause trouble?"

"Waiting is hard," Vicenzo agreed. "It is like something crawling around inside of you, trying to get out."

Then one of the Greeks joined the men in their tent, bringing a bottle of wine with him. "Here, drink this and have a good time. Let them on the hill hear you," he said.

"The train?" Joe asked.

"They don't get so many bullets as they think," the man answered and left.

"They hit the train," Joe guessed. Vicenzo thought of what Frank told him about the train from Texas but that was too far for them to have returned already. They must have gone to Denver as Joe had said.

During the rest of the night laughter rang out in the colony. The Greeks had dispersed themselves throughout the camp so that it would appear that they had never left. Inside the tent where Vicenzo sat with Joe and the others there was little laughter and the men barely concentrated on the cards in their hands.

"What do you think the company will do when they realize what the Greeks have done?" one of the men asked.

"They will not know which men did it," Joe answered.

"That will not matter," Vicenzo said, "They will think they know and that will make all the difference. In war it is not what the other side can or cannot do that is important, but what they *believe* they can do. If they believe it they will act."

"You think that they will attack tonight?" one of the men asked.

"If the Greeks were as successful as they sound right now, there will be no attack tonight. They will not have the bullets to carry on a fight, especially if they are rushed by the men. If they are smart they will catch us at our disadvantage," Vicenzo said.

"You mean the women and children," Joe said.

Vicenzo looked at him momentarily and then at his cards. The men fell silent again. A short time later the card game broke up and Vicenzo went outside and sat in the cool night air. Sometime during the early morning the Greeks quieted down, Vicenzo still sat staring out into the darkness. There must be something he thought. Every day comes and there is nothing. He thought of Frank and how it would be to have a house in town with his family. Perhaps Carmela would come and he would have the solidness of a home, and she would be there like his mother was when his father came home the day the landlord threatened him.

When morning came there was little movement in the camp. The women did not stir until they were sure that the company would not attack. Many feared that the actions of the Greeks the night before would cause a retaliation.

Before long a group of men from Trinidad arrived. They called for a meeting in the main tent. Lewis was there along with all the representatives of the various nationalities. "It is important that there is as little violence as possible," Lewis said. "Reports are going to Washington that the union is trying to prevent violence, and if this is not true, then we will lose the support that we have worked hard to get."

"They have not seen the machine guns that the company has placed on the hills or the searchlights," Tikas said aloud. "That would convince them of the company's intent."

"You have to set an example for the people," Lewis said. "They respect you and look to you for leadership. They listen to you if you tell them that we're walking a thin line right now. The newspapers in Denver are beginning to help us out, so we can't become careless now."

"It would be a good time to take the machine gun on the hill. The company is low on ammunition," Tikas said.

"We can't do that and you know it," Lewis retorted. "That would give them the chance to bring in every thug from here to Virginia and they would have the excuse they need not to be interfered with by the state. We need the federal troops here and we need them on our side."

"You do not think that they would come to help us?" Tikas asked sarcastically.

"No, but if they come, all the guns will be taken away, including the one on the hill." Tikas became silent.

"I want you to make sure that the men understand that it is necessary for us to avoid any acts of violence. The company needs time to act now, and if we can get the attention of the governor it might be the break that we have been working for."

"There is still one other thing," Tikas broke in again. "There are men coming from Texas to work the mines. We cannot allow this."

"When and if that time comes, we will deal with it," Lewis answered.

The sound of a train disrupted the meeting. The men left the tent and saw a train coming from the north. It stopped and two men in suits and ties got out and walked over to the first rail car. One of them slid the door open and men began to get out. The men from the camp had seen the train and a number of them gathered on the edge of the tent colony. Word spread quickly through the camp and soon many others joined them.

Lewis hurried over to the train. "These men are here illegally," he said to one of the men in suits. The man made no reply as more men got off the train. "These men are here illegally," Lewis persisted, but he was ignored by the men.

Then a shot rang out and the men stopped getting off the train and turned toward the tents. Tikas stood near them, his rifle pointed at the train. "You must get their attention before they will listen," he said calmly.

"You tell him to put that thing away or there is going to be trouble," one of the suited men said. Then he pointed to the hills. Lewis looked and saw a line of guards coming from the canyon.

"If there is any more shooting the gun will open fire," the man finished, pointing to the machine gun.

"It seems that you do not know when you are at a disadvantage," Tikas said, pointing his rifle at the man, as the other Greeks came in behind him.

"Come into the car," one of the men said to Lewis. "We'd better talk before the shooting starts."

"All right," Lewis answered, "but you better keep that damn thing quiet."

"And you make sure that those men don't get trigger-happy," the man answered.

Lewis went into the train with the two men. Vicenzo joined Frank as many people gathered near the train.

"We did not expect them so soon," Frank commented.

"Those two men, they look familiar," said Vicenzo.

"They are the same who were at Hastings the day of the explosion," Frank answered.

"The people have been waiting to take revenge," Vicenzo said. "I can see it in their eyes. Since the day the mine exploded they have been waiting."

"The men in those cars could give them what they have been waiting for."

As Frank spoke, a voice came from the crowd. "Send the sons of bitches back where they came from!"

"Yeah, they have no business here," another voice said. A low rumble started and Frank went quickly over to the miners.

"Go back to the tents! We will handle this," he told them, but they did not move. "It is best not to be here in the open. Go back to the tents." Still they did not move. More and more men came from the tents. The crowd grew larger and the rumble grew louder. A car came into the camp. The crowd quieted and turned to look as the sheriff got out. Frank made a path through the people to get to the car.

"What's going on here?" the sheriff asked him.

"Lewis is inside with Osborn. They have sent men on the train." The sheriff paid little attention to what Frank was saying. He walked through the crowd to the railroad car and went in. Many of the men from Texas returned to the railcars and sat waiting for orders from Osborn. The company guards now stood outside the tent colony.

The crowd grew impatient and some of the people began throwing things at the cars. Frank called out to them again. "It will do no good to show violence while the men are inside. It will only give the guards on the hill the chance to use their guns," he said.

A woman called out, "These scabs have no business here! We must protect our homes and our families."

"Then protect your families and go back to the tents! You will do no good out here. Don't give them the chance to use their guns. See," he said, pointing to the hill, "they are waiting to use them." The people stopped throwing rocks but began to talk among themselves again.

"When the men are let out of the cars there will be violence," Frank said to Vicenzo.

"There is little that anyone can do now," Vicenzo answered. "The cards have been played."

The men in the railcar finished talking. Lewis came out first. He stopped and said to the people, "You must return to the tents."

"We are not going to give them our jobs!" A voice came from the crowd. "You want us to turn our backs like cowards while they take the food from our tables!" Lewis walked on without answering.

Frank ran up to him and stopped him.

"We have to tell these people something or they are going to take things into their own hands.

Lewis looked nervously at Frank. "Help me get them back into the tents." Frank read his eyes. "They will fire on the tents," he said in a desperate whisper.

Lewis gave one quick nod and began walking again. Frank walked beside him. The guards who were positioned on the outskirts of the camp began moving in the direction of the train. When the people saw them they stopped following Lewis.

Shouts arose from the men and many of the women picked up stones and began running back in the direction of the train.

"We've been tricked," Tikas called out. The Greeks broke into a run toward the tents. When the women reached the Texans they started throwing the stones at them. "Scabs, maggots, thieves," they shouted.

The Texans scrambled for protection. Some crawled under the train and others jumped back into the railcars and pulled the doors shut.

"Cut them off!" Tikas shouted to his men, pointing to the company guards who by now had their rifles and were taking their positions.

Frank tried to get the woman back to the tents. He grabbed one and said, "Your children need you in the tents. Tell the others there is going to be shooting and the children are in the tents." The woman turned and ran and some of the others followed.

Vicenzo had gone to get his gun. Now he followed the Greeks. The machine gun fired down into the camp. The bullets left a ragged trail of dust through the dirt street. The Greeks responded by falling into cover, some of them returning the fire. Then more shots tore through the streets. Silence followed.

The company guards were trapped in the open. They had entered the colony and had come a short distance when the firing started. Now the Greeks had them surrounded and they stood helplessly, looking in all directions.

"Don't move," Tikas shouted to them. "You move and you're dead."

Osborn came from the train with the other man. Lewis hurried to meet them. "If anyone in the tents is hurt by that damn thing, you'll die with them." Lewis said, clutching his rifle.

"I told you that the Texans are going into the camp. If anyone is killed it's your fault," Osborn said, pointing to Lewis. Then he walked back to the train. The machine gun opened fire again, spraying the street and ripping a few tents. The Greeks answered the shots and several of the guards fell. The rest of them ran toward the plain. The machine gun continued, forcing the Greeks to take cover along the edge of the colony. The blasts came again and again, directed at the Greeks. The bullets did not go into the tents where the women huddled with their children.

Frank ran toward the train and went into the railcar where Osborn had gone. "You stop that machine gun!" Frank yelled, breaking into the car. "Or you will die here."

Osborn looked at him as he squeezed the gun he held, "You kill me and this gun will cut the tents to shreds," he said calmly.

"Come on," Frank said. "Then you'll be the first." Osborn went with Frank. Outside, the shotting had stopped. Frank and Osborn walked to the edge of the colony where both the Greeks and the company guards could hear them.

"Tell them to stop," Frank said.

Osborn waved his hands to the men on the hill. "They won't shoot unless someone starts shooting here. If they do, it will be at the tents. The men from Texas are going to the camp," he continued.

Back at the train the man who had come with Osborn started opening the doors to the railcars and the Texans moved toward the canyon.

"Louie!" Lewis called out. "Louie! Tell your men not to shoot." Tikas came toward Lewis. "They will fire at the tents so tell your men not to shoot!" Lewis said.

"You tie our hands and they will hang us," Tikas said.

"There is no choice," Lewis answered.

"We have them all in one place. Now is the time to stop them."

Osborn looked at Lewis. Lewis turned. "You will not fight the men," he said. "You stinking coward. Let the Texans through," he said to Tikas. Osborn turned to go to the train. "You dirty bastard. There could have been blood shed all over this stinking plain today and you wouldn't give a goddamn. People mean nothing to you, you goddamn animal! You've killed them in those damn mines but you're not going to kill them in their homes," Lewis called after him. Osborn continued to walk away.

"Save your words," Tikas said. "They are worth nothing." Lewis looked at the Greek. The two forces tore at him like wild stallions pulling in opposite directions. The look on the Greek's face called him traitor and it cut him deeply. The helplessness that comes with exhaustion hung heavily upon his shoulders.

Osborn began to lead the Texans through the tents. Then he and his men were stopped by the Greek.

"These men have been paid to come here to do a job and they are not going anywhere until they get the work done," Osborn said.

"Then they are going to have to go through me and my men," Tikas said.

"That's enough!" Lewis said. "I won't have you two playing with the lives of the people." Lewis moved toward them and the Greeks begrudgingly opened a path for the Texans.

"Scabs!" one woman called out. "You would take the food out of the mouths of babes and put it into your own."

"Scabs! Scabs! Scabs!" the people began to chant. Several threw mudballs. One struck a man in the face.

"Scum, you have crawled out from hell to come here to see us starve!"

The hatred spilled out like blood from an open wound.

"You will never cover the sores that this company has caused. They will bleed you to death, like they had bled us. May your souls burn while you are yet alive."

When the Texans reached the entrance to the canyon the company guards moved them quickly.

Lewis returned to the tents where he and the other union bosses met with leaders of the men.

"Politics have failed," Tikas told them. "It is time to start using our knowledge of these canyons to our advantage." His green eyes flashed as he spoke. It was time for leaders to begin preparing the men and there was not a more impressive war leader in any of the camps. His black hair and olive skin gave him the appearance of an ancient warrior who had fought in defense of Athens and now stood on American soil. He spoke softly but with force.

"If we cannot fight them here we will go into the canyon where the women and children cannot be harmed. We must act tonight and take the positions nearest the portholes to prevent anyone from entering the mines. The miners will draw the fire from the machine gun away from the colony. We will take the hill if we can get behind it."

"You will be on company property," Lewis said.

"It is better to fight the enemy on his soil than on ours," Tikas answered. "I am going as soon as I talk with my men. You make sure that the men keep the machine gun busy," he told Lewis.

Vicenzo watched as the other Greeks organized themselves into units and then left for the camp. They headed south of the camp and into the smaller canyons. From there they would approach the portholes to the Hastings and Delagua mines. When they had gone, Lewis began preparing the other men in the camp for the battle with the machine gun. Vicenzo was given a rifle and told that he would be one of the men who would disperse on the plain leading to Watertank Hill and come in around the gun. Then they waited in the tents on the edge of the colony for the sound of gunfire from the canyon.

Vicenzo sat in his tent, cleaning the rifle and practicing inserting the bullets.

The Greeks made their way slowly through the canyons. When they reached the hills overlooking the camp they crawled to the side where they could watch the porthole. There was little movement in the camp and only the guards could be seen. The men from Texas had been put into the company buildings and the Greeks knew that many of them were armed.

Tikas looked at the camp closely. I will not give the order to fire until most of them are outside, he thought. Then we will scatter them. If any enter the mine, we will dynamite it and seal them inside.

The sun began to set and a cold chill permeated the air. The men on the hill looked like dark shadows to Vicenzo.

Frank returned to the colony just before nightfall. He went first to the main tent and then to Vicenzo's tent.

"Here," he said, handing Vicenzo a box of shells.

"Where did you get them?"

"I loaded them," Frank answered. "Has there been any more shooting?"

"No."

"Word has been sent to Trinidad that today's shooting may bring the federal troops."

"We have heard this before," answered Vicenzo. "If they do not come too late." A shot echoed from the canyon and the men quickly went outside. Vicenzo waited for the signal to move to the plain. The order did not come. "Why does he wait?" Vicenzo wondered.

"The shot was isolated. Someone got careless. We do not want to act prematurely." The men moved back into the tent.

There was little movement in the camp or on the hill. The men sat and waited.

It is too quiet, Vicenzo thought. It would be easier if it came and ended. More shots cut through the night and he was on his feet.

"It's started," Frank said. "You watch yourself tonight. Draw the fire away from the tents, but don't be stupid."

"Are you staying here tonight?" Vicenzo asked Frank.

"I'll be at the main tent."

"What about Marietta?"

"She is cared for. She understands that I must be here now." He hurried back to the main tent and Vicenzo joined the men who started out onto the plain. Several fired at the hill and the machine gun responded. They headed away from the hill so that the guards would fire away from the tents.

Vicenzo ran a short distance. Again the machine gun opened fire. He threw himself to the ground. A light from the hill cut through the darkness and swept over the plain. The bullets followed it. When it passed, the miners returned the fire. They could not see any part of the top of the hill but they fired anyway. Other men fired from the west of the camp and soon the machine gun fired in one direction and then the other.

Farther up the canyon the shooting became intense. The company had positioned machine guns and lights near the entrance of each mine. Before they attempted to get the men into the mine they opened fire on the Greeks. The light came a few seconds before the fire and they only had time to look up into the blinding beam before the bullets came. For one of the men his reaction was too late and he fell to the ground. The others scattered to closer positions.

The miners directed their fire in the direction of the lights; they could see no definite target to shoot at. Shapes began moving between the mining office and the electric house. They attracted the shots of the miners and soon their progress was halted. Two lay on the ground. The machine guns sprayed the hills and the shots from the miners stopped. Inside the electric house the Texans refused to go to the mine.

"You bastards were paid to work and you're going to work if we have to turn the guns on *you!*" the company man with them shouted.

"Then you will die with us," one of the Texans said. "We are workers, not militia. We did not come here to get killed."

"You were paid your first wages before you came, and you owe the company your first day's wages. Now get the hell out of here and into the mines."

"You have had your first day's work. Today out on the plain when we were spat upon for coming to your damned mine."

Another Texan grabbed the company man and began to push him toward the door. "You want the coal dug, you go dig it yourself!" he said.

"You bastards will pay for this. I hope to hell that the scum out there kill all of you."

The man took off, running in the direction of the mining office. Shots followed him.

Inside the office he met several of the other officials.

"They won't work!" he told them.

"The hell they won't," Osborn said. "They have been paid."

"They don't give a damn about that. You go over there, and you better be preapred to fight them."

Osborn thought for a moment and then said, "Then there is only one thing left to do. Get word to the men on the hill. Tell them to shoot into the tents. If we can get the miners to stop firing, the Texans will go to work. Tell the men at Ludlow to spray the tents good so that it will get those damned Greeks away from the mine shafts."

At Ludlow, Vicenzo lay hidden behind a small mound of dirt. The old rifle he had been given was wrapped inside his jacket to keep off the moisture of the night. Again shots rang out and he listened for them to hit so that he could tell in what direction they had been fired. He did not hear them hit. He thought for a moment that the guards had directed their fire to the other end of the hill. But the shots continued. A cold feeling crept over him. He listened for more. The shots came at regular intervals. He thought of Frank and the tents.

"Joe," he called out in a loud whisper, "Joe, the shots. They are not at us. Shoot at the hill."

The two opened fire at the hill and the light passed quickly to them. Then shots came, but it was not the shots of the machine gun. Those continued but it was not at the men.

"The tents," Vicenzo called out to Joe. "They're shooting at the tents!"

The women had placed the children in the corner of the hospital tent where they had gone to sleep. Most of the supplies were also in this tent so that the children and the sick would be given first use of them.

The women had begun to pray when the shots first rang out. They had finished saying the rosary when the first of the bullets tore through the canvas. They ran for the children. The first to die was a boy of eight. The next was a woman who took a bullet between her shoulder blades. She fell face down among the tables and chairs that had been knocked over when the women ran to the children.

When the men arrived from the plain, three were dead and two wounded. The men moved the women and children into some of the other tents.

Vicenzo and Joe entered the colony and immediately went to the hospital tent. In the darkness Vicenzo could not see what had happened. "Frank," he called out. "Frank?"

"I am here," came a voice from the darkness.

Vicenzo hurried over to him.

"The men did not take the hill?" Frank asked.

"When we heard the shots hit the tents, we came," Vicenzo answered.

"That was their chance to take the hill!" Frank said in angry surprise. "You must go to the end of the colony where the road from the canyon enters the colony."

"What happened in the camp?"

"The company could not get the Texans to work. Now it is war. Three have been killed already. Keep the guards from rushing the tents." Frank continued moving the women into other tents, again leaving Vicenzo alone. Joe had gone to look for his mother so Vicenzo started looking about the camp for the other miners. He came across one who was running through the streets and said, "We musta go to the roada. The guards willa try to destroy the colony and we musta stopa them."

The man looked at him dumbly and when Vicenzo turned him loose he ran in the direction of the hospital tent.

Vicenzo ran to the road where Lewis had gathered many of the men from the plain. They positioned themselves on both sides of the road to ambush the guards, should they come from the canyon. The gun on the hill had stopped firing and silence fell over the plain. Cries of fear and anguish rose from the tents and isolated shots came from the canyon.

In the tents Frank and some of the others were digging cellars so that there would be protection from the bullets should they start again. They worked quickly, pushing shovels into the earth and piling the dirt alongside the tent. They moved like machines, silently.

A half-hour after they had begun digging, one of the Greeks entered. "Where is Lewis?" he asked. The men stopped digging and moved toward him.

"Who wants to know?" Frank challenged.

"Tikas sent me," the man answered.

"And what do you want with Lewis?"

"I have a message from Tikas."

"And what is the message?" Frank said, getting close enough to see the man's face.

"You are wasting time! I must find Lewis."

"I will take you to him. Keep digging," Frank told the men. He quickly left the tent with the Greek. The two moved between the tents and toward the road where they found Lewis.

The Greek spoke. "Tikas says that the guards are trapped in the canyon and that you should take the hill."

Lewis looked toward the hill, but from where he stood he could not see the gun.

"Can you trust this man?" Frank asked.

"I have seen him with the Greeks many times," Lewis answered.

"You must act quickly," the Greek said. "It is difficult to see what we are shooting at and we do not know how long we can keep them there."

Lewis passed the word to the men that they should divide themselves as they had during the first attack. They moved from the road toward the hill.

Frank returned to the tent with the Greek. "I was afraid it was a trap," he said.

"It is better to be safe," the Greek answered. "If the gun starts again it will be at the tents. Tell Tikas that they have fired on the tents."

"They cannot fire much more. They have not received any ammunition," the Greek said, and left. He knows about the train, Frank thought. I hope he was with the Greeks.

Out on the plain the men moved toward the hill. Again the search-light swept the plain. The machine gun fired but this time the bullets did not strike the ground. In the colony, the tents were torn by the bullets which centered in on the main and hospital tents. The men inside scattered for protection. Several of them ran outside.

Frank lay on the cold ground, waiting for more shots. Several hit the tent next to him and the ground outside. The words of the Greek flashed into Frank's head. "The only scourge worse than war is not to prepare for it." He thought of Marietta. "Pray for us." he whispered. "Pray for all of us."

Out on the plain the men realized that they were no longer being fired at. Lewis and some of the men ran up the hill. When they reached the top, they fired at the machine gun. The two men nearest the gun fell. The other two backed away with their hands up.

"Take their guns," Lewis ordered. He walked over to the machine gun and pushed it over with his foot.

Vicenzo and Joe reached the top of the hill a short time after Lewis. "Whata willa we do witha them?" Vicenzo asked. The miners looked at the guards. Lewis did not answer. "Iffa we take them back, the court willa let thema go."

"There were women and children hit in the camp tonight," one of the miners said. "If we kill them no one will know."

Shots echoed from the canyon. "The fighting continues in the camp," Lewis said to one of the men. "Go down through the colony and to the canyon behind Hastings and get word to Tikas that the gun has been taken."

When the messenger ran through the camp he stopped at the main tent. "The gun is stopped," he said breathlessly. "The hill has been taken." The men threw down their shovels.

"We will finish," Frank said. The men looked at him without understanding. "We will finish the cellars," he repeated starting to dig again. The others picked up their shovels and also began to dig again.

When morning came the holes in the ground were deep enough to enter. The men sat eating bread and cheese. Some of the men from the hill came toward the colony, carrying the machine gun. Others remained to make sure the guards would not bring another. Vicenzo walked wearily to his tent, washed his face in cold water, and rested for a moment. Then he left to search for Frank.

The sound of muffled crying came from one of the tents and Vicenzo walked in the direction of it. If there is something wrong, Frank will be nearby, he thought. When he got near the sound he halted. The crying had stopped and a moaning sound like that of a woman who could no longer cry came from the tent. Vicenzo neared the tent; he had heard the sound before. A burning began in his stomach and moved into his throat as though he had swallowed a piece of coke from the ovens. He went toward the entrance of the tent but was stopped.

"You are the father?" the man asked.

"No. I comma froma the hill."

"Do you know what happened here last night?"

Vicenzo stood silent. The man motioned toward the tent. Vicenzo moved the flap of the tent and saw the woman he had heard. She sat rocking back and forth as gently as a breeze sways the branches of a tree. Her eyes were shut and her arms were wrapped around the small boy in her lap. Vicenzo let the tent flap fall as he felt the fatigue of the night before begin to drain him of all energy. "The stakes are too high," he said in Italian.

"Do you know her?" the man asked. Vicenzo did not answer but walked in the direction of the main tent. His feet felt heavy and his shoulders sagged.

Frank's voice came from the main tent. "We did not want to think that they would fire on the tents," he said. "But we knew that they would."

"You should rest," Lewis said. "The gun is finished and the guards are pinned in the camp."

"What happens now?"

"I don't know. One miner was killed, that's four all together. I must get to Trinidad and let the papers know what has happened. The company will try to cover up the truth so I must act quickly," Lewis replied.

"Will there be more guards sent?"

"Not this time. The governor will have to listen now." Lewis spoke in disgust of what price had to be paid before they would listen to him. On his way out of the tent Lewis passed Vicenzo.

"How many were killed last night?" Vicenzo asked as he entered the tent.

"Four. Three in the colony and one on the plain. I don't know how many in the camp." Vicenzo tooked at the lines on Frank's face. Dirt had caked at the ends of his mouth and his eyes were bloodshot. "You should rest," he said.

"And you too, my friend. I think that we can rest for a short time, but there is still much work to do."

Vicenzo shook his head and left for his own tent. A chill again passed over his body but he was too tired to care.

The tent colony was quiet except for the crying that came out of the tent where the bodies had been placed.

In the camp a white flag appeared from the mule barn where the men from Texas has spent the night.

"Don't shoot, we are coming out," came a voice from the barn.

Tikas answered them. "Throw out your weapons before you come out."

"We do not have any weapons." Then the first appeared. "We do not want to fight you, only to return to Texas," the man said.

"You better talk that over with the company that paid you to come here," Tikas said.

"Then let me leave here and I will."

The man came out warily but the miners did not shoot. He went into the main office and disappeared inside. After a short time he returned to the mule barn and called out to Tikas, "They will not let us leave but we will not work. We want to return to where our belongings are. We will not work, so don't shoot."

"Are you going to believe them?" one of the men with Tikas asked.

"I don't think they will work," he replied.

"After what has happened you are going to let them return to the company houses? They will give them guns and they will fight us."

"They have no guns to give them and they will not fight unless we force them to. If they wanted to fight they could have last night."

The Texans started moving up the hill to the company homes. Before they could reach them the machine gun fired at them and they scattered for shelter.

"They are trapped in the middle now. There is nothing they can do but wait for one of the sides to give out," Tikas said.

The morning passed quickly. The guards did not come from the company buildings and the Greeks sat patiently and waited for them. In the colony each minute passed painfully. Inside the hospital tent the bodies of two children and one woman lay upon tables with sheets over them.

The mothers of the children sat motionless near the table; one staring at the table and the other with her head on her arm. Outside the tent the husband of the dead woman walked back and forth, crazed with rage.

"They are destroying us. They are tearing us apart like wild animals. We cannot fight the devil. We will all die like my wife did." The man broke down and cried.

Lewis returned to the colony by early afternoon. Vicenzo returned to the main tent, where Lewis was talking to the other men.

"They will listen now," Lewis said. "They realize what we have been fighting and they will send troops. I will be back as soon as I can. I'm going up into the canyon to see Osborn. If I have to drag him here he's going to come." Then he left.

Frank saw Vicenzo at the entrance of the tent.

"What are we to do now?" Vicenzo asked.

"Nothing for tonight. The women and children will stay in the tents with the cellars."

"There will be more fighting?"

"If there is, we must be ready. I don't know when the federal troops will arrive."

"And today?"

"I do not know about today but we must be ready."

Vicenzo did not move.

"Go to the springs and bring more water. We used most of it last night. Take someone with you and bring as much as you can," Frank said.

Vicenzo did as Frank asked.

As Lewis moved toward the mining camp he could hear isolated shots coming from the hills. The company had run low on ammunition and was keeping the machine guns quiet, expecting the Greeks to rush the buildings. This Tikas knew was not possible for too many men would be cut down by the machine guns.

When Lewis neared the camp he called out, "Hold your fire, Tikas." Silence came over the camp. "Tikas! Hold your fire! I'm going to the office!"

"Get the hell out of here!" came the reply from the hills. "They'll cut you down."

"I'm going to talk to Osborn. Osborn! Can you hear me?"

"I can hear you, Lewis."

"I'm coming in. I don't have any weapons with me," Lewis said, continuing toward the main office.

"Stupid bastard," Tikas said. "Be ready to cover him," he ordered his men a few minutes later when Lewis came out of the office.

"Osborn has refused to come out," Lewis said, wiping his mouth of blood.

"You fought him," Tikas said.

"He would not fight. He had two of his henchmen throw me out of the office. How many men were killed in the camp last night?"

"Three guards. We lost two men. Five were wounded."

"What about the Texans?"

"Two of them were killed. I don't think we will have any more trouble with them. They left the machine shop early this morning carrying white flags. They have asked to leave in peace."

"Osborn will not let them go," Lewis said.

"He has no choice. He'll have to kill them or let them go. It does not matter now. We will clean out that devil's den once and for all."

"By tonight the government troops will be here to put an end to this insanity."

"There will be no end until the deaths of the children have been paid for," Tikas declared. "I have heard what happened in the colony."

"There will be no more fighting," Lewis said.

"There will be no more fighting when the company learns that the more killers they send the more they will bury," Tikas answered.

"Do you know what's in the hospital tent?" Lewis asked.

"I have heard. It is they who have done this," he said, pointing to the company office.

"And we cannot afford to have it happen again. If we kill the guards that are here, they will send more and more. There will be no end to them. Our only hope is to have the federal troops disarm the guards. I have contacted the papers in Trinidad and Denver. The governor will not be able to ignore them. The whole country will know what has happened."

"These damnable games," the Greek declared. "All they are good for is to give those bastards up there a chance to put us in a position where we cannot fight while the women are being slaughtered."

"You do not realize yet what is happening here." Lewis said, turning in anger. "We have no friends here who can help us, and if we try to get rid of those guards ourselves the results will be the same. Look at the guns your men have. They are nothing compared with the guns that Rockman's money can buy, and soon there will be more trains with more ammunition. You cannot split your men up, some to stay here and some to go stop another train. What do you think will happen while you are gone?"

"There must be suffering if there will ever be a change in these camps," the Greeks retorted. "If your federal troops come, they will take away the guns and the men will have to return to the mines where they will die. I would rather die fighting in the sunlight than down in those stinking holes."

"The federal troops are coming to take the weapons. The fighting will be over. The company is going to pay for what they have done and you're not going to give them any way out by shooting the men in the camp. They're going to pay this time, and every person in this country is going to know what kind of men run these mines. If we lose this chance we may not get another. Kill those men and the papers will make it look like we caused this fight. The company is getting ready now with every trick they have and you're not going to give them another."

Everything that Lewis said went against what Tikas knew as a military leader.

"I am going to the colony and I don't want your men to ruin our chance to rid this canyon of these murders once and for all." Lewis turned to go back to the colony. He was followed by Tikas. "Where are you going?" Lewis asked.

"I am going with you. I want to see this miracle," he replied.

"What about your men?"

"I will leave them with a leader. He will know what to do."

Back in the colony the men waited for Lewis. The miners on the hill looked down over the plain and saw the colony as the guards had.

"It must have been easy for them," said one of the miners. "All they had to do was point and pull the trigger."

"And they did not miss," another miner said.

"I do not think I like their company," the first man said looking over at them. "You would like it even less if they were alive," the other replied.

A car approached the canyon south of the hill. It stopped. A man with a camera got out. He approached the hill and when he got to the top, he spoke to the men there.

"Hello, gentlemen. I'm from the newspaper in Trinidad," he said. The men did not reply. Suspiciously, they clung to their rifles.

"Were you here when the shooting started?" the newsman asked.

"We were here," one answered slowly.

"What happened?"

The miner hesitated. "We took the hill," he said finally.

"You are from the tents?"

"We are."

"Then you can tell me what happened. The people in Trinidad want to know."

"Perhaps it will be better if you speak to Lewis. He is in charge."

"I have spoken to him already. He sent me to you."

The men said nothing.

"How did the shooting start?" the reporter persisted. Again the men did not answer.

"Look," he said, "the people of Trinidad have a right to know what happened. Surely you all have friends in town. Don't you want them to find out what has happened?"

"They started shooting at the tents," said the miner who had talked first. "Then we rushed the hill. They shot for a while but then they started shooting at the tents again so we returned to the colony to try to protect our families."

"How many were up here?"

"Four," another answered.

"How could they hold off so many men?"

"They had a machine gun. Our guns were no match for it."

"How did you finally get up here?"

"After we went to the tents, Mr. Lewis ordered us to the road that leads to the camp, the one you came up. We waited for the guards to come from the canyon but they did not. Then he ordered us to take the hill."

"How did you make it the second time?"

"The gun did not fire much the second time. I think they were running out of bullets. We did not find many when we got here."

"Where is the gun?" the man asked, looking around.

"It is in the camp. Some of the other men took it there this morning."

"Are those the guards who manned the machine gun?" The newsman pointed to the bodies on the ground.

"That's them," the miner answered.

"I would like to take some pictures of you near them." Again the men did not move. "It will be on the front page of the paper. You men are heroes and you deserve credit for saving the colony. Now why don't you get the credit you deserve?" The newsman moved his camera into position and several of the men stood by the dead guards.

"Lewis should be here," said the man who had done the talking. "I will go get him."

When he disappeared over the ridge of the hill the newsman hurriedly took several more pictures.

In camp, Lewis and Tikas waited inside the main tent for the Federal troops.

"We wanted the hill so bad last night that the men would have been willing to give up their lives for it, but we did not take it soon enough. We should build a cross and erect it where everyone can see it so that no demon can come from hell through that sore on the earth again," Frank said.

"There will be no more guns," Lewis said. "When the federal troops come, all the guns will be taken." Tikas looked at him in disgust. Vicenzo took his rifle and went outside. He walked to the tent where Joe and his family were. Outside the tent, Vicenzo told Joe to give him his gun.

"For what?" Joe asked.

"Lewis says that when the troops come they will take the guns. I am going to take mine to the hills where I can find it later if I need it. I will do the same with yours."

Joe went back into the tent and got his rifle. "It is better to trust no one," he said, handing it to Vicenzo.

Vicenzo hid the guns in the hills not far from the colony. Then he lay under a pinon tree and rested.

Later in the afternoon he was awakened by the sound of a train whistle. He rose quickly and the blood rushed to his head. The dizziness made him take hold of the tree that he had rested under. When he was steady again he looked towards the train coming on the tracks from the north. It moved slowly until it reached the platform next to the colony that had been used to unload the tents. Men in uniforms began getting off but the uniforms were not those of the state militia.

The federal troops, Vicenzo thought, it must be them. Many men had gotten off the train by the time Vicenzo reached the colony. He saw Frank talking to one of the soldiers, a man Vicenzo thought must be of high rank, for his uniform was not like the others. When they parted, Vicenzo approached Frank.

"It looks as though they are here to stay for a while," he said.

"They will be here long enough to stop the violence," Frank responded.

"What will we do now?"

"The fight is over for now, Vicenzo. Look at the number of men they brought. The company would be foolish to try anything now. These men are better equipped than any I have ever seen. I think that not even Rockman has enough money to equip so many men so well. The fighting will be over as long as they are here, and it will be best to cooperate with them. They will collect the guns of both sides. Go tell Tikas to get word to his men at the camp at Hastings. We don't want them to mistake these men for more company guards."

"I will hurry," Vicenzo said and was gone.

Suspicion spread through the colony as the people watched the troops unload their provisions. Their uniforms, tents, guns, and equipment were all better than any they had ever seen. For the Greeks they meant occupation, but for the people there was only the experience of seeing wealth that they had never shared and had come to America to find. For Lewis they were the saviors and the people watched him now as he welcomed the troops he had so often talked about.

The troops looked upon the people of the colony as the foreigners that many Americans had gone to Europe to fight for, and for many of the soldiers this was foreign soil. But they could not help but see the ragged tents, the pieces of furniture that had been broken when the people fled the camp, or the ragged clothing that had been used to protect them from the snow. This was a part of the America they had not known existed on the other side of the great plains.

The troops were busy unloading the train when the miner from the hill entered the camp. He went to the train where he knew he would find Lewis.

"Mr. Lewis," he said as he approached him. Lewis turned. "The man from the newspaper is on the hill taking pictures of the men with the dead guards. I think that he wants your picture with them," he said.

"What newsman?"

"The one who was in the camp this morning."

"There was no newsman here this morning. I talked with them in Trinidad but they were not here. "Which paper was he from?" Lewis asked.

"He did not say."

Lewis began walking in the direction to the hill. He saw Frank and called to him. "Did you talk with a newsman in the colony this morning?"

"No."

"There is one on the hill who says he was here this morning."

"I have not seen one."

"Then we better have a look." The men began moving toward the hill. Before they got very far, they saw a man, carrying a camera, coming down the side of the hill. He moved quickly.

"That is him there," the miner said, pointing.

Frank broke into a run, angling to cut the man off before he reached the car. The newsman too ran, but the tripod on which the camera sat was awkward to carry and he fell.

He scrambled to his feet, leaving the camera. Frank reached the point where the camera lay on the ground just before the man reached the car. Lewis and the miner came hurrying to where Frank stood over the camera. The newsman got into the car and sped down the road.

"Do you know him?" Frank asked Lewis.

"I did not see his face but I know who sent him. He was from the company paper."

"Now another battle begins," Frank said. "They have replaced the gun with another weapon."

"What did he do on the hill?" Lewis asked the miner.

"He took pictures of the men."

"Doing what? Be exact!"

"Standing near the guards."

"And what else?"

"Of the hill and of the colony."

"With the pictures they would know what fortifications we have," Frank said, "but it will not be so important now with the troops in the colony."

"Yes, as long as they are in the colony. What did he say while he was taking pictures?"

"He asked questions."

"What questions? Be specific!"

"He wanted to know what happened last night."

"What did you tell him?"

"That we attacked the hill."

"Is that all?"

"That we attacked after the gun started to fire into the colony."

"Are you sure that is what you told him?"

"Yes."

"What else did you tell him?"

"Nothing. That is all we said."

"But you were not there all of the time that he was. Let's go to the hill."

"They have exhanged the gun for the paper," Frank said, picking up the camera. "This is the kind of battle we have never won against them."

"We cannot afford to loose this time," Lewis answered grimly.

They found the other miners waiting for them on the hill. Lewis asked them the same questions and received the same answers. He gave them instructions that no one was to come to the hill unless they recognized them or received orders from him. He told several of the men to take the dead guards to the edge of the colony where they would be buried. Then he and Frank returned to the colony with the camera. As they approached the train, Tikas met them.

"I am going to the canyon to get my men," Tikas said.

"What are you going to do?" Lewis asked.

"The guards will begin collecting the guns as soon as they finish setting up their tents. I am going to take my men to another canyon. We cannot live without our weapons."

"I don't want any trouble," warned Lewis.

"That is why we cannot stay here. Without weapons we are better off dead." Tikas walked toward the canyon. Lewis and Frank watched him.

"We have a great deal to thank him for," Frank said.

"I know."

During the early afternoon the troops were sent into the colony to search for and confiscate the guns. They were stopped by a funeral procession. Two wooden carts drawn by horses moved up the canyon to Hastings were the cemetery was located. In the first were the two children. The parents rode on the cart and the relatives walked alongside. The other cart bore the bodies of the woman who had also been killed in the hospital tent and the two men who had died on the field. The carts moved up the road slowly and several men, playing the funeral march on worn instruments, followed. The crying of the women combined with the notes in a strange harmony of death. The troops stopped their work to watch the people walk toward the canyon.

"When we got on the train last night I didn't expect this," one of the younger men in a federal uniform said.

"What did you expect?" an older one asked.

"I'm not sure, but it wasn't this. Some of the men said that the miners had taken the law into their own hands and were shooting up the mine property. But we ain't even in the camp here. And those people, did you see the way they looked at us? It was like we were here to destroy them."

"Somebody already tried that. I went into some of the tents with Major Benson before we started setting up the equipment and I sure as hell am glad I wasn't them last night. Some of the miners started digging cellars in the tents for protection but the dirt smelled like newly dug graves. Something's bad here," the older soldier said.

"What do you mean?"

"Did you see those carts? Those weren't all miners that they were carrying. Two of them were children. And I ain't seen anybody being arrested. I ain't even seen the local law. It just don't figure."

At the cemetery the people gathered around the graves. The priest began the prayers. Only the crying broke the still air. The sky was clear and blue and the sun shone brightly but gave little heat.

"I'm sorry for the way the funeral had to be conducted," Frank said to the priest after the funeral.

"Yes, it is unusual to have burial before mass is said," Father Zacardi answered.

"I hope it is not an inconvenience for you to stay tonight, Father."

"Of course not," the priest replied. "The mass will be held in the hospital tent tonight and the rosary after. We will do whatever is necessary."

"It is best this way, Father. We do not know what tomorrow will bring."

"I will see you tonight in the hospital tent," Frank said, turning away.

After he returned to the tents, Frank met with Lewis and Major Benson, the commander of the troops.

"I'm sending a man who can speak the languages of these people with your men, Major Benson, to explain to them that they must give up their weapons," Lewis told him.

"We expect a great deal of mistrust after what we saw in Hastings today, Lewis, and any help that we can get from you will be greatly appreciated," the major responded.

"There will be mistrust, but if the people understand that the company guards will be disarmed also, it will make it easier for them," said Lewis.

"They can be sure they will be. There will be no killing of children while I am here."

They left the tent. The people returning from the funeral were entering the colony. Major Benson watched them as they gathered about the tents.

"Where was the law when the shooting started? Surely the sheriff was aware of the tension between the miners and the company," he said.

"The sheriff did not intervene. Much of the land is owned by Colorado Coal and Fuel. They have their own system of law."

"But this colony is outside their property. Doesn't their property begin at the mouth of the canyon?"

"Yes, where the barbed wire fence begins."

"I don't see why a county sheriff cannot enter the company's property. He should have been here in the colony," the major said.

"Then he would have stood the risk of being killed by the people who pay him," Lewis explained with a grin. "That would have been interesting to see."

"I am begining to see why we have been sent here. We were expecting to go to Europe, but from what I have seen it is better that we end the killing on our own soil first."

"We do not expect a trial. It is better that you stay until their ability to make war on civilians is destroyed."

"You mean there will be no trial?" Major Benson asked, in surprise.

"We have been in court before. We stand no chance there. Who are they going to put in jail? The guards? The company bosses? Or maybe Rockman himself? No, in court we stand less of a chance than we do here." They continued to walk in the direction of the hospital tent where the people were making preparations for the mass to be held that night.

"Your men brought the bodies of the dead guards into the camp. Where did they die?"

"There," Lewis said, pointing to the hill.

"But that is behind the fence, on company property."

"They had the machine gun on that hill. From there they fired into the colony. You cannot fight a war and worry about boundaries once the shooting starts. It is suicide," Lewis said.

"I am going to have the guns collected here and then we'll go to the camp and disarm the men there. If there is any more shooting, we will end it once and for all," the major promised.

Frank and Vicenzo went with Major Benson's troops to collect the guns from the Italian miners. At the first tent, Frank spoke.

"You must give your guns to these men," he told an Italian man outside his tent.

"Who are they?"

"They are from Washington. They are the men sent by the president to protect you."

"Why do they take our guns? Do they not know that we have enemies that will kill us and our families if we have no guns?"

"They are going to take the guns from them also."

"It is very easy for the guards to get more guns. For us there are no more."

"The soldiers are going to stay. If there is any more trouble with the guards they will be here to protect you."

The Italian looked at the men in uniforms who stood a few feet from him. Each soldier had a handgun strapped to his side; each wore a round-brimmed hat and boots that reached nearly to the knee; each wore the brown uniform of a highly organized army.

"Ask him if I can see his gun," the Italian said.

Frank went over to one of the soldiers and talked with him for a moment. Then, after removing the bullets, he handed the miner the gun.

The man turned it over. Then, pointing it in the air, he opened the housing and looked down the barrel. Then he closed the bolt and handed it back to Frank. "I will get my gun," he said, turning to go into his tent. When he came out he had an old rifle with him.

"This gun cannot compare with the weapons that these soldiers have. I have faith in you, Frank. Make sure that these soldiers are not the same animals that the others with uniforms are," he said.

# CHAPTER

# 15

Time passed slowly in the colony the first months after the battle. The miners had learned to hate uniforms and their suspicion of the troops would not die easily. But the guns were gone from the Hill and the federal troops made it a practice that whenever possible their guns were left in their tents. They only carried them when they patroled the outskirts of the colony. The memory of the guards remained in the minds of the people and, like a bad scar, would not be erased by time.

Two days before Easter rumors flew that that the miners would attack the company guards when the federal troops left. The men knew nothing of the plans, but the story circulated among the troops and then to the people. Many of the men laughed but Tikas knew better.

Vicenzo listened and said nothing. He knew the bitter hatred between the miners and the company would not let the guns be silent for much longer.

On Easter the people forgot the mines and the strike. But that night the commander of the federal troops received a telegram: ATTACKS ALONG THE ARIZONA-MEXICO BORDER HAVE RESUMED. STOP. LEAVE COLORADO IMMEDIATELY TO JOIN TROOPS AL-READY PURSUING ENEMY. STOP.

The governor notified General Cooke of the state militia. He moved his men quickly toward the colony so that as soon as the federal troops were out of sight, the position could be reoccupied. Early that morning his men climbed the hill behind Watertank Hill. When the sun came up, General Cooke looked closely at the colony through his field glasses. He did not know if the Greek had somehow received the information concerning the federal troops. He remembered the first attack in the fall and how his men had been trapped by the Greek. Now he looked for any defenses that they might have set up.

Five uniformed horsemen rode down the canyon toward the colony. When they reached the canyon entrance they broke into a run. At first the camp did not respond. Then two miners disappeared into a tent on the outskirts and returned with rifles that they had hidden the day the guns had been collected by the federal troops. Two more men positioned themselves, then another and another. Cooke counted fifteen.

"The lousy Greek is good," he said to himself.

The horsemen continued until they were a short distance from the camp. Then they pulled the reins on their horses, turned them, and headed back in the direction of the hills.

Cooke continued to watch through his glasses while his men set up the machine gun.

"It won't be long now," he said, "and I'll see just how you earned your reputation as sharpshooters. Wait ten minutes and then set off the charges."

Inside the camp one of the miners came running up to Tikas. "Five horsemen came from the canyon," he reported. Tikas was talking on the telephone.

"I'll call you back," he said, hanging up. "Did they enter the camp?" he asked the miner.

"No, they stopped a short distance, then turned around."

"He is testing us," Tikas said. "But it is foolish to let the federal troops see this. They will know that it was he that started the fighting. Come with me. We are going to the federal camp." Tikas, with two men, left the tent and started toward the canyon. They were picked up by Cooke with his glasses.

"The gun is ready. Set the charges off now!" he ordered.

The explosion broke the quiet in the tent colony. Many of the people were just getting up and others were still asleep. Those who were outside turned in the direction of the hill where the blast had come from. The air around it was filled with dirt. Then the dreaded bullets of the sharpshooters tore through the camp. Tikas fell to the ground, bleeding from the shoulder.

"You got him." Cooke shouted.

Tikas lay on the ground. One of the men turned him over.

"Get to the camp," Tikas said. "Get the women and children in the cellars." One man took off running, and the other helped him up. Bullets flew around them as they moved toward the camp.

On the road leading to the colony, Frank moved the cart along slowly. The morning air was cool but he knew it would be warmer by mid-morning. As he and Vicenzo neared the colony, faint shots echoed through the hills.

"Did you hear that?" Frank asked. The two became quiet. Frank stopped the cart.

"They are shots," Vicenzo said. "There are many shots."

Frank started the cart again and they hurried on to the colony.

"They are being attacked!" Vicenzo said, standing up in the cart. "Listen! It is the machine gun!"

"They would not attack with the federal troops here," Frank said.

"I must go to the hills," said Vicenzo, getting out of the cart.

"Where are you going?"

"I have hidden my rifle and Joe's in the hills. I must get them."

Frank watched as Vicenzo ran toward the hills. Lewis is in town, he thought, he must know what is happening. He turned the cart around and struck the horse hard with the reins.

At Ludlow the men struggled to save their families from destruction. Tikas moved about, his shoulder bleeding, directing the people to the tents that had cellars. Bullets filled the air and ripped through the canvas of the tents as the men realized that there were no federal troops to protect them. Their worst fear was that the company men might be allowed into the camp.

"Move quickly!" Tikas ordered the people. "Go to the cellars and stay there until it is safe."

The Greeks quickly retrieved their hidden weapons and took their positions out on the plain between the colony and the hill. They had been told that if the company guards occupied the hill again, they would have to take it from them at any cost. The plan they had was much the same as the first time they had taken it: circle from behind and attack from both sides. One group of Greeks split off from the main group and moved toward the canyon, attempting to reach the hill from behind, but they were stopped by another machine gun that stood at the entrance to the canyon. One of the men attempted to reach a position closer to the hill and was cut down before he could reach it.

The fire from the two guns seemed continuous and the Greeks soon realized that any attempt to rush the hill would be suicidal. Then the guns stopped for a few moments, fired a burst, stopped, and fired again. To the Greeks it was a dare.

This battle was different from the first. It was the guards who were ready this time. The Greeks hid in the small gullies and ravines caused by melting snow. They could not be seen by the guards, but the guns were fired anyway. The Greeks knew the guards would not run short of bullets this time.

A cold realization settled over them as they lay trapped between the colony and the hill. They knew that if the guards attacked they would have to give up their positions for the ravines could be approached from the hills with the machine guns to support them. Isolated shots came from the entrance to the canyon as the company guards joined in the firing. The Greeks did not return the fire. They were too well trained to shoot at something they knew they had no chance of hitting. Word was sent to Tikas of the situation.

"We cannot reach the hill," the messenger told him.

The words brought sudden emotion to the Greek. "What happened?" he asked, trying to bring it under control.

"The machine guns fire without stopping. The men are trapped in the gullies and the others have been stopped from entering the canyon."

Tikas looked around the colony. The people needed someone to tell them what to do, where to go. They are helpless, he thought, and out on the plain my men need me.

"I'm going to try and get in touch with Lewis again. Tell the men to hold out until I can join them. The people cannot be left alone. Tell the men that they must prevent the guards from entering the colony or we are all finished!" he said. The machine gun again sprayed the streets. "Tell the men to shoot *only if they have a target.*" The messenger left quickly.

My men are well trained, Tikas thought as he continued to go from tent to tent, trying to get all of the people to the cellars. But I need more than I have. The others are not trained to fight.

In the hills Vicenzo dug desperately as he listened to the chatter of the machine gun. When he came to the rifles, he brushed them off and took from his pocket a box half full of bullets. He took three out of the box and slid them into the chamber of one of the guns. He aimed at a cactus plant about thirty yards away. I would like to know if you are accurate, he said to the gun. He licked his thumb and ran it over the sight. "Be true," he murmured. "Today you must be true." Vicenzo looked at the camp, still under heavy fire. It was about three hundred yards from where he knelt. The roads have been cut off, he thought. If I try to enter from the road, I will make an easy target. The terrain provided no protection once he left the hills. There were no trees or even large rocks to use as cover. The area was empty except for the union building, about two-thirds of the way from where he was, and then the tracks. The colony looked deserted but bullets continued to leave pieces of canvas flapping in the breeze.

Shots came from the plain between the tents and the hill and Vicenzo knew that the men were once again trying to draw the fire away from the tents.

When the shots of the machine gun were no longer aimed at the colony, Vicenzo ran. He slipped and expected bullets to strike, but none did and he quickly rose and continued. A bullet struck near his feet but it was not the repeated fire of the machine gun and Vicenzo did not worry. He knew that with a rifle a man would have to be an excellent shot to hit him if he ran hard.

When he reached the union office, he took cover behind the wall, breathing heavily. They did not fire the big gun, he thought. But they fire again at the tents, a target that will not return the fire. If only they would put down the rifles and come out to fight with their fists.

When the gun fires at the tents again, I will break, Vicenzo decided. He didn't have to wait long. As he ran to the camp, the sound of exploding bullets reached his ears. A short silence came, followed by the whizzing sound of the bullets again as Vicenzo dove to the ground and began to scramble for the nearest tent. When he reached it the machine gun riddled the canvas with shots.

He began running again toward the hospital tent, using the others for cover and stopping behind one every so often to rest so that when he did run it would be fast enough for the guards not to be able to get a bead on him. He passed other men who were lying on the ground next to tents. They watched as Vicenzo ran by them and into the hospital tent. Tikas sat inside, his shirt sleeve torn to the shoulder. His face was lined with deep wrinkles. Vicenzo could see the change that was taking place inside the Greek leader. His wounds had begun to bleed again and a woman with a red rag tied around her arm stood over him, working quickly to rebandage them.

"Tikas," Vicenzo said.

Tikas turned quickly, the look of exhaustion leaving him as he summoned strength. "What news do you bring?"

"I come to aska where you wanta me to fight." Vicenzo said.

"The train has come from Trinidad?" Tikas asked.

"I come froma the hills," Vicenzo said.

"Lewis has not come from Trinidad?"

"I know ofa no train."

"Lewis was suppose to come from Trinidad with five hundred men," the Greek said. Vicenzo was silent. "We have done nothing for four hours but wait for that damnable gun to cut us to pieces. They set us up. The troops left and the company beat us to the positions and now we are paying for it. Hurry," Tikas said to the woman, "I must return to the field."

The shots of the machine gun cut him off. "Listen," he said to Vicenzo, "you hear those bullets? You hear the way they explode when they hit? That's how you win a war. Half of the bullets we use misfire because they are old. I should have bullets like that. Then I would show those bastards how to fight a war." His face was flushed and he looked directly at Vicenzo. "You're the one who was always with Frank."

"I have been with him often," Vicenzo said.

"You have not been here long but you picked a lousy time to come to this country."

"Hasa there ever been a good time?"

"You sound like you know this place."

"My brother come here before. He wassa no here long and . . .," Vicenzo stopped and the Greek did not pursue it. Instead he asked, "Do you know what is going on out there now?"

"I have fought before."

"My men are lying on their bellies, waiting for the guards to attack," the Greek said, not listening to Vicenzo's answer. "All they can do is try and keep the women and children alive. They are used to attacking an enemy. It's suicide to fight a defensive war and they know it. But now we have no choice."

"What do you wanta me to do?" Vicenzo asked.

"You know something about the train?"

"It did not arrive inna Trinidad thisa morning."

"If it left Denver this morning it is stranded somewhere out there. We could use it if we could get it here," Tikas said, taking hold of a metal poker leaning against the stove. He marked two lines in the dirt floor. "If these are the tracks, the camp is here and the machine gun is mounted here. Most of the fire comes from rifles that are here.

"The Black Hills are here, east of the camp. If we can get the train here between the camp and the hill, we can use it as a barrier against the shots. That will give us time."

"You mean for the troops to come from Trinidad?"

"Time to get the hell out of here," Tikas said, standing up. We cannot rely on what we do not have."

"Whatta you mean? Where you gonna go?"

"The men are short of ammunition. They only fire enough to hold the guards back, but before long there will be no more bullets."

"And ifa the train is nota there?"

"Then we move the people out as soon as it is dark. Come. It is important that we do not waste time. Take three men with you and move quickly up the tracks. If you come to the train, take it any way you can and bring it here. If you are not here by dark, then we start moving the people into the hills."

Vicenzo left the camp with three of Tikas's men. As they moved along the tracks the number of shots increased. Vicenzo paused for a moment to look back toward the colony. The guards were coming from the canyon along the road that led to the camp. Twelve horsemen were in the lead. The Greeks began firing at them and were supported by the miners whose rifles hit far from their targets. Some of the Greeks ran along the bottom of the gullies toward the road. When they reached the end of the gully they ran on the plain to the side of the road. The machine gun followed them with bullets. The guards began to move toward the colony but when the horsemen were forced to turn back, they too retreated.

Tikas had joined the men along the road. He watched as the horses left a trail of dust behind them. "They forced us to use many of our bullets," he said, "and I saw only three horses fall."

In Trinidad, Lewis moved the body of men that he had brought together to form his army. He came close to the five hundred that he had told Tikas he would get, but there were only half as many guns. He moved them out of Trinidad along the tracks in hopes of meeting the train and getting it switched toward Ludlow.

"Move quickly," Lewis told them. "The camp is being destroyed." But the men were not trained to move and fight like the ancient armies of Rome, and their leader was not Caesar who had fought and handled men. Some lost heart and returned to Trinidad. The others continued, but the train did not come.

From the colony, Tikas sent word to the men in the gullies that every other man was to go to the road and the rest were to fall back to the edge of the colony. Then what he feared most began to happen.

"There are some who have very few bullets left," one of his lieutenants told him.

"Tell them to return to the colony and get the people ready to abandon the tents. We will take them to the Black Hills. Make sure that they move quickly but take care that they do not panic." He stopped for a moment, then continued, "If we fail they are all dead, and for us there will be nothing but disgrace and defeat!"

The men quickly began gathering the people near the hospital tent. "We are going to leave camp," they said. The words were repeated in several different languages so. "We are going to the Black Hills where we will organize and move through El Moro and then south into Trinidad. Take nothing with you and *do not stop.* If you do, you will risk your life and the lives of those who travel with you."

"Everything we have is here. If we leave it we will have nothing," one women said, clinging to her child.

"You have your life and it is the only thing that is important now. I cannot guarantee that you will keep it if you do not leave immediately."

Out on the plain the shooting had stopped. Tikas knew that the first attack had two purposes: to see how the men defended the colony and, more important, to make them use bullets. He knew that Cooke watched them from the hills that the next time they attacked the men would have to hold their fire until the guards were much closer.

"Use your bullets wisely," he ordered the men near the road. "Make them come close so that every bullet counts. Time is important. We must keep them away long enough for the women and children to escape. Remember you are Greeks! Your ancestors defended their homes many times.

Now you must do the same." Then he smiled. "You are good men. Do your duty well and you will be remembered."

In the colony the small group of Greeks who had left the main body on the road continued to organize the people. The first group waited inside the hospital tent.

"Go to Tikas and tell him that we are ready to begin moving the people," the man who had been put in charge told another.

Five miles south of Trinidad, Lewis moved with his army at a slow and awkward pace. The men who had developed their legs and arms to dig coal made poor recruits. Their senses had been dulled from their toil in the earth and their bodies would not respond to the order to move swiftly across the plain to the field of battle.

"We must move quickly," Lewis appealed to his troops. "The men cannot hold out long." But he watched as some turned back, with no weapons with which to fight and no words to understand.

"We must have courage," Lewis told them while he walked back and forth along the line of men. "Women and children will be killed if we do not arrive in time. The Greeks cannot hold out much longer. They will run out of bullets soon. They will have no one to protect them from the company guards. Think of your families and those guards who will destroy them next if we do not stop them here. The guards will not be happy with destroying one camp. The others will follow and they will continue until we are all destroyed."

The men continued walking. Some understood what was said but many could not. The sun was beginning to lose its warmth and soon Lewis knew that they would have to follow the outline of the hills. It will be dark in the hills, he thought.

Lewis tried to quicken the pace but the men became strung out along the tracks. He fell back and tried to encourage them again. They moved for a half-hour and then one of the men left the ranks and started back in the direction of Trinidad. Lewis ran back to stop him.

"Where are you going?" he asked as he grabbed the man by the arm. The answer came in another language. "Where are you going?" Lewis repeated.

"He said he is going back to the colony at Cokedale where his family is," another of the men answered. Lewis grabbed the rifle from the man and handed it to one of the men who did not have one.

"Go," Lewis cried, "but we need the rifle. Let's go, we must hurry."
The column began to move again.

The cold, early spring air was settling over the colony. Tikas started
the evacuation to the hills. Moving the people all at once made it impossible
for his men to protect them so he organized them into smaller groups.

"Some of the men have no more bullets," one of his men said, entering
the tent. "They will have to pull back or be shot."

"Have they left their positions?" Tikas asked.

The man answered only with his eyes. The Greek knew that they would
not, until the order was given.

"Tell them to move back to the camp, but it must be done quickly and
smoothly so that the guards do not realize what we are doing."

"There are still some who can fight."

"Tell them to wait for movement from the hill before they use what
they have. The guards will charge as soon as they realize that we cannot
fight." The man left quickly and Tikas again turned to the people.

"You will have to move to the Black Hills. Go quickly and do not stop.
From there we will take you to Trinidad where you will be cared for."

He led the people out of the tent and into the street. They moved quickly
past the tents. Before they reached the edge of the colony the machine gun
began to fire. The bullets struck the canvas of the tents and ripped through
them. Then they struck the streets. Tikas knew that if he could get the
people to the farthest edge of the colony, the machine gun could not reach
them. Then he would only have to fear the guards rushing the colony.

More people were brought to the hospital tent and given instructions
on what to do. When the bullets struck the tent they took shelter in the
cellar. When they too were ready they left the tent and began moving
toward the hills.

Tikas watched as the first group of people moved away from the tents.
It was starting to grow dark and he knew that he must hurry. There was
no hope that the men from Trinidad would arrive in time. Then he went
to the next tent and started moving more people. The second band was
not so lucky as the first. Two fell victim to the machine gun. But the rest
also disappeared into the night. After the third group was moved out,
Tikas stopped.

"They know by now that we are moving them," he told one of his men
who had come from the field, having run out of bullets.

"We cannot draw the fire away from the camp," the man said. "There are not many who have bullets."

"Too many were killed when we moved the last group of people."

The man could see that something had changed in Tikas's face and his his voice. He did not look or sound like the same man who had directed the men on the field of battle.

"We need that train," he said finally.

"What train?"

"The train that we do not have."

"We have no train. There are some cars on the tracks that were used to haul coal, but there is no train."

"Yes. There is no train, and we cannot count on having one. We must continue to move the people out of the camp before there are no bullets."

The Greek went to the next tent with a cellar where the people were waiting. "We must move," he told them and they moved into the night.

Each trip took enough time for the sun to drop farther behind the hills. In the darkness the horsemen came again. The Greeks watched as they came nearer and nearer. When they were within thirty yards, the first of the Greeks fire. A horse stumbled and a man fell to the ground. Then more shots rang out and they were answered by the machine gun. Two more men fell from horses and another was pulled from his when he reached the Greeks. The others turned back toward the hills as the machine gun sprayed the tents.

A cold, insane, subtleness settled over the plain. People huddled in the Black Hills east of the camp, and bodies scurried through the camp trying to avoid the bullets that came like a death rain. Others huddled in the cellars waiting for word to leave. There were these who would never leave. The tents stood like monuments to that animal side of man that will never let him live in peace. Monuments that meant victory for the companies and governments that let loose the savage to vent its hatred. Monuments to the price of civilization. For every pyramid, forum and theatre there was an empty tent torn apart by the thoughts that progressed man to the stars and buried him after competing.

An hour after darkness had come, the train pulled into the Ludlow station. When Tikas saw it he knew what must be done.

"Move the people out of the tents!" he shouted from one of the coal cars. Standing against the dark hills he looked like a giant. "You men with the bullets, line up here along the cars." He directed them under the cars of the train so that when the guards charged they could make a last defense of the colony, and hopefully it would be in defense of empty tents. The people ran from the tents as the men hurried them out onto the plain.

"Here isa the train," Vicenzo said to Tikas, running to him from the now stopped train.

"It is like sun to me. Where did you find it?"

"It wasa ona the tracks. There wasa no one there. One you' men ran it," Vicenzo answered.

"Do you have any bullets?"

"Yes, Thisa halfa box,"

"Take your place under the cars. If you see them coming from the hills, shoot. But be careful with the bullets. They are precious."

Vicenzo ran along the train and then ducked under one of the cars. There were other men there and when he got close to them he asked, "Havea you seen Joe Bonacquista?"

"I do not know him," one answered.

"The machine gun now rattled the sides of the train. They could hear the steel jacket casings striking the metal sides.

"Joe Bonacquista, the one who fights in the camps," Vicenzo persisted, moving along the underside of the car.

"I saw him earlier," one man answered, "back at the tents. He is helping move people to the hills."

"You sure? I want the one who fought in the ring and plays the baseball. The one witha the bigga chest."

Vicenzo ran to the colony as the bullets continued to hit the cars."

You seen Joe Bonacquista?" he asked one of the men who was returning to the tents from the edge of the colony."

"I don't know anybody. They all look the same," the man answered, moving away.

"The one who fights," Vicenzo insisted, grabbing him by the arm.

"He could be anywhere." The man jerked his arm away. "Or he could be dead. You got ammunition for that rifle?" Vicenzo did not have time to answer. The man went on, "We need help getting the people from the tents. If the guards rush the colony, we are all finished. Start looking into the tents. If you see a cellar, go into it, and if there are people, get them moving to the hills."

The man took off running toward the center of the camp. Vicenzo began to walk to the other end of the camp. The streets were littered with things that people had dropped and with the bodies of those who had been killed. There seemed to be many dead but Vicenzo did not look to see who they were. He must do what the man had said. He went into the tents. The first he came to was empty, as were the second and the third. Then he came upon one filled with people. Twelve faces looked toward him.

"You must all come, with me," he said slowly. "You all gotta get outta here."

He could see that they were becoming frightened by his harsh voice. "They no canna understand me," he said aloud. "You musta go to the hills. The guards are going to attacka the camp!" he persisted, motioning to the hills. "You gotta go now," he said, pulling at one of the boys who ran up the steps and out of the tent. The others began to follow him. Soon they had all left the cellar. Vicenzo was afraid that they might go to another tent to hide, but they ran toward the hills and Vicenzo was relieved when he saw them disappear.

A sudden silence covered the camp. Vicenzo listened for bullets but there were none. Then several men ran by him from the direction of the train. There were no people coming from the tents and the only noise that broke the calm was the canvas slapping against itself. They have run out of bullets, Vicenzo thought, or they are waiting for the final charge by the guards.

The silence did not last long. It was broken by a strange scream from the hills the chatter of the machine gun followed.

In the hills outside the camp, Lewis arrived with his men. Their progress was stopped by the guards who had been posted by Cooke to cut off any entry into the camp from the main road.

"We can go into the hills and approach the camp from the west," one of the men that Tikas had sent to Trinidad for help told Lewis.

"We do not know where they are," Lewis responded. "Tikas said that the sharp shooters are somewhere in those hills. If we go in not knowing where they are, they will cut us down before we have a chance. "We must wait until we hear from Tikas. He will know what is the best way to get into the camp."

Inside the colony, Tikas' men prepared their last defense. The first assault came from horesmen who rode down the canyon and then split up and rode around the train and into the colony. Several of the men ran to stop them and they were joined by the others who had been moving the people.

Vicenzo saw them coming from both ends of the train. He fired twice but did not know if anyone fell. Then he saw several of the men taking position next to tents where they could shoot from closer range. The horsemen rode down the streets, cutting at the tents with sabers. Several of the Greeks came from beneath the train to meet them. Shots rang out and one of the guards fell from his horse. One of the Greeks was slashed across the chest.

Tikas sent several more of his men back into the colony to check the tents for any who had not yet left and to send the other men to the Black Hills. The word was passed quickly around the camp and the men began to retreat into the hills. Before Vicenzo could get far, he heard the sound of the machine gun. The fire was answered only by isolated shots and he knew that it would not be long before there would be no resistance at all.

The men at the train also heard the machine gun bullets and they knew immediately that the gun had been moved from the hill closer to the camp, on the ground level. Tikas knew that the charge would come now.

He looked around for any more people in the tents and saw only his men. Small fires began appearing throughout the colony and Tikas knew that they were torches. "They are going to burn the tents," he cried out. "Fire what you have left and make every bullet count. Make them pay with their mothers' hearts for what they have done."

But the men split as did the men who had come on horses. Instead of coming at the Greeks, they too went around the train toward the camp. The machine gun continued its assault upon the train, attempting to keep the Greeks and miners pinned down. When Tikas realized this, he ran to the other side of the train, directing the men to go into the colony.

Two fell before they could get out from under the train but the others ran after the guards, waiting to fire the remainder of their bullets. When he saw the number of men who came from the hills, Tikas knew that Cooke had had time to move the main body of men into the canyon and that the ones who were with him were his selected company thugs, who had been known for their harassment.

As the Greeks shot the last of their ammunition, they pulled out of camp. Tikas looked with bitter hatred at the guards who ran from tent to tent, searching for anything that they could carry away. Several of the tents had been set on fire and the gentle breeze that had cooled the hills spread the flames from tent to tent.

"You filthy scavengers," Tikas shouted. "You do not know how to act like men! You should die like the filth you are." He ran into one of the tents and caught a guard from behind. Grabbing him by the throat, he buried his thumb and fingers in the man's flesh like a steel vise, tighter and tighter. The man gasped and pulled at Tikas's arm. His face grew red. Another guard smashed down the butt end of his rifle upon Tikas's head.

"It's Tikas!" one guard cried out. "Cooke will pay for him, more than we could find here. Help me get him out of here."

The others carried on their plundering. They had been around the camp long enough to hear the rumor that the miners hoarded their money in their mattresses. But the ransackers found little.

Inside the hospital tent fifteen women and children huddled together in the cellar. They listened as the sound of gunshots gradually faded into the distance and. was replaced by the sound of men running near the tent.

"We should leave now," one of the women said.

"What if the men outside the tent are guards?" another asked.

The woman took her small son in her arms. "I think that we should leave. We have been here too long."

Voices came from the tent above them and the women became silent. Several of them held their children close to their bodies to muffle their crying. Above them two guards had entered the tent.

"There is nothing here," one said.

"It's the hospital tent. They stored the supplies here, there must be something," the other answered. Then came the sound of objects being thrown on the floor. Outisde the tent a guard ran his torch against the cold canvas and the noise stopped.

The women fixed their eyes on the earthen steps. A red glow appeared above the entrance to the cellar. More shots came from above. The small underground room grew hot as the flames consumed the canvas and ignited the contents of the tent. The crackling sound of burning canvas became louder as the flames shot high into the air.

"We must leave," one of the women screamed. "They are burning the tent."

"The guards," another answered, "they will shoot if we try to run."

Smoke began to fill the cellar and the women tried to cover the children with their bodies. The flames became hotter. The woman who said they should leave picked up her child and ran up the steps into the burning tent. When she reached the top she began coughing. The smoke filled her lungs and the flames ignited her dress. Her skin burned as she turned, looking in every direction for some way through the flames but they shot up all around her. As the earth became blurred, she fell screaming to the ground.

The smoke continued to pour into the cellar and the air became thick and heavy. The women breathed hard but with each breath their lungs filled with smoke. Then a drowsiness came over them. The red glow above them began to fade into a gray haze. As the children clung to their mothers their limbs suddenly relaxed. But their mothers didn't notice. The cold isolation of death invaded as the coughing and crying faded into clouds of smoke.

In the Black Hills, a messenger from Lewis arrived.

"What has happened?" the man asked.

"We were forced out of the camp," one of the Greeks answered. "There were no more bullets."

"I am to give a message to Tikas. Do you know where he is?"

"He has not yet come from the camp. Have any of you seen him here?" he asked the others.

"I saw him looking in the tents when we began pulling out," another of the soldiers answered.

"You did not see him leave with us?"

"He did not appear to be heading out."

"Then he is still back there."

"We must go back after him."

"With what? There are no more bullets."

Vicenzo was standing with them. He reached into his pocket and took out three bullets. They were all that was left of the half box that he had had. There was one left in the rifle.

"Save them," one of the men said when he saw them. "If they have not amused themselves with the tents, they will come here after us and you will need them." Vicenzo put two of the bullets into the chamber.

"Return to Lewis," said the Greek who had taken charge in Tikas's absence. "Tell him to come here with the men. They can do no good in the camp. There is nothing left."

"But if Tikas was looking, there may still have been people in the tents," the soldier answered.

"And if we leave these people unprotected there will be nothing to stop a massacre. Now go and tell him to come here as quickly as possible. We cannot protect them with what we have."

Tikas's body lay at the feet of Colonel Cooke, the back of his head bleeding from the blow delivered by the guard.

"Get some water," Cooke said. "Bring him to."

When the water hit Tikas he began to move slowly. Before him stood a hazy figure. The high boots worn by Cooke began to be clear.

"Help him up," Cooke said. "I've waited for this, you lousy Greek! You've been poison in my veins for a long time. But you knew those son-of-a-bitchin' federal troops would get the hell out and I knew it too. You should have gotten the hell out of here when you could still hide behind them."

"We don't hide behind anybody," Tikas said, slowly rubbing the back of his neck. "Yes, we knew that the troops would leave, but we knew too that you were lurking in the bushes like the hyena that you are, waiting to attack something that cannot fight back."

"You stinking Greek, you come here and think that you belong here. Trash like you should stay where the hell you belong."

The sound of the burning tents filled the air. Tikas looked around at the blur of flames. He could see the guards running through the streets but they only appeared as shadows.

"Your demons do their work well," he said. Then he opened his eyes wide and looked directly at Cooke. "Well, Lucifer, are you proud of the hell you've created?"

Cooke's right fist caught Tikas on the face. He fell to his knees. "I could kill you now," Cooke said, drawing his pistol.

Tikas looked up, a small stream of blood running from his lip. "You talk big with your guns. Why don't you walk on the streets and see what they have done? Go and look at the women and children you have destroyed. You're a brave man to use your uniform in such a way," he sneered.

"I've rid the country of plenty of scum like you. They had no business here. When the Irish left ten years ago because of this damnable union business, it was the same thing. Then these foreigners came in hordes. It was like someone had swept the sewers of Europe and emptied them. But we'll get rid of them, these Wops and Slavs and Greeks."

"You bastard," Tikas said, staggering to his feet and throwing his body at Cooke. Two of the men grabbed him by the shoulders.

"You will pay. . . ." Before he could finish, Cooke struck him across the mouth. Tikas fell. "For one more bullet," Tikas said, "for one more bullet, I would give my soul."

A new sound rang in the air. "Dynamite," Tikas gasped.

"Yes, dynamite. There will be no bodies in the streets. Then let's see how well your union will be able to prove that we fired on the tents."

Tikas let out a yell and broke the grip the men had on him. He lunged at Cooke. His hands tightened around Cooke's throat as the man fell to the ground. Tikas slammed Cooke's head against the ground, trying to kill him with one blow. Then all went black for him again.

"Kill him!" Cooke ordered, getting to his feet.

The guards, startled by Cooke's outburst, backed away.

"You want bullets! Here! Have them!" Cooke said, taking his pistol from his holster and pointing it at Tikas who lay unconscious on the ground. He fired until the gun was empty. The bullets passed through the body and into the ground. The dirt became red with blood.

Throughout the camp the guards continued their work. The flames from the tents grew hotter. In the hills the people waited for Lewis to arrive. Those who had extra clothing gave it to those who shivered in the night air.

"Everything we had is back there," one woman cried out.

"There is no back there," the man who was in charge told her. "You cannot think of back there," he said, loud enough for all of them to hear him. "There is only one way to move now, to Trinidad. When Lewis arrives we must move as quickly as we can to Trinidad." The thought of the burning tents brought fear to him. He knew that the men who did this were capable of going after them when they were finished in the camp, but Lewis must come soon and bring more men with ammunition.

When most of the tents were ablaze, many of the guards stopped looking for anything of value. Some took rings and watches from the bodies and when they thought there was no more they began to leave. Cooke realized that he could not keep them from deserting.

"Shoot them if they try to leave. Shoot them!" he ordered his lieutenant.

"We can't stop them from leaving. Have you seen what is in the streets?"

"You mean the bodies?"

"Not the bodies of the miners or of the Greeks. The bodies of women and children."

"What's the matter with you? Who the hell did you think were in the tents? Is your stomach too full of shooting and you mind soft from killing?" Cooke roared.

"We can't hide all of them. They will come back and find the bodies. When they do they'll hang us."

"They won't hang anybody," Cooke said. "Put them in the tents and use the dynamite. If we miss one or two, the miners attacked us and we had to defend ourselves. The courts will take care of the rest. We paid them enough."

"It's different this time. There's too many and the men want to get the hell out of here."

"Nobody leaves! The next one who tries gets shot. Get the machine gun and post it in the hills near the south entrance of the colony. Anyone who knows what has happened will come from Trinidad. No one is to be let near the camp." The guard hesitated. "Don't worry about bodies. The courts will clear us, just as they always have."

Lewis finally arrived in the Black Hills. From there, the colony appeared as a faint blurry glow. Smoke rose into the black night.

Lewis organized a defense. "You men stay here," he said, leading them to the bottom of the hill that faced the colony. "If they come it will be from the direction of the colony. If they come, cut them off before they can get close enough to use their rifles." He became aware of a man standing close to him. He turned to see one of the Greeks.

"My men will cover the movement of the people. We will move alongside them at a short distance between them and front range of hills," he said.

"Your men?"

"Tikas did not return from the colony. He was still there when the last men pulled out."

Lewis looked back toward the colony. Tikas had always been there. From the first day that he had come to Colorado, he remembered him. He was half the struggle, the half that gave courage by his strength.

"Yes," Lewis said, "it is a good plan."

The people began moving slowly toward El Moro, a small farming community where Frank and others from Trinidad had brought supplies.

Their eyes adjusted to the dark but walking on the uneven terrain was difficult. Many volcanic rocks lay scattered about the ground and the small gullies left by the water from the melting snow made it easy to turn an ankle.

Lewis knew that the movement of the people must be steady, but he also knew that the women would become exhausted if he pushed them too hard. One woman stopped and tried to get her small son to continue. He sat upon the cold earth crying. Lewis went to them and picked up the boy. He carried him as he walked. Soon many of the men who had come with him did the same.

Darkness surrounded the people as they moved slowly in the night. The air was clear and cold and the stars glistened against the pitch black sky. The men were afraid to light a torch lest the people be seen. The terrain grew increasingly difficult as small hills began to encroach on their path. The area was also full of scrub brush that tore at the flesh. Men who herded cattle here had always worn chaps to protect their legs but there was no such protection for these people. As they passed through the bushes they scattered, trying to avoid what they could. Some moved too far to the east and others stopped to rest. Lewis realized what was happening.

"We must stop," he told several of the men with them. "We must stop and bring them together." The word was passed quickly and the refugees were brought to where Lewis was standing. "Check to see that those who left with you are still here," he said loud enough for all to hear. Voices began breaking out.

"Quietly, you must do this quietly." Voices rose again. They all cannot understand me, he thought.

"There is a stream near here. We can follow it to El Moro. It will take longer but it is safer. You men circle behind and make sure no one gets lost." The people began to move again, over the patches of dried grass and small bushes, away from the scrub brush and hills.

A short distance from El Moro, the people were met by a group of men who had left the Black Hills before Lewis's arrival. With them were those who had left the colony when it became evident the guards were going to attack. One of these men was Joe Bonacquista.

"It's good to see you," Vicenzo told him, "and it is good to hear that your family is safe."

"There are many more who are not. We do not know if there are any left in the camp," Joe said.

"Most of the tents were destroyed by the guards."

"We are going back," Joe said. "There are some from the families who left first who are missing."

"They will kill you if they see you."

"We know this. That is why there will only be a few of us. Some who were very close to me are not here. If they are still alive they will need our help."

"What will you use to fight?"

"Lewis brought ammunition with him. It looks as though the guards will not follow. Some of the men said that they saw the guards looting the tents, so they will not be bothered with us. We will take some of the bullets with us. Will you go?" Joe asked.

Vicenzo looked at Joe's face. Gone was the look of youth that he had had when he fought in the ring or played baseball. Now his face wore the hard expression of a man trying to survive.

"I will go with you," Vicenzo answered.

The men moved back toward the hills. Before they reached the camp the sun began to lighten. The men moved cautiously among the debris. Blackened earth marked that area where the tents had stood. Within the scorched squares were broken dishes, charred metal frames of beds, smoldering mattresses. Most of the fires had gone out during the night. Some of the men turned over the bodies that lay in the streets, searching for Tikas. All of them looked toward the hills for the guards they expected to see when they neared the colony.

"Vicenzo," Joe called. Vicenzo looked to where Joe knelt over the body of a small child. "I know this boy," Joe said, picking him up in his arms. "He's my cousin."

Vicenzo looked around the devastated area. There was something about the row of tents that seemed familiar to him. He moved a few feet in the direction of the nearest tent. It was larger than the rest and there were more beds in it. The hospital tent, Vicenzo thought.

He passed through what had been the entrance. The sight that met his eyes filled him with horror. There was the black hole, the cellar that he watched people descend to, hoping they would be safe from the bullets.

He could not go to the hole. For a moment that passed like an age, he stood still. Then he forced himself to walk over to it. A cover had been placed over it. It was charred but Vicenzo pushed it aside and put his foot on the first step. It was dark, for the steps were dug at an angle into the earth. The air was still thick and he gagged as he neared the bottom.

Then he froze. The horrors of the Hastings mine explosion returned. Before him were women and children who had taken refuge from the bullets and had hidden in a grave. Their faces were darkened by the smoke and fire.

"It is not possible," Vicenzo muttered. Most of them were sitting along the cool earthen wall on small wooden benches. One women held a small child in her arms. Another had three huddled about her body. Joe came in slowly behind Vicenzo.

"It is done," Joe said when he saw the figures in the room.

"Was it worth it?" Vicenzo murmured. "Was this worth anything? The price has gotten too high. There is no union or cause that would make dues like this."

"It is finished," Joe said. "The rest does not matter." He backed slowly away from the bodies. His face remained fixed upon them, his eyes did not move. "It is best that we leave now," he said. "They must know what has happened."

Vicenzo looked at him but did not move.

"Come, we must get back to the others."

The two moved up the steps. Bullets were striking again. One of the other men ran up to them.

"The guards have seen us! We have to get out now!" he said.

"There are many dead here," Vicenzo said, "women and children."

"There is nothing we can do here," the man said as he turned and started in the direction of the Black Hills.

"We cannot leave them like this," Vicenzo said to Joe. Several bullets hit the ground near them.

"What can we do?" Joe asked. Vicenzo looked back toward the hole.

"Vicenzo!" Joe said. Vicenzo looked at him. "There is not time now." Joe took him by the arm.

"The world is round," Vicenzo said as the two men moved through the colony. All around them the tents continued to smolder. The colony that had been the last resort of a people struggling to survive lay in ruins.

When Vicenzo and Joe reached the hills, Vicenzo stopped. Joe continued a short distance and then turned.

"What is the matter?" he asked. Vicenzo did not answer. "You are not thinking of going back there?" Joe said. "We must go to Trinidad. We must tell Lewis what has happened before the guards find the bodies. They will try to hide them."

"Go, tell them," Vicenzo said.

"What are you going to do? You cannot stay. There is nothing that you can do for them now."

"Yes, I know." Vicenzo turned to Joe. "You tell them. Tell them that they must get to the bodies. They must bury them."

"What are you going to do?"

"What is there to do now? It is too late," Vicenzo said.

"I know you, you think too much," Joe said.

"What can I do now? Give them life? It is too late. Go tell them what has happened. Tell them everything, but they must get to the bodies."

"Vicenzo," Joe said, "it is too much. Do not add to the dead. You are alive now, and it is important that you remain so."

"I will not die," Vicenzo said.

He watched as Joe ran in the direction of El Moro. Then he began moving across the plain south of the colony. He crossed the plain and moved into the hills.

# CHAPTER

# 16

The morning sun rose over the quiet streets of Trinidad. Many conflicting reports had entered the town the day before. The residents received them with the skepticism that had come from years of conflict. The early morning papers were beginning to leave the presses and each carried a version of what had taken place at Ludlow. But like the news from Europe, it seemed thousands of miles away.

By eight o'clock the quiet had not left the streets. The store owners began to open the stores. Several businessmen finished breakfast at the Columbian Hotel, another cranked the awning down over the sidewalk in front of his store, still another swept the walk in front of his. The morning hours passed as they always had.

At mid-morning, the people neared the town, led by Lewis.

"We need a place for them to stay," he told Frank, "and we will need food and water and some place where those who need a doctor can be taken care of."

"I will see what I can do. Bring them to the East Side Theater for now. I will see to it that it is open. They can rest there until we can find a better place."

Frank hurried ahead of the group while Lewis kept the people moving slowly toward town. They reached the road that entered the town from the east and the outline of the buildings became visible.

As soon as Frank reached town, he went to the bank and asked to see Mr. Johnson. "The colony has been destroyed," Frank told him. "The people were driven from the tents with bullets and the tents were burned."

"Then the reports were true," Johnson replied.

"The worst," Frank said. "The people are east of town now. They need some place to stay, food, water, clothes . . . everything." Frank's voice faded.

"You do not look well," Johnson said. "Were you at Ludlow?"

"No. I met them at El Moro. They came from the Black Hills. It has been a long night."

"Bring them to the town hall. I'll call the mayor and tell him what has happened. We'll get the merchants together and do what we can about food and clothing."

"It will take money," Frank said.

"I'm sure many will help. It's a different game now. Too many have stood around and done nothing for too long. Now go and see that the people have a place to rest."

Frank went outside. The people had entered the main section of town and had stopped at the intersection of Main and Commercial Streets. There they sat on the sidewalks, resting against the buildings.

"I could not get them to go any farther," Lewis said to Frank as he came from the bank.

"It is all right for them to rest here. We will bring the food to them. I am going to see other men who will help."

"I must contact Denver," Lewis said. He took a few steps and remembered the machine that came to town the day the men had Cooke trapped in the Columbian Hotel. "Watch the streets carefully. If you hear anything unusual, come for me quickly," he ordered one of his men and went to the telegraph office.

All became quiet as exhaustion forced sleep on most of the people, but the Greeks would not sleep. Some of them positioned themselves at the intersection of the two streets and others went to the end of the streets to watch for any guards that might have followed them.

As the minutes passed, the people of the town began to hear of the refugees from Ludlow. A few came at first, then, as the word spread, more and more began to come from all parts of the town. Some brought blankets, others brought clothing or food. Some of the people from Ludlow ate while others continued to sleep when a blanket was placed over them.

There on the streets of Trinidad the history of man stopped its hideous progression of war long enough for humanity to reach out to its children and provide what fate had denied. A calm replaced the violence of the day before. Many of the people slept peacefully in the warming sunlight, their faces worn and haggard, their bodies tired of struggle. The children were quiet. Many of them slept after eating. There were no thoughts of the future or of the past. With time there would only be memories.

In the telegraph office, Lewis sat pounding the teletype. I must make them realize what has happened, he thought, they must understand.

LUDLOW COLONY ATTACKED AND DESTROYED. ALL 200 TENTS DESTROYED BY FIRE. MANY DEAD AND MISSING. WOMEN AND CHILDREN SUFFERING, HOMELESS WITHOUT FOOD OR WATER. FEAR SPREADING THAT THE OTHER COLONIES WILL BE ATTACKED AND DESTROYED. HELP NEEDED IMMEDIATELY. CONTACT ALL NORTHERN CAMPS TO SEND MEN AND AMMUNITION OR ALL WILL BE LOST.

Lewis sat and waited for a reply.

MESSAGE    RECEIVED.    WILL    DISPATCH    IMMEDIATELY.

Lewis stood up.

"Have you see this?" The telegraph officer handed him a newspaper. Lewis took it and began to read. The expression on his face reflected the hatred that burned within him.

"They've made it sound like the workers attacked the guards and they responded in defense. The explosions were ammunition stored for the attack, taken from my tent. This is what they'll be reading in New York," Lewis said, looking up. "They won't get away with this." He crumpled the paper with his fist. "Not if I have to bring the bodies of the dead and lay them on the steps of the capitol."

Lewis was interrupted by two men who entered the telegraph office.

"This man says he has just come from Ludlow. I think you better hear what he told me."

Lewis looked at Joe Bonacquista. "What is it?" he asked.

"We lefta the colony a little while ago. Before we lefta we found, inna one ofa the cellars, ten, maybe twelve dead. Itta was harda to tell. There was stilla smoke."

"My God," Lewis said. "Are you sure?"

"I'ma sure."

"Who were they? Could you tell?"

"Women anda children."

Lewis felt the blood drain from his face. "It is worse than I imagined. We must find Tikas. He'll have to get his men organized to go back," he told the man who came in with Joe. "They'll attack the other camps, sure as hell. They'll have nothing to lose."

"You willa not finda him," Joe said quietly. "He isa dead."

"Did you see him?"

"No. The Greeks witha me said he wasa dead. They saw him."

"Get word to the other camps quickly. Tell them to expect to be attacked. Go now, quickly," he told the man with Joe. Lewis returned to the teletype. He sat for a few moments thinking. Then he began:

WOMEN AND CHILDREN DEAD IN THE CELLARS AT LUDLOW. FEAR SPREADING THAT THE BODIES WILL BE DESTROYED TO PREVENT RECOGNITION. MUST GET TO THEM. EXPECTING OTHER CAMPS TO BE ATTACKED SOON. WILL RETURN TO LUDLOW AS SOON AS MEN CAN BE ORGANIZED. INFORM SOURCES OF RECENT DEVELOPMENTS.

Lewis rose quickly when he was finished. Joe still stood in the office, waiting. "What else did you see?" Lewis asked.

"There were others inna the streets who were dead. We dida not find anyone who was alive. The guards came."

"The guards. Were there many?"

"They were looking through the burned tents, likea scavengers."

"What about the machine guns? Did you see them?"

"We werea shot at by the bigga gun."

"Are you sure it was the machine gun?"

"I'ma sure. I never forget the sound. It comma from the road."

"Come with me," Lewis said, leaving the office.

They hurried up the street. Many of the people were asleep, others were eating. More carts had arrived with necessities. Frank returned with the news that the doors of the city hall had been opened.

"Count how many are here," Lewis told him. "We need to know how many have died," Lewis hesitated, "how many are still out there," he added.

"You have heard what was found at Ludlow?" Frank asked.

"Yes."

"We must get to the bodies."

"Yes. But they will be waiting for us. We cannot be careless." Frank waited for more. "They have the gun positioned near the camp. We must get the men ready. The Greeks are the most experienced so the others must be organized around them. Get me a number on how many are missing."

Frank began to move about the street counting the people who had come from Ludlow. By mid-afternoon, Frank again found Lewis.

"There are at least eighty missing," he said. "It does not mean that they are all dead. Some left the colony before the full attack came. They could have gone to the other canyons."

"It will take time for the men to prepare to return to Ludlow. They are not soldiers and they have little with which to fight. The men from the other canyons cannot come. It would leave the other colonies open to attack," Lewis said.

The men knew what must be done but they knew too that it would take time. So often time had prevented success for the miners, and it seemed that again time would be against them.

Later in the day Lewis sent two of the best fighting Greeks back to Ludlow to find out what they could about how the former colony had been fortified. He knew that luck could not be counted on and it was important that he be exact.

Lewis paced the street, reviewing the events that had taken place. Decency demanded the burial of the bodies, but at what cost, and providing they had not been destroyed by the guards. Later in the afternoon the two Greeks returned.

"Where are the guns?" Lewis asked.

"They are here and here," one of the Greeks said, taking two rocks and placing them on the ground. "With the hills here." He wet his fingers and marked the sidewalk. "There is also a garrison of guards encamped here," the Greek finished.

Lewis stared at the ground for a moment. "The one gun is on Watertank Hill?" he questioned.

"Yes."

"Then we cannot approach from the south or the north, and we cannot enter from the hills."

"No." the Greek agreed. "The only way is from the east, the Black Hills. It will not be easy. It is a wide open plain with little protection."

Lewis studied the ground for a few minutes. The sun was sinking fast and with it went his last chance to act for the day. That night he slept in the telegraph office waiting for word from Denver.

When the first rays of sun broke the darkness in the hills that overlooked the Ludlow colony, Vicenzo sat beneath the pinon tree where he had hidden his gun the day the federal troops arrived. He sat watching the colony, his eyes fixed upon the spot where he thought the hospital tent had once stood. No one will disturb the bodies, he said to himself. He no longer thought of how the women and children had died. It was enough that they no longer suffered. The taste and smell of death had not left him, and he knew that they never would.

He watched the guards search through the ruins as the sun became bright in the eastern sky. It had the feel of spring. It was time to till the soil and bring it to life. But there was no life in the darkness of the mines or in the ashes of the cellars.

A cloud passed between the earth and the sun. I have come a long way to watch women and children die, and when it is over they will bury a part of us all. There will always be leaders and there will always be come cause, but in the end there is only us. Yet they will not kill me this day. I will be here when all of their mines are empty, and their houses have decayed into the earth.

Vicenzo placed his gun across his lap. "You have been a good friend to me," he said.

Before night came, more guards entered the camp. They did not act like those who came first. This group began to set up a defense of the colony, for they knew the men would return.

In Trinidad, Lewis prepared the men to march and fight again. A new leader had been chosen by the Greeks and he listened carefully as the scouting parties told him where the guards had positioned the big guns. Lewis knew that they would revenge Tikas's death and that once they started he would not be able to control them. Then word came from the telegraph office and Lewis hurried back down the street.

"There is a message for you." The telegraph officer handed Lewis a sheet of paper:

MESSAGE GIVEN TO SECRETARY OF STATE FEDERATION OF LABOR. RESPONSE IS AN OFFICIAL CALL TO ARMS. SUP-

PORT IS WIDESPREAD BY OTHER UNIONS. EXPECT 2000 MEN WITH GUNS AND AMMUNITION BY MORNING. ANOTHER THREE THOUSAND WILL ARRIVE WITHIN A DAY. MONEY AND SUPPLIES ARE BEING SENT TO HELP THE PEOPLE FROM LUDLOW. SENTIMENT IS HEAVILY IN OUR FAVOR.

"It will be different this time," Lewis said half-aloud, then hurried back to his men.

The word spread quickly through town. For the men it meant power in numbers and supplies; for the people of the town it meant fear that the battle would spread from the camps into the town. When the mayor heard of the reaction the destruction at Ludlow had caused, he quickly sent a message to the governor in Denver, demanding the return of federal troops.

The governor was already aware of the situation. He sat in his office with both Osborn and the Canadian.

"I don't know if Wilson will send the troops back. I don't even know if they are available," the governor said.

"You really botched it," the Canadian said to Osborn. "You were supposed to control Cooke. You knew what he was like."

"They haven't won yet," Osborn retorted. "They can't prove Cooke's men fired first, and I've reports that there were ammunition and explosives stored in Lewis's tent."

"Who'll give a damn! If it's true that there are women and children burned to death in the cellars, every humanitarian will be all over us like flies on shit! We've given them a cause and that's all they needed. This isn't like the explosion. What're we going to say, that it was their fault that they were hiding in the cellars?"

"I hope to God he's smart enough to get rid of the bodies before they can get to them," Osborn muttered.

"Well, it better be soon, because men from Denver to Wyoming are heading to Ludlow. Not just from the mines either. When Lewis started sending messages to the miners' union, they talked with every union in this city, and I'll tell you they're all behind him," the Canadian said.

Osborn began pacing.

"We're going to have to send reinforcements to Cooke. Some of his men have deserted and he's going to need as many as we can send him," he said.

"You're talking about a goddamn war!" the governor broke in.

"What the hell do you think has been going on?" Osborn growled.

"There's going to be a lot of questions asked if I start sending state troops down there. And where the hell am I going to get the money?" asked the governor.

"You might as well face it, your administration is shot to hell. You better let us handle it from here on out. We'll come up with the money," Osborn said.

"The tide is turning against us," said the Canadian.

"Yeah," Osborn said. "What has Rockman been told?"

"Rockman? He's been given the usual snow job. It helps keep him white. At least he's smart enough to stay away from here. That's why he pays a stooge like me to take the heat. It's a luxury of the rich."

"You're going to have to send for federal help," Osborn interrupted. The governor turned away. "I told you what has happened to your administration. If the miners take control of the mines down there, there's going to be a lot more blood shed than there was yesterday. Get in touch with the president and *demand* federal troops! Not request, but demand. And do it now. You're going to tell him you've lost control of the situation and the troops are necessary."

"All right. But you two get the hell out of here while I talk with him."

In Trinidad, the army of miners grew by the hour. A group of Greeks came over Raton Pass and another from the western slope. But the main body from the north had yet to arrive.

"We will meet the miners from the north on the railroad tracks east of Ludlow," Lewis told Frank. "It's like a dream! People from as far away as New York are sending money. Money for food and clothing, men and ammunition. It is as though it has fallen from the sky!"

Frank said, "We could have used it a week ago."

"It is enough that they are willing to help now."

"When will you be leaving for Ludlow?" Frank asked.

"As soon as the train is ready. The people are safe here. The men will not have to worry about them while they are fighting."

Early that morning the men boarded the train and left for Ludlow. Thoughts of what they had left behind them haunted their minds; the sound of the machine gun was still in their ears. They had been told that many more men would join them before they went for the bodies. They hoped it was true but they would go for the bodies if the others were not there.

Vicenzo still sat on the hill overlooking the colony. The sun would be coming up over the plain soon, and he did not know if he had slept the night before. If they do not come today . . . , he thought. No, they *will* be here. A small streak of light appeared in the east. Then slowly, as though it were being squeezed from the earth, it began to rise. In the distance, Vicenzo could see a large group of men coming from the Black Hills. Perhaps I am dreaming, he thought, there could not have been so many men in Trinidad. . . .

In the colony, Cooke looked toward the rising sun.

"They're coming," he said out loud. "Osborn was right. They've come by the hundreds. Tell the men at the machine guns I don't want any shooting unless I give the order," he said to the lieutenant standing next to him.

"The men don't trust them. They think that after the miners take the colony, they'll hang us," came the reply.

"It's a possibility."

"Then why don't we fight? We still have the machine guns."

"They won't be enough. When reinforcements didn't come last night I knew what was happening in Denver. Even before I talked with Osborn on the phone I knew. It was a risk we had to take. The stand-off couldn't last forever."

"The governor will send more men, won't he?"

"Like the scum that deserted after the colony was burned? It won't be the governor who sends men like that. They'll come from the same holes in the East that the deserters came from, if they can get them here." Cooke picked up a white flag.

"What's going to happen to us?"

"If we're lucky, we can talk our way into some time. The governor has requested federal troops. Maybe they'll come before the shooting starts. I'm going to talk to Lewis. I know he'll want to try and avoid more killing."

Cooke started in the direction of the approaching army, holding the flag high in the air. As he approached them he could see that Osborn's estimates of how many had joined them was true. When he was near enough, he waved the flag in the air.

"Lewis! Lewis!" The army stopped. "Lewis! Can you hear me!"

"I can hear you, Cooke!"

"I want to talk to you!"

"It's too late, Cooke! A couple of days late to be talking!"

Cooke hesitated. "Lewis, we can avoid a lot of killing."

"I could take him from here," the new leader of the Greeks said.

"No." Lewis said. "They kill that way, we don't!"

"I want to talk to you alone!" Cooke insisted.

Lewis began walking toward him.

"Take this," the Greek said, offering his rifle.

"I have my pistol," Lewis answered. "If there is any shooting, I will see to it that Cooke is the first to die." He walked slowly, looking in the direction of the machine gun. When he got within thirty yards of Cooke he stopped.

"I can't let you on company property," Cooke said.

"We did not come to destroy the company's property. We have come for the bodies. When we have them we can talk of what to do with the company's property," Lewis said bitterly.

"Bodies? What bodies?"

"What bodies? The women. The children. Tikas. We've come to see that they are buried. You're going to have to kill all of us if you think that you can stop us from taking them."

"I know where Tikas's body is. I will take you to it. But I don't know of any women or children," Cooke said.

"We will see for ourselves."

"You go back and get ten men. They can look for any bodies," Cooke said.

"I'll bring a thousand."

"I still have the guns and enough ammunition to kill half of them. They can be on your conscience," Cooke answered.

"The lives of the men. That is one thing that you have never had to worry about. I will bring the ten men and we will see for ourselves if there are women and children. Then we will talk again."

Lewis walked away. When he got back to his men he called for nine men and Joe Bonacquista. "Bring a cart," he said. "Show us where you found the bodies, Joe."

As the men walked back to where Cooke stood, Vicenzo started toward the colony. He moved slowly. He could feel the eyes of the guards upon him as he neared the camp.

"I will not die," he said half-aloud. He thought of the machine gun and the bullets that exploded, and he thought of the short distance that the trigger of the gun traveled before the fire started.

The colony was quiet. There was no breeze and only the eyes of the guards moved as Vicenzo came within striking distance of the gun. He walked slowly, his rifle at his side. He could see the guards following him with the gun. They had set up wooden barricades to hide behind for there was nothing left of the colony except dark black spots of earth where the tents had once stood. He went directly to the spot where the bodies lay beneath the surface of the earth. There before him was naked reality. A few minutes later, Lewis and the other men, led by Bonacquista, arrived.

"They have come for the bodies?" Vicenzo asked.

"Yes."

"They have brought many men," Vicenzo said.

"Many came to Trinidad when they heard," Joe answered. "They are still in the cellar?"

"They have not been disturbed."

"What the hell are they saying?" Cooke said. Lewis did not answer.

"They are inna there," Joe said to Lewis, pointing to the spot. Lewis went down the steps and in a few moments came out.

"Get them out of there," he said to the men. The cart was brought to the opening of the cellar and two men went down. When they returned from the cellar they carried the body of a woman. As they were laying it on the cart, two more went down. The opening was too small for more than two to enter at a time, so the others waited. When the next two surfaced they carried the bodies of children blackened with death. While they were removing the bodies, Cooke took a couple of steps backward, turned, and walked away. The men continued to work in silence. When they were finished they covered the bodies with blankets.

"Tikas's body?" the leader of the Greeks asked.

"I will get it," one of the other Greeks said. He walked a short distance from the tent and picked up the body. He brought it to the cart and laid it with the rest. The cart began to move toward the Black Hills.

"Get ready for an attack," Cooke told his men as he watched the cart move away.

"Take the bodies back to Trinidad," Lewis told Joe and Vicenzo. Before they had gone very far they heard shots.

"The fight continues," Joe said.

"It always will," Vicenzo said, "but for the women and children it is over. They cannot hear it."

In Trinidad they took the bodies to the mortuary. People gathered around in frozen disbelief. When their work was done, Vicenzo and Joe walked away from the mortuary in the direction of the main street.

"There are many men who will fight now," Joe said. "When the other workers joined us we became very powerful, more powerful than I ever thought possible."

"Yes, when the men unite we are very powerful," Vicenzo agreed in a low voice.

"Do not be sad, my friend. The price that they paid could very easily have been paid by us. But now it is our turn."

"We will be victorious, but it will not wash away what we paid in defeat. Sometimes we forget that. Where will you go now?"

"To my mother and father. And you?"

Vicenzo hesitated for a moment as a picture of his mother and father standing on the dock at Naples flashed in his head.

"I will go to Frank's house," he said. When they reached the intersection they stopped. "You take care of yourself," Vicenzo said, "and don't trust anyone you cannot speak to."

"Yes, my friend," Joe said. The two parted.

Vicenzo went to Frank's house, ate and slept. He said little and Frank and Marietta understood. Early the next morning, Vicenzo told Frank, "I am going back to Ludlow."

"There is no need. The guards at Ludlow have been pinned in the canyon. All over the hills miners have attacked the mines. Some of the buildings have been burned. There will be a great deal of destruction before they are stopped."

"What will happen now?"

"The federal troops will be here soon. Then the fighting will stop."

"I am going to town," Vicenzo said.

"Watch yourself," Frank warned. "You have fought well for what you believed." Vicenzo did not answer.

On the third day after the massacre, the bodies of the women and children of Ludlow were to be buried. A coach led by two black horses crossed the brick streets on its way to the church. It was followed by another and yet another; six in all.

A large crowd waited for them in front of the church. They stood quietly and some cried. Everything that could be said had been gone over too many times, with little good.

Forty-five minutes passed before the caskets were all brought into the church. Vicenzo watched from across the street. He saw the crowd slowly disappear through the large wooden doors. These were the people he had come to know. He crossed the street and went into the church. The priest had already begun the prayers, and the Latin that he used sounded almost familiar. Everywhere there were statues, and in front of each, candles burned in rows. Before the mass was over, Vicenzo left the church and walked silently toward the hills.

# CHAPTER

# 17

When the sun was high, the old man sat on a large rock near the chicken coop. I must clean the rabbits, he thought. If they are not cleaned, they will die.

The sun's rays warmed the air and felt good on the old man's skin. The hill that stood opposite his house was like many hills that surrounded the small valley in which the town had been built. The top of it was exposed rock, smooth and straight, so that it was almost impossible to climb. Pinon trees grew on the top.

"Hey, Mr. Caputo, you want something from Bonfadinis'?" a small Spanish boy called out from a house above his.

"No thanga you," the old man replied. "Nothing today."

I will go to see if the boy has come home yet, thought the old man when the sun had risen higher in the sky. He will take me to town. The old man began to walk slowly to the boy's house. The road descended and then rose as did the hill that it was built on and it was difficult for the old man to walk. He moved slowly, leaning heavily upon his cane. He remembered when it was a dirt road and there were few houses along the sides. There were a few people still alive who had moved to town when the mines closed, and these were not like the houses they had lived in in the camps. When he got to the top he could see his son's house, but he knew that his son would not be there.

The old man continued along the top of the hill until he came to the school that bore the same name as the church he had gone to the mass in the first Easter he was in America. Here he rested and looked down on the row of houses that he had come to know when he met Frank. Although Frank had been dead for many years, his house still gave the appearance of having been built by a man who took pride in his work.

"It has been many years since I have seen you, my old friend," Vicenzo said, looking at Frank's house. "You came to this country and figured it out better than the rest of us. You tried to help us do the same but there were too many against you. If only you had had the money that the owners had, how many people would not have been destroyed! But fate is not like that. Too often she does not allow a good man to change what many bad ones have done." Vicenzo faded into the past slowly. "You even tried to help those in the old country when Ludlow was finished."

"Why do you go to this war?" Vicenzo asked Frank.

"Because it is what I have to do," he answered.

"But it does not make sense. You came here from Italy to live in peace, and now they are sending you back there to fight."

"I have chosen to go," Frank said. "It is still our country."

"Then we all should go," Vicenzo said.

"No, my friend, you must stay here. Carmela will be here soon. The war will not last much longer."

"Then why do you go? You did enough here."

"I was never near the bullets. But do not worry, I shall return as soon as there is peace."

"It is bad over there. The letters that my mother sent said there is much destruction and many are dying."

"Yes," Frank said, "this planet knows little rest. In a way it will be good to see the old country again. It has been a long time."

"The company says that we owe them money, that we cannot leave until it is paid back," Vicenzo said.

"Yes, the strike settled little."

"It is different at work now. There is a hatred for the work we do," Vicenzo said. "What will happen to Lewis?"

"I do not know if they will let him out of jail. The legal battle is just starting, but there is much support for him now."

"We got a lot of support after Ludlow. Men came from everywhere to help. We could have used some of it sooner."

"It is a lot like that in Europe. Things are very bad there for the people. Now that we have entered the war, we can help finish it."

"I do not think that this business will ever be finished, here or over there. It is like a curse."

"Have faith, Vicenzo, and endure,"

The old man shifted his weight upon the cement step away from the side of the hip that he had injured when he fell outside of Savina's bar. The brick school that he sat in front of had been built a long time after the church and was only a short distance from it. His son had bought a house on the same block as Frank's, and from where Vicenzo sat he could see both of them. It was easy to picture Frank standing in front of the house, Marietta next to him. She had never remarried and had told Vicenzo that no one would ever share her bed, that there was only Frank.

I remember the day Frank returned from the war, Vicenzo thought. He looked good in his uniform. He was not gone long but he said that the old country would never be the same. But the camps did not change. There had been another trial to determine what had happened. Many came to help us but it did little good, the old man recalled. I stood in the back of the courtroom and listened and they called me up to the witness stand to tell them what I had found in the cellar. But nothing was done.

Vicenzo began walking down the hill. "They did not believe anything that we said." he mumbled. "When the hearings were over they put Lewis in jail for the murder of one of the guards. The company said three had died during the fighting. They said that Lewis had killed one of them. There were more than three that died. I saw more fall and I knew that there had been others. The others that had been killed they got rid of because they were wanted in the East for killings that they had committed during the strikes back there. None of the company officials was ever tried."

When Vicenzo reached the bottom of the hill he crossed the highway, the same road that led to the camps. He went to his son's house and knocked on the door several times. As he waited he leaned heavily on his cane. His hip had begun hurting as he came down the hill and now it caused him a great deal of discomfort. Again he knocked but still there was no response.

He looked about the street and all was quiet. Then he sat on one of the lawn chairs that his son always put on the front porch when spring came.

It was a day much like today that we went back to work, Vicenzo thought. After all the suffering and hatred, when the trials were over we went back to work . . . back to the ovens and to the mines. He thought of the porthole and how it descended sharply into the earth. He would not think of the years that he had spent in the mines.

The spring sun was warm and it felt good to be in the shade of the porch. When he had rested, he got up slowly from the chair. Then he began walking down the block in the direction of the Volunteer Inn. He passed two houses after leaving his son's porch and then there was Frank's house. On the porch sat Marietta with two other elderly women.

"Vicenzo. Come stai?" Marietta asked.

"Bono, Marietta, e tu?"

"Not so good today. My back hurts all the time and I cannot eat."

"You need a little wine and you'll feel better."

"It would kill me," she said, throwing up her hands.

The other two women greeted him with a nod and smile. One of the flower pots near the steps was broken and Vicenzo asked about it.

"A couple of days ago someone broke it. I don't know who it was. I wanted to replace it but nobody makes them any more."

The news brought a moment of sadness to Vicenzo. He knew how Frank took pride in his house and how he liked everything in just a certain way.

After a few moments of conversation, Vicenzo went on his way.

I would like to see Frank again, he thought as he walked. I would like to sit and talk with him. Both he and Carmela died when they were too young. And how I would like to see my Carmela again. She gave me reason to live many times and now she is not here.

The old man sat at a table in the Volunteer Inn, drinking coffee mixed with whiskey. The bar was empty except for himself and the bartender. "Vicenzo, you feel alright?" the bartender asked.

"I fella OK."

The bartender returned to his newspaper. "Here's something that'll interest you." "It says here that people have been stealing bricks from the old coke ovens."

"They steala the bricks?" the old man asked without looking up.

"Ya. They use them to cover the fronts of their houses. You used to work the ovens didn't you?"

"I worked them."

"There ain't much of anything there now," the bartender said.

The old man became silent as he had many times.

I remember the first time I saw the coke ovens, Vicenzo thought. And I remember the night they burned.

"You crazy."

"Come! Look!" He went out to the front yard. There was an unnatural glow in the hills. Carmela dressed hurriedly and followed the men. Many others had joined them, all their eyes fixed in the directions of the ovens.

"I cannot believe this," Vicenzo said when he got close enough to see the flames. The ovens stood before him, their bricks glowing like fanned hot coals. Flames rose from and pieces of burning coal tossed in the air.

"It is as though the earth has opened up her insides. Like the volcanos that I have heard about in Italy." A hundred ovens burned and the heat forced them back as their faces became hot and their skin dry and tight.

In a short time everyone from the camp came to look. Some stood in the night air half dressed, others wrapped blankets around themselves and the rest stayed close enough to the flames to keep warm. Vicenzo watched only a short while, then began walking home. Carmella followed.

"What will you do now?" she asked with emotion.

"I am going to bed."

"Tomorrow, when it is time to work. What will you do," she persisted.

"I will know when tomorrow comes."

"But if the ovens are destroyed there will be no work."

"There is always work."

"No. If the ovens are destroyed there will be no jobs."

Vicenzo stopped. "There is always work. I have been here long enough to know that. As long as there are mines there will be work."

They walked in silence the rest of the way. When they were in bed, Carmella wished to talked to be reassured, but Vicenzo said nothing and fell asleep.

On the television set two men walked on the moon. Vicenzo sat and dazed into the past as he did too often. They died too young, he thought. When you have to struggle to live too many times you cannot die, it becomes hard to do the natural things and only when you struggle is it possible to live. I thought it would be easy to die. The homes we lived in were theirs, the stores were theirs and the coal we dug was theirs. When the ovens were gone there were the mines, but Carmella did not have to bury me.

The old man put his head down on his shoulder and slept. Late that afternoon, the old man's son came to the bar. He found his father sleeping at one of the tables.

"Pa, it's time to go home," the son said softly, shaking his father's shoulder gently. "Pa, wake up." The old man picked his head up slowly. "Joe," he said, "sitta down."

"No, Pa, it's time to go home," The son helped his father to his feet and gave him his cane. On the way home the old man drifted in a half-sleep. He unconsciously shifted his weight away from his injured hip.

"You hip's bothering you,isn't it?" the son said.

"A little bit," the old man answered.

"Do you have the pills the doctor gave you for pain?"

"Atta the house." When they got to the old man's house the son helped him inside to his bed and found the pain pills on the kitchen sink.

"Pa, you were supposed to take these when the hip bothered you, but most of them are still here," the son said.

"They hurta my stomach," the old man said.

"Why didn't you tell me? I would have taken you back to the doctor and he would have given you something else." The old man did not answer. "I'll call the doctor in the morning," the son said, putting the pills in his pocket.

The house became quiet. The son looked around. The memories of the past flashed through his mind. His family had moved from the camps shortly after he had left for the war against Japan. He remembered his mother crying the day he left and her smile the day he returned. He remembered how proud she was of their new house. The kitchen still had the coal stove that Carmela used to cook on. There was also an electric range but she would not let them remove the old stove and she continued to bake bread in it after the other one had been delivered.

"Joe," the old man said. The son went over to the bed and sat down in the chair next to it.

"It will be Easter soon?"

"In about a week," the son answered.

"It is time to plant," the old man said.

"On Sunday I have the whole day off. I will come up and get the ground ready," the son said. He remebered when the old man had planted a large garden, and during the years of the Depression it helped keep the family alive. But a few rows of lettuce and spinach with some horse beans were enough for him to take care of now. The old man became quiet again and the son thought that he might fall asleep. Then he heard the sound of the porch door open and he got up to see who had come into the house.

"What are you doing here?"

"I finished exams this morning so I thought I'd come home," the boy said.

"You didn't cut any classes?"

"Of course not. All my exams were scheduled for yesterday and today. Where's Nonno?"

"He's resting."

"Joe!" The words came from the bedroom.

"I'll see what he wants," the boy said.

"Don't stay too long, he needs some rest."

"I'll stay until he falls asleep." The son left through the porch door and the boy went into the bedroom. "How do you feel, Nonno?" the boy asked.

The old man opened his eyes. "Whosa you?" he said.

"It's me," the boy said, turning on the light.

"Turna offa the light," the old man said. The boy did so. The room became dark as the light went out. The boy could see only an outline of the old man as he lay upon the bed.

"Sitta for a little while," the old man said. For a short time the old man was quiet and the boy thought that he had fallen asleep. Outside the April sun set over the hills and cast its rays through the windows of the kitchen.

"Boy," the old man said.

"I'm here."

"Good." The old man became quiet again. A short time passed and the old man raised one of his hands. "Boy," he said again.

The boy took the old man's hand and the old man brought them both gently down to the bed.

"You remember you' nonno?" the old man asked.

"I remember you from when I was small," the boy answered.

"You remember him when he'sa gone?" The boy did not like to hear the old man talk that way.

"You will outlive me, Nonno," the boy said with a smile.

"I have hada my time. You live one day, one life. I have lived too long." The old man became quiet again and it made the boy uncomfortable. He knew that the old man drank often, and that it was not good for his body. He did not know if it would be worse if he stopped.

"Whena you' nanna die a long time ago it woulda been a gooda time to die. She likea this house whena we moved froma the camps. She wasa very happy. It has been lonely here withoutta her. I donna thinka she knows it."

"She knows, Nonno, she knows," the boy said.

"I never say nothing whena she wasa here."

"Don't worry, Nonno, she knows."

"You' nonno would likea to see her again but I donna think so," the old man said. He became quiet again. Then, "For forty years I worka inna the mine," the old man said. "Now I no canna forget how hard I become. It isa no easy. You no worka inna the mine!"

"No, nonno, I do not work in the mine."

"Whenna a man isa dead he goes inna the ground. When he'sa alive he should be inna the sun. It isa no good to be under the ground. You aska you' uncle, he tella you whatta the mine isa like. You aska him. You' daddy isa smart, he no go into the mine."

The old man's hand relaxed in the boy's as he became quiet. After a short time the old man spoke again. "You go now."

"I will wait until you are asleep," the boy said.

"You go now," the old man said. "I do notta like it whena people wait until I am asleep before they leave. You go now so I canna rest."

The boy hesitated, then got up from the chair. He went into the kitchen and stopped, and remembered when the old man had told him about the mines when he was younger, and how it had hurt him when he had looked at the scars that marked his body the day they had taken him to the hospital, and when he had felt his clawlike hands. He felt his head fill with emotion and water filled his eyes.

"You locka the door whena you leave," the old man said, "and whena you come back tomorrow you canna turn over the garden for me. And donna forget!"

"Sure, Nonno, I'll see you tomorrow." The boy shut the door behind him and pulled on it to make sure it was locked. Then he waited outside the house. The sun had gone down over the hills and the air had become cool. He is asleep by now, he thought, and then he left.